The Fighters of Peace

Book 1

The DragonStaff

By Emily Woods

Cozy Coop Press

Morganton, Georgia

Copyright © Emily Woods

All rights reserved. No part of this book may be reproduced or used in any manner without written permission of the copyright owner except for the use of quotations in a book review.

First paperback edition September 2024

Book design by Emily Woods

Published by Cozy Coop Press
Morganton, Georgia

ISBN: 979-8-9913159-0-6 (paperback)
ISBN: 979-8-9913159-1-3 (hardcover)
ISBN: 979-8-9913159-2-0 (ebook)

Library of Congress Control Number:
2024916754

Printed in the U.S.

PROLOGUE

Midnight in Cloudairia—the Cloud Kingdom—a huge party was being held in an old casino that was converted into an apple cider restaurant. Only the powerful and rich were invited, but to a spy, you can always invite yourself. In the dark night sky, on the roof of the huge restaurant, an uninvited Cloudairian looked through his bag of supplies. Like all Cloudairians, or Cloud Dragons, he had weird wings. Some don't even call them wings. They were long and skinny; they don't flap like other dragon wings. Instead, the dragon must get a running start to catch the wind with his wings and move his entire body with the wind. The Cloudairians were also much longer than other dragons and had stronger legs, but they were still four-legged. Their scale colors were always cloud-like. This one was pure white. The dragon on the roof pulled out a couple of sharp gadgets and tightened his two belts that went around his chest and waste like a sash, crossing each other on his chest. He attached blasters, bombs, and all sorts of dangerous weapons to his belts. Then he grabbed a small chain with a metal stick as a pendent and put it around his neck. He attached a dagger to his left back leg, then he pulled out his hologram phone with a blue screen rising above it. He clicked a disguise button, making all the belts around him look like a fancy suit. "Time to crash a party," he said to himself.

The music played loudly in the party room on the bottom floor of the huge old apple cider restaurant in Cloudairia, the Cloud Kingdom. Many Cloud Dragons were at the party, eating and dancing and just having fun—a perfect place for a spy to get some answers. Three of the Cloud Dragons were talking to each other, one of them was kind of old. His scales had blue swirls in his white scales. Another dragon that was a little younger had light grey color scales, like dark clouds. The third had to be one of the youngest in the whole restaurant, his scales were pure white. "All right, here's another one," the oldest dragon said to the two others. "Why did the chicken cross the road? Any takers? To get to the other side!" The three of them all burst into laughter.

"That is obvious..lee a hilarious joke," the pure white dragon said.

"Why, thank you," the oldest dragon said. "You said your name was Sky, correct?"

"Yes, that is correct," Sky responded, taking a sip of apple cider. He wore a fancy suite and a necklace with a metal stick as its pendant.

"Well then, cheers to Sky, for thinking that an old man like me has funny jokes, even when they are about plants and butter making."

The three of them raised their glasses of apple cider, saying, "Cheers."

A vibration came from the old dragon's belt pocket, "Ooo, I got to take this. Nice meeting you, Sky," he said, walking away.

"Nice meeting you," Sky responded.

"His jokes are terrible," the other dragon said, taking a sip out of his apple juice.

"I know," Sky said, doing the exact same thing.

The other dragon laughed, "I knew you were too young to think that *those* were funny. You must be a good actor."

"Back at you," Sky said.

"Thanks."

"I'm sorry, but what is your name again?" Sky asked.

"Wilbert, but my friends call me Will," he responded.

"Ok, Will."

"Willbert."

"Oh…," *Alright Wilbert, time to get some answers.* "Man, I can't believe what happened last night," Sky said.

"I know," Wilbert said. "Of course I wasn't sure if anyone else knew about it, but now I guess they do."

"Hmm? Oh no, that's not what I'm talking about," Sky said, shaking his head. "I'm talking about the *other* thing that happened last night."

"What other thing? And how would you know what I'm talking about?" asked Wilbert.

"Oh, I just know something else happened, (*or is happening*, Sky thought) but I don't want to spoil it for you, because some say that I have a tend to over exaggerate," Sky responded.

"Oh, I'm sure I already know," Wilbert said.

"I don't know…..."

"Oh come on, I'm sure it's about the Alliance isn't it?"

Sky's heart began to pound in his chest. He needed to know, but he couldn't show that he was interested. "You know there is a lot of alliance stuff, it's kind of hard to know which is which," Sky responded calmly.

"You know……," Wilbert said, "the King of the Lightning Dragons finally gave in to King Omega's forces. The Lightning Dragons are not with the Represenetor anymore, whoever the Represenetor is, he is probably going to die, because he's one of the Three Bounties."

"Three bounties?" Sky asked.

"Yeah, you know, the leader of the Fighters of Peace, the criminal, and the Represenetor," Wilbert said. Of course Sky knew what the Three Bounties were, but he liked hearing *everyone's* opinion.

"Anything else you know?"

"Yeah, get this: Omega thinks that there might be a spy at this party, so he sent soldiers here to make sure there isn't. They are guarding the outside so they can trap him in and kill him," Wilbert said. Sky felt sick to the stomach, he was horrified. "So…… what is it that you know?"

"Well, you basically just described it, except I was going to say that the humans blew up a part of the Peace Forest and took a lot of tree wood, and a couple of prisoners. They also set up some bases," Sky said, slowly moving his eyes across the party room, studying the large room for a chance to escape.

"Know anything else?" Wilbert asked.

"Maybe, what about you?"

Wilbert smiled, "Listen carefully." He leaned over and whispered some of the most important secrets in Annorlia. Sky had never heard anything the man said before.

"Excuse me, but I have to go," Sky said after he heard everything. He didn't want to be sudden, but this information was far too important. He had to get out, but movement from the other side of the room caught his attention. *Oh no.*

"Oh! Sky! There's one more thing you need to know."

"Quiet," Sky interrupted.

"No! Really, you need to know this," Wilbert urged.

"Get down." Sky pounced onto Wilbert, knocking him to the floor.

"What are you doing?" Wilbert asked in horror.

"If they see you with me, they will kill you. So be quiet," Sky said, staring into Wilbert's eyes intensely.

"Who is it?" Wilber asked in horror.

"Umm," Sky gently tipped the table over and looked above it. Creatures that looked like wingless dragons in black armor were coming in from all of the doors. *Diammonites,* Sky thought in disgust. "Someone who doesn't like me."

"You do know Omega doesn't like anyone who is spying against him, right?"

Sky paused, "What do you mean…."

"Sky, you know exactly what I am talking about," Wilbert said. "You're a spy for the Fighters of Peace."

"Am I that obvious?"

"Not really, I just know how younger dragons talk, and you're what? Twenty?" Wilbert responded. "Most Cloudairians these days aren't so calm and respectful at that age, unless they are extremely rich. But, I've researched on you. Sure, no one knows your name or anything, but they know there is a master spy of the High King. You are famous."

"So, let me guess," Sky said, "You're going to turn me over, aren't you?"

"I could… or I can do what I have always wanted to do."

"Which is…?"

"Listen Sky, if you want to tell all of your information to the Fighters of Peace, who will tell it to the Represenetor, then you *will* do exactly as I say."

"I would still like to know what you have always wanted to do," Sky said warily.

"Look," Wilbert said. "Fifty-five, zero, six, and one hundred twelve. I don't know exactly what it means, but I do know you have to keep it away from Omega."

"What do you know about it?"

"I think it's some sort of code that can rig something."

"Rig what?" Sky asked.

"I don't know, but I do know that this is just a little bit of the codes," Wilbert responded. "The human man named Pilot knows the rest."

"How do you know all of this?"

"Let's just say I have a very good ear and that Diammonite was not very good at whispering," Wilbert responded.

"But why would you even be near a Diammonite like that?" Sky asked.

"King Saul said that I had to be in a meeting."

"Why?"

"Because I can help him with financial issues," Wilbert responded, rolling his eyes.

"Oh."

"Now listen," Wilbert said, "I will distract them while you run to tell the Fighters of Peace." Wilbert began to stand up.

"Will, wait," Sky said before Wilbert left. "Why are you helping me?"

"All my life, me, Wil*bert*, Omega, and King Saul has made me do terrible stuff that I really regret," Wilbert said. "I have always wanted to go to the Fighters of Peace and the Represenetor, but I didn't know how to contact him. I figured that telling you everything can finally help the Fighters of Peace do a major strike against the Diammonites."

"Oh, well I guess I will have to tell the Represenetor that it was you who helped the Fighters of Peace," Sky said with a smile.

Wilbert smiled, "Remember, Sky, just because the Cloudairian, the human, and many other kings have all gone against the Represenetor, it doesn't mean that everyone is bad. There are still good people and dragons out there who are willing to fight if someone leads them. You know that, right?"

"I know," Sky responded.

"Well then, I guess this is goodbye," Wilbert said.

"Yeah, I guess it is," Sky said. "And Wilbert…"

"Yes?"

"Thank you," Sky said. "I really couldn't have found this out without you, Will."

Wilbert smiled, "Wilbert. And you're welcome."

"Good luck."

"To the true High King," Wilbert said.

"The true High King," Sky said with a nod.

Wilbert smiled and edged away to where Sky couldn't see him.

The music stopped, and a large Diammonite stepped onto the stage at the end of the room. He looked like a commander or something. The Diammonite's voice was loud and authoritative as he yelled, "Attention! There is a spy in our midst! If you see him, please notify us. If you do not notify us, then you will suffer the same consequences of the spy. Now do us a favor and don't get in our way."

"Excuse me! Excuse me!" the voice of Wilbert called, walking up to the commander. "Man, I am so glad you are here!"

"Why?" the commander asked.

"I know where the spy is!" Wilbert said.

Wait a second, is he telling the truth? Sky thought in horror.

"Where?" the commander ordered.

"It was horrible!" Wilbert responded, "I barely made it out a live! The spy has a Fighter of Peace with him!"

"Where are they?" the commander demanded.

"I'll show you!" Wilbert said, running as far away as possible from Sky.

A couple of the soldiers followed him, but the commander slowly walked behind, stopping in the middle of the crowd of tables. He wasn't going to be tricked. *Will did his best.*

Sky waited for what felt like forever till he glanced above the table to see what he was up against. He guessed that the Diammonites made everyone else leave, for only creatures in full body black armer were everywhere. *Man these guys really want me dead.* He edged over to another table where the commander was talking to a soldier. Sky perked his ear up to listen. "Report," the commander said.

"We got one of them, but I think the spy got away," the soldier responded.

"Xero6 is scouting the area to find him, he won't get far," the commander said.

"You're right," the soldier agreed. "The spy won't get far."

"Hm? No, I'm saying Xero6 won't get far," the commander said. "That guy's an idiot. The only reason I sent him alone was so he would leave *me* alone. But don't worry, I sent *real* soldiers to look far the spy. The spy also won't get far either."

Sky's heart was racing. *I need to get out of here. I need to tell him.* Sky looked to see if there was a way out, but everywhere in sight was crawling with Diammonites.

Sky edged his way under each table to get to the wall with folded tables and chairs leaning against it. He gently slid a circular folded-up table that was against the wall aside. *I guess nobody found this,* Sky thought as he carefully picked up the piece of the wall that had already been cut off. He glanced behind him to make sure no one was watching, then crawled inside the wall. He pulled out a small laser and sealed the hole shut behind him. *I may as well un-camo this,* Sky thought as he made his fancy suit disappear. Sky made his way up by climbing on the studs inside the wall, thinking back to when he was climbing down it. *I should be two stories up by now.* He felt against the wood of the wall until his claw got caught on a crack. Sky quickly pulled out the laser and cut where the cracks went, forming a small opening.

"Here comes the fun part," Sky whispered to himself. He braced himself and jumped for the opening. "Ow," he said, trying to squeeze through. He grabbed hold of something on the other side and pulled himself out into an old attic. The room was filled with shelves of dusty books and barrels. Sky shifted his wings from being uncomfortably squeezed from crawling through such a small hole. *If I go to the roof it would be expected, but if I go to the ground would it be too unexpected to where it is expected?* Sky's ear perked up, *Something doesn't feel right.* He slowly stood up onto his four talons and looked around. Slowly, he twitched for his blaster around his belt. He glanced as much as he could behind him without turning around, keeping his heartbeat completely under control. He grabbed his blaster and turned to fire. Quickly, a

Diammonite soldier jumped from behind the shelves and kicked the blaster out of his claws before he could even aim.

"You must be the idiot," Sky said with a smile. Sky's small metal stick turned into a sword as he yanked it off the small chain around his neck. There was the sound of metal as the Diammonite somehow blocked the swing of his sword using its tail. "Ok, I have to admit," Sky said, staring at the unharmed tail, *"that* is pretty impressive." *But very annoying!* Every time Sky would swing his sword, the Diammonite would block it with his long whip-like tail. Again Sky struck, but this time the Diammonite hit too, then wrapped his impressive tail around the sword and yanked it out of his claws. Sky shrugged a small laugh, then tackled the Diammonite to the ground. Another thing Sky found annoying about the Diammonites was their insanely quick reflexes.

Immediately the Diammonite kicked Sky off of him, but Sky's reflexes were insanely quick too. Using his strong Cloudairian legs, he kicked the Diammonite in the stomach, sending him into the shelves. Sky bolted for the way out on the other side of the room before any other Diammonites could show up. But this Diammonite soldier wasn't done with the fight yet. The Diammonite jumped behind him and wrapped his long powerful tail around Sky's neck. Sky choked as the Diammonite pulled hard. *If he wanted me dead he'd kill me, he prefers me alive. No! I have to get to him!* Sky grabbed his dagger out of the holder on his back leg and stabbed deep into what felt like the Diammonite's left back knee. The Diammonite lost his grip and fell to the floor, allowing Sky to catch his breath and run as fast as he could, leaving his dagger. The second Sky opened the door, the Diammonite grabbed a pistol-blaster and fired. Sky nearly screamed when the red blast hit his shoulder. He tumbled into the hallway and limply threw himself into the first door he could see, which seemed to be the janitor's closet. He closed the door shut, locking himself in. Breathing hard in pain, he leaned against the wall, clutching his shoulder. He looked at his hurt shoulder then quickly regretted it when he felt queasy. "I have to tell him," Sky whispered to himself. He reached into one of his pockets and pulled out a small metal ball. Squeezing it, he rolled it onto the floor. Almost immediately, a large blue dragon-like figure appeared in the air, coming from the ball. The dragon-like figure spoke in an echoey voice, **"Did you find out if the rumors are true or not?"** It asked.

"I'm not happy to say this, but it's true. The Lightning Dragons have abandoned you and joined Omega," Sky responded.

The figure sighed, **"Well, I'm hoping since you called me to tell me this that you are not going to betray me too? All who have left used to be quite close."**

"Trust me, I will never do that," Sky promised. He clutched his shoulder and moaned. He could hear Diammonites running in the hallway looking for him, he guessed the rest of them made it to the other Diammonite.

Sky's master heard it too and noticed his wound, **"Sky, are you alright?"** he asked.

"No, I need backup," Sky admitted. "I have some of the most important information in all of Annorlia and the galaxy. This can cause a major blow against the Diammonites and maybe even possible victory."

"You seem worried."

"If Omega knew about everything I found out tonight," Sky said, "it could be the end of the Represenetor forever."

"Very well, I will send my most trusted pilot and crew to pick you up, then I personally will come to your aid."

Sky heard the soldiers coming to the door he was leaning against. "This is getting way out of hand," Sky said with a sigh. "This is the fifth time this year someone has betrayed you. Even rebellions are giving up and turning against you."

"I know, and I'm about to do something about it," the figure said.

"What do you mean?"

"It's time for me to train and recruit the last Fighter of Peace member. I have known where he is, I just wanted to wait till he is ready."

"Well, then I hope he's ready," Sky said, holding the door closed as the soldiers were banging on it.

"He is."

CHAPTER 1

THE PLAN

The only thing really different about Jacob, a young teenage boy, was that he actually loved to run…… sort of. He wasn't exactly into the sweaty part, but when you have a brother *obsessed* with trying to figure out how to destroy all of the dragons and win the war, and a sister who, well…… let's just say that his brother Michael and sister Hazel didn't exactly have too much in common. Hazel's biggest dream was to have a pet dragon, or even *see* one. Like most citizens, Hazel didn't know what a dragon looked like or really know anything about one. The only thing everyone knew was the dragons were evil in every way, which, of course, Hazel did not believe. Jacob still loved his brother and sister, but sometimes he wanted to have his alone time and just run without anyone trying to convince him that the dragons are probably innocent, or that we have to find out how to kill them all in one big hit. Every single conversation always ended one way: Michael and Hazel would get into a huge argument and then would *always* turn to Jacob and say, "How about *you?* Tell us *your* decision so then *you* can end this argument once and for all." Of course, Jacob knew that he was with destroying all of the dragons, but, for some reason he always had a feeling that if he said that in front of both of them it would ruin his relationship with Hazel. So every time they put him in the middle he would always just shrug and say, "I don't know." Jacob still regretted the one time he made the huge mistake of secretly telling Michael that he did agree with him and wanted to help him come up with a plan to win the war. Ever since then, Michael had been waking Jacob up early in the morning, interrupting him from doing homework, and—worst of all—Michael would tap on the window of Jacob's classes at school and call out to him *just* to tell him that he had a plan. That was when Jacob decided that he needed to find a hobby. His favorite place to run was the huge public park right next to King Luther's castle, Kings Park. The park had nice running trails with beautiful bushes with almost any kind of flower you could think of growing along the trails. But Jacob's favorite thing about the whole park was the medium-sized dog that always sat on a bench, waiting for Jacob to come and run with him. The dog had long black fur with white on the tip of its tail, white paws, and one big white spot on its face. Because of this he named him Spot. He looked kinda like a Belgian sheepdog but with white spots. He was the prettiest looking mutt ever.

"Spot!" Jacob called to the dog that sat on a bench. "Are you coming?"

With a bark, Spot hopped off the bench and ran with Jacob along the long trail.

Just like what they always did after running on a trail, Jacob and Spot sat on the same bench and stared at the castle. Even though Spot was a dog, whenever they went to that bench Jacob would always tell him everything that was going on at home, and how he was feeling. "I hope my dad is ok," Jacob said with a sigh. "My mom keeps telling me that he is, it's just, I have a feeling that he's not. Of course my brother thinks I'm crazy," Jacob sighed. "I don't know, maybe I am crazy, what do you think?" Jacob asked. Spot barked. "You're right," Jacob agreed. "And I am still trying to convince everyone to let me bring you home. I'm working like crazy with that." He pet Spot's head, "What do you think about coming home with me? Would you like that?"

Spot barked.

Jacob smiled and stood up, "Well, I guess it's time to head back home. Want to walk with me?" Spot hopped off the bench and looked up at him, wagging its tail.

It was almost immediately after Jacob had taken a shower from running when he heard his name being called. "What?!" Jacob called back.

"Come here! I want to show you something!" It was the voice of Michael.

Probably another plan, Jacob thought. He walked downstairs, through the dining room and into the kitchen. Sitting at the four-seater breakfast table with pieces of paper in front of her (as usual) sat Jacob's sister, Hazel. Hazel had long, smooth, brown hair and brown eyes. She was a little over a year younger than him. Hazel's skin wasn't as pale as Jacob's, but Jacob by far had the palest skin in the family.

"Another plan, I'm guessing?" Hazel asked, looking up from her papers.

"Most likely," Jacob responded, walking through the door into the two-step playroom. The playroom was a long, dirty-white carpeted room with two sets of shutters on the wall; one pair that opened to the dining room, and one pair that opened into the breakfast table. Both were closed. In the middle of the room, Jacob's brother, Michael, was rummaging through a box of papers.

"There you are," Michael said, brushing his brown hair out of his eyes. His hair was shorter than Jacob's, but it was longer right above his eyes. He usually gelled it a lot. His eyes were brown like Hazel's, and he was a little taller than Jacob. "Why do you always run for so long?"

"Spot likes to talk."

"More like you like to talk and he has no choice but to listen. Or maybe even stare off into the distance and try to ignore everything," Michael responded.

"He's going to be my dog someday."

"You keep telling yourself that."

"Where did you get that box?" Jacob asked, changing the subject.

"Dad's stuff from last night," Michael responded.

"But we didn't see him last night, or any night for that matter," Jacob said with a sigh.

"Yeah, but Mom did, and she brought back some stuff," Michael said, nodding to the box.

“When?”

“When we were asleep, but you know, I’m *never* asleep.”

“Right,” Jacob said. He wasn’t too sure if he wanted to ask how he got ahold of the box. “So what’s in it?”

“Only everything we need!” Michael said energetically. "Look at this stuff! It’s all of dad’s work papers.”

“Why do we need *work* papers?” Jacob asked, a little confused.

“Because he was *working* on the DragonStaff,” Michael responded, excited. “See look. This is all his journaling from his travels.” Michael was basically jumping up and down as he handed Jacob a few pieces of papers from the box.

“‘My journey to find the DragonStaff,’” Jacob read out loud from the piece of paper. "I don’t remember Dad doing obvious names, he was always good at that kind of stuff.”

“See!” Michael said. “Proof that the DragonStaff is real!”

“Not really,” Jacob said. "Just because you search for something doesn’t mean it’s real.”

“True,” Michael agreed, "but if we keep looking, I bet we’ll find something.”

“Fine,” Jacob said, sitting down and digging into the box of papers.

The next day Jacob woke up to his brother Michael yelling, "Jacob! Jacob! Wake up! Aren't you going to help me search for it?"

"Less searching, more sleeping," Jacob mumbled.

Michael took a deep breath, then yelled right into his ear, "WAKE UP SLEEPY HEAD!"

"Grrrr fine!" Jacob said, sitting up from his bed. His eyes widened when he looked at his alarm clock. "It's seven-thirty!"

"So?" Michael asked.

"*So,* I still have two hours," Jacob said.

"Of doing what?" asked Michael.

"OF SLEEPING!" Jacob nearly yelled.

"Oh come on," Michael said, as if sleep wasn't a big deal.

"Though I *really* want to keep sleeping, I probably can't go back asleep. So I guess I'd rather do something that's *very important* with you than just lying in bed awake," Jacob said, rolling his eyes.

"*YES!*" Michael said happily. Jacob just loved seeing his older brother being happy, even though SOMETIMES he would wake him up at seven o'clock in the MORNING when they're *supposed* to wake up at ten! *COME ON MICHAEL, WHY DO YOU HAVE TO DO THIS TO ME!?* Jacob wondered.

"So what are we going to look at this time?" Jacob asked.

"That box from yesterday. I was thinking we'd keep looking in it more," Michael said with a smile.

"Ok."

"Great! You get out of your pajamas while I go get that box!" Michael took off running.

Jacob moaned and reluctantly got out of bed and went to the mirror. He stared into his messy reflection. "I still think I should let my hair grow more. It looks awkward." He tried to brush it, but it kind of made it worse. "Yeesh." His slick, jet black hair *refused* to not look like a jumbled wilderness on the top of his head. It wasn't an afro or anything, it was just *messy*. Jacob wasn't the only one with black hair in the family, but he *was* the only one with bright, teal blue eyes. He yawned, "If Michael does this again, I'm throttling him."

When he left his room and tip-toed down the stairs, he found Michael sitting on the living room floor opening the same big box from yesterday. "So why are we still on that?" Jacob asked.

"Yesterday might not have gone well, due to *someone* deciding we needed to go to the store. Honestly, I think Hazel *knew* that we'd find something against the dragons. She sabotaged us! But not today! With all of Dad's paper work from his journey," Michael reminded, "we *have* to find what he found."

With a yawn, Jacob walked over to the box and sat down.

"I want to look at this," Michael said, showing Jacob a journal that read: 'My journey to find the DragonStaff.'

"That's the same one from yesterday."

"I didn't get to read it all," Michael responded.

"It might be interesting," Jacob said with a shrug. *A little too interesting.* Seriously, Jacob's dad was *not* the person that made everything obvious.

"You can find something else that you want to look at," Michael suggested. Jacob dug into the box and picked up a piece of paper that said, 'A Dragon Attacked Me.' *Why is this so obvious?!*

"I guess I'll look at this," Jacob said, setting the papers on his lap.

"Ooo that looks good."

"I guess I'll look at this while you're looking at that and then we'll switch."

"Ok," Michael agreed, opening his journal.

Jacob sat down on the floor and started reading the paper: *To all of those who wanted to hear how my journey to the Dragon Forest was, here we go. I saw many things in the Dragon Forest including, of course, a dragon!! I cannot remember how exactly it looked, because I only saw it for a split second. All I can remember was that I was searching through the forest and I fell into a hole. I looked up and saw a glimpse of what I think was the DragonStaff. Then I saw green eyes and a black dragon attacked me. When I woke up, I was in the hospital. I don't know what happened to the dragon, but all I know was that for some reason it spared my life.* Jacob's mind exploded with questions. *Why is Dad writing so weird and obvious? He literally writes for the king! But what happened to the dragon? How did my dad end up in the hospital? How did the doctor find him? And... why did the dragon spare his life??*

"WE HAVE TO GO ASK THE KING!" Michael suddenly yelled, standing up and running to the box, throwing papers around. "Here it is!" Michael yelled, holding up a piece of paper.

"What is it?" Jacob asked.

"A map to the DragonStaff!!" Michael yelled in excitement.

"*What?* Let me see that," Jacob said, confused.

"We can go to the king and tell him everything and then *we* can go and find the DragonStaff, then we can destroy them once and for all!" Michael said, handing Jacob the paper. Jacob looked at it. It wasn't the best map, but it would do, because at the end of all the lines there was an X that read: DragonStaff. Jacob looked up at his brother.

"You thinking what I'm thinking?" Michael asked.

"Oh yeah," Jacob responded.

"Well then, what are we waiting for?" Michael asked, excited.

"Ok then!" Jacob said. Jacob ran upstairs to his room to get his shoes on. His heart was pounding. His hands were shaking. His joy was lifting. He was excited. After he got his shoes on, he ran to his window and looked outside. "Victory, here I come," he said.

Jacob and Michael were just outside the door when Jacob realized something. "Um Michael, what if Mom wakes up and finds out we aren't there?" Jacob asked.

"Don't worry, it will be fine," Michael assured.

"You sure?" Jacob asked, unconvinced.

"Positive," Michael said. "Now let's go!"

"Ok," Jacob said, walking across the street, "It's kinda weird that there aren't any cars out today."

"It's good for us cuz we don't have to worry about getting ran over," Michael pointed out.

"Yeah," Jacob agreed. After they had walked about one or two miles, they turned right to the entrance of King Luther's castle. It stood on a huge hill so big that if you looked down, you could see the edge of the Dragon Forest. Once, Jacob and Michael had watched the forest all day, thinking they would see a dragon, but they never did. King Luther's castle was massive with a wall all around. Inside of the wall stood one huge tower with a large spike on top of it, which some people had said that if a dragon flew by, the spike would shoot up and hit it. Of course that was just a rumor that Michael always believed was true. "Do you think King Luther will be excited to see us?" Jacob asked nervously.

"I hope so," Michael responded, then paused and more confidently said, "he should be excited to see us! Because our father works for him! He should be jumping with joy to see his best searcher's sons!"

Are you sure? Of course, Jacob knew that his dad was the *only* searcher King Luther had, but he wasn't sure it was a good time to point that out. Jacob had always gotten nervous while walking towards the guards at the gate.

"Who goes there?" A guard called.

"My name is Michael and this is my brother, Jacob," Michael said pointing to each of them. "We are here to see King Luther."

"Oh! You're Matt Bennett's kids, aren't you?" the guard asked.

"Apologies for your father. He was a good employee and an amazing friend. I do hope he gets better and will come back," another guard said, sounding upset.

"Thank you for your generosity," Michael said, bowing his head in a kind way. "And I talked to my mother the other night and asked her how he was doing. She said he was doing better and should come home in around five days," Michael said. A stab of guilt hit Jacob like a lightning bolt. He had never asked Michael how Dad was doing. He had only asked about the box that Mom brought home.

"How amazing!" the second guard said.

"We didn't know if he was even going to make it!" a third guard said.

"So he should be back in five days?" clarified the first guard.

"Yessir!" said Michael happily. They all looked happy, but not as happy as Jacob felt. *Five days, Dad! I'll see you in five days!*

"Well, I guess we should let y'all in," the first guard said.

"Thank you, kind sir," Michael said. The gate to the castle opened and they happily walked through.

It was always so cool to walk into the castle. The door led into an open room with one large chandelier. Staircases spiraled along the high walls, and hallways were everywhere. It was like standing in the middle of a maze. Jacob and Michael always wondered where all the hallways went, but they didn't dare go in them. The one on the right was the only one that was allowed without special permission, since it led to the Throne Room. Most people were either still at work or in bed, so no one else was visiting. "Excuse me," Michael said to one of the soldiers who was in the room.

"Yes?" the soldier asked.

"Is King Luther here?" asked Michael. *Did he seriously just ask that question?*

"Of course he is," the soldier responded kindly. He was dark-skinned and had extremely short black hair.

"Can you take us to him?" Jacob asked. The guard nodded and walked to the hallway on the right. Jacob knew it led to the Throne Room. The hallway twisted a lot, then went to the left, ending at a gold, double door. Inside was the Throne Room.

"This is as far as I can go," the soldier said.

"Thank you," said Michael.

"You're welcome. Good luck with whatever you are doing," the soldier said walking away. Jacob was excited and scared at the same time. Even though he had visited and talked with the king a lot, this time felt different. Jacob knew whatever was about to happen was either the start of the war ending or the start of defeat.

Here we go.

They opened the door and walked into the Throne Room. It was a large room with two hallways, one on the left, and one on the right. In between the hallways there was a three-step stage with a throne of pure gold. Sitting on the throne was King Luther, the ruler of the humans.

King Luther had short brown hair, but it was hard to see all of it, due to the large gold crown. The crown had one large ruby in the front and smaller sapphires around the rest of it. King Luther looked bored, but when Jacob and Michael walked in, he looked relieved.

"Jacob! Michael! What a thrilling surprise to see you!" King Luther greeted joyfully. "No, no, no, you better not bow at me!" King Luther said while Jacob and Michael started to bow. Michael gave a confused look. "And that's an order," King Luther added with a smile.

"Well, I guess you can't disobey an order," Michael said with a shrug.

"No, you cannot," King Luther said.

"Is that new?" asked Michael, pointing at a glass box with something inside of it.

"Oh yes!" King Luther responded.

"What is it?" Michael asked.

"Come and see!" King Luther was quick to leave his throne and stand next to them, staring at the box. The glass box sat on a wooden platform. Inside of it looked like a panther with wings. Jacob shuddered.

"What is that!?" Michael asked.

"My worst nemesis," King Luther responded. "He is the one who started this war. He's evil."

"Well, I guess he isn't anything anymore," Michael said, grinning.

King Luther sighed, "I wish it was him. But it's only a stuffed panther that I sewed wings on. The real one has red eyes."

"Oh," Michael said in a sad voice.

"So that's your nemesis's name?" Jacob asked, pointing at the plate that said a word he had never heard of before. Severein.

"Hm? Oh! Yes, yes of course! It's a weird name. Dragons always have weird names," said King Luther.

"How do you say it?" Michael asked.

"Severe-in," King Luther responded. Jacob was starting to have goose bumps. *That's a weird name. Sounds very 'severe.'*

"Well, maybe if we run into him, we can kill him," Michael said.

King Luther turned around to look at him, "You didn't come all this way here just to see me, did you?"

"King Luther, we came here to show you the map to the DragonStaff," Michael announced.

"What do you mean?" King Luther asked.

"We went through our dad's stuff that he was working on and we found it! The DragonStaff is real!" Michael said, pulling the map out.

"Not here," King Luther said, looking at the door as if people were listening from the other side. King Luther speed-walked to the hallway in the back left. "Come with me," he said quietly. Jacob and Michael followed. The hallway led to a huge, metal, spiral staircase. After a while, they finally got up the several flights of stairs, which went into another large room. It looked like not many people were allowed in. Of course, Jacob had never been in before. It was a large square room with a pole in each corner and a glass wall. It might have been the last story of the palace, for outside of the glass was the blue sky. *Talk now, look around later,* Jacob thought. King Luther closed the barn door they came through.

"That ought to do it," said King Luther. "Now let me see that map."

"Yes, sir," Michael said, handing him the map. He sounded a little out of breath from all the stairs.

"King Luther, if I may ask, why are we in here?" Jacob asked, confused.

"Because I do not want everyone to hear this conversation. I want this to just be me and you two," King Luther said. "This isn't the best map I've seen, but it will do."

"So it really does exist!" Michael said in an excited voice.

"I think so, everyone knows Severein is a man of his word... but of course, I don't trust him. I definitely trust your father.... so... yes, I do think it exists," King Luther responded in a worried voice.

"What exactly does it do again?" Jacob asked. "I know it can defeat the dragons, but how?"

"If the rumors are true, then I believe it has the power to control them," King Luther responded.

"Whoa," Jacob said. "But how is that possible?"

"Some type of power," Luther said.

"Like….. magic?"

"King Luther, this is something me Jacob and I have always wanted to do…. please allow me and Jacob to go on this journey to find the DragonStaff," Michael nearly pleaded. "Please. We are ready! And we want to destroy the dragons! Please let us go on this journey!"

We could be heroes, then people won't laugh at us for thinking that the DragonStaff is real. Instead, people would be so happy to see us…. Then we could be called the Kids Who Saved the World.

"But aren't you two a little young?" King Luther asked.

"I'm fifteen," Jacob said.

"I'm almost seventeen," Michael responded.

"Little young," King Luther said in a soft voice.

"Some people say that it's good to learn young, because if you wait to learn when you are older, you would be old and forget everything," Michael pointed out.

King Luther laughed, "So, you are calling me old and forgetful?"

"Uhh….No! No! No! No! That's not what I meant, no! You're not old! No! I mean like old, old! But like, no! I mean like, no!" Michael said trying to not sound offensive.

"I'm just messing with you!" King Luther said, laughing.

"So, you *will* let us do this journey?" Jacob asked.

"I don't know, I will have to think about it. But I will let you know tomorrow. Be prepared because it will be early in the morning. So just let me think about it today and I will let you know tomorrow, ok? King Luther asked.

"Yes, Your Majesty," Jacob and Michael said in unison.

"Now go home before your mother gets worried about you. One of my soldiers will drive you home," King Luther said.

"Thank you," Michael said. They turned back and walked the way they came. After a long time from walking down the stairs, they came out of the Throne Room. The same soldier that had led them to the Throne Room was waiting for them. Jacob waved and he waved back.

"Samual, can you please take them home?" King Luther asked.

"Of course, Your Majesty," Samual said with a bow.

"Go with Samual and come back tomorrow," King Luther said.

"Thank you for everything," Michael said as they left.

"You're welcome! I will see you tomorrow!" King Luther called.

CHAPTER 2

A DISAPPOINTMENT

"Thank you!" Jacob and Michael called, waving at Samual.

"Anytime," Samual said through the open window. The limo pulled out of the driveway and drove off.

"Seriously, we need to visit the king more often! A limo? Awesome!" Michael happily said.

"That was pretty cool," Jacob agreed.

"Yeah. I hope everyone is still asleep, especially Hazel," Michael said. They unlocked the door and walked quietly inside, but not quietly enough.

"What are y'all doing?" asked a voice from in front of them. They froze and slowly looked at the breakfast table, where Hazel sat. "Where were you guys?"

"Uh….. King Luther's," Michael responded.

"Why?" Hazel asked.

"Um…" Michael hesitated.

"I can't believe this! You went there to talk about destroying the dragons, didn't you?" Hazel asked, annoyed.

"Maybee," Jacob answered innocently.

"We talked about this!" Hazel said, sounding upset.

"No, *you* talked about it," Michael pointed out.

"But you agreed to it!"

"I don't recall 'agreed'," Michael said. "You can't expect us to be like 'hey there's a dragon! Let's be friends with it and talk about how horrible this war is!'"

"There's no point in arguing about it right now," Jacob pointed out.

Hazel took a deep breath. "Ok," she said. She stomped back to the table, sat down, and continued to draw.

"I'm going to go keep looking in Dad's box," Michael whispered.

"Ok," Jacob responded as Michael walked down the two steps into the playroom. Jacob nervously walked over to Hazel. "What are you drawing?"

"Umm, you wouldn't like it. You might would kill it," Hazel said dryly.

"Let me guess? A dragon?" Jacob asked.

"My master piece! But….yes," Hazel responded.

"Aren't they all your master pieces?" Jacob asked.

"Yeah, but this one is pretty good," Hazel said, showing him the drawing.

"Wow, Hazel that *is* good!" Jacob complimented. It was a drawing of Hazel petting a pink-scaled dragon. "Are you going to draw one of me?"

"I already have," Hazel responded, showing him another piece of paper.

"Oh…um… that looks uhhh… pretty good," Jacob managed to say. *And creepy.* It was a picture of a dragon lying on the floor, and Jacob stabbing a spear into its heart. Blood was everywhere.

"This…this is what you want to do to the dragons, and this is how I feel," she said, holding up another piece of paper. It was a drawing of herself with her hands over her mouth and tears running down her eyes.

32

"Very accurate," Jacob said.

"Thank you," Hazel said, pleased.

"Hey Jacob, come look at this!" Michael called from the playroom.

"What is it?" Jacob called back.

"Umm… something."

"What?"

"JUST COME HERE!" Michael yelled loudly. *Michael what are you doing? Are you trying to wake Mom up?* Jacob thought, then realized, *Oh I better get down there before he yells loud enough to wake her up.*

"Coming," Jacob finally said.

"Bout time," Michael said in an unhappy but joking voice. While Jacob was walking in the room he heard steps behind him. *Oh no! Is Mom up already?* But when he turned around, he realized it was just Hazel.

"Oh, uhhhh…whaaat are you…doing?" Jacob tried to asked.

"What? Am I not allowed in the playroom anymore? What am I going to do, tell the dragons your oh *so* secret and amazing plan?" Hazel asked, rolling her eyes. "Why would I care?"

"Ok, I guess I will allow you to join us," Jacob said, grinning.

"Oh, you don't have to allow me," she joked. They stopped when they saw Michael. "What in the world are you doing?" Hazel asked. "No wait, I know what your doing: you're making a *MESS*." Pieces of paper were *everywhere.* It looked like Michael had picked up the box of their father's papers they were looking at, stood on the couch, and completely threw the box in the air, letting all of Dad's work fly around wherever they wanted to. *Which he probably did*, Jacob thought. They were on the floor, some on the couch, even some on the two chairs.

Michael was running in a circle, picking up papers, reading it, then throwing them back on the floor.

"I'm *trying* to find clues," Michael said hurriedly, then stopped, noticing Hazel. He gave Jacob an 'are you sure?' look. Jacob nodded.

"What kind of clues?" Hazel asked, trying to walk towards Michael without stepping on any papers.

Michael took a deep breath, "Well you know, what does the DragonStaff look like? Why did the dragon attack Dad? Where exactly is the DragonStaff and-"

"Whoa, whoa, whoa, *whoa,* a dragon did what?" Hazel asked, confused. Of coarse Hazel didn't know about why Dad was in the hospital. She only knew he was hurt for some reason, but Jacob and Michael had only just found out the real reason. Jacob knew Hazel needed to know.

"Ok, but you might want to sit down so I can tell y'all the whole thing," Michael said, walking over to a pile of papers, the only thing that was organized. Jacob and Hazel sat on the floor next to each other as Michael sat in front of them to explain.

"I can't believe this!" Hazel said again. "Why would a dragon attack Dad?!"

"Can I see that picture you found?" Jacob asked.

"Ok," Michael said, handing the new papers over. Jacob studied it intensely.

"So, this is what the dragon that attacked Dad looked like?" Jacob asked.

"That's what it says," Michael answered. Jacob didn't want to admit it, but it looked kind of cool. It was mostly all black, but it looked like Dad had tried to draw…scales? But the tips of every drawn scale was blue.

"That looks kind of…cool," Hazel said carefully.

"Whether it looks cool or not, if I ever see that dragon, I'm gonna… I'm gonna stab a spear into its throat for attacking my dad!" Michael said angrily.

"Eww….grows!" Hazel yelped.

"You know what? We should go to the forest and do that exact thing!" Michael said angrily.

"Wait, what?" Hazel asked while Michael stood up and went for the door. "But he spared Dad's life! He never killed him!"

"You don't know that! He could have tried to kill him, but the police came and saved him!" Michael said angrily.

"But we don't have permission from King Luther yet!" Jacob called after him.

"Grrrr, but I just really want to do *something!*" Michael said angrily.

"Guys," Hazel said.

"We have to wait for King Luther's permission," Jacob argued.

"Guuys," Hazel said again.

"That dragon needs to be punished!" Michael argued back.

"But…" Jacob started.

"GUYS!" Hazel interrupted.

"What?" Jacob and Michael asked at the same time.

"Mom's awake," Hazel said. They paused, listening. Hazel was right. Footsteps were coming from upstairs.

"The papers," Jacob realized, looking at Michael.

"We have to clean them up," Michael said quietly. He turned around and ran back into the playroom. Jacob followed him with Hazel close behind. *Huh, through all of that she is still going to help us with cleaning the papers up?* Jacob thought. *She must really forget about arguments fast.* They ran into the playroom and began to pick up all the pieces of paper. "I'll put these all up before Mom sees them," Michael whispered.

Jacob nodded, "Hazel, turn on a show or something."

"Good idea, that way Mom will think that we have just been watching stuff all morning," Michael said. Hazel nodded, then turned the TV on. Jacob and Michael were stuffing all of the pieces of papers into the box when a song began to play. Michael looked up at the TV, "Hazel, what are you doing?!"

"What? Y'all said turn on a show," Hazel said innocently.

"Not the Fighters of Peace show!" Michael nearly yelled. *Oh boy.* Jacob thought just as the theme song began to play: *"Peace at last! We all come together! No more fights! Humans and dragons living in PEACE!!!!"*

"TURN THAT DISRESPECTFUL JUNK OFFF!" Michael yelled.

Hazel laughed.

"What's going on down here?" someone asked from the doorway. They all turned around as their mom walked down the two steps and into the play room. She had short, blackish-blond hair. She looked up at the TV. It was still playing the theme song. She frowned, "Hazel, I know you like that show but Jacob and Michael don't, so can you please turn it off?" Mom asked.

"Ok," Hazel said, picking up the remote and turning it off. Michael had just covered the box from the chair's footrest just before Mom had walked in.

"Are we going anywhere today?" Jacob asked.

"Let me eat breakfast, then later we need to go to the store and eat…or would y'all rather go for lunch or dinner?" Mom asked.

"Dinner!" they all said at the same time.

"Ok, then we'll wait a little while so we can go to the store, then eat dinner," Mom said.

"Ok," Jacob said.

"I'm going to go eat breakfast," Mom said, turning around and walking out of the play room.

"K," Michael said.

"Want to go to my room and draw?" Hazel asked.

"Sure," Jacob answered.

"I'm going to my room to think," Michael announced.

"Ok, Mister Thinkie Pants, Jacob and I are going to go draw *or* play Legos, maybe both," Hazel said with a grin.

"Alright. Oh and by the way, I'm not 'Mister Thinkie Pants.' You were the one who told me to be more thinking and less doing, remember?" Michael asked, walking towards the stairs.

"And yet you still do it. Come on, Jacob," Hazel said, running up the stairs.

Before he followed her, he wanted to ask Mom something. "Mom?" Jacob asked, walking over to her as she cracked some eggs in the kitchen.

"Yes?" she asked.

"Um…do you want the war to end?" Jacob asked.

"Of course I do," she responded.

"So, you do want us to destroy the dragons?"

Mom didn't answer, she only sighed. *Grrr why does she never want to talk about these things?!* Jacob wondered. "Mom, don't you want the humans to win?" Jacob tried. Jacob's mom looked at him with an unreadable expression on her face.

"It's not that I want the humans to lose, and it's not that I want the dragons to win, it's just that…I guess… I guess I just don't know what I want. It's complicated," she said. This was how all conversations ended whenever Jacob tried to talk about dragons with Mom. Mom would get so upset about something that Jacob did not know, then she'd just stop talking. "Why don't you go play with Hazel?" Mom asked.

Jacob nodded, then made his way to the stairs. *One day,* Jacob thought, *one day I'm going to find out why Mom gets so upset about dragons!* The first bedroom upstairs on the left was Jacob's room, with the bathroom right across from it. The second bedroom on the left was Hazel's room, and then right across from her room was Michael's room. Way in the back of the hallway was Mom and Dad's room, where the hallway ended. Jacob stopped and opened Hazel's door. Hazel was laying on her stomach on the floor, looking at a piece of paper. Her room was a soft green color with some sparkles here and there, and a white carpeted floor. Jacob sat on the floor next to her.

"So what are we doing?" Jacob asked.

"We are going to draw, but first…I have a few questions about this," Hazel said, showing him a piece of paper. To Jacob's surprise, it was the drawing of the black and blue dragon that Michael found in the playroom.

"How did you get that?" Jacob asked.

"When Michael turned around to look at the Fighters of Peace show, I grabbed it and put it in my pocket," Hazel responded with a grin.

"Sneaky," Jacob complimented. "And that has got to be a very deep pocket. But I don't see how you have any questions about it. It's easy, the dragon attacked Dad and then Dad drew a picture of it."

"No, that's just it! The dragon attacked Dad and then he woke up in the hospital. When Michael read the story to us, it said that Dad didn't see much of the dragon. How would he know what the dragon looked like? *And* Dad was in the hospital, so how would he have drawn this?" Hazel asked. Now that he thought of it, he was starting to get those questions too. *How did Dad know what the dragon looked like?*

"Can I see the picture again?" Jacob asked. Hazel nodded and gave to him.

"And the biggest question that I have, is how would Dad be able to draw the dragon in this position?" Hazel said, "I—of course—am an artist, so I know for a fact that you can't look at something for a split second, then draw it in this position and make it look so real," she said matter-a-factly. Jacob hated to admit it, but Hazel was right. Now Jacob was studying the whole picture. He never paid any attention to what the dragon was doing. In the picture the dragon was laying on a couch, resting its head on the side with his tail dangling on the end. The dragon was looking forward. There were two couches, one on the end looking forward, and one that started on the side. The picture ended at the edge of the other couch. "Man, Dad must be a *good* artist," Hazel said.

"If you're right," Jacob said, "and Dad would have had to be looking at the dragon, then…he would have lied about seeing a dragon for a split second…right?" Jacob asked uneasily.

"I just don't see how he would have come up with all of this on his own," Hazel said.

"Wait a minute, I see where this is going," Jacob said. "Do you really think Dad would betray us?"

"Of course not," Hazel responded. "But let me ask you something."

"What?" Jacob asked.

"Michael said that y'all found a map, is that right?" she asked.

"Yeah," Jacob answered slowly.

"And didn't Michael say that it looked horrible?"

Jacob looked at her, surprised.

"Dad doesn't draw bad maps," she said.

"You've seen one of his?" Jacob asked. She nodded. Hazel put down the drawing of the dragon and picked up a blank piece of paper and started to draw. Not knowing what to think, Jacob sat there, a thousand thoughts whirling in his head. But they were so hard, he couldn't make it out. *Dad would never lie to us…right?*

Jacob was quiet for the rest of the day. He just could not think right. Something was nagging him, like he was so close to something, but he just couldn't make it out. They had already eaten dinner and gone to the store, and he was already in bed. But Jacob couldn't sleep. Everything Hazel had said was just stuck in his head. It was pitch-black dark in his room. He looked at his alarm clock and groaned "Ughhh, why can't I go to sleep? It's one o-clock!" he said. An idea popped into his head. He gently got off his bed and walked over to his door, gently cracking it just enough to squeeze through. *Hope Michael hasn't thought of this yet.* He crept down the stairs and into the kitchen, past the table, and into the playroom. He got down on the floor and lifted the blanket off the chair. *Yes!* The box of Dad's work papers were still there. He picked the whole box up and took it to his room. To his surprise the box was heavy. "Let's see how many answers I can get from here," he whispered to himself. He put the box on his bed and sat down. Then leaned over to his lamp and turned it on. One by one he looked at all of the papers. "How am I going to find anything in here?" he whispered to himself. He reached his hand in the box to pull out more paper, but paused when he felt something tear. *Whoops.* But when he looked in the box it wasn't paper that tore, it was the box itself. *Wait… is there something inside it?* He looked at it more closely, then gasped. There was a pocket with a folder in it on the side of the box. *What else are you hiding in here, Dad?* he wondered. He reached his hand inside and pulled it out, then shoved all the other papers aside and opened the folder. When he looked inside there were more papers, but not only papers. There were… pictures. But the pictures weren't of Jacob, Michael, or Hazel, but of people that he did not recognize. The only person he recognized was his father, but he looked younger. The picture had to be taken about the time when his dad and mom were married. But his dad was with someone else who Jacob did not know. The person had a brown cape and a brown cowboy hat on, and he was holding something…a little cat? There were a lot of pictures of the strange person, but without the cat. *Who is the weird…and cool person with Dad? I know Dad's old, but he is NOT old western!* After several yawns, and his eyes getting blurry, Jacob figured it was time to try to sleep again. With a yawn, he put all the normal papers back. But when he started to put the special papers back in the folder, he found a piece of paper that he had missed. His eyes widened when he picked it up. "What? How!" he nearly yelled. It was a map, but not just any map, it was a map of the entire Dragon Forest. It was the best map Jacob had ever seen. Jacob studied it carefully. One of the multiple routes ended in small words: 'The DragonStaff Cave.' "How can there be two maps?" Jacob asked himself. But the weirdest thing about it was there were a lot of lines, but the biggest one ended and said in larger letters: 'His Cave.' *Whose cave?* Jacob wondered. *Should I show this to King Luther? But… for some reason Dad hasn't shown this to him, so maybe I shouldn't.* But then a plan began to form in his mind. *Well, maybe there is a way to find the DragonStaff even if Luther says no; that map that we gave him might not be real. So even if Luther says no, Michael and I are going to find the DragonStaff, whether he likes it or not. Well then, looks like we're going on a journey tomorrow.* Jacob closed his eyes and drifted off to sleep.

King Luther paced back and forth in the tallest tower of his palace. "What to do...what to do... Should I let them do it? Can I even trust them?" He looked down at the map Jacob and Michael had given to him. "Hmmm, this really is a bad map." King Luther continued. "What if they do what their father did?" He stopped and looked out his window. It was dark outside, but Luther could still see the Dragon Forest below, or rather, the Peace Forest. "I can't trust them. I will send my best soldiers to find it, and when they do, you'll be dead, Severein. I *will* kill you, and I am not going to let two little kids stop me from doing it."

It was eight o-clock when Michael came storming in Jacob's room. "Rise and shine! Wake up sleepy head! We have a big day today!" But when he pulled Jacob's blanket away he saw that Jacob wasn't there. "What? Did he leave without me?"

"Under here," Jacob called up to him.

"What?" Michael got on the floor and looked under the bed. "What are you doing?" he asked.

"Oh nothing, just getting ready for our big adventure...you know what I mean?" Jacob asked from under the bed.

"On the floor?" Michael said in a funny voice.

"Packed my backpack."

"On the floor?"

"Got everything I need.

"On the floor?"

"Will you stop saying that?"

"On the floor?"

"Ok, now you are starting to sound like Hazel," Jacob joked.

Michael laughed. "What are we going to do? Eat breakfast and then go to King Luther? Or go to King Luther and then eat breakfast?" Michael asked.

"How about…eat breakfast first," Jacob answered.

"Ok," Michael said, running to the door. "You coming?"

"Oh yeah, be right there," Jacob called as Michael ran out the door. As soon as Michael was gone, Jacob jumped back to the floor under his bed and grabbed the secret folder, sticking it into his backpack. *I can't tell him yet.* Jacob got off the floor and walked downstairs. Michael was sitting at the table eating a bowl of cereal, and to Jacob's surprise, Michael was shaking all over with nerves. "You ok?"

"Uh yeah, of course, why wouldn't I be?" Michael answered weirdly.

"Oh I don't know…. Maybe it's because you're shaking all over and you are actually looking at the bowl of cereal and not just staring out into the distance like you usually do."

"Ok, so maybe I'm a little nervous."

"Mmm-hmmm."

"Alright, so maybe a lot! But you can't expect me to not be," Michael admitted.

"Yeah I understand." Jacob hesitated, "Michael…. if King Luther told you to kill someone….or something….would you?" he asked very nervously.

"Why do you ask?" Michael asked suspiciously.

"I'm just wondering."

"I guess it depends on what it's like….if it's a human then I don't know, but if it's a dragon, then any time, any day," Michael said. But something about his face looked unsure. Of course Jacob and Michael had never actually seen a dragon, so they didn't even know if they could kill one.

"I don't want to talk about it though," Michael said.

"Yeah, it was a weird question any way," Jacob admitted. Jacob poured milk and cereal into a bowl and began to eat. When Jacob had finally sat down Michael was already getting up. "You're not going to eat that?" Jacob asked, pointing at all the cereal that was still in his bowl.

"Eww, no! The cereal got all soggy and gross," he said in a funny voice.

"Ok," Jacob said, rolling his eyes.

After they ate and got ready, they ran to Luther's castle, but when they got there, everything was quiet.

"What happened here?" Michael asked. "It's like everything is deserted."

"Yeah," Jacob said nervously.

"I'll go check the speaker on the gate," Michale said, walking over to the castle's gate. The gate usually wasn't closed though. Everything felt weird.

Jacob, feeling spooked, walked over to the edge of the railings and looked down to the Dragon Forest below. Chills ran through his body for no reason, and a strange desire to run into the forest grew. His hands twitched for a sword, even though he had never held a sword in his life. He saw dragons flying towards burning houses and fields. Soldiers attacked soldiers as dragons attacked dragons. Lightning lit up the sky as a strange voice said, "Tonight...we attack." Jacob gasped in fear. "What was that?" Jacob breathed. It was all just a vision in his head, but it looked so real.

"Jacob, are you alright?" asked Michael, looking curiously at him. Jacob hadn't even noticed that he had come over.

"Did you feel that?" Jacob asked.

"Feel what?"

"N-Nothing.

"Are you ok?"

"Ummmmm...yeah...yeah. I'm alright."

"Ok," Michael said. "The guy on the speaker said to come on in. I don't know why everything seems so abandoned, though. It's usually pretty busy this time of day.

Cold fear was running through Jacob like water. *What was that? Is something going to attack tonight? Is it the dragons?* Michael walked up to the gate to see if anyone was there, but there was no one in sight. "This is really creepy," Jacob said nervously. He looked back at the forest.

"Yeah… we should probably go," Michael said. He tilted his head at him. "Are you sure you're alright?"

"I'm fine," Jacob responded.

"Ok," Michael said. "Now, come on. We don't want to keep him waiting."

They kept walking as the castle gate opened. *What. Was. That?! Did I like fall asleep or something? Was it a daydream? It all just looked and sounded so real! What was that?* Then a strange feeling took hold of Jacob as a weird buzz hummed in his mind. **"And who might you be? The part you will have in this world is strange, isn't it?"** An airy voice echoed in his mind. But it was so clear, it sounded like someone was talking right in front of him. Jacob shrieked and jumped back, too horrified to scream.

"Jacob, Jacob come on," Michael called. The buzz stopped, the voice was gone, and pure silence fell in his mind. Jacob looked around in horror. "Jacob! Come on! We're gonna be late!" Michael called impatiently.

"C-coming!" Jacob forced out of his mouth, breathing hard. *What. Was. That?!!!*

"I'm sorry guys," Luther apologized, looking out the huge window. They were in the same hidden room as before. "I just can't let you go, it's too dangerous."

"But…" Michael tried to protest.

"No buts," King Luther said. "Besides, you are needed at home with your mother and your sister. Without your father there, you guys are the men of the house, especially you, Michael." It always felt weird when people said that. Of course, Jacob was glad that Michael was the man of the house….but Jacob had always felt that he would probably beat Michael in combat. Even though Michael was older, it seemed like he could beat him with cleverness and strength, but of course Michael didn't believe that.

"But…but I just want to do something!" said Michael disappointingly.

"Why do you think we can't do it?" Jacob asked. Michael looked at him with an expression on his face that clearly said "Stop!" But Jacob only gave that exact look right back at him. *You might be older than me, but that doesn't mean you can boss me around in front of the king…maybe at home but not here.* King Luther looked at Jacob as if he just realized something, studying him from top to bottom with a worried expression on his face.

"Well, umm you see," said King Luther, then hesitated. "Well….um…you're a little young and I just don't think you're ready," he said worriedly.

"If I may ask, why not? Is there any way we prove it to you?"

"Why don't y'all go home," King Luther said without answering his question. "You never know when a dragon decides to attack, cuz really, you never know. So how about y'all run along and head home?"

"Ok," Michael said, turning around and walking out of the room. Jacob walked slowly behind him.

"Remember, Jacob," Luther said, right before Jacob was completely out of the room, "if you ever run into a dragon, or something like a dragon, don't believe a word it says."

"Ok…" Jacob responded slowly.

"Oh, and Jacob," Luther called again as Jacob started to turn around. "Meet me at the FreshCod restaurant tomorrow morning, before breakfast. Just you…alone…no one else. Be there, ok?" King Luther said in a serious voice.

Jacob slowly nodded and walked away.

After Luther knew they were gone, he said with a chuckle, "Looks like I found him before you did….. " He turned around and tossed a picture off of the wall, revealing the hidden portrait that had the picture of the prophecy on it. "Too bad I beat you to him," he chuckled. But little did he know that he didn't beat him at all.

CHAPTER 3

THE VOICE

Fires were everywhere as two dragons with glowing swords fought. A black ship with orange stripes launched into the sky, only to crash down to the ground. A door opened, and in the darkness, red eyes opened.

"Young one, young one, wake up!"

Jacob shot up from his bed, breathing hard. *What a horrible nightmare!* Of course, Jacob knew far too well that the denied permission from Luther was real, but this? This he had no idea. Everything looked so real, but was it? Jacob looked out of the window and into the dark night sky. Then the buzz set off in his head again. **"I'm guessing you don't know how to control yourself, young lad,"** the voice said so clearly in his head. Jacob shrieked in horror and jumped out of bed.

"Where are you?" Jacob asked in fear. "Who are you?!"

"May I ask the same thing again; who are you?" the voice asked in response.

"I will not tell you until you tell me," Jacob said, trying not to sound afraid as he searched his room.

"Neither will I."

"What do you want?"

There was silence, then the voice said, **"You know. I sense your presence, but do you sense mine?"**

Jacob froze. Of course, Jacob did feel something, but without answering he said, "Stop! Go away! I don't have anything you'd want! Leave before I call my mom!"

"Very well, I will let you sleep. But remember, tomorrow at seven when you wake up, why don't you turn the TV on and check the news? You might find something interesting. Goodbye, sleepy head." Then the voice and the buzz vanished. Somehow, Jacob sleepily laid back, forced himself to think it was all a dream, and fell asleep.

All night Jacob's dreams were haunted by the fear of something seeing him, and the fear of something catching everything on fire, until finally he woke up. Just as the buzz in his head vanished, he looked at the alarm clock next to his bed. "Hmmm seven o'clock….the TV!" He shot up out of bed and ran downstairs to the playroom and turned the TV on.

"Breaking news," the reporter said. "Last night, many citizens' houses and fields about to be harvested mysteriously caught on fire. One owner even claimed that he saw a giant beast in his field, but when he looked there were no prints in the mud."

"MOM!" Jacob called running upstairs. He ran to the end of the hall and into his mother's room. His mother was awake but still sitting on the bed with the TV on. She looked up at Jacob, tears were in her eyes.

"Go get your brother and sister," she said in a sad voice. Jacob nodded and ran to Michael's and Hazel's rooms, woke them up, then sent them to Mom. They all huddled around their mother's bed, as the TV showed pictures of fields on fire and houses in ruins. A reporter was saying, "Still, firemen are searching for more things that have not yet been found. Now, we are going to one of our top reporters, Susan McCarthy," said the TV.

"I am here, live at one of the fields that was destroyed," said the reporter. She was tall with short blonde hair. Jacob had never known why this reporter always wore so much makeup; it made her look like a ghost.

"Isn't that old Marty's field?" Hazel asked.

"Mr. Marty, and yes," Mom said.

"As you can see, the fire was somehow put out, but, I have a few interesting facts that I would like to say," she continued. "I talked to the owner of this field, and he told me that it was a lightning bolt that hit directly in the middle of the field. I know what you're thinking folks. Why would we be so interested in lightning? The weird part about it is when we got here, ice was all around the field. Everything around the field was wet with ice and water, the fire never escaped the field. This is the same for many other fields as well. Millions of dollars have been lost in this attack. A significant price raise is to be expected for all produce. Considering a beast was seen, we are assuming the dragons are responsible. I am not sure how we will retaliate for this, but I will report all the information I receive. But the remaining question I have regarding this attack, is who put the fires out? And how did a lightning bolt strike when zero storms were reported? I'm Susan McCarthy, reporting for one of the biggest war attacks of the year."

Jacob heard enough. He walked out of the room and walked gloomily to his own room. "Grrrr, why do these things have to happen?!" he said to himself angrily. Then he remembered what Luther had said and eagerly threw his socks and shoes on. "Mom, I'm going for a walk!" he called. He immediately ran downstairs and outside. When he got outside, he slowed down and started to walk.

"Going somewhere?" the voice asked as the buzz turned on. Jacob shrieked and ran. **"Hmmm, how long does it take for someone to get used to something?"** the voice asked himself wonderingly.

"You knew, you knew about the attack!" Jacob gasped for breath.

"A human's temper….ever so strong and quick. You know, you can figure out a lot about someone if you know how quick they are to get angry," the voice responded.

Jacob growled in frustration. "You started it. You started the fire, didn't you!?" Jacob nearly yelled.

The voice didn't answer, until finally it asked, **"Why are you running?"**

"You didn't answer my question."

"Neither did you."

"I asked you first."

"Stop."

"You stop."

"You stop running."

"Oh, so you *want* me to stop running?" Jacob asked mockingly. "Well then, I guess I'm going to do the exact *opposite!"*

"Oh sweet niblets, how much does it take to get a kid to stop?" the voice asked. Jacob all of a sudden tripped as if he ran right into a wall.

"Ah!" he shrieked in surprise. "Did, did you just…" Jacob started, but then he was interrupted by the voice.

"Look beside you," the voice instructed.

"Whoa," Jacob said in amazement. Gasping for breath, he stood up and stared at the burned-up house and yard beside him. "How did this happen?" he asked himself. Something glittered in the dirt and he squatted down to look at it. Touching the dirt he tried to make out what it was, but the dirt was cold and wet. His hand fell on something freezing. "Ice?" he asked, looking down at the chunk of glittering ice. "But that's impossible."

"How is it impossible?" the voice asked.

"Because of the sun, and it's summer, so it's too hot for ice. How could it just appear?" he asked wonderingly.

"One day young child, you will see that it is not impossible," the voice responded.

"But how did it get here?" Jacob asked, confused.

"That question will be for another time, but for now, isn't there a place you are trying to be?"

"Oh yeah, I forgot! I have to be at the restaurant! I've got to go!" Jacob realized.

"Well, then I guess I'll talk to you later. See you soon," the voice said and then the buzz and the voice, once again, vanished. *I really need to figure out what that is,* Jacob thought, getting up and running towards the restaurant where Luther wanted to meet.

The FreshCod restaurant that they were going to meet at was on First Monroe Street, which was right off Luther's castle. The bells to the restaurant rang when he walked in. Looking around for King Luther, he walked around the store till finally he found him. King Luther was sitting down at a small circle table next to a window, a couple of pieces of paper were laid out in front of him. A worried expression was on his face. "Ah, Jacob, there you are. I was beginning to wonder if you would show up," King Luther said in a delightful, welcoming voice. Jacob began to bow. "Oh no, please don't. I would rather not draw much attention," Luther said. "Please, please sit down." An unsettling feeling went over Jacob; it was odd that it was just him and King Luther sitting there alone with no guards in sight. It was also odd that no one was noticing Luther's presence, everyone around them was acting normal, a little too normal. People around them were all just drinking coffee and minding their own business, but still, Jacob had a strange feeling that he was being watched. As if something was there that wasn't supposed to be there.

Good grief, what is wrong with me? Jacob thought. *Why do I keep feeling like something might happen when it obviously isn't going to?*

"Why do you want me to be here?" Jacob asked. *Whoops, that didn't come out right.*

"Oh, well, um," Luther said, a bit shocked. "Well, you see Jacob, I see something in you: greatness. Amazing skills, that you probably never even knew were there. There's just something about you, that's just so unique," Luther continued. "I believe you could get the

DragonStaff…" Right at that moment—while Luther was still talking—the buzz snapped on in Jacob's head. "And…… Jacob, are you ok?" asked King Luther.

"Hmm…oh uh, yes of course!" Jacob said in a worried voice.

"Who are you talking to?" asked the voice. *Oh no!* Jacob thought. *Please don't talk to me, please don't talk to me, please don't talk to me,* Jacob thought over and over until finally—to Jacob's relief—the buzz left. *Whew.* "So, you do think we can go?" Jacob asked.

"Of course!" King Luther said. "I am just afraid you would get hurt."

"So we can go?!"

"Of course, of course you can go. In fact, I am now ordering you to go there, and that's an order you can't refuse," King Luther said calmly. A little too calmly.

"Wait," Jacob said. "What about my mom? What if she doesn't want us to go?"

"Don't worry," Luther said. "I will take care of your mom, but what you need to do is go back home, gather what you need, and then go to the Dragon Forest."

"Isn't my brother coming too?" Jacob asked.

"Hmm, oh, oh yeah. Why not?" Luther said, as if he didn't think about that. "Now, go grab your brother, and go find that DragonStaff," King Luther commanded. Although, it kind of sounded like he was trying to convince a kid to give him something, but Jacob tried not to think about it.

"Yes sir!" Jacob said happily.

He started to get off his chair when King Luther said, "And Jacob, if you run into any dragons or anything, don't believe anything they tell you, no matter what it is. Oh and if you get captured, I want you to be my spy, so act like you're their friend, and get them to trust you. Then, lead them right to me," Luther said, handing him something. "This is a tracker. It will track all of your steps after you click the button, and you will also be able to text me, but only my number is on there, so you can't text anyone else. Put it in your pocket, and don't lose it," King Luther said.

"I won't," Jacob promised. "And thank you."

"You are welcome, Jacob the spy," Luther said. Jacob smiled and walked out the door.

Jacob was just off First Monroe Street when the buzz turned on. **"Hmm, seems like you are starting to get used to this,"** the voice noticed when Jacob didn't jump.

"Why me? Why are you talking to me when there are so many others to bother?"

"Because, I feel your presence," the voice responded. **"And I know you feel mine, so you need to stop trying to run away from me."**

"Why not?"

"Because you can't run away from your own shadow."

"So, you are just my shadow?" Jacob asked jokingly.

"It's just a metaphor, a little something you kids probably don't understand," the voice responded mockingly.

As Jacob walked over to the railings at Luther's castle, the leaves shuffled from the breeze in the Dragon Forest below. More than ever, something was calling him to the forest. He sighed, "Why don't I know who you are?" Jacob asked. "Have I ever met you?"

"Not exactly, but you know what you must do, I know what you must do, so why won't you just do it?"

Jacob sighed.

"Listen to that odd voice inside of you. You have always wondered in your heart why it is that you feel the way you feel. The call to the forest, and that strange feeling that something is about to happen. And it does happen. Always," the voice said.

Jacob looked up, "How did you?.."

"I know why you're different. You have questions, I have answers. Just come to me, and I will tell you everything."

"How, how would I find you?" Jacob asked.

"Listen to that feeling, and you *will* run into me," the voice responded.

"Why can't you come to me?" Jacob asked.

"I already have," the voice answered. **"But you did not get out of bed, sleepy head."**

"Yeah, I am still a bit tired because someone kept me up last night," Jacob said.

The voice chuckled, **"Yeah, see you soon young'n."** The voice and the buzz both faded out.

Jacob took a deep breath, "What am I doing?" he asked himself. Jacob knew he needed to obey King Luther to find the DragonStaff, but that feeling he had always kept deep inside was urging him to that voice. Of course, Jacob wanted to find the DragonStaff, but how could he refuse to do this? All his life he always had something nagging him with strange things. Something inside him knew what he had to do. A plan began to form in his mind, but how could he drag Michael into this mess? *I have to find this voice. Even if it means not being able to find the DragonStaff.* Jacob sighed. *I need to know. I need to know what this is, and I want to find out today. I need to know who I am.* He turned to walk home.

When Jacob came around to the house, he immediately saw Hazel outside playing baseball. "Where have you been?" she asked when Jacob walked up next to her.

"Uh, nowhere," he answered. "Hey Hazel, do you know where Michael is?"

"I think he's inside plotting revenge against the dragons, unless he took off walking like you did." Hazel swung the bat at the stick holding the ball.

"Ok."

"And Jacob," Hazel said as Jacob walked up to the door, "where did you walk to?" she asked.

"First Monroe Street."

"Why?"

"Because I wanted to."

"That's right off of Luther's castle."

"Yep."

"Does that have anything to do with anything?"

"Does it matter?"

"Ok," Hazel said dismissively. "Oh, and Jacob, good luck." She swung the bat one last time. Walking inside the house, Jacob immediately walked up stairs.

"Michael," Jacob said, knocking on the door. Without waiting for an answer, Jacob opened the door. "Michael, are you ok?" Jacob asked. Michael sat on his bed looking down on his hands.

Yep, he's definitely upset.

"I just don't understand!" Michael said angrily. "Why do the dragons have to attack? What have we ever done to them? What do we have that they want so much!"

"I don't know what they want from us," Jacob said. "But whatever it is, we are going to find out."

"I wish."

"Oh, I think we will," Jacob said.

"Wait, what are you talking about?"

"Michael, Luther said yes."

"What! But he said no, right?

"But then he wanted to meet me at a restaurant on First Monroe Street......."

"And then......"

"And then he said yes!"

"No way! This is awesome! We are going to find the DragonStaff, use it to destroy the dragons and save the world!" Michael cried excitingly.

"Pack your stuff cause we're going today!" Jacob said with excitement.

"Today?"

"Today!"

"Today!"

"Today!"

"Yes!" Michael yelled, "We are going to finish this war today!" Michael said.

"Why don't you go pack some food; we don't know how long we will be gone," Jacob said.

"Good idea! I'll go pack some sandwiches or something," Michael said, getting off the bed and walking out of the room.

"Ok," Jacob said.

"Wait a second," Michael said walking back, "what about Mom? She probably won't want us to go, then what will we do?" Michael asked.

"Michael, this is a command by King Luther, we can't disobey him," Jacob said. "And also I already asked, and he said he will take care of her."

"Oh, ok," Michael said relieved. Michael ran out the door and down the hall. Jacob had decided not to tell Michael the whole story about what King Luther had said. He had thought Michael wouldn't really take that well, especially the part that King Luther wanted Jacob to be the spy. Jacob didn't know exactly how he would get the dragons to trust him, or even how to find the dragons at all, or find the voice. No matter what happened, Jacob really wanted to find the voice. Excitement hit Jacob like a cannon ball. *I'm going to find the DragonStaff!* Jacob got up and ran to his room and grabbed the backpack from under his bed. He sighed with relief when he found the folder safe and secure. *I wonder why Luther didn't give the old map back?* Jacob thought, looking down at the nice map. It had nice lines and writings leading to The DragonStaff, and "His Cave" and a lot of others. *Judging by the map, The DragonStaff is only about three miles or so from here. Shouldn't take too long.* He still wondered why King Luther didn't give the old map back, and how he was going to find that voice without Michael knowing about it. He decided not to think about that, besides, he was about to go on a journey to save the world. *Maybe we could even be called "The Kids Who Save The World,"* he thought with a laugh at how stupid the thought was. Jacob looked out of his window. *Although, for some reason, no matter what happens, I feel like I am going to help save the world.* "Victory, here I come."

CHAPTER 4

THE DRAGON FOREST

After Jacob and Michael said their goodbyes to their mom and Hazel, they set out on their journey. Now they stood staring into the Dragon Forest. "Are we really about to do this?" Jacob asked in disbelief.

"Looks like it," Michael responded.

"I really hope we find the DragonStaff," Jacob said.

"Me too," Michael responded."

"You ready?"

"As ready as I'll ever be."

They took a deep breath and made their way into the borders of the Dragon Forest.

It felt like they had been walking for miles and miles. Jacob's legs felt like jelly. He sighed with exhaustion. Michael—on the other hand—was even more exhausted than Jacob. "Are we almost there?" Michael whined.

Jacob looked down at the map, "It looks like about four to five miles to go," Jacob responded.

"What?! How many times are you going to say that! You said that was how far it was from when we left!" Michael said. "That's it! I'm gonna to sit down and rest! And you will too!" After they found a nice patch of green grass, Michael sat down dramatically, as if he had never sat in his life. Jacob dug into his backpack and found two bottles of water, handed one to Michael, and then sat and relaxed. The sunlight was soothing as it shown through the trees. Everything was so pretty. Birds chirped and flew everywhere, the trees were huge. And the overall forest seemed so peaceful. Despite the beauty, an unsettling feeling went over Jacob.

"Michael, you know what's weird?" Jacob said.

"What?" Michael asked.

"This entire time we have been here we haven't seen a single dragon," Jacob said nervously.

"Maybe we won't."

"I hope so," Jacob said.

"Should we get back walking?" Michael asked.

"I guess," Jacob said. The strong buzz set off in his mind. It was so strong it was starting to give him a headache, but the voice wasn't speaking. He stood up. Something was calling. It felt like it was pulling him more into the trees, away from the trail.

"Jacob, are you ok?" Michael asked. Jacob could hardly hear him.

"How about we go this way," Jacob said pointing left, towards the buzz.

"But isn't that the wrong way?" Michael asked, looking down at the map. "The map says we should keep going straight." Jacob could hardly notice Michael, he only kept on walking into the trees, following the call. "Jacob, are you ok?" Michael asked. Jacob still didn't say anything. "Jacob!" Michael ran over to him. "Jacob, snap out of it!" Michael gave him a shove. The buzz stopped in his head. He shook his head violently. "What just happened?" Michael asked.

"We're not alone," Jacob whispered, looking around.

"Jacob! Is there something you aren't telling me?" Michael asked.

"Shhh," Jacob shushed.

"Jacob, I don't know wha……"

"Shush!" Jacob interrupted. Something was off, it was like he could feel the presence of someone or something. There was a rustle in the leaves, then everything went silent. "Run," Jacob said.

"What?"

"RUN!"

Something took off into the sky, followed by the sound of wingbeats. Jacob took off running with Michael close behind him. "WHAT IS THAT!" Michael yelled in fear.

"We're in the Dragon Forest! What do you think it is!" Jacob yelled back. With sharp claws, the dragon dove to the ground in between the two brothers, the force of its wings caused them both to fall. Jacob knew they wouldn't be able to outrun a dragon, so he hid behind a strange boulder he found. Michael did the same and hid behind a tree, where Jacob could see him. Jacob tried to make out what the dragon looked like, but all he could see was a black blob. The dragon looked around for them but saw nothing, until a twig snapped. The dragon jerked around and looked at the tree that Michael was hiding behind. Slowly, the dragon walked to the tree, its tail rolled right next to Jacob. *No!* Jacob thought, *I can't let it find Michael! Looks like it's going to have to be Michael or me, and I know exactly who it needs to be.* Jacob jumped up and stomped the dragon's tail. The dragon quickly jerked around and saw Jacob. Its glowing green eyes met his and as soon as they did, the buzzing returned to his mind. For a split second, Jacob had a vision of a dragon lifting into the sky with a human on its back. And then the same human pulling out a double-bladed purple glowing sword that swirled with white. Jacob breathed hard, then looked up to see the dragon was gone. *What is happening to me?! Well, at least the dragon is gone.* But it wasn't gone. Out of nowhere the dragon pounced onto Jacob. With sharp claws it gripped onto his shoulders and his back. It spread its wings wide and leaped into the air, holding onto him. Jacob nearly screamed so loud he was afraid his lungs would burst. They were above the tree line and flying away fast. Jacob didn't know why, but he turned his arm and grabbed what felt like where its wing started, then pushed on it as hard as he could. To his surprise, it made a pop. The dragon shrieked in pain and surprise. It missed a beat, then another. Almost immediately, they found themselves toppling down towards the trees. The dragon's grip loosened and Jacob was able to break free, but not from the fall. He was too busy screaming to notice a tail wrapping around his leg as the dragon was able to grab a tree branch to soften the fall, then let him go. Jacob tumbled with a thud on the forest floor. His back ached, but somehow he was alive! *How is that possible?* he wondered.

"Michael?" Jacob asked looking around. He moaned in pain, tiredness, and fear. There was a rustle in the trees and twigs snapping. Jacob stood up in alarm. "Where are you?" he asked in fear. "Like a dragon can talk," he said to himself. He grabbed a stick, even though his hands were shaking so much he could barely move them. "Show yourself, you monstrous beast!" He failed miserably at not sounding afraid.

"Aren't you a feisty little one?" A soft voice chuckled from behind him. Jacob paused. Slowly he turned around. Sitting on a large branch with its tail wrapped around it, with eyes as green as emeralds and large wings possibly as big as Jacob or bigger, was the first dragon Jacob had ever seen.

"What's your name?" the dragon asked. Somehow it sounded nice. Jacob was horrified, pure *horror*. The dragon moved his head from side to side, examining him. *Probably trying to decide what part of me to eat first!* Jacob thought in a panic. The dragon hopped off the branch and landed in front of him. Being right in front of him, the dragon didn't look tall at all. Even though it was long with its back, tail, and neck, the dragon was around the same height as Jacob. Maybe shorter. All of the dragon's scales were pure shiny black, but on the tips of every scale was a cool blue. It looked like the color of blue lightning, as if lightning had hit them and the color stayed on it. Jacob couldn't take his eyes off it. The dragon was definitely four-legged with sharp talons. Then Jacob's gaze fell on its wings. The left one was bent and twisted up; it looked painful. *Did I do that?* Jacob wondered. The dragon must have noticed his gaze. "Oh, my wing there," it said. "Don't worry. I've had that ever since I was born."

"Oh," was all Jacob could say.

"Well, anyway… Hi. My name is Lighter, what's yours?" it asked.

"Ummm, Jacob," Jacob responded, shocked that Lighter was acting nice to him.

"How old are you? You look about my age," Lighter asked, examining him. He circled around him curiously.

"Umm, fifteen," Jacob responded, not letting Lighter get behind him.

"Ok," Lighter's face brightened. "So.... you're only about two years older than me. Although, my birthday was a few months ago…so…. Sorry, I can't really focus enough to do math." Now that Lighter was standing *right* in front of Jacob, he could tell Lighter was little bit shorter, but if he stood on his back legs, he would be taller. "Oh! Big idea!" Lighter said excitingly. He was pretty hyper. "You could come with me and meet all my friends!" Lighter continued. "I can introduce you to Glider, Glazer, and Tortoise! And then we could become like best friends! And sit and talk and talk! And maybe even pick a subject, ooh! I know a perfect one! We can talk about how *HORRIBLE* this ridiculous war is! We could also come up with plans to stop it! *And* put those plans in action! Don't you think that would be awesome?!"

Jacob was *so* confused. *What is wrong with this dragon? Are all dragons like this?* Jacob wondered. Jacob's hands and legs were still shaking in fear. Lighter frowned. "You know, you don't have to be afraid of me," Lighter said. "I'm not going to hurt you. I've just been bored all day. Someone told me that something was lost in the forest, so I came here to look for it. And also, someone mixed coffee in my hot chocolate this morning. I get really hyper whenever I drink that." Lighter sighed, "That Glider."

Jacob couldn't believe this! Why would this dragon, his enemy be nice to him? *Wait a second…* "Did you say someone told you to look for something?" Jacob asked.

"Hmm? Oh yeah!" Lighter said. "Yeah, he said that something was just wandering around, so of course...… I got curious…"

"So, do you know who told you?" Jacob asked.

"Of course!" Lighter responded. "What? Do you want to meet him?"

"Sure!" Jacob said, trying to mimic Lighter's excitement.

"Great!" Lighter said. "Follow me!"

"Ok!"

Lighter started out, walking happily on his four talons for Jacob to follow. Jacob acted like he was about to follow, but immediately turned and ran the other way.

Jacob ran as fast as he could from the dragon known as Lighter. Even though he acted nice, Jacob was not ready to be led into a trap by a dragon. *I will not be a dragon's prisoner! I'm sorry King Luther, but I don't think I have the strength to be your spy.*

Jacob ran as fast as he could through the forest, but all the tree roots and rocks made it really difficult. Even though he had a feeling he lost Lighter, he felt like something else was chasing him.

"Running is your favorite sport, isn't it?" the voice asked as the buzz cut on in his head.

Once again, Jacob's foot hit something and he fell to the ground.

"Ow…..." Jacob moaned.

"Why are you running the wrong way?" the voice asked.

"I'm not!"

"Is that so?"

There were growls coming from the bushes and trees. Jacob looked up to see wolves slowly stepping out in a pounce position.

"May I suggest running the other way?"

Jacob quickly got up and ran. Immediately, the wolves barked and howled, chasing after him. Everywhere he would turn, a wolf would jump in front of him. Jacob had no idea how he managed to run for even a second without getting eaten. In a matter of seconds, he found himself in a small clearing with a big stone rock in front. The wolves circled around him, blocking his path in all directions, ready to pounce. Just before a wolf started to attack, there was a loud roar.

The wolves jumped back and looked up in fear. Noticing the wolves backing away, Jacob turned around. On top of the giant stone was a growling black panther.

The panther, with its dark, black fur and strange, scary eyes as red as red can be, continued to growl, staring at the wolves and Jacob. The wolves looked from the panther to Jacob, contemplating on attacking Jacob or running. Jacob didn't know what to do. In all directions he was either blocked by a panther or a wolf. He didn't know which was worse. Finally, a wolf made up its mind and pounced for Jacob. With a roar, the panther attacked the wolf before it could hit the terrified kid. The panther's force caused the wolf to fall to the ground with the panther on top of it. The wolf whined in fear and tried to jump away, but the panther wasn't finished yet. The panther gripped onto the wolf with its mouth and tossed it on top of another wolf, causing them both to fall. The wolves jumped back up and circled around the panther, growling. The panther's eyes followed each of the wolves warily, being prepared to fight. One by one, each of the wolves would try to bite or scratch, but the panther would quickly snap its jaws, making the wolves jump back. The wolves continued to circle around the panther as a pack, fighting over Jacob. The panther didn't exactly attack the wolves first, the wolves would attack first, then the panther would double it back. The biggest wolf jumped from behind onto the panther's back and tried to bite, but the panther's reflexes were too quick. The panther whipped around and grabbed onto the wolf in mid-air, then slammed it against the rock. As if that was the only wolf that could fight, all the wolves jumped back and looked even more scared. The bigger wolf got up from the ground and did a pouting bark as if it was reasoning. The panther growled in return that made the wolf step back in fear. The big wolf howled, and the others joined in, then the panther let out its massive roar. Immediately, the wolves took off running, barking at each other. Jacob gasped in fear. He knew there was absolutely no chance he could outrun a panther. Slowly, as if it had forgotten about him, the panther turned around and growled. Jacob took as many steps back as he possibly could, searching for a way out. He thought about jumping onto a tree and getting out of reach, but then realized how stupid that would be. He looked back at the panther, but it was gone. *Where did it go?!* Jacob thought in panic. His heart beat fast, waiting for the large cat to pounce out of nowhere.

"The woods are no place for a child."

"*Aaah!*" Jacob shrieked in fear and shock. He jumped back and looked up at the rock. The panther just sat on top of the rock and stared down at him. "Did. That. Thing. Just. Talk?" Jacob asked himself in horror.

"What're you call'n 'thing'?"

"Ah!" Jacob shrieked again.

"Ugh, humans these days," the panther said to itself. "Know nothin' of what's around them."

"You can talk!" Jacob yelped in alarm.

"Oh, and you can hear. How amazing!" the panther said teasingly. "Of course I can talk, ya dummy!"

"You have an accent!" Jacob said, surprised.

"Yeah, and that accent is called a voice," the panther snapped. "But I do have to admit, there are a few letters, especially 'r's' that I have a hard time with. Plus, I guess in some cases I do kind of sound a little…… well…. strange."

"What in the world!" Jacob said to himself. "This is not possible!"

"You do realize I'm right here, right?" the panther asked, tilting his head curiously. "It's not the smartest to talk like that to your rescuer."

Rescuer? Jacob realized. "Are you going to eat me?" he asked uneasily.

"Not unless you give me a good reason," the panther said with a strange smirk-like smile.

Wait, was that sarcasm? Jacob thought. *What in the world is this thing? And how is it smiling? Cats shouldn't be able to smile!*

"What are you?" Jacob asked.

"Name's Krennicx," the panther answered, jumping off the rock and landing soundlessly in front of him. "You?"

"Er… human," Jacob said, feeling awkward and taking a step back.

"Ok, Human, what are you doing in the woods?" Krennicx asked.

"No, my name isn't *human,*" Jacob said feeling stupid, "but I am a human."

"Wow, I had no idea," Krennicx said sarcastically.

Ok this thing is getting a little annoying.

"So human," Krennicx said, "what is your *actual* name?"

"Jacob," Jacob answered. "What are you *actually?*"

"Krennicx," Krennicx grinned, "I am not a human."

"I noticed," Jacob responded.

"Where did you come from?" Krennicx asked.

"The land of the humans," Jacob responded.

"Which one?"

"What do you mean?"

"You don't know anything do you?" Krennicx asked. Jacob was really wishing he hadn't run from Lighter.

"I know enough!" Jacob said, offended.

"Do you though?" Krennicx asked, tilting his head curiously.

Jacob's fear of Krennicx was the only thing that kept him from wanting to talk back and prove him wrong. He kept finding himself looking into its large, strange, pure red eyes. Jacob had chill bumps from looking at them. It felt like he was staring into a pool of pure, red blood. The only part that wasn't red was the blackness of the pupil—which of course—only added to the effect of falling into a dark pit. He had to pull himself away from the terrifying sight and the cold sweat.

"Where am I?" Jacob stupidly asked, trying to distract himself and not look at its eyes. He didn't know why that question blurted out, he knew it was stupid, but he had to say *something* to distract himself.

"A forest," Krennicx responded flatly.

"I had no idea," Jacob said, even more annoyed as he recovered from the chills.

"Not surprising. Although I didn't know humans had no sense of direction," Krennicx said.

There's a lot about us you probably don't know! Jacob thought.

"Is there anywhere else you can be?" Krennicx asked.

Jacob thought for a second, "Do you know anyone who goes by the name Severein?"

"Who doesn't?" Krennicx snorted.

"Do you know where I can find him?" Jacob asked.

"Hmm," Krennicx said thoughtfully. "He's pretty tricky to find…. If he wasn't he'd be dead already…."

"So do you know where he is?" Jacob asked, aggravated.

"Now, I didn't say that, did I?" Krennicx asked, walking back and forth. "But it depends who's asking."

"Me," Jacob responded.

"So, if it's you asking, then I don't know what to respond with," Krennicx responded weirdly.

"What?" Jacob asked flat-out confused.

"But I might know someone who might know someone who knows ol' Severein."

"Can you take me to him?" Jacob asked, ready to get away from the weirdo panther.

"Maybe…. But you must be aware of the weirdness that follows him," Krennicx responded, acting even *more* weird.

"Ok, please," Jacob said, desperate to get away from Krennicx.

"Follow me," Krennicx said, walking away.

CHAPTER 5

THE INSANE PANTHER

Jacob kept silent as the strange, talking panther led him thru the woods. Jacob wondered what Michael's response would be when he would ever be able to tell him. *I wonder if he'd believe me? He would probably go: "Panthers don't talk! At least a dragon talking is somewhat believable, but a panther?! Really?" yeah…… maybe I will have to show them talking before I tell him.*

"Excuuuse meee," Krennicx said.

"Hm?" Jacob asked.

"Are you alright?" Krennicx asked. "I've been trying to talk to ya for a few minutes."

"Oh," Jacob said feeling awkward. "What?"

"Do you like to climb trees?"

"Why?" Jacob asked.

"Cuuurious," Krennicx responded.

"Ok……" Jacob said slowly. *Why is this thing so weird?* "So……" Jacob said, trying to break the silence, "who are you taking me to?"

"Someone who might be better at human kids than me," Krennicx responded.

"Where?" Jacob asked.

"Do you always ask so many questions?" Krennicx asked. "The village."

Panthers have villages? Maybe I should try to act like I know everything, that way no one will think anything. Another thought crept in his mind that scared him. *How will I not be noticeable? I'm a human!*

"Are you afraid?" Krennicx asked. *Oh no! Can panthers smell fear?*

"Whaat?" Jacob asked. "Why would I be afraid?"

"I don't know," Krennicx responded. "You *look* afraid."

"I don't look afraid!" Jacob yelped in panic. *"You* look afraid."

Krennicx gave him a weird look. "I would have more of a reason to be," he said, "but I'm not."

"Why?" Jacob asked.

"Because I'm not."

"No, I mean," Jacob said, "why would you have a reason to be?"

"Never mind that."

Why oh why did I run from Lighter! Jacob thought miserably. *I think I prefer a dragon over this thing.*

"I have got to be dreaming!" Jacob said in panic. "Surely I'm just going to wake up in my bed, and I never actually came here."

"You are a sad, strange, little kiddy aren't you?"

"Kitty!" Jacob yelped, offended.

"What? Isn't that what you are?" Krennicx asked.

"A kid! Not a cat!"

"I didn't say *kitty,* I said kid*dy,"* Krennicx said. Jacob growled in frustration. "There, there, kiddy," Krennicx said, jumping up and patting Jacob's head. Jacob had a very strong desire to rub his head and get the panther's germs off.

Jacob took a deep breath, *I guess I may as well try to get some answers from this thing,* "So……"

"So….?" Krennicx asked.

"Erm……" Jacob said, trying to think of something to say. "How long have you been in the forest?"

Krennicx looked at him in a way that said, 'Really? That's the best you can come up with?'

"Let's see……." Krennicx said with a slight smirk. "Yesterday was around twelve hours maybe? The day before that was probably like seven hours, and then the day before *that…*"

"Not like that!" Jacob said. "I *mean,* have you like lived here your entire life?"

"Not really," Krennicx said. "I mean, it depends."

"Oh," *Absolutely nothing.* "So, who are you taking me to?"

"Didn't you already ask that?"

And did you answer? NO!

"So, does he know Severein?" Jacob asked.

"I did say I might know someone who knows someone, did I not?"

"So…. he doesn't?" Jacob asked.

Krennicx only chuckled… *very* creepily.

"So how much longer?" Jacob asked, accidentally sounding very annoyed…but then again, he was.

"Hmm, this kiddy doesn't seem to have much patience," Krennicx said to himself. *He has got to stop calling me kiddy!* Krennicx's ears perked up, "Oh no."

"Oh no, what?" Jacob asked. Krennicx smirked a smile and glared behind him.

"Oh no, what?" Jacob asked again in frustration. Krennicx only chuckled. "What is it Krennicx?!" Jacob asked, starting to lose it.

"Quick, get behind that bush," Krennicx said.

"Why?" Jacob asked.

"Just do it."

Jacob obeyed and went behind the bush Krennicx was talking about. "What am I doing?" Jacob asked. Krennicx jumped onto a long branch high up a tree.

"See that hairy-thick vine?"

"Yeah."

"Toss it to me."

"What?" Jacob asked, confused.

"Just do it," Krennicx responded. Jacob grabbed onto the long, thick vine with strange, long hairs and pulled it off the tree.

"Here," Jacob said, trying to toss it to him, but it was heavy. Quickly, Krennicx caught the end of it and pulled it up. "So what are you doing?" Jacob asked.

Krennicx only did a small insane laugh as he tied the vine around the tree branch. Jacob watched curiously as Krennicx brushed all the long hairs of the vine backwards. *What in the world is he doing?* Jacob wondered as the panther wrapped the entire vine around the tree branch. When Jacob thought that it couldn't get any weirder, Krennicx laid down on the branch and looked asleep.

"What in the world?" Jacob said out loud. *What is wrong with this thing!* Jacob looked at the panther with its eyes closed, laying on the vine wrapped around the branch. There was the sound of wing beats in the air that made Jacob jump behind the bush. A shimmering-white dragon swooped from the sky and reached its claws out towards Krennicx.

Krennicx jumped from the branch just as the dragon dove for him, causing it to grab the vine that Krennicx wrapped around the branch.

"Yow!" the dragon yelped. It jumped away from the vine and landed on its back legs, in front of the panther.

"Ha! That is what ya get for terrorizing any panther ya see!" Krennicx barked.

"Ow, ow, ow, ow, *OW,*" the dragon said shaking his claws. Standing on his back legs, he was way taller. "Why did you *do* that?!"

"I didn't do anything except protect myself from idiotic beasts like *you,"* Krennicx said.

"Idiotic? I'll show *you* idiotic!" The dragon dove for Krennicx again. But this time Krennicx took a step aside, causing the dragon to crash into a thorn bush.

"YOOOW!" the dragon yelped again.

"Boy, will you ever learn?" Krennicx asked calmly.

"Don't call me a boy!" the dragon said, getting out of the thorn bush and standing in front of Krennicx on all fours. His scales were the color of ice. The many spikes that lined his neck, back, and tail looked like icicles. He had two horns right above his ears, pointing straight back. His eyes were dark blue.

"Ok, child."

"Don't call me a child either!"

"I don't think you want to know what's lower," Krennicx said, tapping his lips.

"Don't you *dare* say it," the dragon growled, showing its sharp too-clean-to-be-possible teeth.

"I don't have to," Krennicx said, with a grin. "You know what it is."

The dragon growled, "Don't you have somewhere else to be?"

"As a very happy matter of fact, yes I do," Krennicx said. "Me *and* the kid do."

"Kid?" the dragon asked, noticing Jacob. "You gonna push him off a tree like the last one?"

"Wait, what?" Jacob asked in alarm.

"For the last time Glider, I did not purposefully push him off the tree!" Krennicx smirked, then said, "And even if I did, you have to say that was a very impressive catch."

"Of course you had to catch him," Glider said. "His mom was standing right there!"

"I would have caught him anyway!" Krennicx defended. "And she wasn't even standing there the whole time. She just so happened to walk by right when he fell."

"That's even worse!"

"How 'bout we turn the tables, *Glider.* I'm sure you'd *love* to be reminded of that one time when you froze that same kid's foot!"

"Well at least it's common for an Ice Dragon to accidentally freeze something than for a panther to '*accidentally*' pick up a kid, take it on top of a tree, and then drop it!"

"I'm guessing you two know each other," Jacob said, feeling extremely awkward……. Again.

"Ya think!" Krennicx and Glider said at the same time. Krennicx smirked teasingly at the Ice Dragon for saying the same thing.

"Glider, Jacob. Jacob, Glider. Can we go now?" Krennicx asked.

"With pleasure," Glider said, turning to walk away. "Ow! Grr, thinks to you I still have to get my splinters out!"

"You do that, and don't follow us!"

"Oh, you don't have to tell me that!"

"Good!" Krennicx said.

"Fine!"

"Fine!"

"Good!"

"Great! Come on Jackiepoo," Krennicx said, starting to walk away.

"Yeah! Yeah, just keeep walk'n!" Glider called.

"With pleasure!" Krennicx called back.

"And don't come back!"

"You don't have to tell me that," Krennicx said calmly.

"Who was that?" Jacob asked after what felt like a while.

"That, dear kiddy, was the biggest nitwit in the world…Glider," Krennicx responded. "He thinks just because he's an Ice Dragon he can scare every single panther he sees."

"Why does he do that?"

"Because he doesn't like me."

Jacob thought about asking why, but he felt like he knew already. *Why would I even care? I don't even like him…. at all.*

"So, there's different kinds of dragons?" Jacob asked.

"Uh…… yeah. You didn't know that?" Krennicx said.

"Well……. I mean…. I knew there'd have to be different colors…. but…. different *breeds*?"

Krennicx gave him a weird look, "What do they teach at schools these days?"

Most of the times it's how terrible the dragons are. Jacob kept silent as they continued to walk, then he realized that he should probably pay attention of where they are going so that he could find his way back.

"Alright, here we are," Krennicx said stopping. "Now go away."

"This is the village?" Jacob asked, seeing only a giant rock.

"Yes, the village is a rock," Krennicx responded. *He is being sarcastic…right? He sounds like it, but it wouldn't really surprise me if he wasn't.*

"Then what is it?" Jacob asked, aggravated. He assumed the panther was joking. Krennicx rolled his eyes and gave the rock three small taps, then it rumbled and slid aside, revealing an entrance to a tunnel.

"And where does this go to?" Jacob asked, turning around, but Krennicx was gone.

"Hello?" Jacob asked. "Krennicx?" *Maybe I should just run, but is that a good idea? Where would I even go?* Jacob sighed, *I guess I have no choice. Why would he even take me here if it isn't anything?* He remembered how insane the panther was, so maybe this was nothing.

"What are you waiting for?" Krennicx asked, somehow standing right in front of him.

Jacob jumped back in surprise. "I didn't know what to do," he said.

"Obviously. Follow me," Krennicx said, turning around and walking into the tunnel.

"Right," Jacob said, following.

There was silence for a few minutes as they walked along the dark tunnel. The only thing he could really see was Krennicx's gleaming, red eyes. He tried to think of something to say to break the awkward silence.

"So," Krennicx said, breaking the silence before Jacob had to. "Why do you come alone?"

"Just looking for something," Jacob said panicked.

"What?"

"Just treasure."

"What kind of treasure?"

Jacob thought in panic. For some reason he just knew that Krennicx could tell if he was lying. "I wanted to find something worth value."

"For your family?" Krennicx asked.

Jacob nodded.

"Get down!" Krennicx shrieked, ducking. Jacob obeyed and fell to the floor. Something silvery flew by above him with a chill.

"What was that?!" Jacob yelped, standing back up.

"Those nitwits!" Krennicx barked. He ran along the tunnel with Jacob following behind him. The tunnel ended into a large, high-ceiling cave where two dragons fought, somewhat.

"Get off of me!" a seaweed-colored dragon shrieked.

"Never!" the silvery-white dragon on top of him said. Jacob recognized him as Glider.

"Remember what we talked about!" a familiar voice came from a dragon in a corner. "Buck him off!"

The seaweed dragon tried but failed miserably.

"Glider!" a silvery girl dragon next to the other dragon in the corner barked. "What did I tell you about not hurting anyone? You're going to hurt his back!"

"He can take it," Glider said.

"No, I can't! It's still hurts from last night!" the dragon yelped and tumbled to the ground.

"Three. Two. One. Knock out!" Glider called, jumping off the dragon. "Boom baby! That's how ya do it!"

"Oh my goodness, are you ok!?" the girl shrieked, running over.

"I'm wonderful," Glider said with a wide smile.

"Not you," the girl said, kneeling next to the fallen dragon. "Are you alright Tortoise?" she asked, helping him to his feet.

"Am now," Tortoise said, smiling. "Although my back still kind of hurts." Jacob caught Krennicx rolling his eyes.

"Wait a minute," Glider said, "I thought you two were supposed to be fighting?"

"We were, before you flew in and tackled everyone," the dragon from the corner said, walking to them.

"The element of surprise," Glider said with a nod. "It always works best."

"Agreed," Krennicx said, suddenly standing in front of them.

"*AH!!*" they all shrieked in surprise.

"That had to be the most pathetic fight I've ever seen in my life," Krennicx said calmly. "And I've seen a lot."

"I thought I told you not to follow me!" Glider barked.

"I didn't follow you Glider," Krennicx said. "I know my way here."

"But you knew I would be here!"

"Unfortunately."

"What do you want?" Glider asked, annoyed.

"More like what I don't want," Krennicx motioned for Jacob to come over. "This is Jacob…… right?"

Jacob nodded, standing in front of them.

"Anyway," Krennicx said, "you've already met Glider the nitwit, and the green egghead is Tortoise. The hyper silver girl is Glazer...oh and that one's Lighter. See yah." Krennicx turned and tried to leave.

"Whoa, whoa, whoa, whoa, whoa," Glider said, stopping him. "You can't just leave him here!"

"Can and am. Goodbye." Krennicx stormed out of the cave without another word.

"Well……" Glider said awkwardly. Jacob turned around to see frosted, light blue eyes right in front of his face.

"Whoa!" he shrieked in surprise.

"Hi, Jacob!" Glazer said, grabbing his hand and shaking it rapidly. "It's so nice to meet you! I've never had a human friend before! Well, I guess I have, but none my age! They're all full grown with a very deep voice. But yours isn't! Your voice is childlike, like me!"

"Excuse me?" Jacob asked. He nearly yelped when he realized how freezing cold Glazer's claws were.

Glazer quickly let go, "I'm so sorry! Sometimes it's so easy to forget about that! You see, I'm super cold because I have…. I'm an Iceling."

"It's fine," Jacob forced out. His hands were so cold they were numb. Glazer frowned. "Really, it's ok." He put his hands in his pockets for warmth. Glazer smiled. Even in the dark cave, Jacob could tell how pretty Glazer was. Her eyes were a frosted light blue, and her pupils were white. She had beautiful, long black eyelashes. Her scales were silvery-white that shimmered like sun dancing off water. She had strange snowflake shapes scattered on her scales. They looked like they were glowing. *This,* Jacob thought, *is Hazel's kind of dragon.*

"Hello Jacob," Tortoise said with a slight bow.

"Erm, hello," Jacob said, feeling awkward. *Am I supposed to bow?*

"Nice to meet you," Tortoise said.

"Nice… to meet you too," Jacob responded. *I guess.* For all Jacob could tell, Tortoise looked a lot different than the others. It was dark in the cave, but he could tell that the dragon was a little longer than the rest, and his wings were a different shape. They were shorter in wingspan but bigger in width. The biggest difference Jacob could tell were strange antennae-like thingies that attached to the back of his head and stopped after what Jacob assumed was the shoulder. Another thing was he didn't have spikes along his back, instead they were strange fins that lined his back all the way to the end of the tail. He really did look like seaweed. All the dragons seemed four-legged.

"How's your back, Tortoise?" Glazer asked, concerned.

"Fine," Tortoise said with a shy smile. Jacob could tell in a heartbeat that Tortoise totally had a crush on Glazer.

"So," Lighter said, walking up to him with a strange look in his face. *Is he embarrassed?* Jacob wondered. "I'm really sorry about that," Lighter said, rubbing the back of his head. "I looked over and you were gone. Are you ok?"

"I'm fine," Jacob responded. Lighter seemed like he was *actually* upset. *He's probably just acting. He was the one that kidnapped me in the first place!* Lighter smiled, and Jacob smiled back, but he had no idea why.

"So……," Glider said, "you met Krennicx, eh?"

"Yep...." Jacob answered.

"Isn't he like the weirdest thing ever?" Glider asked.

"So it's not just me?" Jacob asked, somewhat relieved.

"Trust me when I say this," Glider said, "he is the most insane thing that has ever lived."

"Sure, he might be a little insane," Lighter said, "but he sure is clever."

"Not really," Glider said.

"Said the one who fell into his trap," Glazer said with a laugh.

"You have to admit, the laughing vine was, I say, *insanely* smart," Tortoise laughed.

"It's not funny!" Glider barked.

"It is a laugh, though," Lighter pointed out.

Glazer laughed, "Oh brother, will you ever stop trying to get that poor panther mad?"

"Not until I win the battle!" Glider said.

"How is it a battle if you *always* lose?" Lighter asked.

"Burn," Tortoise said.

"Oh, stop it," Glider snapped.

Glazer walked over and whispered something into Lighter's ear. Lighter nodded. "Jacob, do you mind if the four of us talked for a second?" Lighter asked.

Jacob nodded. They went to the other side of the cave as far away from Jacob and began to talk. Realizing they weren't looking at him, Jacob pulled out his tracker and began to type. "I am with a group of dragons. I am your spy." Not being able to think of anything else, he sent it. A part of himself urged him to run away and find Michael, but for some reason, he had a feeling that this group was probably the safest one. He sighed, *I hope Michael is ok.*

Michael walked along the Dragon Forest; he somewhat knew where he was going, but had *zero* clue how in the world to get there. Michael sighed. *Should I find the DragonStaff or Jacob?* Of course, the love for his brother screamed at him to find him, but how would he? A twig snapped and Michael jumped back in terror. There were thumps of footsteps as a group of human soldiers stepped out of the thick trees. "Halt!" the soldier in front commanded. They stared at Michael in shock. Then suddenly they pointed their swords at him. "Stay back you traitor!" one of the guards yelled in fury.

"Wait, what?" Michael asked in confusion.

"You know what I mean! You're a traitor to King Luther!" the guards started to move their swords closer. *They think I'm a traitor? Pffft, never!*

"I'm not a traitor!" Michael protested.

"Oh yeah! Then why are you in the Dragon Forest?" they asked.

"I'm on a mission from King Luther himself."

"I doubt that! Why would the king send a kid? Do you have a clearance or anything?" the leader asked.

Michael didn't know what to say to that, but he had to say something. "He didn't give me something to show to you. But he *did* send me and my brother to find the DragonStaff. See?" Michael said showing them his map, then continued, "But they took him! The dragons took my brother! I'm not good at reading this either, that was his job. I don't know what they're going to do to him." Hot tears began to claw their way past Michael's eyes. He didn't like playing the kid in distress, but that's what he *was.* "Please, you have to help. He's my little brother. Please!"

The soldier frowned, "Did you say you were looking for the DragonStaff?"

Michael wiped his eyes, "Yessir."

"That's odd," the soldier said, tapping his chin. "Samual, bring over the map."

Samual?! Michael realized. Sure enough, Samual came to the leader, holding a piece of paper. The leader thanked him and took the map.

"That looks like the map we gave King Luther," Michael realized out loud.

"Really? This map is terrible. We already went where it said and all that was there were ruins. What does yours look like?" the leader asked. Michael handed him his highly detailed map of the forest. "Strange," the leader said, "this one is definitely better. And it leads somewhere different. What was your name?"

"Michael Bennett," Michael answered.

All the soldiers looked at him in shock, but Michael didn't know why. The leader cleared his throat, "Well, Michael, we better get going. Maybe we'll find your brother on the way, but if we don't, as long as we get the Staff, we can force those terrible creatures to give him back. Don't worry."

Michael smiled, "Thank you."

"We're moving out," the leader announced. *Don't worry Jacob*, Michael thought as he walked next to Samual. *We will find you. And we'll make those dragons pay.*

Jacob was still waiting for Lighter's discussion to end, but little did he know that it would change his life forever.

"All I'm saying is do we really *need* another member?" Glider complained. "Cuz we've been doing *pretty well.*"

"Getting our butts kicked is *not* pretty well," Tortoise pointed out. He rubbed his back, "Man, that soldier hit my back good. It still hurts."

"I still should have been there," Lighter said quietly.

"It's not your fault," Glazer insisted. "You were needed somewhere else. But you still made it right when we needed you the most."

Lighter sighed.

"Glider really needs to stop putting coffee in your hot chocolate," Tortoise observed. "It makes you super hyper…then you crash. Huh, I guess you haven't crashed yet."

"Glider did *what?*" Glazer yelped, turning to her brother.

"I mean, are we sure we even feel it?" Glider asked, jumping back to the original subject. He grinned at Glazer's sigh.

"I know what I felt," Lighter insisted.

"I'm sure Lighter knows," Glazer said. "And as a matter of fact, I feel it too."

"I'm surprised you *don't* feel it, Glider," Tortoise said.

"I mean, I do. It's just…it's been us for *so* long… it's going to be weird to have someone new," Glider said, glancing at Jacob, who was still waiting on them.

"Change can be good sometimes, and it's time to get a new person on the team. He's… the last one. You guys in?" Lighter asked

"I'm in," Glazer said.

"Me too," Tortoise said.

"It's going to take a lot of work," Glider said.

"Yep," said Lighter.

"We're going to have to train him."

"Uh-huh."

"It might be a disaster, and he might turn us over."

"Most likely."

"I'm in," Glider said with a smirk.

"Well, it looks like it's settled. We will take him to our place and teach him everything we know," Lighter said. They all nodded in agreement.

CHAPTER 6

JACOB THE SPY

Jacob was sitting on the floor when Lighter, Glider, Glazer, and Tortoise were done talking. "So," Lighter said as he bounced up next to Jacob, "we talked about it and finally agreed that you can come and stay with us! We're going to have so much fun!" Lighter cheered. *Wait, what?*

"So what should we do first?!" Glazer jumped up and down in excitement.

"Wait, what do you mean?" Jacob asked in surprise.

"Well, you know, we can play, or swim, or do whatever!" Glazer cheered.

"Well, first thing's first, I need to go pick up Turtle," Tortoise pointed out.

"Aw, man!" Glider groaned. "Do you have to?"

"Oh come on guys, y'all like Turtle," Tortoise said.

"*You* like Turtle," Glider moaned.

"I like Turtle," Glazer said.

"Me too," Lighter chimed in.

"Who's Turtle?" Jacob asked, wanting to know as much as he can.

"More like what's Turtle," Glider said. "And to answer that, it's Tortoise's pet."

"I didn't think you were going to pick him up till after.... the....ummm...." Glider eyed Lighter in an 'are we supposed to talk about it' way. Lighter shook his head. *Yep, there's definitely something going on here.*

"Jacob, where do you want to go first?" Lighter asked.

"What are the options?" Jacob responded.

"Well……" Lighter paused, "how about we stay here for a little bit, then go to my house?"

"Why?" Glider asked

"Just…. because," Lighter responded.

"What all is there to do here?" Jacob asked.

"We could go in the game room and play pool or air hockey," Lighter suggested.

"That sounds fine," Glazer said. "You in?"

"I guess," Jacob said, not really wanting to very much.

"So, who wants to play pool?" Tortoise asked, walking towards the pool table. They had gone into a different cave. This one was a lot brighter than the first one and it had some furniture.

"You and Glazer can go on ahead," Glider said. "Yo Jacob, you wanna play air hockey?" he asked.

Jacob was still shocked that they would want him to play with them. A human? Of all creatures!

"I guess," Jacob responded.

"What is Lighter going to do?" Glazer asked, looking up from the pool table.

"I think I'm just going to read a book or something. Y'all can go on ahead," Lighter responded kindly.

"You sure?" Glazer asked.

"Yeah, I'm sure," he responded with a yawn.

"So…. What do you think about Krennicx?" Glider asked as they were setting up the air hockey table.

"Honestly, pretty creepy," Jacob responded. "I noticed that you two don't really like each other."

"Oh yeah, that."

"Why do you guys hate each other?"

"Well…. No, no, it's not that…. it's just we've known each other for so long and have done so much. We just like to mess with each other sometimes; plus, I was getting back at him for something," Glider said.

"What did he do?" Jacob asked.

Glider answered with a sigh, "He changed my profile name to Smell-ma-pits."

He couldn't help it. Jacob cracked up with laughter.

"Oh come on! Really? You laugh at what he did to me, but not what I did to him?! Now you're starting to remind me of him!" Glider complained.

"I think you might be beat," Jacob said with a small laugh. *Wait a second, what am I doing! Why am I laughing at something a dragon said? Dragons are my enemies!* Jacob realized. *I have to be careful.*

"So… Jacob, how long will you be staying?" Glider asked.

"Oh…. I don't really know," Jacob said.

"How did you find Lighter?" Glider asked as if he knew the answer.

What does he know that I don't? Jacob wondered. "Umm, well......." Jacob didn't exactly want to tell him that Lighter kidnaped him. "I was kinda just walking through the woods, and Lighter swooped in and grabbed me." Jacob didn't dare tell them about Michael and the real reason he came. *I hope Michael is still searching without me.*

"So.... You're saying Lighter kidnapped you?" Glider asked

"I don't know," Jacob said as his insides were screaming 'yes'.

Glider barked a laugh, "Ha! Lighter! Kidnapping and scaring! Ha! When pigs fly!"

"Oh, come on, really? Why wouldn't you believe me? Isn't kidnapping usual for a dragon?" Jacob said. Glider paused and just stared at him. *Oops.*

Glider studied him from head to toe, kinda like what Lighter did. "Where were you born?" Glider nearly whispered.

"Three Point Hospital. Why?" Jacob asked.

Glider took a deep breath, "Ok, I was just wondering."

"Oookay," Jacob said.

"Maybe we should start the game."

"Yeah.... maybe we should.

"Bet I'll beat you," Glider said with a grin.

"Oh, I bet you won't," Jacob said.

"Boo yeah!" Glider cheered for the hundredth time. Literately.

"Grrrrr, how are you so good at this?" Jacob asked in defeat.

Glider was too busy doing his victory dance to notice.

"Now do you see why we never want to play air hockey?" Tortoise called from the other side of the room.

"Oh yeah! Glider is undefeated!" Glider cheered to himself.

"You know you don't have to rub it in," Glazer said as she hit the q-ball with her stick. "Oh yeah, I forgot to tell you that Krennicx said that you are banned from the blueberry bushes."

"Why would he tell you and not me?" Glider asked, his victory dance ruined.

"Probably because you put coffee in his honey suckle juice, and you know how much he loves that," Tortoise said.

"But Lighter didn't get mad when I put coffee in his hot chocolate!" Glider said.

"Because he's *Lighter,*" Tortoise said. "He never gets mad at anything."

"Where is Lighter anyway?" Jacob asked.

Glider smirked, "I don't think he ever intended to read that book."

They all looked over to the green couch in the middle of the cave. Lighter laid on his back with a large open book over his eyes. He was totally asleep.

"Glider…" Glazer moaned.

"He crashed," Glider said with a grin.

"I thought coffee keeps you awake?" Jacob asked.

"Usually," Tortoise responded, "but not for Lighter. Usually he gets extremely hyper for a couple hours…. then he crashes. Hard."

"So hard," Glider laughed.

"Glider, you have *got* to quit doing this," Glazer said with a frown.

"I agree," Tortoise said.

"Thank you, Tortoise," Glazer said with a smile.

"If you don't think that's funny," Glider said with a smirk, "just wait till you see *this!*"

"Glider no!" Glazer shrieked.

Jacob almost lost it.

There was a bang as Glider flipped the couch completely over with Lighter still on it. Lighter yelped as the couch fell on top of him.

Glider was laughing so hard it sounded like he would pass out.

Lighter pushed the couch off of himself and stood up. He looked at everyone in confusion, "Did…did I fall asleep?"

"You crashed twice!" Glider laughed.

Jacob crossed his arms and put his fist over his mouth, trying hard not to laugh.

"It's not funny Glider!" Glazer said.

"Is toot!"

Jacob finally lost it.

"Aha! See? He thinks it's funny!" Glider said, pointing at Jacob.

Glazer started to say something, but Lighter jumped in. "It is actually pretty funny," Lighter said with a laugh.

"It was hilarious!" Glider laughed.

Glazer shook her head.

"Sorry for falling asleep like that," Lighter apologized. "I really don't know why coffee does that to me. But hey, at least I shouldn't be going crazy now," Lighter smiled. "Y'all ready to go to the other cave?"

"Other cave? How many caves do y'all have?" Jacob asked, sounding a little more interested than he wanted to.

"Aw man, that cave isn't fun like this one; that one's boring," Glider said with an eye roll.

"Just because it doesn't have air hockey, doesn't mean it's boring," Glazer said.

"I actually think Lighter's house is even more fun," Tortoise said, "cause we can *swim!*"

"Yeah, Glider," Glazer said. "Let's go swim."

"Doesn't that sound fun?" Lighter asked.

"I mean, I guess it's adequate," Glider said.

"Where is your house?" Jacob asked.

"It's in a cave nearby," Lighter answered. "It's not far at all," Lighter said, leading the way into a tunnel.

"How many tunnels and caves are there?" Jacob asked as they walked in the twisty tunnels.

"Oh, there are thousands," Lighter said.

"How do you keep up with them?" Jacob asked.

"Man, you sure do ask a lot of questions," Glider said from behind them. The tunnel came to a split, they immediately turned right.

"Well… I guess we just got used to it, and now we know it by heart," Lighter answered Jacob's question.

"Sure is a lot to memorize," Jacob observed. They turned left, then right, then right again, then left. Jacob was *so* confused. *How in the world do they keep track with all of this? Surely they have a map or something.* A sickening feeling hit him. *How am I going to lead the army down here if I can't show them where to go? If there's so many tunnels that lead out, then a dragon could escape!* They were coming up out of the tunnel when Jacob saw light. Everyone stopped. Lighter turned to Jacob and whispered,

"Now Jacob, we're about to come to the surface of the forest, these dragons are pretty nice but some of them do not like humans very much."

"Most of them do, it's just there's a couple of them that you really don't want to mess with," Glazer added.

"And we don't exactly come to the surface in the day that much....so...... try not to look like you are hiding something. Oh, and act normal, and just speed walk through, but not too fast. You got that?" Lighter asked.

"Ok... what's so big about you coming up here?" Jacob asked.

"Well.... let's just say, there are some dragons who don't really like us. We kind of just stay in the caves a lot," Lighter responded.

"Why do they not like you?" Jacob asked.

"It's complicated," Glider said.

"Just, don't be afraid," Tortoise said.

"Everyone here is usually nice, there's just like two or three that you really don't want to mess with," Glazer said again.

"Now, just stay calm," Lighter said. Finally, they left the tunnels and walked outside. Jacob was prepared for violence and anger. He was prepared for anything, but not this.

Young dragons laughed and played in the sunlight. Older dragons clipped grapes off vines with smiles on their faces. And beautiful tall trees were all around the dragon village. The dragon village was beautiful. Some of the houses were made of stone, others were wood, and some were even inside the tree itself. *But how is that possible!* Jacob wondered. *No houses can just grow like a tree, how did they do that?* To

Jacob's surprise, most houses were in the trees, some even dangled from the trees. Everyone looked so happy.

"Jacob, welcome to the Peace Forest," Lighter said with a slight bow.

Peace Forest? THAT'S what it's actually called?!! "Are all villages like this?" Jacob asked, trying not to sound surprised.

"Like what?" Lighter asked.

"Like this calm. Is every day like this?" Jacob asked.

"Well…. It depends on what is going on," Lighter said. No one seemed to pay any attention to Jacob, which was surprising. Everybody just walked right past him. *This is weird.* Something about the village felt so off, but not in a bad way. He couldn't put his finger on it. *Why does it feel so weird here?*

"See! I told you I could still do it!" a baby dragon yelled. Jacob looked up. A tiny blue dragon, probably a dragon's version of a young toddler, was in the air above them. He was flapping his little wings violently. "And I'm not going to fall this time!" he cheered in excitement.

"He's doing it! He's doing it!" his friends cheered on the ground.

"Wee!!!" the little dragon yelled. Jacob couldn't help but smile. *He's so cute!*

"ZACH!" Jacob guessed that was his mother calling. "Time to come down!"

"Why?" the kid called back. "I'm doing great!"

"I know you're doing great sweetie, it's just time to come down! It's lunch time!" she called.

"Can you take a picture first?" the kid called.

"Fine, one picture," the mom said, "and then you're coming down."

"Ok!"

The mom ran inside one of the houses to look for a camera. But that was when the baby dragon lost his rhythm. He dropped out of the sky fast. The dragon screamed in horror as he tried to flap his wings. Glider opened his wings to take off, but something else was faster.

Something shot from the trees and, as fast as an arrow, grabbed the child just before he could hit the ground. Whatever it was, it was fast. It jumped onto another tree, then climbed down to the ground. He gently put the kid down in front of him. Zach immediately ran to all his friends to hug them.

"Oh my goodness! Are you ok?!" Glazer shrieked. She ran over with Lighter, Glider, and Tortoise right behind her. Jacob followed from a distance.

"*YOU!*" the mother yelled furiously. She grabbed a club and flew over.

"Whoa!" Krennicx shrieked, dodging a swing. He jumped onto the tree and stared at her like a scared cat. Probably because he *was* a scared cat.

"Mom!" the little dragon yelled, running to her.

"STAY AWAY FROM MY SON!" She put her son on her back and stomped away.

"Krennicx!" All the other kids yelled.

"Heyyyyyyy, kiddos!" Krennicx said, hopping off the tree and smiling like nothing just happened.

"You saved Zach!" the kids cheered.

"Oh really? When?" Krennicx asked. They jumped onto the panther and play-tackled him to the ground. "Oh, I don't know if we should do that," Krennicx said on his back. "I've been having back issues."

"Really?" one of them asked, jumping onto his stomach.

"Oof!"

The kids giggled. "Try to get me off," the kid on top of him dared.

"You asked for it." Krennicx angled his claws underneath the dragon kid and flung him into the air. He rolled onto his claws and stood up just in time to catch him with his mouth, holding him like a kitten.

"You strong," the kid complimented.

Krennicx opened his mouth, letting the kid fall to the ground. The kid giggled.

"I'd hope so," Krennicx said with a grin, "I *am* a panther."

"Are you fast?" a different kid said.

"Fast enough to outrun you, I'd hope," Krennicx said playfully.

"Awest him!"

"You mean arrest?"

They only looked at Krennicx as if he was an idiot. "Awest him!" the kids shouted, jumping onto the panther.

"Ahhh! Oh no! I'm being *arrested!* Somebody help me!" Krennicx fake yelled as he tumbled to the ground.

"On behalf of the Fighters of Peace, I awest you!" one of the kids announced. *Fighters of Peace?* Jacob wondered. *That's an old myth. I guess dragons have it too?*

"Wait," one of them said, "I thought I was going to be the Fighter of Peace."

"Aren't there more than one?" Krennicx asked.

They looked at each other, "Ok."

"Can you give me a ride?" a little girl asked from on top of his stomach.

"I thought I was arrested?"

"How 'bout re welease you if you give us ride," the girl asked.

"*We* release you," Krennicx corrected. "It's a w and r, very difficult to say close to each other."

The girl giggled, "You're funnily stupid."

Krennicx laughed, "Well *that* was unexpected!"

"Well, wha't gonna be?" she asked.

"As long as your parents are ok with it."

"MOOOM!" all the kids yelled as they ran over to their houses.

Krennicx rolled over and stood up, "They're adorable."

"Come on Jacob, we should get going," Lighter said.

"Hey wait!" Krennicx called as they started to walk away. "I can come with you. I could help y'all with whatever you're trying to do."

"Nah, no thanks. I think we're good," Lighter responded.

"Plus, aren't you supposed to be 'awested'," Glider mimicked.

"It's arrest, Glider," Krennicx sighed. "It's arrest."

"What's up with *him*," Jacob asked, looking behind them.

"Who? Krennicx?" Lighter asked. "Oh, he likes to follow us around for some reason."

"Huh, he sure does seem to like kids. But...didn't he hate y'all like an hour ago?" Jacob asked.

"Yeah...... he's weird," Glider said.

"He's not weird!" Glazer barked.

"Right......" Glider responded.

"I don't think he's weird," Tortoise said.

"Thank you, Tortoise," Glazer thanked.

"Nobody is weird," Lighter said, sounding a little aggravated. "Now come on, we're almost there."

"Kind of what someone would say if they were defending someone who's weird," Glider mumbled. Jacob wondered why Krennicx followed them around everywhere. It was weird though, only around an hour ago, he acted like he hated the group of dragons. *Something is definitely going on, and I'm going to get to the bottom of it.*

For all Jacob could tell, Lighter's house seemed nice for a dragon's house. The entrance was the only part of the cave that could be seen from the outside, everything else was covered by flowering vines. Right next to the entrance was a stone tree about six feet tall. The inside of the house/cave had two couches and a little kitchen. Everything was in one relatively large room with a fireplace. From the looks of it, Jacob guessed they didn't have air conditioning, but there was one thing that was awesome: the pool. The pool was like an awesome waterfall with a rock wall next to it that could be climbed. The waterfall itself was smooth enough to slide down. There were also vines so you can swing into the pool. Jacob had to admit it was pretty cool.

Jacob and Lighter stood at the edge of the waterfall, looking down. "So, Jacob," Lighter said, "are you alright with getting your clothes wet?"

"Well," Jacob said, "it depends on th....." With no warning, Lighter pushed him into the waterfall slide. He screamed but his voice only floated up into bubbles. Jacob swam up to the surface of the pool.

Water was stuck in his eyes and nose to where everything was blurry. "Really!" he yelled.

Lighter only laughed, "Cannon ball!" Then he grabbed the vines and did a back flip in the air. With a splash, he cannoned into the water.

"How dare you push a human over the side of a waterfall!" Jacob mimicked, somewhat copying something Michael would say.

Lighter laughed, "No wonder humans are so grumpy, they never have any fun! I know you're probably thinking about the other humans but come on! Let's have some fun!" Lighter cheered. They laughed.

"Hey! No one swims without us! But specifically me!" the voice of Tortoise called.

They looked up, "Oh no," Lighter and Jacob said, looking at each other. Tortoise, Glider, and Glazer, all at the same time, cannonballed into the water. What had to be the biggest wave Jacob had ever seen sent him and Lighter under water.

They played in the pool all day. It was kind of cool to see Tortoise swim so professionally. Since he was a Water Dragon, he could breathe underwater, and his finned tail and webbed talons could make him go extremely fast. Jacob hated it whenever the Water Dragon swam underneath him though. Whenever Jacob's toes touched Tortoise's cold scales, he would shriek because it felt like a snake. Glider loved it when that happened though. The Ice Dragon definitely knew how to laugh and *keep* laughing for a *long time.* Tortoise had also told Jacob that the large antenna-like things on his head allowed him to sense fish from miles away, which Jacob thought was impressive. Overall, Jacob had a good time. When the sun was beginning to set, it was time to go back inside. "Come on Tortoise!" Glider called from the edge of the pool.

"Come on! Just a little longer," Tortoise begged.

"No! I'm hungry," Glider responded.

"Come on Tortoise, don't you want to eat?" Glazer asked.

Inside, Jacob and Lighter were talking about.... just about everything. "Man, my clothes are soaked, thanks to you," Jacob teased.

"If it wasn't for me, you wouldn't have gotten in the water," Lighter pointed out.

"That is probably true."

"So, I guess a 'thank you' is in order?"

"No, no not really," Jacob said.

"What!" Lighter said. "But you had fun, right?"

Jacob somewhat didn't want to admit that he had fun with a few dragons, even though he did. He decided to change the subject. "Where are they?" Jacob asked.

"I'm guessing they're still trying to get Tortoise out of the pool," Lighter responded.

"Hmm, so what are we making?" Jacob asked.

"Cubed steak, mash potatoes, and gravy."

"I've never had that before."

"You haven't?!" Lighter yelped in surprise.

"What? Is it good?"

"You have no idea."

"So what am I making?" Jacob asked.

"You are going to do the honor of the mashed potatoes. The cubed steak has been cooking all day," Lighter responded.

"Is that what smells so good?"

"Yep."

Jacob put the potatoes in the bowling pot. "You said that you're thirteen, right?"

"Right."

"So, why does a thirteen-year-old kid live alone in a cave?" Jacob asked.

"Well, not really," Lighter said. "I don't live alone……. of course, Glider, Glazer, and Tortoise stay here a lot but…."

"But… when they leave, then you are alone," Jacob finished for him.

"Well…… no, there's still someone else who kinda always stays with me," Lighter said.

"Your parents?"

Lighter sighed, "I don't remember my parents. I've been an orphan all my life."

"Oh….er…. sorry to hear that," Jacob said feeling awkward. Even though Jacob was against the dragons, he still felt strangely bad for Lighter. "So, how are you not in an orphanage?"

"Well…… let's just say, someone saved me from it," Lighter answered.

"Who?"

"A relative."

"The same one you're living with?" Jacob asked. Lighter nodded. Jacob wanted to know more, but inside he just tried to find a different subject. "So, mashed potatoes and gravy, now that sounds delicious."

"You don't know but half of it, but the cubed steak is good too," Lighter said.

"I bet."

"Why do you have to make this so difficult?!" the voice of Glider yelled.

"What are you doing?" Lighter asked, looking at them. Glider and Glazer had Tortoise laying on the ground while they were trying to pull him from his feet.

"How many times do I have to tell you? I need water in my squirters, so I can defend myself from you!" Tortoise said as he tried to pull himself away from them.

"I think your spit can wait!" Glider teased.

"Grrrr, how many times do I have to tell you……" Tortoise started.

"Come on Tortoise. Can't you just drink some water?" Glazer interrupted.

"I could……. But it would be way faster if I just dove into the water," Tortoise argued.

"Don't *make* me freeze your talons!" Glider threatened.

"Ahhh, no! Too cold!" Tortoise shrieked.

"Then stop struggling!" Glider commanded. Tortoise stopped, then a powerful blast of water shot from his mouth. Glider and Glazer were sent back and upside down.

"Oh would you look at that," Tortoise said, free from their grasp. "Looks like I had a little bit of water left. Well then, looks like I could use some more." Tortoise spread his wings wide and pounced into the air, diving outside towards the pool.

"Oh no you don't," Glider said, running towards the opening. He opened his mouth wide and shot out a blast of ice frost. Glider perked his ears up.

"Ahhhhh! My foot!" a yell from Tortoise echoed.

"Hah! That's what ya get for spit'n at Glider!" Glider called.

"NOT SPIT!" Tortoise called back.

"Science!"

"Actually, science says that it is *not* spit," Glazer pointed out.

"It's spit," Glider assured.

Dinner was delicious! Jacob loved every bite. All the gravy and steak and mashed potatoes! He was upset when it was all gone.

"Do I go ahead and put out the fire?" Glazer asked a few hours after dinner.

"Yeah, isn't it supposed to get hot tonight?" Glider asked. "Can I please turn the cold up in here?"

"You mean down?" Tortoise asked.

"Can I please turn the cold down in here?" Glider asked as if nothing just happened.

"Yeah, I guess you can freeze all of the walls tonight," Lighter responded.

"YES!" Glider said happily.

"Lighter, are you going to be ok with it being colder tonight?" Glazer asked. "I know Nighters don't like the cold as much as Icelings and Waterlings do."

"Who said I like the cold?" Tortoise asked.

"I should be fine. What about you, Jacob?" Lighter asked.

"Probably," Jacob responded. *How could it get cold in here? There's no air conditioning!*

"Ok," Glazer said.

"Jacob," Lighter said, "you can go pick your sleeping mat in the closet."

"Ok," Jacob said. *Man, it's going to get hot tonight,* Jacob thought, walking to the closet. *I should probably get the thinnest one.*

"Don't y'all get hot in a cave like this?" Jacob asked as he arranged his sleeping mat on the floor.

"Not really," Lighter responded. "Glider and Glazer do, but not me and Tortoise. If anything, we get cold."

"How?" Jacob asked.

"You see that big metal thing on the ceiling that circles around the whole cave?" Lighter asked.

"Yeah."

"It has holes in it so all you have to do is freeze it. It cools down the whole cave, kinda cold too," Lighter explained.

"Hmm, I've never seen anything like that before," Jacob said.

"Yep."

"Goodnight," Glazer announced.

"Night, night, Tortoise," Glider teased.

"Night, Glider," Tortoise grumbled from his mat. Everyone went to their own sleeping mats and snuggled into it. *Better be prepared for a horrible night sleep,* Jacob thought as he closed his eyes to fall asleep.

CHAPTER 7

DRAGONS ARE WEIRD

The sound of laughter, the cries of children. The dreams Jacob kept having were horrible. Most, he didn't even understand. Who were these strange creatures? For some reason, every dream had one amazing fighter, but it was hard to tell what it was. One second it would be a dragon, then another it would be a tiger. But at all times it had the same sword and green eyes. *Wait, green eyes?* Jacob shot up in alarm, breathing hard. He turned over to see Lighter sneaking past all the sleeping mats. Lighter seemed to know what he was doing, for he was walking so silently and dodging whatever was in his path. Jacob wondered if he had night vision. *I don't think that's what woke me up, but what did?* Lighter crept out of the cave and outside. *Don't follow him,* Jacob thought. *I'm not going to do it, I'm not going to do it,* Jacob repeated in his mind. The buzz set off so hard in Jacobs' head, it hurt. *Wait a second,* Jacob realized, *the buzz is coming from where Lighter is at. Ok, I'm following him.* Jacob slipped off his mat and tip-toed after Lighter. *He couldn't have gone that far, right?* Jacob stepped outside in the pitch-dark night; it was kind of chilly. Jacob was still surprised about the fact that Lighter pushed him into the water. He liked swimming, but he hated the wet clothes. *I definitely wish I had my backpack with my extra clothes. Another thing thanks to Lighter.* A lot of thoughts came in his head as he walked in the woods, the biggest thing was if Michael was ok. Each step Jacob took, the buzz became stronger and the dreams clearer, until everything stopped. Jacob shook his head. *I lost it!* He took his eyes off the path. *Where is Lighter?* "Oh, there you are Lighter," Jacob said after bumping into something. "What are you doing out here?"

"And who are you?" the dragon turned around to face him, and it had purple eyes. *That's not Lighter,* Jacob realized in horror. "Hey everyone look!" the dragon called. "I finally found something!"

"What did you find this time?" another dragon asked as it stepped out of the trees.

"Looks like a little human," another one said. "I am pretty hungry."

Jacob gulped in fear. "You wouldn't want to eat me," Jacob tried, "I'm too bony."

The dragon chuckled. "We have traveled nonstop from Dylavore itself. We have found nothing to eat the whole time. So when you're hungry like us, you really don't care," the first one said. All three dragons began to growl and get into pounce position.

"Oh, come on guys, we can talk about this." Jacob took a step back.

"Oh, don't worry," it growled, "we'll make it quick." With a growl, it jumped at its prey.

Something shot from the trees and cannoned on the dragon in mid-air. The dragon was knocked off its feet and pushed into the trees. "What is that?!" the other two dragons shouted. "Grab it!" They jumped up and down trying to grab it. There was a sound of sharp claws scrapping against scales after one of the dragons tried to grab it. The dragon roared in pain and fury. The attacker hovered in the air, waiting for the others to make their move. The first one that was pushed into the trees pounced into the air and tried to knock the attacker out of the sky. The attacker only caught him in the neck and slammed him onto the ground, then the attacker returned to the trees to remain unseen. The purple-eyed dragon was the only one standing. "Where are you?! Show yourself!" he shouted. Nothing happened, except for the two injured dragons moaning on the floor. "SHOW YOURSELF OR I WILL DESTROY THIS HUMAN!" the dragon shouted. Nothing happened. "Well," the purple-eyed dragon breathed, "I guess it's gone."

The attacker bolted out of nowhere at the dragon, aiming for its neck. It pinned the purple-eyed dragon to a tree, using something on its tail to pin the opponent's neck. The attacker remained hovering in the air with its wings as he did it. The dragon shrieked in horror as the attacker flung him onto the forest floor. The attacker was still hovering in the air as it pinned the dragon on the ground. "Let me go!" the dragon yelled. He stopped struggling, then took a deep crackling breath. The dragon's mouth began to glow red as smoke started to cloud up around his mouth. He was about to shoot a blast of fire when the attacker's tail shot up and stabbed the dragon's tail. The fire stopped, as the dragon shrieked in pain. The other two dragons on the floor scrambled up and began to scream, "Run away! Run away! Retreat! Retreat!"

The attacker let go and hovered in the air, watching the two dragons below running around in circles. The dragons continued to scream in horror.

"RUN!" they yelled as they rushed to their brother. They kept tripping from their injuries. Both of them grabbed their brother and took off into the sky.

Jacob was horrified. First, he almost got eaten by dragons, then there was a small terrifying battle (more like a sneak attack) and now he stood in terror with an attacker hidden somewhere.

"W-who are you?" Jacob asked in fear.

"Well, well, well, look who it is," a familiar voice said. "It's the human, Jacob, right?" It stepped into the light, and Jacob knew who it was.

"Krennicx? What are you doing here?" Jacob asked.

"The real question is, what are *you* doing here?" Krennicx responded, tilting his head curiously. His pure red eyes glowed terrifyingly.

"Ummm……. well….it's confusing," Jacob answered.

"Hmmm."

"How did you do that?" Jacob asked.

"Do what?" Krennicx asked, confused.

"What do you mean?! You know, you just beat up those dragons," Jacob said. "Didn't you? But… you were flying too…. with wings."

"Me?"

"Yes, you! Right?"

Krennicx's expression was blank, for he knew nothing. "What are you talking about?" he asked.

"How can it not be you?" Jacob growled in frustration.

"How can what not be me?" Krennicx asked, still confused.

"Never mind," Jacob sighed. *He clearly knows nothing, maybe whoever just saved me is the voice.* Jacob still had no clue who or what it could be. *Maybe I should ask Lighter about it, he might know something.*

"Are you lost?" Krennicx asked curiously.

"Pffff, no! I think I can find my way around," Jacob said. He turned and started to walk away.

"Do you, huh?" Krennicx asked. "I don't know if you're testing me, but you should know that that is the completely wrong direction."

"Hm? Oh yeah! Yeah, I know that." Jacob turned around and walked the other way.

"Know where you're going, right?"

"Right!"

"Going to Lighter's house?"

"Yep!"

"Then you're going the wrong way," Krennicx calmly said, then started to laugh.

Jacob stopped and took a deep breath. "Ok, so maybe I don't know where I'm going!" he admitted.

"Of course you don't," Krennicx said. "Humans never like admitting their wrong-ness."

"And dragons do?"

"Oh no, dragons are even worse, and super stubborn."

"Sure does seem like you're talking against yourself," Jacob teased.

"I am no dragon," Krennicx pointed out.

"Right…….so…….do you know the way to Lighter's?"

"Follow me."

"So, if you're not a dragon," Jacob said as they wondered through the woods. "And panthers really are not supposed to be able to talk. So if you're not a panther who talks, then what are you?" He asked.

"That…is undecided," Krennicx responded. "Some call me different things."

"What do you call yourself? If you are just a panther, how do you talk?"

"I don't really want to talk about it," Krennicx said.

"Ok…. so… how do you know Lighter?" Jacob asked.

"Well……. It's complicated," Krennicx responded.

"How complicated?"

"You sure are curious," Krennicx observed, avoiding Jacob's question.

"Is that a good thing or a bad thing?" Jacob asked.

"Depends."

"On what?"

"So how did you meet Lighter?" Krennicx asked. *Man, he is good at dodging questions.*

"It's complicated," Jacob mimicked.

"How complicated?" Krennicx mimicked back. Jacob almost laughed but stopped himself.

"Do you know anything about the Cloud Kingdom?" Jacob asked.

"Pfff, Cloud Kingdom, why would you want to know anything about the Cloud Kingdom?" Krennicx asked nervously.

"What do you have against the Cloud Kingdom?" Jacob asked.

"Well…. let's just say me and um…. King Saul aren't exactly…….
well…...friends…….. at the moment……" Krennicx stared off into the
distance.

"Wait a second, you know the king?" Jacob asked.

"Hmmm? Oh yeah, yeah, yeah I know him……... sorta," Krennicx
responded.

"How?"

"Complicated."

"What isn't complicated with you?" Jacob asked.

"Come to think of it, not much," Krennicx answered with a grin. *Grrrr!*
Why won't this guy tell me anything! Like something important and useful!

"So what were you doing out here?" Jacob asked.

"I was just going home. What were you doing?" Krennicx asked.

"Nothing……"

"Nobody does nothing."

"Ok! So maybe I was a little curious…. I'm a kid, we are always
curious."

"Right……"

"How did this war start?" Jacob blurted out.

"Welp, here we are," Krennicx immediately said. "You better go back
to bed before they realize you're gone."

"Right, well I guess this is goodbye then," Jacob said.

"Fortunately, yes, I'll probably see you again though. According to
Glider, I always show up at the worst times," Krennicx said. "But if
you're with Glider, every time is the worst time."

"Yeah…. bye," Jacob waved.

"See ya," Krennicx said, then jumped into the bushes.

Jacob tip-toed back into the house-cave-thing and into bed. He couldn't tell if Lighter was back or not. As Jacob laid there, he wondered why Krennicx changed the subject on so many things, and why he acted so weird. Whatever the reason was, Jacob needed to find it and fast.

Krennicx walked into the building in his back yard. After flipping the light switch, he sighed, for nothing happened.

"Well, well, well, look who it is. The one with the very un-normal name," a voice said in the shadows.

"Like yours is more normal," Krennicx responded, knowing exactly what it was.

"Well at lease mine wasn't made up," the voice said.

"Weren't they all? Now show yourself, you coward!" Krennicx commanded. Black smoke rolled from underneath a table, then took the form of something like a dragon in front of Krennicx. "Proof of your cowardice and your master's, you always come as smoke and never yourself. And he always sends you instead of himself," Krennicx mocked.

"Look who's calling who a coward," the smoke said, "when you have been running your entire life, you criminal."

"Why would I run if there's no one chasing me, Klaus?" Krennicx asked.

"Speaking of which," the smoke—Klaus—said, "I heard that the King of Firea has finally told my king that they are considering on joining the new Annorlia. He has also agreed to the requirements of the three bounties. Don't forget you are one of the bounties, criminal."

"Of course they did," Krennicx sighed.

"Four kingdoms down, six to go. Your hiding spots are crumbling. Sooner or later, you will be found and put to justice."

"I haven't been found yet, what makes you think I'll be found now?" Krennicx asked.

"I have a few ideas." The smoke curled up into a ball and vanished into thin air.

Krennicx's phone vibrated on the table with the caller's name on the screen.

"Hey Ben, what's up?" Krennicx asked through his headphones that were always in his ears. "What? Ok, ok, I'm coming, bye."

"Dangflabbet that guy wants me dead more than a chicken wanting to eat bread!" There was a flicker of lightning as Krennicx turned from a panther to what he really was. Spreading his wings wide he took off into the dark night sky.

"RISE AND SHINE!" Glider yelled in the morning.

"Just a few more minutes," Jacob moaned. Oh how awesome the blanket over him felt, it had gotten *so* freezing cold that night. He still regretted not getting a thicker blanket.

"Come on sleepy head," Glider said, thumping Jacob's head.

"What time is it?" Jacob asked sleepily, pushing Glider's talon away.

"Six."

"Six in the *morning!?*" Jacob groaned.

"No, six in the afternoon," Glider said sarcastically.

"Don't worry Jacob," Tortoise said from his sleeping mat, "Glider usually *never* gets up when we're supposed to."

"Yeah, in about a day or two he's probably going to get back to normal and never get up," Glazer chimed in.

"I get up!" Glider defended himself.

"Ha!" Tortoise laughed.

"Where's Lighter?" Jacob asked, yawning. He stretched and slowly got up.

"He's on the phone," Glazer responded.

"Today's going to be SO AWESOME!" Tortoise said excitingly.

"Tortoise's version of awesome is my version of torture," Glider pointed out.

"Well, not today it isn't," Tortoise said, "because today we're going to pick up Turtle, and then we're going to go to the beach! How awesome is that?!"

"One out of two things in there I *really* don't like, and I'm not the craziest about the second one either," Glider said.

"I know, I know you're not the craziest about Turtle, but I still don't get why you don't like the beach that much," Tortoise said.

"No, I like the beach," Glider said. "It's the beach *with* Turtle I don't like."

"Sure… You keep telling yourself that," Tortoise said, "but we all know that you like him on the inside."

"No, no I don't." Glider said, shaking his head.

"Change of plans," Lighter barged in. "We're not going to the beach."

"What?" Tortoise yelped.

"Yes!" Glider cheered.

"We were actually never going to the beach, but we are going to go pick up Turtle," Lighter said.

"Yes!" Tortoise cheered.

"No!" Glider yelped.

"So now where are we going?" Glazer asked.

"We need to pick up something so…… we're going to the Cloud Kingdom," Lighter answered.

Wait, what? Krennicx and I somewhat talked about the Cloud Kingdom last night. He had said something about knowing the king.

"Why?" Glazer asked.

"We need to……. pick up something," Lighter responded.

"So, are we taking the ship?" Glider asked.

Lighter gave him a strong glare. "Actually, we're flying today," Lighter said. *What ship?* Jacob wondered.

"But that's going to take forever!" Glider complained.

"Are you sure you can make it that far?" Glazer asked.

"Yeah, I should be fine," Lighter responded.

"Is Jacob coming?" Tortoise asked.

"Not on my back!" Glider protested. Everyone looked at him. "And…. I just volunteered myself…. Didn't I?" Glider asked. Everyone nodded.

"Are you coming, Lighter!" Glider called from outside the cave. "What is taking him so long!" he complained.

"Remember, Glider, it is kind of difficult for Lighter to fly that long," Glazer said, "and the Cloud Kingdom is pretty far away."

"It's not *too* far," Glider said.

"How is Lighter's wing like that?" Jacob asked. They all looked at each other hesitantly.

"It's complicated," Glazer responded.

"How?" Jacob asked.

"He probably wouldn't want us to talk about it," Tortoise said.

"Ok."

"READY!" Lighter called running out of the cave.

"'Bout time," Glider complained.

"You ready to have Jacob on your back?" Lighter asked, half teasing. Glider moaned.

"How long of a fly is it?" Jacob asked nervously.

"Not too long," Lighter answered.

"Just depends on if you just so happen to fall off," Glider said, trying to scare him. Jacob gulped. "Oh, I'm sorry, did I scare you?" Glider teased.

"Lighter, please don't make me do this," Jacob said.

"Oh, you don't want to go? Well…… I mean I guess you don't *have* to," Lighter said.

"Oh no! No, no, it's fine, I want to go.," Jacob responded quickly. *What are you doing!* Jacob thought. *I have to stay with them to figure out how to beat them and find the voice.*

"Ok…" Lighter said. "Well, then I guess get on Glider's back."

Jacob walked over to Glider in fear. *Ok, Jacob,* he thought. *You're not going to fall, Glider's a good flier…… I hope.* Glider was not that much bigger than him, but it still felt like trying to get on a horse, (or pony to be more accurate) "Ok, so how do I do this?" Jacob asked as he stood there, standing in awkward positions to try to pull himself up on Glider's back.

"Don't look at us," Glazer said.

"You think we've ridden on a back of a dragon before?" Tortoise asked.

"Right," Jacob said. "Ok, can you please be still?" Jacob asked as he tried to climb onto Glider's back.

"I am still!" Glider barked. Glider began to walk in circles with Jacob trying to grab him.

"Stop it! Glid*er*…." Jacob said.

"I've got a better idea," Glider said. He shot into the sky and then turned back, and without any warning, grabbed Jacob's shoulder and tossed him onto his back.

"Glider, what are you doing!" Jacob yelped in fear. Glider hovered in the air with Jacob on his back. Jacob was terrified. "Glider, there's nothing for me to hold on to!" Jacob gulped in fear.

"I'm sure there's a spike or something back there," Glider responded calmly.

"*Spike*?" Jacob yelped, looking down at what he was sitting on. Spikes went down Glider's whole body, sharp and……. cold spikes. It took a second for him to realize it but… all of Glider was cold. "Glider, why is your skin so cold?" Jacob asked, still shaking with fear.

"Obviously, I'm an Ice Dragon so my *scales* are cold," Glider corrected.

"Are you sure you're going to make it all the way to the Cloud Kingdom?" Lighter asked, flying up with the others behind him.

"Sure…… hopefully," Jacob said looking down, then regretting it.

"Ok." Lighter shut his wings and dove towards the ground fast like an arrow. At the last second, just before hitting the ground, he flared his wings wide. One by one the others followed, doing the exact same thing.

"Oh no," Jacob realized. "No, no, no, no, no, no." Glider began to tip over and do it too.

"Oh yeah!" Glider cheered as he dove towards the ground flying fast.

"AHHHHHHHHHH!" Jacob screamed in horror, holding on for dear life. Glider zoomed through the trees, flying like an arrow, dodging all obstacles in his way.

"Isn't this fun?" Glider called out.

"I think I'm going to be sick," Jacob called back. He looked up to see where the others were. "Hey, uh Glider."

"Yeah?"

"Where did Lighter, Glazer, and Tortoise go?" Jacob asked. "I don't see them anywhere."

"Hmm, Oh! Yeah, they never usually come this close to the ground," Glider said. "I only do it to practice for my races, and, well…. I can actually do it… most of it."

"But I thought I saw them come down here and……. wait, what do you mean *most* of it?" Jacob asked.

"Well……. I have never really been able to make it at a certain part," Glider said.

"What part?"

"This one."

"WHAT!" Jacob looked up to see a giant rock with trees all close around it. Glider tried to shut his wings completely to shoot through an opening from the tree and the rock, then Jacob saw the floor flash before his eyes.

"Found 'em," a familiar voice said. Jacob opened his eyes to see red eyes right in front him.

"Jacob, are you ok?" Lighter asked, running over to him.

Jacob moaned, "I think so, what happened?" He started to try to stand up.

"I would probably stay sitting down, just in case you got a concussion or something," Krennicx advised.

"How did you know where we were?" Jacob asked, leaning back against the rock.

"Well, we ran into Krennicx while we were looking for you, then he said that he saw you guys fly by, so we asked him to help us," Lighter responded.

"When you say 'ran into him,'" Glider said, "do you mean you caught him trying to steal your wallet?" Krennicx gave him a strong glare. "No comment? He's hiding something guys, I know it!"

"You know how I found you?" Krennicx asked, "I just heard girl sounding screams and branches snapping. So I thought to myself, 'Huh, who do I know who has a girl scream and crashes into stuff *a lot?'* And then it hit me, Glider is *super* clumsy and screams like a girl."

"Oh yeah," Glider said daringly, "well, you scream like a.... umm.... Like a……. a panther! Yeah, you scream like a panther."

"A panther?" Krennicx asked. "That's the best you can do?"

"What? You scream like a panther."

"Alright, first off, panthers don't scream, Glider," Krennicx said. "If anything, they make a cool sounding roar, so thank you Glider for saying I can do a cool sounding roar. Second… I *am* a panther."

"Weirdo."

"Dumdum."

"Ok! I think that's enough of whatever this rivalry is," Lighter said, standing between them. "How are you feeling Jacob?"

"I'm fine," Jacob responded standing up.

Krennicx coughed, "Uh hem, no thanks to Glider."

Glider opened his mouth to say something.

"Glider…" Lighter warned.

"Oh, come on. Why can't I?" Glider asked.

"Well, for one reason, he knows a short cut and can help us," Lighter said.

"And the other?" Glider asked. Lighter only stared at him.

"What short cut?" Jacob asked.

"Apparently, Krennicx knows a short cut to the Cloud Kingdom," Tortoise said.

"Short cut?" Jacob asked. "Don't y'all just fly?"

"Don't cars just drive?" Krennicx mimicked.

"Ooo, he got you there," Glazer said.

"What I mean," Jacob said, glaring at the annoying panther, "isn't flying just a straight shot?"

"It *would* be if we didn't have to drag a *walking* panther," Glider said, glaring at the crazy thing.

"It is," Krennicx responded, ignoring Glider, "but if you go through a couple of caves and stuff, it will be faster."

"How?" Jacob asked.

"You'll see."

CHAPTER 8

THIEF AS A GUIDE

"I still don't see how this is supposed to be any faster," Glider called out in the air.

"Glider, we haven't even passed the forest yet," Krennicx called back.

"Well, the sooner we get there, the sooner I can get this human squeezing my neck off!" Glider complained. Since Krennicx was a panther and they needed to follow Krennicx, they had to fly extremely close to the trees to stay in eyesight with the creepy feline. Jacob was surprised at how fast Krennicx was as he jumped from tree branch to tree branch and was keeping up with dragons flying in the air. They were flying a little slower than usual though.

"How are you doing, kid?" Krennicx called to Jacob.

"Do you want the lie or the truth?" Jacob asked.

"What is the truth?" Krennicx asked.

"Well, I am on top of a dragon in the sky with nothing to hold onto except for freezing cold spikes and scales, so what do you think?"

"I think it sounds awesome."

"Not awesome!" Jacob called.

"Well, you know we can always turn back...."

"NO!" Jacob nearly yelled. "I mean, no I'm fine, I'm fine," he added when everyone stared at him.

"Well, good," Krennicx said, "because things are about to get bumpy." Krennicx jumped off the trees and dove down to the ground into huge bushes.

"Is he crazy?!" Tortoise called. "We're too big to go into bushes! And why are we even going into bushes any way?"

"Like I said," Glider said, "Krennicx is insane! And a thief! Why are we even letting him come along with us?"

"Because he knows more about the Cloud Kingdom than we do," Lighter responded. "And he knows about a special short cut so…… you are just going to have to suffer through it." Lighter closed his wings shut and dove after Krennicx. Tortoise shrugged and did the same.

"You heard Lighter," Glazer said, diving towards the bushes.

"Hang on, Jacob," Glider said, starting to close his wings.

"Not again!" Jacob yelped as Glider dove down in the bushes.

Yep, it's official, Jacob thought, *I hate flying.* Jacob stood up from the floor after falling off Glider when he landed.

"You're looking a little tired there, Krennicx," Glider said teasingly.

"You're looking a little slow there, Glider," Krennicx said, catching his breath.

Glider growled, "Faster than you."

"A dragon flying fast isn't *nearly* as impressive as a panther *running* as fast as a dragon," Krennicx pointed out. "Plus, all dragons fly fast so…… there really isn't anything different."

"Oh yeah! Well, uh……. You probably can't beat uh…a… a cheetah! Yeah, cheetahs run faster than panthers."

"Do they Glider? Do they really?" Krennicx asked, giving a funny, smirky smile.

"Are you sure this is the right place?" Tortoise asked. "I don't see any caves."

"You see, that's how you dragons think," Krennicx said. "If you don't immediately see something, you don't think it's there, when really…." Krennicx pushed a button on a small remote. All of the big bushes around them disappeared, revealing a massive tunnel. "Still think I'm an idiot, Glider?"

Glider didn't say anything. They flew through the twisting tunnel, going deep into the ground. Jacob tried not to look anywhere because he was already terrified. The tunnels twisted around and became narrower to the point that Glider nearly fell because he scrapped his wing on the wall. Jacob was scared he would hit his head on the ceiling. The tunnels became steep and went straight down. For a second, Jacob thought that he saw a lightning bolt.

"Tree!" the voice of Lighter called.

"How in the world could there be a……."

"I can't believe you guys fell again," Krennicx said, looking down at Glider, who was still laying on the floor.

"My head hurts," Jacob said.

"Did he fall asleep or something?" Krennicx asked.

"Is he unconscious?" Glazer asked worriedly.

"Do I hear him snoring?" Tortoise asked.

"Ok, he is literally sleeping," Krennicx said. "How is that even possible? Wait, why am I even asking this? It's Glider."

"Man, you dragons are weird," Jacob said, rubbing his head.

"I completely agree with that," Krennicx said.

"But dude, you're a dragon too," Jacob said.

"Dude, how many times do I have to say it? I'm not a dragon. Do I even look like a dragon? No. No, I do not."

"Dude, then what are you?" Jacob asked.

"Dude, I'm not a dragon, that's for sure!"

"Ok then, dude, *all* of whatever you guys are, are weird," Jacob said.

"Dude, I totally agree with that," Krennicx said.

"Dude, but that would mean you too."

"Dude, yep."

"Dude, you're crazy."

"Dude, thanks."

"Dude, that's not a compliment!"

"Dude, I know."

"Dude, you're insane!"

"Dude," Krennicx said, "I'm starting to like this kid."

Whew, Jacob thought in relief, *why did I just do that? And why in the world did I say dude?*

"All right Glider, time to get up," Krennicx said, giving him a little kick on his leg. "Glider," he said again.

"Let me try," Tortoise said walking over. "Sometimes all you need is to do a little tickling." Tortoise snapped a branch with leaves off a tree and rubbed it on Glider's face, or snout.

"That's gotta be the weirdest thing I've seen all day," Krennicx observed.

"Still not working," Lighter said.

"I don't get it!" Tortoise said. "Were there any Zillow plants in there or something?"

"What's a Zillow plant?" Jacob asked.

"It's a certain kind of plant or flower that can cause a dragon to fall asleep if it's touched or breathed in," Krennicx responded.

"Some people make weapons out of it," Glazer added.

"Did Glider hit the wall or anything in the cave?" Krennicx asked.

Jacob thought for a second then a flash of memory hit him, "He hit one of his wings against the wall just before we came out."

"Well, that would explain it," Krennicx said.

"How long should it last?" Glazer asked.

"Usually a few hours, but don't worry, this will make anyone wake up," Krennicx said, going over to the snoozing dragon.

"What are you going to do?" Tortoise asked. Krennicx only smirked a smile in response.

Krennicx went to the right side of Glider, bent down, and burped loudly *directly* in his face. Quickly, a fist shot up and punched the red-eyed panther in the face.

"What was that for!?" Krennicx yelped, staggering back.

"EW!" Glider yelled angrily. "That's disgusting! What is *wrong* with you?!"

"What is wrong with me? What is wrong with you! You just punched me in the face!"

"You burped in my face!"

"Well, at least I didn't punch you!" Krennicx said, rubbing his face.

"How about I do it again?" Glider asked threateningly. "Besides, you can't do it that hard, so I don't have to worry."

"Oh you do that and I'll *show* you how hard I can do it!" Krennicx threatened.

"Can you guys please work this out?" Lighter asked.

"Yeah, you owe me," Glider said.

"Oh, come on. Why do I owe you? Do you think I owe him?" Krennicx asked.

"Yeah, you do," everyone responded.

"Oh, come on. How?"

"Where do we start?" Lighter asked.

"Fine," Krennicx said. "Here's my wallet, get whatever you want," Krennicx said, tossing a black leather wallet to Glider.

"Wow, Krennicx," Glider said, catching it. "I honestly did not expect this from you."

"See, I'm not that bad," Krennicx said.

"Wait a minute," Glider said, looking down. "This is *MY* wallet!!"

"Man, you got to be more careful on where you stash all of your money, because someone can easily steal it," Krennicx said, smiling.

"But how is this possible!" Glider said angrily. "I don't even have pockets!"

"A true master never reveals his secret," Krennicx responded with a grin.

Glazer felt her ear, "Where's my earring?"

"Like I said, I'm a master." Krennicx tossed something shiny to Glazer.

"Even though I absolutely hate that he just did that, I have to admit *that* is impressive," Glazer said, holding up the dangly snowflake earring.

"So that's it, you didn't take anything else, right?" Lighter asked.

"Well, let's see," Krennicx said, "here's Tortoise's bracelet."

"It's a watch," Tortoise corrected, taking it from him.

"Lighter's wallet," Krennicx said, handing it to him.

"I'll take that, thank you very much," Lighter said.

"And Jacob's...what is this?" Krennicx asked, holding up Jacob's tracker.

Jacob felt like he had stopped breathing. He reached into his pocket, feeling for the tracker, but it wasn't there. Somehow Krennicx had gotten it.

"How did you get that?" Jacob asked, trying as hard as he could to not sound worried.

"What is it?" Krennicx asked, pulling it away from Jacob's reach.

"Uh...."

"Is it a phone?"

"Sure....... Yeah, it's a phone for kids," Jacob said.

"What, is it to text your girlfriend or something?" Krennicx asked. "Because trust me, don't get into that at your age, because if you go in, you don't come out.

"I thought you said you've never had one before?" Glider asked.

"I haven't," Krennicx responded. "I'm saying it's best to wait until you're a tad bit older." Krennicx tossed the tracker to Jacob, who caught it with his heart racing. *I think I underestimated this guy,* Jacob realized. *I need to be more careful.*

"How old are you?" Glider asked, still continuing with the conversation.

"Eighteen," Krennicx responded.

"I still don't think we can trust this guy," Glider said to the others.

"You know I'm standing right here," Krennicx said. "You don't have to call me 'this guy.'"

"I don't think we should trust 'He Who Shall Not Be Named'," Glider said, tilting his head towards Krennicx.

"Seriously?"

"I'm not a big fan of it either," Lighter said, "but…. Krennicx knows more about this place than we do, so, he can help us around."

"What is this place like?" Jacob asked. Everyone turned to Krennicx, for he was the only one who knew the answer.

"Let's just say the king and his friends are very rich," Krennicx said, sounding either annoyed or stressed.

There must be something about the city that Krennicx doesn't like. He seems sad.

"So how many have punched you in the face there, Krennicx?" Glider asked.

"Don't talk to me," Krennicx responded.

"Will you guys ever get along?" Glazer asked.

Glider and Krennicx looked at each other for a second, then said at the same time, "No."

"How far away are we from the city?" Lighter asked.

"Not far," Krennicx said. "Just past these trees and down the cliff."

"What cliff?" Glider asked. "You didn't say anything about a cliff."

"Just did," Krennicx said. "And what? Do you not know how to fly or something?"

"'Do you not know how to fly or something?'" Glider mimicked. "Of course I know how to fly! I flew here! And my name is literally Glider!"

"Gliders don't exactly fly though," Krennicx said. "They need an engine...... in other words a brain," he smiled. "So yeah, I guess you are a good *glider.*"

"Thank you," Glider said happily.

"Glider, you do know that wasn't a compliment, right?" Lighter asked.

"Hmm?" Glider asked. "Yeah it was, he just called me a good glider."

"Glider...... you know what? Not even going to say it," Lighter started.

"What?" Glider asked in confusion.

Krennicx did a small laugh walking past him. "Very good glider," he said.

"What?" Glider asked again.

"We will walk to the drop off then make our way to Cloudairia," Krennicx said, leading the way through the trees.

"Cloudairia?" Jacob asked. "That's a strange name."

"Yeah, the Cloudairians are very strange," Krennicx said. "I think you'd fit in quite well, Glider."

"Haha, make fun of me all you want. At least now I know that you think I'm a good glider," Glider said.

"Right...." Krennicx said.

"How far do we have to walk?" Glazer asked.

"Not far," Krennicx responded.

"Not far he says!" Glider groaned. "We've been walking for hours! Where is this so called Cloudairia we've heard so little about?"

Jacob's legs felt like he was about to fall from tiredness. *Don't complain, don't complain*, Jacob thought to himself over and over again. *I can't show that I don't really want to be here! That could ruin everything. I have to just suffer through it....... Come on Jacob, suffer through it!!* A movement in the sky caught Jacob's attention. "Did that cloud just move?" Jacob asked.

Krennicx stopped and gave Jacob a weird look. "Did those words really just come out of your mouth?"

"Was kind of hoping you didn't hear it," Jacob said, feeling like an idiot.

"Yeah.... I think I heard it," Krennicx teased.

They kept walking, laughing here and there about Jacob's odd words, and even Jacob laughed at some of the hilarious things they said. All of their talks and laughs ended when Krennicx stopped in front of them.

"What are we doing?" Glider asked, alarmed. Krennicx was always creepy, but he was acting even creepier.

"We're at the drop off," Krennicx said, staring out into the distance.

"So," Glider said, "that means the city is just down there. Why don't you just jump?"

"There's something you need to know." Krennicx whipped around with a weird gun in his claws and shot twice into the sky behind them and then once in front of them. Before Glazer even had time to scream, three dragons with armor on fell from the sky into the trees.

Jacob had no idea who to run away from. Krennicx? Lighter? The soldiers? He knew he should run away, but something inside him told him to stay.

"What are you *DOING*?" Glider asked in alarm.

"They know we're coming," Krennicx said with authority in his voice. "Or... they know I'm coming."

"Uh…." Lighter said, looking into the woods.

"Relax," Krennicx said, putting the blaster away. "It's set to stun."

"Were those Cloudairian soldiers or Diammo…." Tortoise started.

"Cloudy's," Krennicx interrupted.

"What do you mean, they're expecting you?" Glazer asked. "Weren't we just coming here to pick up Turtle?

"Well… You were…... Do you really think I would travel with *you* just to pick up a pet?" Krennicx asked.

"Then why did you even come with us?" Glider asked.

"Cause I….er….. I kind of needed to…...."

"Oh, you got to be kidding me," Glider said angrily. "You are wanted in the Cloud Kingdom, aren't you?"

"Well…" Krennicx started.

"Of course," Glider said. "That makes perfect sense. You just wanted to come with us so you could sneak into the Cloud Kingdom, am I right?"

"Wow, how long did it take for you to figure that out?" Krennicx asked mockingly.

"What? I figured it out before they did," Glider said, confused.

"Wait, you didn't know before now?" Tortoise asked. "It's kind of obvious; he's been wanted by the Cloud Kingdom for… how long?"

"About ten years," Krennicx responded.

"Wait, didn't you say you're like eighteen?" Tortoise asked.

"Some say I was a handful," Krennicx said thoughtfully.

"Ok, so then why are you wanting to go to the place with the biggest bounty on your head?" Glider asked.

"Oh, you think I want to go there?" Krennicx asked. "Name anywhere in Annorlia or even space and I'd rather go there than here."

"Then why do you have to go there?"

"There are things you don't understand, and I don't even want to try to explain it to you, because you know how long that would take," Krennicx responded.

"If you are not coming with us…." Glider said, "then I guess this is where you leave, right?"

"Unfortunately, no," Krennicx responded. "I still need you to help me slip into the town, then we go our separate ways."

"If you can't get in, then how do you expect to get out?" Jacob asked.

"I have my ways," Krennicx responded. Then without a word, he continued to walk closer to the edge of the cliff.

"What are we supposed to do with those soldiers?" Glazer asked.

"They should be fine," Krennicx answered, "but if you're going to have nightmares about it, you can go check on them." Without a word, Glazer, Glider, Tortoise, and Lighter walked back into the woods, leaving Krennicx and Jacob alone.

A part of him really wanted to ask Krennicx what happened between him and the Cloud Kingdom, but after Glider tried asking him, he thought better of it.

"Wanna see something sad?" Krennicx asked.

"What?"

"Come here."

Jacob walked over to where Krennicx was, then he saw what he was staring at. Just below the cliff, ruins of scorch-marked buildings were everywhere. What once looked like tall buildings were now nothing more than old, rotted bricks. The destroyed place looked bigger than Jacob's entire city. It was monstrous.

"What is that?" Jacob asked, staring at the ruins.

"This is Cloudairia," Krennicx responded.

"Why is there smoke there?" Jacob asked, looking at the rising smoke.

"He never even tried to fix it," Krennicx said to himself, staring at the ground in pain. "Instead, he built his own place for the rich and never let anyone else in, so now they have to stay here in these ruins." Anger and sadness were in Krennicx's eyes; then he stared at the very center of the massive kingdom. Jacob noticed what he was staring at. It was a tower with weird looking burnt marks. The tower was barely standing in the middle of the town; it looked like it used to be huge. It stood somewhat taller than the other buildings. The top of the tower almost looked like it had exploded and pieces scattered everywhere. *Everything* looked like it exploded. But there was still something different about the tower in the middle.

"What happened here?" Jacob asked.

Krennicx sighed, "Terrible things, but only few know the truth."

"Do you know the truth?"

Krennicx didn't respond, instead he only went back to stare at the tower again. Jacob opened his mouth to say something but was interrupted by Lighter walking towards them.

"I don't know how in the world you managed to hit those guards into a tangle of vines," Lighter said.

"It's a gift," Krennicx said, turning around to face Lighter.

"Well, that gift is wrapped around their wrists," Glazer said, coming behind Lighter, "and I'm not really good at untying."

"One of the many things," Krennicx whispered.

"What did you say?"

"Hmm?

"I thought you said something."

"What?"

"Never mind."

"Huh?"

"Never mind!"

"Ok," Krennicx said.

"I still don't get why you're trying to get to the Cloud Kingdom," Glider said.

"None ya business!" Krennicx snapped. "Now don't say a word to me or about me. Just talk to the guards, then we'll never have to see each other again, right?"

"Right," Lighter agreed.

"What are we supposed to talk about?" Glider asked.

"I don't care! As long as it isn't about me," Krennicx said. "Just stop at the gate and ask them something."

"How is that going to help you?"

"Just do it."

"Ok," Glider said. "We won't be in trouble if you die, right?"

"Right," Krennicx responded.

"How would he die?" Jacob asked.

"Well, it's not exactly because he'd die, it's just because…. Well…." Lighter said.

"Because what?" Krennicx asked.

"Well…. Come on! He's a talking panther! It's not every day you see a talking panther," Lighter said. "And with the red eyes you look a lot like……"

"Ok, I get it!" Krennicx interrupted.

"Looks a lot like who?" Jacob asked.

"Let's just get this over with so I can stop having to answer Sir-Asks-A lot," said Krennicx.

Oops, Jacob thought, *I guess I should try not to ask too many questions anymore.*

CHAPTER 9

CLOUDAIRIA

After a few minutes of walking, they finally made it to the wall at the edge of the town. Dragons in silver armer stood in front of the entrance to the gate with a few guards on patrol around the wall too. Jacob wanted to ask why there were so many guards but figured it would be best not to talk and bring attention to himself; plus, he didn't want to use the few questions he could ask on a silly question. He also kind of wanted to know what the Cloud Dragons looked like but couldn't tell from the armor. The only thing he could tell was that they looked longer and either had smaller wings or no wings at all, but it was hard to tell with armor surrounding them.

"Ouch!" Lighter all of the sudden yelped, right before they walked to the gate. "You just stepped on my claw!"

"I wouldn't have done it if you weren't walking so slowly right in front of me!" Tortoise responded angrily, although he kinda looked like he was faking it.

"Ow!" Lighter yelped. "You just stepped on my tail!"

"You're lucky I didn't hit your wing!" Tortoise said.

"Passport?" the guard that was in charge of opening the gate asked.

"Here you go," Lighter said, as he and Tortoise handed the guard a silver card. *Uh oh,* Jacob realized. *I'm a human, dragons don't like humans.* He thought about the night before, how horrified he was when he ran into the three dragons who tried to eat him, and the weird events of the attacker who saved his life. He was lost in thought when he realized that the guard had asked him something.

"I'm sorry?" Jacob asked nervously.

"Passport?" the guard asked.

"I don't think I have one," Jacob said, looking at Lighter, who shrugged.

"Hmm……. Wait, never mind I got it," the guard said. "Enjoy your visit to Cloudairia and let us know if you see the spy, or the criminal. Just make sure you look at the wanted signs." The guard swiped a card on the machine and immediately the gate to the Cloud Kingdom opened.

"Ow!" Tortoise yelped.

"OOPS! Sorry," Lighter said after he stepped on Tortoise's tail.

It had been a few minutes after they walked in the town when Jacob realized that Glider, Glazer, and Krennicx were not behind them.

"Lighter?" Jacob asked.

"Yeah."

"Where's everyone else?"

"Who else?" Tortoise asked.

"You know," Jacob said, "Glider, Glazer, and Krennicx?"

"Krennicx might be somewhere around here, but I don't know exactly where, but Glazer and Glider won't be able to come in here, they have to go somewhere else," Lighter said.

"How did I come in?" Jacob asked.

"Easy, you walked through the door."

"I don't mean that!" Jacob said, feeling stupid. "I mean…. why did they let me in? I didn't think dragons liked humans."

Lighter gave him a weird look. "Oh yeah, I guess you're a kid, so you don't know," he said.

"Don't know what?"

Lighter didn't respond, he only kept walking.

Grrrrr, why is it the things I'm the most curious about? "I guess this town isn't too bad," Jacob said, looking at the rows of houses they were walking by.

"This isn't the town," Lighter said.

"What?"

"We are still *in* the gate." Lighter paused in front of a tall, old rackety gate. "This," Lighter said with a frown, "is the town." Lighter pushed the gate open, and what Jacob saw had to be the worst scene he had ever seen in his life.

The so-called town was a whole bunch of ruins. All of the destroyed buildings were the color of ashes; dust and smoke were everywhere. Jacob suddenly realized why Krennicx didn't want to come here. "What happened here?" he breathed.

"No one really knows," Lighter said. "Apparently it used to be a beautiful city, but then one day it was just…… Destroyed."

"Does anyone still live here?" Jacob asked.

Lighter stopped and stared, "Look for yourself."

They turned into a busy street, the sale calls of dragons and cries of babies filled the street. Jacob was able to tell what a Cloud Dragon looked like. They all seemed to be a white-ish kind of color like the sky. They seemed to be longer than the other kinds of dragons that Jacob had met, and their snouts were longer too with two antenna-looking things under their ears. Somehow the strange antenna things pointed back, barely waving in the air. The weirdest thing about the Cloud Dragons were the wings. Their wings were more on the back instead of the side, and they were skinny and bizarre looking. They didn't even look like they could flap to fly at all. Jacob looked curiously at the Cloud Dragons. A lot of them looked skinny and dirty, but he guessed that was probably from living in a horrible place like this. "Why do they still live here?" Jacob asked. "Why don't they just fly away?"

"That's just it," Lighter said sadly, "they can't."

"Why?" Jacob asked.

Lighter sighed, "You see those wings?" Lighter asked.

"Yeah."

"They are Cloud Dragons," Lighter explained. "They can't fly without a running start and wind."

"How do they stay flying?" Jacob asked.

"When their wings catch the wind, they go high in the sky where it's always windy," Lighter said.

"Did you know," Tortoise chimed in, "that the reason they are called Cloud Dragons is because when they are high in the air like that, they have a strange, hazy, smoke kind of thing that makes them look exactly like a cloud. And when they're up there they can take a rest and just go along with the wind just like a cloud! How cool is that?"

"So where is the wind?" Jacob asked.

"The wall," Lighter responded. "The stone wall prevents all the wind gusts, so *no* Cloud Dragon can escape." Jacob didn't know what to feel, but quickly realized that he felt horrible for the dragons. No matter how hard he tried to convince himself that they were the enemy and not to think about it….. he did. *Who would do such a thing?!* he wondered. Jacob realized that wanted signs were everywhere; on poles, on market booths, and on destroyed buildings.

"What's with all of the wanted signs?" Tortoise asked. "I know there's usually a lot, but I don't know about this much. Is Severin second most wanted now?"

"No, he's kind of tied with a spy right now," Lighter responded. "Apparently there was an intruder at the party the other night. Rumor has it that it was a Cloud Dragon."

"A spy for what?" Jacob asked. Again, no response for his most important questions.

"What are we supposed to be looking for?" Tortoise asked, looking around.

"A couple of things," Lighter said, stopping in the middle of the alley. "How about we split up? Tortoise, you could go look on that side and me and Jacob look at this side."

"Why can't Jacob come with me?" Tortoise asked.

"If he wants to go with you, he can… but it's all up to him," Lighter said. Tortoise gave Jacob a hopeful smile. Staring at the floor, Jacob took a step closer to Lighter.

Tortoise frowned. "I guess I'll just go shopping alone, no one with me, all… all alone," Tortoise said, taking a step back.

"Yeah… you do that," Lighter said.

"Bye, Tortoise," Jacob said. Lighter and Jacob slowly backed away, leaving Tortoise alone in the shopping strip. "Now where are we going?" Jacob asked when Tortoise was out of sight.

"A different alley," Lighter said.

"What are we looking for?"

"A lot of things," Lighter said. "But…. I guess you don't have to go shopping if you don't want to,"

Lighter continued. "You can go look around and meet me here before or after dinner."

"When is lunch?"

"I guess whenever you want it to be," they turned to a less busy alley. "Here," Lighter said, handing him a small card, "this should be enough for lunch and dinner, and probably a souvenir."

"How much does it have?" Jacob asked.

"It should be enough," Lighter repeated. "Just try not to get lost." *Is he letting me go?* Jacob thought, *this could be my chance to escape….* He quickly pushed that thought away. *No, I would never escape this place and even if I could, I wouldn't know how to get back, plus, I need more information.* "So…… where do I meet up with you?" Jacob asked.

"I think this alley is called Gloom Alley, so I guess we'll just meet here," Lighter said.

"Ok," Jacob responded.

"Be careful."

"I'll try." In shock, Jacob went to explore Gloom Alley.

Probably the weirdest part about Gloom Alley was the name because it wasn't as gloomy as the other alleys but… it was still pretty bad. To Jacob's surprise, no one really paid any attention to him, which was odd considering that dragons and humans were at war with each other. But here he was, a human walking all around in a dragon kingdom. Jacob finally ate lunch when he found a fried chicken restaurant that was actually really good. He didn't know if it was expensive or anything because he had zero clue what dragon money was, but he was able to pay for it with the card Lighter gave him. The water tasted gross, but he figured he would need to drink it throughout the day so he won't get dehydrated. As Jacob walked along the road of Gloom Alley, a couple of dragons in their sales booths were nearly begging him to buy something. Gloom Alley was definitely not the happiest place to be, but still, Jacob was having a good time looking at all the strange dragon products. He wasn't planning on getting anything, but he was really tempted with some things. He was doing good until something caught his eye. Jacob stopped to look at it. It was a pair of strange human shoes. He couldn't tell if they were small boots or shoes, but they were nothing like he had ever seen before. They actually looked like his size, which was strange. He couldn't take his eyes off them; they were shiny black with silver latches, which was odd. *Don't do it Jacob*, he thought to himself. *They probably are not even comfy, and they might be like boots, and I don't like boots, or they might be like high-tops, and I*

don't like those either. He continued to stare at them. *Well……… I guess it wouldn't hurt to try them on or at lease ask how much they are. Why would human shoes be in a dragon kingdom?* He walked into the small line to the counter of the booth. Only two dragons were in front of him in the line, but he heard the first one at the counter arguing with the owner.

"It's an awesome deal! If you ask me, it's actually *WAY* more than what it's worth!" the dragon customer said angrily.

"What you are asking is way too little!" Jacob guessed the owner arguing back.

"What?! But this is all the money I have right now," said the costumer. "Maybe there's something else you would want to bargain for, or *maybe*……… play for?"

"You might have lost a game for your wings, but I'm not interested in any body parts or even stupid enough to do it."

The dragon in front of Jacob lost his patience and walked out of the line, allowing Jacob to see the argument between the owner and the costumer. Jacob looked in shock at the angry customer; he wasn't a Cloudairian. This new kind of dragon had a strange, really cool lightning blue color underneath the scales, making it show in-between each scale. Its scales, underbelly, and spikes were dark purple. The blue looked a lot like Lighter's, but he didn't look like him. He looked like a bolt of lightning in a dark purple sky, with purple eyes too. It took a few seconds, but Jacob realized that the dragon didn't have any wings. It looked like it was supposed to, but there wasn't anything there.

"Well, I am NOT stupid enough to play for any of my body parts!" the purple and blue dragon said. "And why in Annorlia would you think that I'd do that?!"

"I don't know, you tell me," the owner said rudely, looking at his wingless back.

"What did you just say?" the costumer asked angrily.

"You know what," the owner said, noticing his rising anger, "I believe it is lunch break… so…. Yeah, we're closed now. Bye-bye." The owner flipped the open sign to the closed side and slammed the shutters of the window.

"Oh, you inconsiderate dummy! Don't you *dare* close on me!" the costumer yelled at the closed shop. "How rude." He turned around and saw Jacob. "Well, what are you looking at, human?"

"Err……. nothing," Jacob answered.

"Oh, so now I'm being called a nothing?!" the wingless dragon said. "Good grief! What is wrong with this place?!" He turned and stomped away.

"What?" Jacob asked, surprised. "No, no, no that's not what I meant!" Jacob chased after him. Technically, all dragons were his enemies, but he did *not* want to make any of them unhappy with him, at least until he could turn them over to King Luther.

"Wait!" Jacob called out to the dragon. Either the dragon didn't hear him, or was ignoring him, but he ran along the alley dodging everyone in his way. "Oops, sorry," Jacob said when he bumped into a Cloud Dragon. The dragon looked at him in concern.

"What are you doing, running around alone?" the dragon asked.

"I was just…. Looking for someone," Jacob responded.

"Who?" the dragon asked curiously.

"I don't know."

"Do you need any help?"

Jacob looked at the dragon curiously. *Why does he want to help? Why am my even chasing around a different looking dragon again?* He realized something strange about the Cloud Dragon. He had strange straps going around his body, kind of like a country outfit with a tight looking cloth around his shoulder; at least Jacob figured that's where a dragon's shoulder would be. The dragon was pure white with sky blue eyes and wore a necklace with a tiny metal stick as a charm.

"I'm probably fine," Jacob responded.

"Oh, ok," the Cloud Dragon said with all curiosity gone. "Well, bye," he said calmly, walking away. *That was weird,* Jacob thought. He stared at the dragon walking away and noticed that he never moved his wings. Jacob had already noticed that whenever dragons walked, they were constantly shifting their wings, but this dragon wasn't. *I am kinda bored....* Jacob thought, *plus I am supposed to spy, and I don't think that shop will open any time soon....... I am supposed to be a spy.* Jacob decided to follow the Cloud Dragon, he didn't know why, but he just felt like doing it for some reason.

Nothing seemed abnormal with the Cloud Dragon, but Jacob still felt like following him for some reason. Jacob was about to stop following until he realized that he was gone. *What am I doing?* Jacob thought. *Why am I just being weird and following any strange thing I see? For all I know it could be normal.*

"OW!" Jacob shrieked. Something really sharp hit on top of his foot and hopped off quickly; he automatically sat down and grabbed his foot in pain. He heard a small whisper in his ear saying, "Sorry," but he couldn't see anything around. Then he felt a small pat on his shoulder, but still, nothing could be seen. *Or maybe it's not normal,* Jacob thought. He stood up and looked around, his foot still hurt but not that much, it felt like a big cat stepped gently on it with its claws mostly in, *or maybe it was a big cat,* Jacob realized. He looked around for any sign of a panther, but still, he couldn't see anything. He stopped when he saw a blue and purple tail slither in between two buildings. *That was that dragon with no wings,* he realized. *I won't lose him this time.* Quickly, Jacob chased after him in-between the buildings, keeping a small distance so the dragon wouldn't notice him. The dragon stopped deep in the rows of buildings in an abandoned alley; Jacob hid behind a dumpster. The dark purple and blue dragon looked around, then whispered, "Where have you been?"

"There's not exactly many places to go," a pure white Cloud Dragon said, stepping out of the shadows. Jacob recognized it as the Cloud Dragon he ran into. "But still, why would you have to know," the Cloud Dragon added. "How do I know I can even trust you?"

"Why else would I come all the way here?" the wingless dragon asked, annoyed.

"I don't know, you tell me," the Cloud Dragon responded threateningly.

"Why do you two have to argue about absolutely *every*thing?" a new voice asked that made everyone jump. Jacob saw with his own eyes a panther that was at first invisible appear in-between the two dragons.

"You have got to quit doing that!" the wingless dragon shrieked in surprise.

"How long have you been standing there?" the Cloud Dragon asked.

"Long enough to tell that you two do not agree with or even trust each other," Krennicx responded calmly.

"So……. How long would that be?" the Cloud Dragon asked.

"Well, let's just say that you were so distracted by each other, that you did not notice the kid watching you." Krennicx smiled, then said, "You can come out now, Jacob."

Uh-oh. He thought about running away but thought better of it. Slowly Jacob got up from his hiding spot and, keeping his head down, walked to the panther and two dragons, not looking up at them. Krennicx smirked a smile and Jacob started to smile back, but stopped when he remembered that he was afraid.

"Weird," the Cloud Dragon said. "I ran into this human earlier."

"Guys, this is Jacob," Krennicx introduced. "And Jacob, this is Sky and Ben. Sky is the Cloud Dragon and Ben is the Lightning Dragon. And Jacob came with Lighter, Tortoise, and me……. And Glider and Glazer," Krennicx added.

"Wait a minute," Ben said. "I think I recognize you from the shopping strip, right?"

"Uh…." Jacob said, thinking back to the whole situation.

"Wasn't that guy being just unreasonable?" Ben asked.

"He did ask for a certain amount," Sky responded for Jacob.

"That was a fair price I offered him!" Ben defended. "It was even more than what it's worth!"

"Kind of like Krennicx talking about you?" Sky asked.

"Good grief," Krennicx said. "You guys are starting to sound like Glider, and do you want to sound like Glider?"

"No," Sky and Ben said at the same time.

"Ok, so let's just shut up…... and fix what I came here to fix, alright?" Krennicx said dismissively.

"What are you even trying to fix?" Jacob asked.

"Oh, I don't know," Krennicx said. "Ben, why don't you answer that question?"

"It wasn't my fault!" Ben protested.

"Sure," Krennicx said sarcastically.

"Krennicx," Sky said nervously, "can I talk to you?"

Krennicx glanced around with a worried expression. "No, not here," Krennicx said, then turned around and started to speed walk away.

"Krennicx!" Sky said, chasing after him with Ben and Jacob following too. "Krennicx, you don't understand," Sky said worriedly.

"Yes, I do," Krennicx responded calmly.

"What?" Sky asked. "But he has to know."

"I know," Krennicx stopped and turned to him. "But if him hearing means them hearing it too, then it's best for neither of them to hear it at all," he said, then started to walk again.

"But then it will all be for nothing."

"Trust me," Krennicx said. Then no one said a word as they followed the talking panther through the alley.

"So… you didn't take anything personal at that shop, right?" Jacob asked Ben.

"Why would I take anything personal?" Ben asked, then laughed. "That was pretty funny though, you were all like 'Wait! Wait! Come back!' And you even chased after me! That was so hilarious!"

"Wait a minute," Jacob said. "You heard me calling out to you?"

Ben did a small laugh.

There was still something weird about Sky. Jacob noticed that he still never shifted his wings at all, and he kept acting weird around Krennicx. There was something he *badly* wanted to say.

"Is there something wrong with Sky?" Jacob quietly asked Ben.

"Other than the fact that he doesn't like me, I don't think so…. Well…" Ben said.

"What?" Jacob asked.

"He is having a hard time though," Ben said. "And he is a….*OW,*" Ben shrieked when Sky stomped on his foot.

"What are you doing?" Sky asked. "Are you crazy? Why in the galaxy does he trust you?"

"He trusts me more than you!" Ben defended. "Plus, why can't the kid know that you're a spy?"

"A *what?*" Jacob yelped in alarm.

"Oh, you did not just do that," Sky said, getting close to exploding in anger.

"Oops…… I guess," Ben said.

"You *guess?*" Sky asked. "Why did you do that! Now he knows!"

"*Now* what are you doing?" Krennicx asked, noticing their new argument.

"He just told this human the secret!" Sky said, pointing to Ben.

"What?" Ben asked. "Why can't he know?"

Sky gave him a surprised look. "We don't even know him. For all we know he could be a spy himself," Sky said, glaring at Jacob. Jacob's heart felt like it skipped a beat. *He's on to me,* he realized.

"Spy or no spy, it doesn't matter," Krennicx said with his calm expression not changing. "He knows and there's nothing you can do except trust…. or, well, hope…. that he is good and won't betray you." For the second time, Krennicx's pure red eyes met Jacob's. A cold chill ran through Jacob's body, and it felt like he had chill bumps from the inside out. It was only for a second, but it made everything feel like it was freezing. *What was that?* Jacob thought. Jacob stared at Krennicx in fear, but he wasn't looking at him anymore.

"What do you want me to do?" Sky asked, still looking nervous.

"It's getting late, and I don't want Lighter to get mad at me so…." Krennicx said, "Take Jacob to find him. He wants to go back to him anyway."

"But what if I…" Sky trailed off.

"I know what happened the other night, Sky, and I'm sorry," Krennicx said. "But this is the only way….and then after that I'll get you a good doctor for your shoulder," he added.

"Good, because Ben's terrible," Sky said with a painful laugh. Krennicx smiled and kept walking with Ben behind him, leaving Jacob alone with Sky.

Either Sky was quiet, or he simply didn't like Jacob. Sky barely spoke at all; the only times he did speak it was not to Jacob, but either to himself or telling a seller that they weren't interested in anything and to back off. Either way, Jacob was kind of glad that he didn't talk that much. He knew that knowing Sky was a spy (most likely highly trained) and he himself was a spy (trained in the head, not in the action) Jacob would not stand a chance if they were to get in an argument. He couldn't help but say something when Sky decided to go hide in a basement of a restaurant and lie down on the floor, breathing hard. "Umm…" Jacob said, feeling awkward.

"Jacob, right?" Sky asked.

"Yes?" Jacob responded.

"Do you have any ice?"

"Uh… no," Jacob responded, thinking how weird a question it was.

"Can you do me a favor?" Sky asked.

"What?"

"There's a restaurant right above us," Sky said. "Can you run up there and get a cup, and fill it with only ice?"

"Ok…" Jacob said. "Why?"

"Just do it…. please."

"How do I get there?"

"Go outside and walk up those stairs, then I think it's the seafood restaurant."

"Ok," Jacob said. "Why do you need ice?"

"Don't ask any questions," Sky responded, "and when you most likely run away from me, don't you dare tell anyone about me, ok?"

Without saying a word, Jacob followed his instructions and walked outside. *Maybe I should run and find Lighter myself,* Jacob thought, but for some reason since Sky said he was going to run away, it made Jacob *not* want to run away. Jacob was still not sure whether Sky always acts like that or if he's in a bad mood. Jacob wanted to say he is always like that, but something just didn't feel right. He was too lost in thought when he realized that someone was calling him. Jacob was shocked at how happy he was when he realized it was Lighter calling him.

"What are you doing here?" Lighter asked. "Have you not eaten yet or something?"

"No, I was just getting some ice for Sky," Jacob responded.

"Oh, Sky's here?" Lighter asked.

"You know him?" Jacob asked.

"Yeah, how did you meet him?"

"I ran into him, Ben, and Krennicx," Jacob responded. "Do you know Ben?"

"Yeah," Lighter responded, "he's Krennicx's best friend."

"Oh," Jacob said, thinking back, "I guess that would make sense."

"Where is Sky?" Lighter asked.

"I think he's hiding."

"He should be."

"What?"

"Uh…" Lighter said as if he said something wrong, "I think Tortoise should be up there eating a disgusting fish snack. So why don't you go up there, and I'll go talk to Sky real quick, ok?"

"Ok," Jacob responded slowly. Jacob walked up the stairs into the seafood restaurant where Tortoise was sitting, but it wasn't just Tortoise.

"For the last time, Tortoise," Krennicx said frustratingly, "I don't like fish!"

"Why?" Tortoise asked in confusion.

"I hate it!" Krennicx said. "It's disgusting!"

"Ah, Jacob," Tortoise said, noticing him, "can you tell him how awesome fish is?"

"Uh…." Jacob said, "I don't really like fish."

"Ha!" Krennicx said in victory.

"What! How can you NOT like it?"

"Because it's gross!" Krennicx said. "And you're fighting a losing battle so just back down and accept your defeat."

"You have no idea what you're missing," Tortoise said.

"I think I do, and man am I glad," Krennicx said with a grin. "So, Jacob, how was the trip with Sky?"

"How did you know I was here?" Jacob asked suspiciously.

Krennicx's expression changed, "Tortoise, can you go get Sky's ice? I need to talk to Jacob… alone."

"Oh," Tortoise said with an understanding look in his eyes. "Ok."

"Good," Krennicx said. "Come along, Jacob."

"Why?" Jacob asked.

"I need to talk to you," Krennicx said, looking into his eyes again. This time, Jacob didn't feel a chill, instead, he heard the vibrating buzz in his head. "You have questions," Krennicx said, "I have answers."

Jacob didn't know what to think as he and Krennicx walked in-between the old buildings of an abandoned alley. *What is he wanting to talk about?* Jacob wondered. *Why is he going so deep into the buildings? Is it a coincidence that I heard the buzz as he was saying something the voice had said?* Many questions whirled in his mind as they got deeper and deeper into the alley. "So…. what are we doing?" Jacob asked, getting a little afraid.

"I need to tell you something," Krennicx said nervously, "but I can't find a safe place to do it."

"Uh…." Jacob said, "this seems pretty safe to me."

"Maybe," Krennicx said. "But you don't know how important this is."

"What is it?"

Krennicx paused and took a deep breath, "Do you still have that tracker with you?"

"Uh…...." Jacob said, putting his hands in his pocket.

"Don't lie to me," Krennicx warned.

"Yeah… why?" Jacob said nervously.

"Oh, why do I have to be such an idiot?!" Krennicx asked himself.

"What?"

"Give me the tracker."

"What?" Jacob yelped in panic. "Why?"

"Just do it," Krennicx said, holding a paw out. Jacob didn't know why, but he obeyed and handed it to him.

"What is going on?" Jacob asked.

"I don't have time," Krennicx said. "Now I need you to run."

"Why?"

"Just run!"

"Where?!"

"That way!" Krennicx said, pointing straight ahead. Krennicx, being a panther, ran fast back the way they came. Jacob panicked. *Do I run? Krennicx said to run, but am I really going to trust a panther? He took my tracker; I need that thing.* Jacob decided that he did not trust Krennicx at all. *Why would I really trust any of the dragons?* They're his enemies after all. *Maybe what's going on is there's a human attack,* Jacob realized.

What if Krennicx is tricking me and causing me to not get back to my home?! Deciding not to obey Krennicx's orders, Jacob turned the other way and ran the direction Krennicx did.

Jacob stopped at an old, large water fountain. Right after the water fountain, there was a strange deep drop off. It looked like something huge fell from the sky and left a massive, deep hole in the ground. He looked around for Krennicx or any human. Jacob was so distracted that he bumped into a Cloud Dragon. "Oops, sorry," Jacob said, looking up to see that it was an angry looking soldier.

"Watch where you're going!" the soldier snapped.

"Sorry," Jacob said, backing away. *Where am I?* he wondered, looking around. *Is this still the same alley? I don't think we came by here before.* Jacob jumped when he heard multiple sounds of gun shots.

"Where is it?!" a soldier in the distance shouted.

"Where did it go?" another soldier asked. Soldiers from everywhere ran from the direction the noise was coming from.

"You there," the soldier that Jacob ran into said.

"Me?" Jacob asked, pointing to himself.

"Yes, come here!" the soldier demanded. Jacob walked slowly and fearfully to the soldier, ready to run. Immediately the soldier grabbed Jacob's shoulder and squeezed it tight, making it impossible to escape.

"What are you doing?" Jacob yelped in panic.

"Quiet, traitor," the solider angrily said.

"They got away!" the distant soldier yelled.

"Not all of them!" the soldier that had Jacob called back.

"Not all of what?" Jacob asked in horror. Loud trumpets blasted in the sky as a fleet of soldiers landed on the ground. In-between all of the guards was an enormous Cloud Dragon dressed in silk, rubies, and sapphires. The dragon had a large crown twisted in gold, rubies, and sapphires that looked a lot like King Luther's crown. The red and sparkling gold silk twisted all over the dragon's body to where no scales could be seen except for the face, but it did not hide the fact that the dragon was extremely fat. Jacob never even thought that a dragon could get fat, but even though he didn't know many dragons, he could tell that this one *HAD* to be the most overweight of them all. "Your Majesty," the soldier said. "I believe this might be the one causing the trouble," he said, bringing Jacob to the fat dragon.

"This is the one I was warned about?" the fat dragon asked, looking at Jacob. "He looks far too puny to do anything."

"What do you want me to do, King Saul?" the soldier asked. Crowds of Cloud Dragon citizens began to circle around the action. Jacob didn't feel the smartest for not guessing he was the king at first.

"Your.... er... Your Majesty?" Jacob said. "I don't.... er... exactly know what you're talking about. Because I...... er.... I don't remember doing anything."

The king gave him an unbelieving look. "So," the king said, "you have nothing to do with the fact that the spy that we just found got away?"

Wait, are they talking about Sky?

"What do you want me to do, Your Majesty?" the soldier asked again.

"Do what I was advised to do," the king said. "Kill him."

Jacob was too horror-struck to do anything. He wanted to scream but it wouldn't come out of his mouth. The soldier pulled a blaster out of his belt and Jacob felt it against his back, ready to shoot. But something pounced out of nowhere onto the soldier, causing him to lose his grip. It was Krennicx.

CHAPTER 10

THE TRUTH OF THE TALKING PANTHER

Krennicx positioned himself between Jacob and all of the soldiers of King Saul, growling in a pounce position. King Saul looked amused. "Look at this," King Saul mocked, "a little cat somehow got into my borders. Are you lost little kitty? Or are you this child's pet?"

"I beg your pardon Your Majesty," Krennicx's tone changed to more of a threatening voice, "but I believe you don't have the one that you are looking for."

King Saul's amusement quickly changed to pure horror at the sight of the talking panther. The guards also took a few steps back from Krennicx too.

"Those eyes," King Saul said after a few seconds of silence, "look familiar……. Bring it closer to me!" he demanded.

"Don't," Krennicx snapped at the guards when they tried to grab him, "touch me. I'll. Walk. My. Self." The guards seemed to be too afraid to do anything to Krennicx, but they had no problem bringing Jacob. Krennicx willingly walked right in front of King Saul, with Jacob dragged behind him.

"Your Highness," one of the soldiers said, "if he really is as dangerous as you say, then are you sure you want him this close to you?"

"Do not interrupt my thinking," King Saul demanded. "I know those eyes from somewhere."

"Your Majesty, if I may," another soldier said, "there has only been one in all of history that has red eyes and that is…."

"The necklace," the king realized, noticing the dark, see-through, blue lightning bolt on a silver chain around Krennicx's neck. Jacob had never noticed it before. "The red eye thing might not be that accurate, but I know that necklace." The king looked into his eyes, then said, "I know who you are, but I wonder how much it would take for you to show yourself."

"What are you suggesting, Your Highness?" the soldier asked.

"Hold the panther down and bring me the boy," said the king. They immediately had Krennicx pinned to the ground and brought Jacob to the king. "Tell me, boy," King Saul said, "what's your name?"

"Uh…. Jacob."

"Last name?"

"Bennett," Jacob responded, hesitating.

"Bennett, huh?" the king asked. "Let him go."

"What?" a couple of guards said at the same time.

"You heard me," said the king. They obeyed and let go of Jacob. "Now before you start to run, I want to show you something."

When Jacob realized that it was a command, he slowly walked to the king. *What does he know about my family?* Jacob wondered. *Does he know how successful we are and is afraid of us?* "What is it?" Jacob asked nervously.

"You see that amazing castle?" the king asked, pointing past the huge deep hole to a ginormous palace on the mountain. "That is my palace," the king said.

"Then why are these dragons living here?" Jacob asked.

"Like I said, that's *my* palace."

"Well your so-called *palace* is big enough for everyone!" Krennicx barked. "Stop being an idiot and let them in!"

The Cloud King ignored him and continued to speak to Jacob, "This is where you belong," he said, waving towards the palace. "Do you want to go there?"

"To the palace?" Jacob asked.

"Where. You. Belong," the king repeated. Jacob yelped as something hit his back. The ground left his feet, as the King of the Cloud Dragons pushed him into the deep, dark hole.

"No!" Krennicx shrieked. He broke away from the soldiers that had him pinned down and dove after the screaming in horror Jacob. There was a small flicker of light as the talking panther showed everyone who he really was.

Just before Jacob could hit the ground, something grabbed him and shot up like an arrow back to the surface. Jacob was dropped onto the ground and his rescuer landed next to him. He looked up to see red eyes and thought it was Krennicx, but then realized something. The thing he thought was a panther had black wings like a dragon, and its paws looked more like razor-sharp dragon/human talons than panther paws. It seemed a little bigger than a panther too. It still looked similar to a panther, but completely *different*. It had no whiskers. Its ears looked more similar to a dragon's, for they were longer and pointed. It had to be the coolest thing Jacob had ever seen in his life. It even beat Lighter. The statue of it looked weird, but in real life, it looked *right*. And *cool*. *It can't be.* Krennicx wasn't a panther. His name wasn't even Krennicx. He was King Luther's nemesis. He was Severein.

"I'm sorry," Severein mouthed.

"You lied to me," Jacob said.

Severein opened his mouth to say something but was interrupted by Saul. "Well, well, well. Little Severin all grown up," the king said. "How long has it been?"

"Not long enough if you ask me," Severein said, facing the king. There wasn't an ounce of fear in Severein's large and terrifying red eyes.

"True," King Saul said, "but to be honest, I was wanting to see you one last time."

"Why? So you can kill me yourself?" Severein asked mockingly. He no longer sounded like an insane panther. His voice was smooth and calm. "Your eyesight must be getting pretty bad if you have just mistaken that kid as me."

"That was on purpose!" the king defended himself. "And you obviously care about him."

"You did that on purpose?!" Severein asked angrily. "I thought that maybe you were being clumsy, which is normal for you, but you actually tried to KILL AN INNOCENT KID?!"

"Keep your voice down!" the king demanded.

"Why?" Severin asked sneakily. "Do you think I'm going to draw attention to your huge mistake?"

The king growled, "Maybe I should kill you now."

"Ooo, that would also be one of many horrible mistakes," Severein said calmly, pushing his ridiculously cool wings back.

"How?"

"If you were wanting fame from your oh *so* precious catch," Severein said, rolling his eyes, "then wouldn't you want to have proof that it is true?"

"That is true….." King Saul said thoughtfully. "And I bet there's a lot of rulers and supporters who would love to watch….." The king trailed off.

"That's not gross at all," Severein said sarcastically.

"I am a genius!" King Saul said. "I'll invite all the kings of Annorlia."

"What about the Represenetor?" Severein asked, smirking.

"Uh…. Represenetor?" Saul asked nervously.

"Yeah, you know," Severein said, "the one who is kind of over the kings just a little bit. Ya know?"

"I don't know what you're talking about," the king obviously lied.

"Listen," Severein said, "I know you're lying, you know you're lying, we all know you are lying, so just admit it."

"You have no proof," King Saul said angrily.

"Then show me," Severein said.

"What?"

"If you want to prove your harmlessness, then show me your representative. You know, the one that was assigned to watch over you? He was chosen by the High King himself."

"Do you think I'm an idiot?" the king asked, changing the subject. "You are just trying to distract me from your execution! And do you think I'm stupid enough to fall for that?"

"No," Severein said, "but I would think that you'd be smart enough to not defend yourself so terribly in front of your own subjects."

Jacob had never seen such an amount of hatred in anyone's face before, let alone a dragon's. Every Cloud Dragon that was watching could tell that the king was not handling a little conversation with the calm faced Severein. When Jacob didn't think it could get any worse, it did.

"Why were you with the kid again?" King Saul asked, as if he knew the answer.

"We ran into each other," Severein responded. "He was just about to betray me when you threw him over the cliff."

"Isn't he a Bennett?" Saul asked.

"Uh…. yeah, that's kind of the whole point."

"I thought the Bennetts were bad," King Saul said.

"Hm?" Severein asked. "What Bennett are you talking about?"

"There's two Bennetts?"

"There's probably a couple," Severein said, studying his razor-sharp claws, "but I'm talking about this Bennett."

"Which one?" the king asked, confused.

"The Bennetts."

"But I thought you said there are a couple Bennetts?"

"There might be, but I'm talking about this Bennett."

"Which Bennett is this?" the king asked.

"Bennett," Severein responded.

"You're not making any sense."

"What?"

"What do you mean, 'what'?"

"What?"

"What?" Saul asked.

"Why are you saying 'what'?" Severein asked.

"What?" King Saul asked, completely confused.

"What?"

"You said what first."

"What?" Severein asked again.

"You just said it again."

"Huh?"

"You're not making any sense."

"Who said I make sense?" Severein asked.

"*What?*"

"What?"

"What were we talking about again?" Saul asked in confusion.

"What?"

"Grrrr," King Saul said, "would you just stop?!"

"Dummy said what?"

"What?"

Severein chuckled a laughed.

"What?" the king asked again.

Jacob felt like laughing when he realized what Severein was laughing at. He noticed some guards secretly smiling too.

"Did you hear about the attack on the human kingdom last night?" Severein asked, glancing at Jacob. "Sad."

Immediately, the King of the Cloud Dragons grabbed a stun gun from his belt and shot Severein with it.

"I don't understand how you criminals know so much," King Saul said.

"Maybe it's because I'm not a part of you," Severein said, struggling to get off the ground. "I do not stand for the King of Shadows."

"Hmm," King Saul said, "that's odd. Usually whenever I do that, they stay asleep for a while." He looked curiously at the conscious Severein, or whatever his name is. Severein stood up and faced the king again with a grin.

"Why do you obey him?" Severein asked. "What has he ever done that is good for you and your subjects?"

"Many things," King Saul said. "He is really the reason we have not fallen."

"Fallen to what?" Severein asked. "The only one you could possibly fall to is the one you ran to. And now look where you are! When will you realize that these are your subjects too? They are starving while you feast on anything you want every day. These are your subjects; you have to help them."

"You're right," Saul said. "These are my subjects, which means this is my territory, which also means you are trespassing! And how do you, of anyone in Annorlia, have the right to even speak to me? Let alone tell me how to rule my kingdom! I don't care if you're the most wanted criminal in the galaxy, I wouldn't even care if you're the Fighters of Peace! And while I'm at it, I wouldn't even care if you are the Represenetor of all of Annorlia! You have no right to even step foot on my land, thief."

"The only thief I would be," Severein said, staring into King Saul's eyes, "is the thief of the truth."

"The words of a true criminal," King Saul responded, looking away from Severein's terrifying eyes. "Send an invitation to all Kings and Queens, and all those who have a bounty on his head. Tell them that tomorrow at two in the afternoon, the criminal known as Severein, will die."

"What do you think you'll gain from this?" Severein asked.

"Respect," the king responded.

"Yeah," Severein snorted, "I guess that is something you need."

Everyone turned slowly to Severein in pure shock, and the king was not happy.

CHAPTER 11

THE THIEF OF THE TRUTH

Maybe it was because everyone was so distracted by Severein—formerly known as Krennicx—that no one even noticed Jacob. Jacob stood alone in the streets of the Cloud Kingdom. *What just happened?* One second he was falling, another second the king was arguing un-king-like to a criminal who was thought to be a talking panther. Jacob's mind whirled with everything that happened. *Why did Krennicx, grrr Severein, talk to the king like that when he knew that he wanted to kill him? Was he trying to tell me something, but what?* Jacob recalled everything Severein had said. Severein made it really clear that King Saul obviously had no intensions on helping his own subjects, *but what did he mean by the King of Shadows? Wait,* Jacob realized, *did he say the Fighters of Peace? Is that a rumor to dragons too? What is a Represenetor? What did he mean by the thief of the truth?*

"Jacob!" Lighter called, running over to him. Tortoise and Sky followed him.

"What happened?" Tortoise asked.

"Are you ok?" Lighter asked.

"I'm fine," Jacob responded, "but Krennicx isn't who he said he was. He's actually a wanted criminal named Severein!"

"They took him?" Sky asked, alarmed.

"Yes," Jacob said responded. "They were going to take me, but for some reason they didn't."

"Do you have any idea what they're going to do to him?" Lighter asked, looking worried.

"Isn't it obvious?" Sky said angrily. "They're going to kill him."

Lighter looked sick, "Maybe they won't."

"Oh, they will," Sky assured.

"He's right," Jacob added. "Tomorrow at two o'clock in the afternoon, actually, but I didn't think you liked him."

"Even if we didn't like him that much doesn't mean he deserves to die!" Lighter said, panicked. "Even if it was an enemy that didn't do anything wrong, why would you kill him? This is a life we're talking about! He's more innocent than the king himself!"

"What are you going to do?" Jacob asked.

"I don't know what you're going to do," Sky said, "but I know what I'm doing."

"Which is?" Tortoise asked.

"Bust him out," Sky responded.

"No, Sky," Lighter said, "let me handle this."

"Why?" Sky asked.

"You don't even have a plan," Lighter said.

"Actually, I do."

"Plus, you can't do it alone," Lighter added.

"I won't be alone," Sky responded. "I'll have Jacob."

"What!" Jacob yelped. "But he wanted to kill me too!"

"He's right!" Lighter said. "You can't take Jacob."

"Why not?" Sky asked.

"Because you just can't," Lighter said.

"Ok," Sky said, "I won't bring him with me."

"Good," said Lighter. "Now can you take Jacob to Ben?"

"Fine."

"And please don't try to break him out," Lighter said. "We definitely don't need to lose you."

"Don't worry about me," Sky said. "Now you go sit at the table for a couple of hours and think about plans that won't work."

"They'll work," Lighter said.

"Ok," Sky said. "Come on, Jacob."

Jacob followed Sky away from Lighter and back towards the direction where they came from. *Why did Lighter let him take me? Isn't that what he wanted?* Jacob tried not to think about that as he silently followed him, still being mad at the fact that Krennicx had lied to him. He still wondered what the king was talking about with his family. *He must be afraid of us,* Jacob thought pridefully. *He must know how successful my dad is, but why would Severein defend us?* Jacob was lost in thought when he realized Sky was talking to him. "What?" Jacob asked.

"Don't run or look afraid," Sky responded. Then Jacob noticed two soldiers were walking towards them. He recognized them as two of the ones who helped arrest Severein.

"You have to come with us," one of them said.

"Why?" Sky asked.

"Not you," the soldier said. "The human."

"But the humans are…" Sky started.

"Not this one," the soldier interrupted.

"And unless you want to get arrested too, you will allow him to come with no issues," the other soldier said.

"But what if he is innocent?" Sky asked. The soldier did not respond.

"What did I do?" Jacob asked, horrified.

"That is the matter of the king," the first soldier responded.

"Is he going to have a trial?" Sky asked, sounding concerned.

"Maybe," the soldier responded, sounding annoyed.

"Why do you care?" the second soldier asked. "He is most likely not on our side, and don't you have other things to do?"

"Yes, sir," Sky said, "I do." Sky took a step back to get out of the soldiers' way. *What is he doing?!* Jacob thought in horror. The soldiers took hold of Jacob and led him away.

Definitely not the brightest, Sky thought, watching the soldiers lead the human away. *It was obvious that they built the huge wall to keep the Cloudairians out of the rich side of the city, but what about the soldiers themselves? Not all of them are highly trained to fly with no wind. So there would be no way for them to make it out without a secret underground tunnel or something…No citizen would dare follow a soldier,* Sky smiled. *But then again, I am no citizen.*

"This has got to be a huge misunderstanding," Jacob said for what felt like the hundredth time. "I haven't done anything." Jacob had been walking for what felt like forever. They were walking through large tunnels lit by torches. It felt like they were going up through the inside of the mountain. Sounds of clattering hammers echoed off the walls. "What was that?"

"Probably the prisoners searching for gold," the second soldier answered.

"Am I going to have to do that?" Jacob asked.

"No," the first soldier responded.

Jacob wanted to ask what he would be doing but was too nervous. Their path went up into a huge, long hallway with barred cells to the right and left. He caught glimpses of angry dragons in the cells as they walked along in the prison. They were walking too fast for him to see if there were any humans in a cell. Something in a cell caught his eye, making him stop to look. It was too dark to see what the dragon looked like, but he could still see its green, glowing eyes. Jacob looked curiously at it as it growled at him. "Come on," the second soldier commanded, pushing him to keep walking. They stopped in front of a cell on the left side. The first soldier unlocked the door with a hoop of keys, then pushed Jacob inside and locked him in.

"I still don't know why I'm in here!" Jacob called out. The soldiers ignored him and walked away, leaving him in the dark prison cell. With a sigh, he looked around his dark cell. For a dragon it would be small, but for a human it was pretty big. There was one mat in one corner and another mat in the other corner. *Wait, why are there two?* There was a scrapping sound of metal chains coming from behind him. Jacob turned to see red eyes gleaming in the dark. "Oh no," he said out loud.

"Well, you sound happy to see me," Severein—formally known as Krennicx—said sarcastically. He stepped into the light and sat down.

"Actually, I'm not," Jacob said.

"And why is that?"

"Sorry, but I don't really want to talk to you," Jacob said, looking away.

"Sorry," Severein said, "but you kind of just did."

"What?"

"Ooo, you did it again."

"No, I didn't," Jacob said, aggravated.

"Stiiill doing it."

"No, I'm not!"

"Ooo wow, someone's getting into a talkative mood."

"Stop it!"

Severein laughed, "Man, you're bad at this aren't ya?"

"I'm not that bad," Jacob said.

"Eh……" Severein said, "So……. Tell me dearie, why don't you won't to talk to me?"

"Because I'm mad at you!" Jacob responded.

"Why?"

"You lied to me!"

"I did?" Severein asked thoughtfully. "When?"

"Uh…." Jacob said thinking, "you said you're a panther!"

Severein chuckled, "You actually thought I was a panther?"

"You said you were!"

"Dude, you actually thought that I was a talking panther?!" he said again. "And even if I said that, in a way I *was* a panther, but I never said what I *usually* am, now did I?"

"Uh…...." Jacob said when he realized that he was right. "You said that it wasn't you that night when it had to have been you saving my…." Jacob trailed off when he realized what he was about to say.

"You mean when I saved your L.I.F.E?" Severein spelled with a sneaky grin.

"Uh…. Well, you still said that it wasn't you!"

"No…. No, I didn't," Severein responded. "Think about it, I never said that it wasn't me. That was when I went dumb with you when you were stupidly wondering around the woods in the middle of the night."

Jacob thought back to that night when all *Krennicx* would say was 'what' and 'huh.' *Kind of what he did with the king,* Jacob realized.

"Well……" Jacob said, thinking about something else. "Ha! Well, you still said that your name was Krennicx when it is really Severein."

"Jacob Bennett," Severein said, counting with his claws. "Krennicx Severein," he counted, then smirked. "Again, I ask, did I lie to you, dearie?" Jacob paused when he realized that it was true. Severein never actually lied to him, but he wasn't exactly very frank either.

Jacob sighed, "I'm still not happy with you."

"I know," Krennicx Severein responded. "I was about to tell you, but you had to run…. So how does it feel after you don't obey me?"

Jacob looked at the bars of the cell, "Pretty good."

"I know you're being sarcastic," Krennicx Severein said.

"Yep," Jacob responded. "So, Severein, is there anything else I need to know about you?"

"Oh please, call me Krennicx. Usually only people who hate me call me that Severein," Krennicx chuckled. "I guess that's why most everyone does."

"Ok, Severein," Jacob said half joking. *Half.*

Severein laughed, "I guess it would be weird to die beside someone I don't know, so how about we change that?"

"Beside?" Jacob asked in alarm.

"Well, you were with me when I was arrested, so they think you're on my side," Severein said. "But I think they might give you a trial."

"What about you?"

"They already know they hate me," Severein responded, "so what would be the point?"

"But what if you were innocent?" Jacob asked.

"Do you think that matters to a king who has the power to kill whomever he hates? Maybe not if everyone else likes him, but nothing can stop him if everyone else also wants him dead." Severein continued, "Here, it doesn't matter if you're innocent or not, it only matters if you are hated or not."

"But why are you hated? In other words, why are you a criminal?" Jacob asked.

"I really don't want to talk about it," Severein responded, looking away.

"I thought you wanted us to get to know each other?" Jacob asked.

Severein sighed, looking at the floor. "For now, let's just say they didn't give me a choice." Now that Severein's ears were long—similar to a dragon's—they pointed all the way down when he was upset.

Jacob had already noticed that dragons were *constantly* moving their ears with their emotions, like cats' ears to the extreme. He wondered if they ever really noticed they were doing it. *I guess this place is a very tough subject.* Jacob decided to try not to ask about his past again no matter how curious he was, well *try* not to. Severein was definitely the strangest dragon—or thing—he had met so far. He was surprised when he realized that he *almost* felt somewhat bad that the crazy thing was going to die, even though he didn't like him or trust him in the least bit. He tried to think of something to say to break the awkward silence, "What was that dragon that I saw a few cells down on the right?" Jacob asked.

"What, was it a Dragonese?" Severein asked, looking back up at him. His ears were already lifted back, although they still didn't point all the way up. He kept them at a halfway position.

"A what?"

"Dragonese," Severein responded. "They're a different type of dragon. They don't have different breeds and they don't speak in any languages that we do. They can be extremely aggressive and will eat you, but they can also be very affectionate."

"Why can't they speak?" Jacob asked.

Severein shrugged, "They just can't." He smirked a creepy smile, "Aren't you so glad that I can?"

Jacob shook his head, trying not to laugh. "So, they're like the roaring dragons that everyone talks about? If they're not like other dragons, then how are they dragons at all?"

"Yeah, their language is a whole lot of roars and growls," Severin responded. "I guess the easiest example is like a house cat and a tiger…they're completely different, but they're both felines."

"Weird," Jacob responded. He thought about Hazel and how she always wanted a dragon like that, minus the aggressiveness. He knew the exact way she hoped it would look like: pink. Of course, she really wanted any color dragon, but pink was the main color. "I doubt there's any pink dragon," Michael would say. "Besides, after we win the war all the dragons would be dead." A small stab of guilt hit Jacob when he thought of all the dragons dying. He looked at Severein, with the chains shackled on his wrists, like a dog leashed to a pole. The chains kept him from walking too close to the door. Jacob tried to come up with excuses of why he felt bad that Severein was about to die. *Maybe he's not a dragon,* Jacob thought. *Maybe why everyone hates him is because he's for the humans.* Still, he knew that could not be true because Krennicx had even talked about humans once. *Why am I doing this! I don't even like him! I have got to control myself! I can't believe I'm starting to care about a dragon I don't even like! Or is he a dragon? Wait a minute! King Luther said that Severein is his nemesis! That means he needs to die! But...if he's King Luther's enemy, why do the dragons hate him too?* The sounds of metal chains rattled as Severein walked to the other side of the cell.

"What are you doing?" Jacob asked. Severein put his claw against the metal bar and tapped it three times. He paused, then did it two more times. A cell in the distance did the same thing. Severein smiled, then walked around the whole cell, tapping three times on each bar. Jacob counted about five different responses of the tapping, but Severein obviously heard more.

"Thirty," Severein whispered to himself.

"Thirty of what?" Jacob asked.

"Not as much as I hoped," Severein said, ignoring him.

"How many are here?" Jacob asked.

"I think a couple of hundred, most likely thousands," Severein responded with a frown. "But there might be more who would respond somewhere else."

"Respond to what?" Jacob asked.

"It's getting late," Severein said, avoiding Jacob's question. "You should probably get some sleep; you have a big day tomorrow."

"How do you know what time it is?" Jacob asked. "It's always dark in here, isn't it?"

"When you have to live underground a lot," Severein responded, "you kind of learn how to tell what time it is…… That and a couple other reasons."

"Wait a minute," Jacob said, noticing something about the sleeping mats. "They put the mat out of your reach!"

"I don't think that was an accident," Severein said, looking amused.

"Let me guess," Jacob said, "you're used to sleeping on the stone floor, aren't you?"

Severein smirked a sneaky smile, "Joke's on them. I *prefer* the cool stone over the dirty hot mat. It reminds me of sleeping in the trees. Plus, can you imagine how many different prisoners slept on that thing? Talk about germs!"

"That sounds more like a panther than a dragon," Jacob said, trying hard to ignore the germ part. *I think the floor would be more germ infested. Wait, but what about mites and lice?!*

"It's not the only thing I have in common with a panther," Severein responded.

"Is it past dinner time?" Jacob asked after his stomach growled.

"Oh……. Yeah," Severein responded. "You passed dinner when you were walking up the mountain, but you might get breakfast in the morning."

"Did you get dinner?" Jacob asked.

"Nope," Severein responded with another smirk.

Jacob didn't even want to ask if he'd get breakfast. He forced himself to lay on the sleeping mat. *It's cleaner than the floor… it's cleaner than the floor. Ew! Is it just me or am I actually feeling mites and lice?!* He couldn't stop thinking about it as he stared at the ceiling for what felt like hours.

"Severein?" Jacob asked after a while.

"Hmm?"

"Do you want to play a game?"

"What kind?" Severein asked sleepily.

"Do you know 'I spy'?"

"Learned that one when I was like two."

"I spy with my little eye," Jacob said ignoring Severein, "something that is…… green."

"The dragon in the other cell wanting you to shut up's eyes," Severein responded.

"Your turn."

"*Fine*," Severein said, "I spy something that is black."

"The ceiling?"

"Nope."

"The wall?"

"Nope."

"The floor?"

"Nope."

"Your fur?"

"Nope."

"Your wings?"

"Nope."

"Your claws?"

"Good night, Jacob."

"My hair?"

"Nope."

It felt like every night Jacob's dreams would get worse than the last. That night he saw fire burning everything to the ground, including his own house. Then he saw a dragon as white as snow destroying everything in its path, but when it turned to Hazel, he woke up.

"Are you awake?" Severein asked.

"Yeah," Jacob responded, trying to calm his fast-beating heart.

"Did you have a bad dream?"

"How did you know?"

"You were kind of screaming in your sleep," Severein answered with a smirk.

"Oh," Jacob said feeling embarrassed. "What time is it?"

"Time to go," a soldier at the door answered.

"Where?" Jacob asked.

"The arena," the soldier responded.

"Which one of us?" Severein asked.

"They're saving the best for last."

Severein rolled his eyes as the soldier unlocked the door and took Jacob out, then locked the door back. They walked in the opposite direction that he came from. Jacob glanced back at Severein, who was still sitting and looking calm. *I'm defiantly not calm!* He was the furthest away from calm; he thought he was going to be covered with sweat.

"What are you going to do?" Jacob asked with his voice cracking.

"If you lose this trial you die, but if you win…. I don't know."

He gulped with fear. The long hall of prison cells turned into a huge metal elevator with bars. The soldier pushed a button that made the elevator go down. They stood there for what felt like forever.

"How high in the mountain are we?" Jacob asked with his voice still shaking.

"How many questions do you have?" the soldier asked. "We're not going completely down."

The sun shown brightly through the bars of the elevator and Jacob could see the huge arena. It was a huge circular dome with a bar ceiling. There had to be thousands of benches around the dome filled with dragons of almost every color, many he had not seen before. On a large stage at the end of the arena stood a huge golden throne with sapphires scattered all over it. On the throne sat the extremely overweight King of the Cloud Dragons, who looked more like a big ball covered in sapphires and silk than a dragon. The elevator stopped when it reached underneath the benches of the arena where prison cells lined all around the arena wall. Jacob stood frozen in fear, staring out into the massive crowd.

"Stay," the soldier commanded. "When the king says it's time, you go out there and stand before him."

The chatter of dragons stopped when the sound of the microphone thundered. "I know why you are all here," the voice of the king said across the arena, "but before we get to the best part, we have to deal with someone who has been charged of being friends with the one we all know and hate. I present to you uh………… Jaco……… I mean Jacob."

"That's your cue," the soldier said.

"I can't do this," Jacob forced out of his lips. But the soldier wasn't going to take no for an answer. He pushed him out onto the arena sand and forced him in front of the fat king. Jacob stood in horror as the soldier who brought him explained the situation to the king.

"What charge should be brought against him, Your Majesty?" an attendant asked.

"Tell me again what happened between him and the criminal?" the king asked forgetfully.

"I believe the criminal sacrificed his life to save him," the attendant responded.

He did? Jacob realized he had never even thought about it. *Why did he do that?*

"So, it is believed that he is friends with the criminal?" King Saul asked.

"Yes, Your Majesty."

"Well, then, no friend of the criminal is welcomed here," King Saul said. "The one called Jacob, is charged with death."

"And then the doctor said to the dragon, "I'm sorry, but I'm too blinded by your stupidity to see your brain.""

The soldiers burst into laughter.

"It's so funny because it's so true!" one of the six guards walking Severein down the prison hall said. They were heading to the arena. "They're idiots, we're idiots, all of us are idiots!"

"Of course we're all idiots!" another soldier said. "I mean, come on! Why do we need six soldiers to guard one prisoner?!"

"I never knew a wanted criminal like you would be such an amazing joke teller!" another said.

"When you have like no friends you kind of have a lot of time to come up with some jokes," Severein said.

"I guess that's true," the first guard said, thoughtfully. "You know this is nothing personal, right? You know, with whole execution stuff?"

"Right, nothing personal," Severein responded sarcastically.

"Good, because we're only killing you because we hate you," the solider said.

"Dude," Severein said, "that is literally the definition of personal."

"Oh yeah, I guess it is," the guard said thoughtfully. "So I guess it is personal," he shrugged.

"That's personal, but this isn't." Severein's blaster appeared in his talon and shot the soldiers on stun. Quickly, all six of them fell unconscious. "He wasn't an idiot for doing six," Severein said, looking at the napping soldiers. "He was an idiot for not doing twelve." He unstrapped his invisible bag of weapons from his waist. Going to every cell that had tapped three times, he placed a small silver magnetic ball on each lock. *I guess they don't remember this,* Severein thought as he glanced at his extremely sharp U-shaped spike at the tip of his tail. He had always wondered why he had that part of his tail, but it sure was useful in battle, especially to trap an opponent's neck underneath it. It was useful, but no matter how many times he'd say that he wouldn't actually stab it into their neck, everyone would always think that he would. He made all of the weapons and gadgets disappear when he decided that it was time to go. *I guess I have to save that kid's stupid butt again.* Severein left the prison cells and ran in the direction of the arena.

"Aren't you going to let us out!?" A prisoner yelled.

Jacob had never been so terrified in all of his life. Sure, when Lighter took him away from Michael was bad, but not like this. That wasn't near as bad as standing in front of a dragon king who gave a command to kill him. The crowd also wanted to kill him, but they were really there because of Severein. "Get this over with!" the crowd yelled. "Severein is why we are really here!"

"Severein is coming very quickly," the king assured. "We just have to use this as an example to all who follow the criminal way. Now, bring out the beast!"

A loud roar filled the arena as a massive creature in chains stepped inside. The creature was a dark blue color. It was way longer and taller than a dragon, and its long tail didn't even drag on the ground. Its entire body was covered in spikes that looked like armor. It had no wings, but its legs were bent in a way that looked like it could jump high like a frog.

It was so much taller than a dragon and way longer, and it looked stronger. It had to have been at least twenty feet tall.

The King of the Cloud Dragons stood up, then said to the crowd, "Let this be an example to all. Never betray me and join a criminal. RELEASE THE BEAST!" Some of the crowd cheered as—to Jacob's pure horror—they locked the doors and released the chains to the beast.

Immediately, the beast charged for Jacob with its mouth open. Jacob's fear glued him to the ground, he was too afraid to move. Knowing it would be the end, he closed his eyes, expecting to feel pain.

A loud, ear-piercing roar filled the arena, causing Jacob to open his eyes. Severein had shot onto the beast's face, stabbing it with his tail. He let go, and the beast jumped away and paced back and forth as if it was trying to recover.

"How did you..." the king started, but he didn't have the words to speak.

The crowd exploded with anger and excitement. "It's true!" they yelled. "The criminal is here! Kill him!"

"Are you insane?" Severein snarled to the king loudly. He stayed in the air, flapping his cool wings slowly. He looked *very* majestic. His voice was raspy but full with authority, "You have no idea who this kid is, do you?"

"It is because I know who he is, that he must die beside you," the king responded.

"But you don't know who he is!" Severein called with a loud authoritative voice. "If you did, you wouldn't kill him."

"Ok," King Saul said, "then who is he?"

"He is King Luther's spy, sent to kill me," Severein announced.

"Luther would pick this pathetic kid?" the king asked. "Even if that was true, why would you want to protect him?"

"Because unlike you," Severein said, majestically landing in front of Jacob, "I don't want to kill even my enemies, but who says we even have to be enemies? And who says we even have to hate each other?"

"Call off the beast!" the king commanded, standing from his throne.

"But Your Majesty…" a soldier started.

"Do it," Saul commanded, "then let me in."

The guards obeyed and pulled the chains to the beast back, then the king himself walked into the arena.

"What are you doing?" Jacob asked, still too shocked and terrified at the fact that Severein somehow knew who he was.

"I have to try to make this right," Severein responded.

"But Krennicx, I thought you said you didn't do anything," Jacob said quietly.

"They don't know that," Severein said, glancing at the crowd. Then he looked at Jacob and gave him a warm smile. *Wait,* Jacob realized, *did I just call him….*

"It's been a long time since you've seen a large crowd like this hasn't it?" King Saul asked, now standing right in front of them.

"You know I never meant for anything to happen," Krennicx responded, the pain in his eyes was strong. His ears were also lowered again.

"You're still on that?" the king asked. "Trying to clear your name? You do know, no one will ever forgive you for what you did? It seems like after ten years you'd realize that."

"I know it was wrong, and I'm sorry," Krennicx apologized, "but please don't take it out on this kid and your own subjects."

"Your flattery might work on the queen of the Sunlazies."

"Sunilians," Krennicx corrected.

"Whatever," the king said, "but it doesn't work on me."

"I know," Krennicx said, "but stalling does."

There was a long pause of weird silence.

"Is something supposed to be happening right now?" the king asked awkwardly.

"Wait for It," Krennicx said, perking his ear up to listen. "Keeeeep waiting."

"You are so strange," King Saul observed.

"Any second," Krennicx continued. "Any minute now……"

"Do you have some sort of disease or something?" King Saul asked.

Krennicx froze. "Oh yeah, I just remembered I have an appointment today," he said, acting insane. "I might be a little early."

"What is wrong with you?" the king asked, confused.

Krennicx continued to stare off into the distance, whispering something about red birds and songs, and something about a dragon of gold. *What IS wrong with him?* Jacob wondered. He shook his head when he remembered something Krennicx had once said about acting dumb. He was *good* at it. Krennicx paused, "Oh, hello, Your Majesty," Krennicx said as if he had just woken up. "How are you?"

"What in the world!" King Saul said, utterly confused. "You have got to be the most terrible criminal of all time!"

"Wait, hold on, hold on. I want to do this," Krennicx said with a happy smile. "I know you're about to try to kill me and everything, and I know you're about to fail miserably, but I really want to do this. Knock, knock?"

"You've got to be kidding me."

"Come on? Knock, knock?"

"Who's there?" King Saul asked, rolling his eyes.

"The interrupting Severein."

"The interrupting Severein who?"

Krennicx's face was pure blank and he didn't say a single word. There was long silence as everyone waited for Krennicx to do something with the joke, but he was flat-out blank. It was pure silence until Jacob and a few guards couldn't help but crack up. Krennicx burst out laughing and so did Jacob and all the guards.

"What in the world!" Saul said, confused. "How in Annorlia can you be so weird?! And I don't even see how it's funny because you didn't even finish the joke! What is the interrupting Severein?"

Krennicx paused and went blank again, causing everyone to laugh even harder.

"What did you *do* to them?" King Saul asked, alarmed.

"No, the question is," Krennicx said, "what did you do to them?"

"I know what I'm going to do you." The king pulled out a weird metal stick-looking rod with electrical flashes at the end of it. He tried to stab Krennicx with it. Fear flashed in Krennicx's eyes as he caught the king's wrist in mid-air and held it there. Guards immediately tackled Krennicx to the ground, freeing the king's hand. Krennicx quickly kicked the guards off of him and, somehow, was *winning* a fight with them. While Krennicx was distracted by the guards, Saul took the strange stick thing and stabbed it right on the back of Krennicx's neck. Krennicx nearly screamed from pain and fell to the ground, clutching his neck.

"I forgot about this handy little thing," King Saul said, looking pleased. "To be honest, I never even tried to use it before. They only said very little of what it does." The king smiled, "I guess some scars never heal." He did it again on the same spot on his neck and held it there, causing more pain. Krennicx laid on the ground, gasping for breath as he clutched his neck.

"This is what you wanted!" King Saul called out to the crowd. "Now, hand me a sword."

"The Fighters of Peace don't like it when innocents are killed," Krennicx warned. He was still out of breath.

"Who said the Fighters of Peace would find out?" King Saul asked as a sword was handed to him. "And who said that you are innocent?"

"Maybe not, but he is," Krennicx said, glancing at Jacob.

"It will be his turn next, but even if it wasn't, this is you and not him."

"Yes, but I'm sadly the only one in your kingdom that would save him."

Saul chuckled and shook his head. The King of the Cloud Dragons raised his sword over Krennicx, then swung it down. But Krennicx was right.

The sword shattered mid-swing as the sky went dark. Lightning bolted everywhere in the sky and the bars on top of the arena shattered. Krennicx jumped onto Jacob, causing him to fall to the ground with Krennicx using his wings to block the pieces of metal.

"How dare you try to kill those who did nothing to you!" a voice shouted. The buzz in Jacob's head went wild.

King Saul looked horrified. "N-n-nothing?" King Saul stammered. "N-n-n-no, no, no, no, you've got it all wrong."

"Do I?" the voice asked. Jacob recognized the cool, airy sounding voice. *It can't be.* It was one of the biggest reasons he came. It was the voice.

"Y-y-you have no proof," King Saul stammered in horror.

"Your fear is my proof." A huge lightning bolt flashed onto the ground of the arena. Then, standing there, was a dragon of pure lightning. He couldn't tell if it was a suit or the dragon itself. It had glowing, green eyes. The lightning flickered, as if it was glitching. Clouds covered the sun as lightning lit up the sky. It flashed everywhere.

"W-w-w-what do you want?" the king asked fearfully.

"We came here for a friend, but now it looks like we are needed for multiple reasons," the dragon-in-lighting said.

"W-w-w-we?"

"We."

Four more appeared in the sky, flying in a circle, too far away for Jacob to tell what they looked like, but they seemed to be different colors.

"Go!" the one on the ground shouted. **"Find what we came here to find!"**

Immediately, the four in the sky separated and flew around the entire kingdom.

The King of the Cloud Dragons ran from them screaming, "Kill them all! All seven of them!"

Many soldiers from everywhere poured into the arena with weapons in hand.

"Krennicx," Jacob said in panic, "what do I do?"

"Well, there's really only one thing you can do," Krennicx said, getting up from on top of Jacob.

"Run?"

"Yep."

Jacob got off the floor and they both took off running in the arena. *Where am I even running to?!* A soldier went to stab him with a sword but was blocked by Krennicx's strange tail. Krennicx, who was surprisingly a very good fighter, kept saving Jacob's life at every turn. There was an ear-piercing roar that made everyone stop. The beast had been let out again, but this time the soldiers were in the arena too.

"Uh… Krennicx?" Jacob asked, horrified.

"Don't look at me," Krennicx said.

"Can you beat that thing?" Jacob asked. Krennicx's expression was blank and he didn't respond. "I'll take that as a no," Jacob said.

The beast growled like a panther about to pounce. Everyone went silent.

"Krennicx…" Jacob said.

"Yeah?"

"Do you know anything about this thing?"

"I know as long as we stand extremely still, we might be ok," Krennicx responded. The silence was broken when a soldier took off running and screaming. "But unfortunately we have an idiot," Krennicx added.

The beast roared and ran fast across the arena, its eyes searched over everything to decide on what to eat first.

"Go!" Krennicx commanded. "Run back to where you came in, there might be someone there who will help you."

"But what about the guards?" Jacob asked.

"Are you seriously worried about the guards?!" Krennicx asked, his voice as raspy as ever. "They're too busy saving their own lives. Now go!"

Jacob took off as fast as he could to the other side of the arena. He ran around in front of the prison cells. Jacob stopped when he realized something was in one of the cells.

"What are you?" Jacob asked, looking into the cell. The dragon jumped at the bars of the cell and making Jacob jump back. The dragon was a dark, midnight blue and it was a little smaller than Jacob, height wise. It had to be one of the coolest dragons Jacob had seen so far. He stared into its green eyes as it continued to growl at him.

"Can you talk?" Jacob asked.

It growled in response.

"I'll take that as a no," Jacob said, staring at the dragon.

Its red tongue flicked in and out like a snake; it was definitely like the dragons Hazel would talk about. *It does look kind of cool...* Jacob shook his head, *I'm a human, I don't like dragons, I don't like dragons. Come on, Jacob, just remember I don't like dragons!* He stared at the dragon and how cool it was. He looked at the cell door and noticed that it didn't need a key. *Ok, I'm not doing this because I like it, I'm doing this because I am just curious...and Krennicx DID say someone might help, right?* He grabbed the cell's handle and twisted it a few times till it opened. Immediately, the dragon jumped out of the cage and stared at him, growling. Jacob took a few steps away in fear, regretting what he just did. *Why am I so stupid!?* It continued to growl, walking in a pounce position. It kept walking towards him until Jacob was against the wall, then it took a deep breath like it was going to breath fire. There was a gun shot and the dragon quickly jumped away.

Sky stood pointing a gun at the dragon threateningly. "I'd get out of here if I were you," Sky warned. Staring at the gun, the dragon backed away, growling. It stopped and stared at Jacob, then it opened its massive wings and took off flying out of the arena.

"You alright?" Sky asked.

"Yeah," Jacob responded. "What are you doing here?'

"What does it look like I'm doing?" Sky asked. "I'm getting you out."

"But you're the one responsible for putting me in here!"

"Never mind that," Sky said, "now where's Krennicx?"

"WHOA!" There was a bang as Krennicx crashed against the wall next to them.

"Found 'em," Jacob said.

"Ow, ow, ow, ow, and ow," Krennicx said, standing up and looking dizzy. "Oh, hey Sky, coming in to join the party?"

"The party of you getting your butt kicked?" Sky asked.

Krennicx smirked, "You have to admit," he said, "I put up a pretty good fight."

"What is that thing?" Jacob asked, watching the soldiers running away from the beast.

"It's a Lyvith," Krennicx responded. "They'll eat anything that has meat."

"They also really love to play with their food," Sky said, glancing at Krennicx.

"Playing with me or not, I'm alive and that's a win," Krennicx said.

"Is it though?" Jacob asked.

"Youch!" Krennicx yelped, somewhat joking.

"Where did the Fighter of Peace thingies go?" Jacob asked.

"Who knows what they're up to," Sky said.

"Where's Ben?" Krennicx asked.

"He's probably late as usual," Sky responded, "that is, if he's even coming."

"How could he get here?" Jacob asked.

"Hopefully not the same way he got to this kingdom," Krennicx said, rolling his eyes.

"How did you get here?" Jacob asked Sky.

"Easy." All of Sky's gadgets and guns showed themselves around Sky, reappearing on his straps. Sky grabbed a gun from his belt and smiled.

"Stun?" Jacob asked.

"Sure...." Sky responded.

The whole arena went quiet except for the Lyvith searching for everyone. Jacob could see all of the soldiers also hiding underneath the stands from the beast like what they were doing.

"Can that thing reach us from here?" Jacob whispered.

"Yep," Krennicx responded.

"The soldiers are getting closer too," Sky whispered.

"Are they still wanting to kill us?" Jacob asked.

"Yep," Krennicx responded.

"Is the audience still here?" Sky asked.

"Yep," Krennicx responded.

"Is 'yep' the only thing you're going to say?" Jacob asked.

"Nope," Krennicx responded.

"Are you a fast runner?" Sky asked.

"I guess," Jacob responded. "Why?"

"He is not going to be able to outrun that thing if that's what you're asking," Krennicx said.

"Just a thought," Sky said.

"The second we move, everybody moves," Krennicx pointed out.

"What is that supposed to mean?" Jacob asked.

"Sky, can you hand me a bomb?" Krennicx asked. Sky immediately gave him a small silver ball.

"So what? We're going to stay here forever?" Jacob asked.

"No," Krennicx responded, "we just have to time it perfectly." Krennicx turned and threw the ball at the beast. When it hit the Lyvith's snout, the bomb blew up. The Lyvith roared in fury, locking its eyes onto Krennicx.

"That was timing it perfectly?!" Sky asked.

"Run," Krennicx said, smiling. He bolted himself at the Lyvith and dodged it in midair.

"Where am I supposed to run to?" Jacob shouted.

"Just follow me," Sky said, running with Jacob right behind him.

Immediately the soldiers chased after them, but this time Jacob had Sky, who had a gun.

"Is that thing on stun?" Jacob called.

"Is now," Sky called back.

Jacob looked behind him to see Krennicx trying to distract the Lyvith. The beast snapped its massive jaws at Krennicx, but he shut his wings and went underneath it. Jacob was surprised at how fast Krennicx was as he flew around the Lyvith. Jacob noticed as they ran that a lot of the crowd had left, and the king was running around in a panic.

They stopped when they reached the other side of the arena. Sky was breathing hard, rubbing his shoulder in pain.

"Are you alright?" Jacob asked, out of breath.

"Hopefully," Sky responded.

"What are we waiting for?" Jacob asked, looking around.

"You'll know it when you see it," Sky responded.

It didn't take long for the Lyvith to get bored with Krennicx. It decided to stop and go for Sky and Jacob on the other side of the arena. It ran towards them fast, but not as fast as it could go. Right when it got really close to them, Krennicx bolted himself from behind at its neck, but it was a trick. The Lyvith whipped its head around and bit onto Krennicx in mid-air. Using its mouth, the Lyvith slammed Krennicx to the ground. Then it picked him up again and threw him hard against the wall. So much of the bricks crumpled from the wall that he almost went completely through it. Immediately, Sky ran to him with Jacob hesitantly following.

"Beat it, huh?" Sky asked when he reached him. Though he sounded humorous, in his eyes, he looked highly concerned.

"Put up a fight," Krennicx corrected, rolling onto his stomach with a small moan. The Lyvith growled in a pounce position.

"Do they eat humans for dinner?" Jacob asked, taking a step back.

"Nah," Krennicx responded, "they're snacks."

The Lyvith kept growling, then it pounced with its mouth opened.

There was a bolt of lightning as the main Fighter of Peace reappeared right in front of them. Lightning flashed from its claws and struck the Lyvith.

"Thank you, Lightning Prince!" Krennicx cheered. The Lyvith roared in pain and fell to the ground, then it ran fast to its own massive cell across the arena. All who were left of the crowd fell over each other trying to run as far away from the Fighter of Peace as possible.

"Thank you," Sky said with a small nod.

"I think it's time for you to leave," the Fighter said with the same voice as what Jacob had been hearing in his head. It was weird to see lighting itself hovering in the air with its wings.

"Ben should be here," Krennicx said.

"There he is," Sky said. "Late as usual."

"I don't see anything," Jacob said, looking around.

"Dude, you gotta look up," Krennicx said.

Jacob looked up to see a massive spaceship in the shape of an arrow tip, a little bit like a stretched triangle. It was black with three large dark orange stripes going down it. Jacob had never seen anything like it before. He had always thought that ships like that were just a myth. It was even bigger than most houses. The ship came to a stop a couple of feet off the ground.

"What is that?" Jacob asked.

"Haven't you ever seen a ship before?" Sky asked.

"I didn't even know they existed! Let alone be owned by a dragon!" Jacob said.

"This particular one isn't," Sky responded.

The large door on the side of the ship slid open and a ramp came out, but it was still high in the air.

"How can we ever repay you for what you've done?" Sky asked.

"You know," the Fighter responded.

"Thank you," Krennicx said.

The Fighter nodded in response. **"Goodbye, Jacob,"** the Fighter's voice said in Jacob's head. Then the Fighters of Peace were gone without a trace.

"Great, Ben just had to do this too high," Sky said, looking up at the ship hovering in the air. The ramp was till several feet off the ground.

"You know you could always jump," Krennicx pointed out.

"Sure," Sky said, "it's only like fifteen feet off the ground."

"That's very specific."

"Because it's precise," Sky said.

"Well, then let's see how pre*cise* you can jump," Krennicx said.

Sky took a deep breath, then jumped.

"That was terrible."

"Sorry, but I can't exactly jump as high as a Lyvith," Sky said.

"You used to jump pretty high," Krennicx said.

Sky tried again.

"A little higher that time," Jacob joined in.

"It might would help if you stopped staring at me," Sky said.

"Ok…" Krennicx said. He grabbed onto Jacob and flew to the ship. Jacob noticed he was very clumsy as he landed. He almost fell off the side of the ramp. Krennicx went to the door and untied a rope ladder and tossed it down.

"Are you alright?" Jacob asked when he noticed Krennicx do a small limp.

"I should be fine," Krennicx said rubbing his neck.

"Someone stop them!" the voice of the Sky King shouted.

"Thanks for the hospitality!" Krennicx called out to the king. His accent was strong, "I especially loved the part when you yourself tried to kill me!" Sky climbed onto the ramp and into the doorway next to Jacob. "Bye, bye," Krennicx said, waving. The door and the ramp closed the same way it opened.

"What is this?" Jacob asked, looking around the strange hallway they were in.

"Jacob," Krennicx said with an excited look on his face, "welcome to the BeetleWing."

CHAPTER 12

THE BEETLEWING

As far as he could see, the hallway went to the left and right. The walls were black with three strange, glowing lines running through the middle. They walked down the hall to the left that led to a triangle-like shaped room unlike anything Jacob had ever seen before. It was like an airplane pilot room but much bigger. There were four groups of two chairs lined up with two on each side of the room, and all of the walls were glass. At the end of the room were the pilot and co-pilot seats right in front of the controls. There were buttons and switches everywhere at the controls, even on the ceiling. Jacob recognized the wingless dragon, Ben, on the pilot seat.

"It looked like the Cloudairians treated you better this time than the last time," Ben said, noticing them walk in.

"Yeah, this time I only almost died twice," Krennicx responded with a weary smile.

"Hey, it must be getting better," Ben said.

"If better is worse… then yeah," Krennicx said, walking to the pilot seat. "Now get off my spot."

"What?!" Ben yelped. "Oh, come on! You're not still mad at me, are you?"

"No, I just want to fly my ship," Krennicx said. "Now shoo."

"Why?"

"Off," Krennicx said. "To the co-pilot with you."

"Co-pilot doesn't sound near as cool," Ben grumbled, getting up.

"I know," Krennicx responded, happily sitting in the pilot's chair. Ben sat on the other chair and started clicking buttons. He *looked* like he knew what he was doing.

"Is this your first time in a ship?" Ben asked, as Sky sat on one of the passenger seats.

"Yeah," Jacob responded, sitting next to the Cloud Dragon.

"What!" Ben yelped in surprise. "Then that means you've never been to space before!"

"Don't you *dare* barf on my ship," Krennicx chimed in.

"We're not going to space, right?" Jacob asked nervously. Ben and Krennicx exchanged looks and did an excited smile.

"Lady and gentlemen, it is time to fasten your seat belts," Krennicx spoke calmly into a microphone, "or you can be stupid and not do so as we leave the atmosphere. Thank you."

"Aren't we the only one's here?" Jacob asked.

"Hey, Jacob," Lighter said, walking past him.

"Where did you come from?" Jacob asked in surprise.

"Peace Forest," Lighter answered, sitting in the chair in front of him.

"Hey, Glider," Krennicx greeted miserably.

"You sound happy," Glider noticed, walking in with Glazer and Tortoise behind him.

"I was supposed to pick them up, right?" Ben asked.

"Unfortunately, yes," Krennicx responded.

"It's been a while since I've seen you, Sky," Glazer said.

"Indeed," Sky responded.

"How are you?" Glazer asked.

"Ready to get back to the field," Sky answered.

"Right," Glazer said awkwardly.

"What field?" Jacob asked. "Oh, spy field, right," Jacob added when everyone started to laugh.

"Oh yeah, about that," Sky said, "if you tell anyone about me, it will be the last thing you ever say."

"Ok," Jacob said, badly wanting to go sit next to Lighter instead.

"Are we ever going to leave?" Glider asked, still not sitting down yet.

"I don't know, Glider," Krennicx said, "you still haven't buckled yet."

"I'm trying to do it at the last second right before we go," Glider said. "Plus, the least amount of time on those un-comfy seats the better."

"Un-comfy, huh?" Krennicx asked.

"Yeah, I mean the pilot seats might be comfy, but the passenger's seats aren't," Glider said.

"Hmm," Krennicx said nodding, "good to know."

"What? So you're going to fix it?"

"I do have a pretty good solution."

"Really?" Glider asked in excitement. "Because you know if you sit on them for a while or even for a second, they start to hurt your back." Glider continued to go on and on about everything terrible about the seats. Smiling, Krennicx shook his head and was obviously not listening. Without a warning, Krennicx calmly grabbed hold of the stick and yanked it to the right.

"Whoa!" Glider shrieked when the pressure of the ship pushed him off his talons. Krennicx smirked a smile as he made the ship violently go up and down.

"Should have buckled up," Krennicx grinned. "Punch it, Ben."

Before Jacob knew anything, everything went bright as the ship shot out of the sky. In a split second, they stopped in a void of black with massive balls of fire and tiny silver dots. They were flying in space. It took a few seconds for Jacob to feel anything, then his queasiness started to catch up with him. Everything looked so amazing and unreal, but his whole body felt like it was going to come out of his mouth.

"How you doing back there, Glider?" Krennicx asked calmly.

"Never better," Glider said from the floor. Glider stood up and fell down again, looking dizzy.

"You're looking a little green back there, Jacob," Krennicx observed.

"What… just…. happened?" Jacob asked, trying his best to not throw up.

"Yes, that was a couple of trillion miles away from Annorlia," Krennicx responded calmly.

"What?" Jacob squeaked.

"Yeah, it usually takes a few seconds for the queasiness to truly hit," Krennicx said, "so if you need to, the bathroom is over there," he said, pointing out of the door. Jacob immediately got up and ran in that direction.

"Humans," Glider murmured.

"Glider?" Krennicx asked.

"Yes?"

"It's best to do it in there than in here," Krennicx responded.

"Ok." Glider shot up and ran to the bathroom.

"Humans, huh?" Krennicx asked, then everyone started to laugh.

Jacob explored the BeetleWing as he was trying to find his way back to everyone else. His mind was still dazed at everything that happened at the arena…and the fact that he was in *space. The Fighters of Peace are real,* Jacob thought, *and for some reason they saved our lives, but why? They saved a criminal, a dragon spy, and a human spy, three things that dragons don't seem to like. And how do dragons have this much technology and humans don't?! That could turn the tide of the war! And…I think there's more dragons than humans! The rest of Annorlia is far more vast than we ever thought!* "And why is this thing called the BeetleWing?" Jacob asked himself out loud.

"Now that is a question we've always asked."

"Ah!" Jacob jumped back in surprise.

"Sorry, I've been scaring you a lot, haven't I?" Lighter asked apologetically.

"Oh, it's you," Jacob said, a little relieved for some reason.

"Are you lost?"

"Not really," Jacob said, "I'm just trying to find the bedroom Krennicx was talking about."

"So… you're not lost... you're just, lost?" Lighter asked.

"Precisely," Jacob responded.

Lighter laughed. "Come on," he said, leading the way. "So, I heard you guys ran into the Fighters of Peace?"

"Yeah," Jacob responded. "How did you know about that?"

"It's kind of easy to know where the Fighters of Peace go."

"What?" Jacob asked. Lighter didn't say anything, it was like he knew he shouldn't have said that. *How does he know?* Jacob wondered, *and where did you go when I got arrested?*

"What was that noise?" Lighter asked.

"What noise?" Jacob asked.

"That," Lighter responded.

"I don't hear anything," Jacob said.

"I think I know what it is." Lighter sped up with Jacob behind him.

"What is it?" Jacob asked. They turned into a dark room with no light-up walls.

"Having trouble finding the light switch again?" Lighter asked into the darkness.

"Maybe," the voice of Tortoise said in the darkness.

"Do you need help?"

"Yes, but if Glider is there, please don't send him, you can definitely see in the dark the best, V," Tortoise said.

"V?" Jacob asked.

"I'll explain later," Lighter said. "I'm coming."

Lighter disappeared into the darkness, leaving Jacob standing awkwardly. After a few seconds, a bright light lit up the room.

"Thanks," Tortoise said, standing in the middle of the room.

"No problem," Lighter said. "Can you turn it down a little though?"

"Sure." Tortoise twisted a black knob on the wall, causing the light to dim.

"That's better."

"Hey, Jacob," Tortoise greeted.

"Hey," Jacob responded.

"How are you?" Tortoise asked.

"Fine……. I guess," Jacob answered. "Um…. How about you?"

"Good," Tortoise answered. "You can come in if you close the door."

"Ok…… What door?" Jacob asked. "There's not a door."

"Just tap the screen on the wall," Tortoise said. Jacob did what Tortoise said, and immediately two sides of the wall slid closed, meeting each other in the middle.

"Are all the doors like that?" Jacob asked.

"Yeah, pretty much," Lighter said.

Jacob looked around the room; there really wasn't that much stuff except for two bunk-bed-like objects. They were weird beds that looked a little like bunk beds, but they were attached to the wall instead of bars. There were big chests in front of each bed instead of dressers.

"How much longer do you really think you can hide Turtle?" Lighter asked.

"Whaat? What makes you think I have Turtle?" Tortoise asked.

"Tortoise, I helped you sneak him in here," Lighter said.

"Oh yeah," Tortoise said thoughtfully, "I forgot about that."

"Who's Turtle?" Jacob asked.

"My best friend," Tortoise answered.

"A dragon?" Jacob asked.

"Nope," Tortoise said, smiling.

"Then what is he?" Jacob asked, surprised.

"You'll see," Tortoise responded.

"Tortoise, where is Turtle?" Lighter asked.

"I put him in the closet," Tortoise responded.

"Tortoise," Lighter said, "we don't have a closet."

"Oh yeah……. We don't, do we?" Tortoise said in a forgetful way.

"Tortoise, where did you put him?" Lighter asked urgently.

"I think I told him to stay in here," Tortoise said.

"Wait," Lighter said, "so you left him in here, and then you left with the door open?"

"Yes…. I think," Tortoise said.

"And do you see him in here?" Lighter asked, knowing the answer.

"Oh…… I guess I don't, but you always see a lot better than me, V."

"He's not here," Lighter said.

"Well, maybe Jacob can see better," Tortoise said.

"No, Jacob cannot see it, you know why?" Lighter asked. "Because he's not here," Lighter said when Tortoise opened his mouth to say something.

"Oh……." Tortoise said, realizing what he was saying.

"Yeah," Lighter said. "Now we need to go look for him, alright?"

"Ok," Tortoise said. "Maybe he's napping in one of the chests in here."

"Oh good grief," Lighter said, frustrated. "Come on."

"Turtle! Turtle!" Tortoise called as they walked out of the bedroom.

"Does he have something wrong or something?" Jacob whispered.

"Legally, no," Lighter responded.

"Turrrrrrrrrrrrtle!" Tortoise called loudly.

"What are you doing?" Lighter whispered. "They're not supposed to know he's here. If he finds out he's gonna...."

"Who finds out about what?" Jacob asked as they jumped to see Krennicx standing right behind them.

"Naah Krennicx," Lighter said, surprised, "what are you doing?"

"Just walking in my ship," Krennicx responded. "Why do you ask?"

"Oh, I was just, I guess surprised you're not flying the ship," Lighter said nervously.

"Nah, it's on auto pilot," Krennicx responded.

"Of course," Lighter said.

"Yeah, the strangest thing just happened," Krennicx said.

"Really?"

"Yeah, I was just walking along, and I thought I saw Turtle."

"Whaaaaaaat? Why would you think that?"

"Weird right?" Krennicx asked.

"Yeah, super weird," Lighter said in panic with a laugh.

"Yeah, welp.. have fun," Krennicx said, starting to walk again.

"We will," Lighter assured.

"And by the way," Krennicx stopped and looked back, "nothing happens on this ship without me knowing about it."

"Ok."

"And when you find Turtle, please keep him away from me." Krennicx continued to walk away and out of sight.

"Why is he so scary?" Tortoise asked.

"He's not," Lighter responded.

"Yeah he is," Jacob said.

Tortoise nodded in agreement.

"I can't find him anywhere!" Glazer said, looking underneath a box.

"No matter where he is, he's not gonna be under a box!" Glider teased. "Come on, Tortoise! You should be glad you don't have to care for that annoying thing!"

"I don't even know what I am looking for," Jacob said, looking into a tiny box. "For all I know, it could be a mouse."

"I wish!" Glider said.

"It's not a mouse," Glazer said. "It's a Sea Skipper."

"See what now?" Jacob asked.

"You've never heard of a Sea Skipper?" Glazer asked in surprise.

"No," Jacob said, "I've also never heard of Ice Dragons either."

"What!" Glider yelped, offended. "You've never heard of the most awesome kind of dragon? You're not even saying the name right!"

"There's other names?" Jacob asked.

"There's actually a lot," Lighter said.

"For some reason Krennicx calls us Ice Brains," Glider said.

"Dude, you do know that's not a compliment, right?" Ben asked from the corner.

"How?" Glider asked.

"Ice doesn't have brains," Ben answered, smirking.

Everyone except for Glider burst into laughter.

"KRENNICX!" Glider got up and ran out.

"Welp, now he's gonna set up a booby trap," Lighter said.

"Yep, and then it's going to somehow end up on him," Ben added.

"It's the circle of Glider," Lighter and Ben said at the same time.

"Where is Krennicx anyway?" Tortoise asked.

"I think he's on the phone with Icicle," Ben answered.

"I promise you, I WILL HUNT YOU DOWN AND DESTROY YOU!" the dragon on the hologram yelled. The hologram made the dragon look blue.

"Oh dearie, dearie, I wonder what I'm going to do with that threat? I guess I'll throw into the pile of *I don't care,*" Krennicx snarled through clenched teeth. "But I promise *you*, if you harm him in any way, I will *personally come and make you wish you NEVER see the light of day again!*"

The dragon chuckled, "Don't make promises you can't keep."

"I don't," Krennicx responded with his jaw clenched.

"Ooo, kitty's got claws," the dragon teased. "But will he *actually* use them? You're not very well known for painful torture, Severein."

"Trust me when I say this," Krennicx Severein responded, staring the dragon flat in the eyes, *"my* type of torture, is *far* worse than physical pain." Krennicx continued to stare into the dragon's eyes. Then the dragon gulped and stepped back.

"Fine," he said, whipping his eyes away, "I won't harm him. At least, as long as *you* live."

"As long as I live, *no one* will."

"I don't doubt that," the dragon responded, terror in his eyes. His talon shook as he reached for the button to make himself disappear. "I hope your death is painful," the dragon spat.

"As long as I'm protecting him, I. Don't. Care."

The dragon clinched his jaw, then disappeared.

Krennicx took a deep breath.

"Wow, you look tense."

Krennicx sighed with relief, "I wasn't really expecting that, I was expecting you."

The white-silver dragon frowned, "I'm sorry. I was late. Is this a bad time?"

"It's fine," Krennicx assured. "Trust me, I'm used to this."

Icicle frowned, "You shouldn't have to be."

"It's nothing you can stop," Krennicx sighed.

"I know," Icicle said with a sigh, "I just wish I didn't make it worse."

Krennicx smiled, "I still can't believe you're doing this; this is crazy even for you."

"I know," Icicle said, "I just can't let this happen to my subjects. You understand right?"

"I understand," Krennicx responded. "Glider and Glazer won't."

"Yeah, I don't know what to do about them," she said with a sigh.

"Oh come on, they're your kids."

"I know that," Icicle said. "It's just... I don't want them to worry."

"Oh, you're only gonna lead a *small* Iceling squad against the Diammonites. Why would they get worried?"

"Wow, that made me feel a lot better," Icicle said sarcastically.

"That's something I'm really good at," Krennicx said, continuing the sarcasm.

"Yeah, you're really not."

"I know."

Icicle arched her eyebrows, "Are you alright? Your eyes look tired. Did you get hurt?"

Krennicx immediately pushed the tiredness out of his eyes. He had forgotten to do it earlier. He stared at his claws, not wanting to answer her question. Icicle sighed, "Headaches again?"

"Somewhat," Krennicx responded, rubbing his *burning* neck, "but something else happened…," he stopped when he realized he'd worry her. "I'm fine."

"I don't think you are," she said, "but I guess I'll let you escape this… for now. I'll *try* to pretend you're not in terrible pain. So… you're sure this is ok?" Icicle asked. "I don't know how long it will take."

"You know I'm gonna say it's ok, but deep down I'm going to be miserable," Krennicx said, relieved that she allowed the subject change. *Plus, you already know you'll disagree with my advice.*

"I really do appreciate this," Icicle said. "It's nice having someone I can trust."

"Back at you," Krennicx responded.

"Oh yeah, which reminds me, I told Sunny that you were going to be there tomorrow and pick up a few things for me," Icicle said hurriedly.

"What?!"

"Thanks again, Krennicx, you are a life saver. Literally." Quickly, the hologram disappeared and was replaced with words that said, 'your call has ended.'

"Oh come on," Krennicx said. "Man, Queens these days are crazy." Krennicx turned off the hologram and left to pilot the ship.

"Turtle!!!!!!!" Tortoise called.

"I don't think that's working," Jacob said.

"It should," Tortoise said.

"What are you guys doing?" Krennicx asked from behind him.

"Stop doing that!" Jacob shrieked, surprised.

"We're still looking for Turtle," Lighter said, a little annoyed.

"He's got to be around here somewhere," Tortoise said worriedly.

"Dude, I found him like an hour or more ago," Krennicx said.

"Where is he?" Tortoise asked.

"Where he belongs," Krennicx responded with a smirk.

"Which is?" Tortoise asked.

"In a cell."

"You put my Turtle in a prison cell?!" Tortoise yelped in horror.

"What? He's safe there," Krennicx said.

"From what?"

"Me," Krennicx answered, "and Glider, and Ben, and probably Sky. I would say Jacob, but I doubt he could do anything, so, everyone but you, Glazer, and Lighter."

"He is not going to do anything!" Tortoise defended.

"Last time you said that he almost blew up an entire city," Krennicx said.

"He didn't mean to!" Tortoise said.

"Yeah, just like how I didn't *mean* to grab it by the collar and drag it to a cell and lock it with a lock that he cannot break," Krennicx said. "Oh wait, I did mean to do that, didn't I? Well, I guess now that he's there he can stay there until he can get off my ship. Uh, bye-bye now." He turned and walked away.

"I'm coming, Turtle!" Tortoise called, running away.

"This ship has a prison?" Jacob asked, a little nervous.

"Yeah, it's just like four or something cells," Lighter said. "He never uses it except for Turtle."

"Why does he hate him?" Jacob asked.

"I don't know," Lighter said, shrugging.

"So what all is there to do in space?" Jacob asked, a little nervous.

"We're not going to be in space for that much longer," Lighter responded, "but we can go to the front and talk to everyone. Mainly to see what Glider's going to do to get back at Krennicx."

"Yeah, I don't care too much about the prank part, but I do want to see if Sky will tell any stories about being a spy," Glazer said.

"He's not going to, but ok," Lighter said. *I really hope they aren't going to put me in a cell,* Jacob thought nervously as they followed Lighter back to the front of the BeetleWing.

"Why! Why did you do that?" Glider asked while Krennicx and Ben were laughing.

"What did we miss?" Lighter asked, smiling.

"That *creature* changed my profile name to Smell-ma-pitts!" Glider said, pointing at Krennicx.

"Dude, you don't even have a profile," Krennicx said, "and even if you did, it's not like anyone would be *looking* at it."

"Well, if I did have one," Glider defended, "it'd be the most popular one ever."

"Well, you know what's funny?" Krennicx asked.

"What?"

"You don't have a profile, but you are still known by hundreds by that name."

"Krennicx!" Glider yelped angrily.

"Saying my name ain't gonna fix yours!" Krennicx said with his hilarious accent. Jacob still had no idea what it was, for he had never heard it before.

"If you don't have a profile, then how did he change your name?" Jacob asked.

"I actually changed it like a month ago," Krennicx said. "I just didn't tell you that it was you until now."

"What!" Glider yelped.

"So how was Cloudairia?" Glazer chimed in. "Was it pretty?"

"Ha," Sky snorted. "What part are you asking about? The king's so-called kingdom of himself, or the city?"

"Well, I just had heard that Cloudairia was the prettiest place in Annorlia," Glazer said, shocked.

"'Was' is a lot different than 'is'," Krennicx responded. "You're right. It used to be the prettiest, but it's not anymore."

"Oh," Glazer said.

"You did say you fought a Lyvith though, right Krennicx?" Ben asked.

"It wasn't exactly a fight," Krennicx responded, "it was more like a……"

"Getting hit out of the air a couple of times?" Jacob chimed in.

"You didn't say that!" Ben said excitedly. "So did it beat you up?"

"I wouldn't exactly say beat up…" Krennicx said.

"I mean, it did bite you," Sky pointed out.

"It bit you!" Lighter yelped, sounding worried.

"KRENNICX GOT RABIES! KRENNICX GOT RABIES!" Glider announced loudly.

"Would you stop that!" Krennicx snapped. "I don't have rabies."

"That's exactly what something that has rabies would say," Glider said suspiciously.

"Dude, anything that would have rabies wouldn't be saying that because they'd be going crazy," Krennicx said.

"Oh, so maybe you've always had rabies," Glider said.

"And maybe you've always had a bad case of ID-10-T," Krennicx said calmly.

"What's that supposed to mean?" Glider asked.

Krennicx smirked a smile and didn't say anything.

"You don't think you could get sick from that bite, do you?" Lighter asked, looking worried.

"I'm fine," Krennicx assured. "I didn't get sick when *you* bit me."

"That was different," Lighter said, "and I don't even remember doing that because I was a baby."

"Ooo I would have loved to do that," Glider said.

"You have," Krennicx said.

"Really? When?" Glider asked.

"You don't remember?" Krennicx asked.

"Not really…." Glider said.

"Remember…. When we first met you hated me so you……" Krennicx trailed off.

"Oh yeah! Now I remember!" Glider tilted his head, "Not much has changed, huh?"

"Haha very funny," Krennicx responded.

"I mean…… you don't think it's gonna scar do you?" Lighter asked worriedly.

"Oh, you're still on that?" Krennicx asked.

"I'm just saying, you might want to get it looked at," Lighter said.

"Why?" Krennicx asked.

"Well… I don't know…. It's just…. you know the last scar you got from the Cloud Kingdom was…." Lighter trailed off.

"Completely different," Krennicx finished for him. Lighter still looked unsure, "Oh come on," Krennicx said.

"Do you think it'll scar?" Lighter asked.

"I mean mayyybeee……." Krennicx responded. "I don't know, I'm not a bite expert."

"If y'all are done with…… whatever this is," Ben said, "would anyone like to tell me where I'm going?"

"Very, very sadly…. To Sunny's palace," Krennicx said miserably.

"Really?" Ben asked in shock.

"Palace?" Jacob asked.

"Ooo, don't know if I have ever been there during your meetings before," Glider said excitedly.

"Why are we going there?" Glazer asked.

"Yeah, why are we going there?" Ben asked.

"Yeah Krennicx, why are we going there?" Glider asked.

Jacob just had to, "Why are we going there, Krennicx?"

"So…… why are we going there?" Lighter asked.

"Why?" Glider asked. "Why Krennicx? Why? Why? Why? Why? Why?"

"Would you stop that!" Krennicx asked in annoyance. "It's like a whole bunch of children in here!"

Everyone went quiet, silently laughing inside. The door slid open and Tortoise walked inside, "Krennicx, why are we going to Sunny's palace?" Tortoise asked. Krennicx took a deep breath as everyone burst into laughter.

"What's so funny?" Tortoise asked, confused.

"Heyy, Krennicx?" Glider asked.

"Glider," Krennicx said, "this is already funny, if you do it, you'll ruin it. Don't. you. dare. say….."

"Why are we going to Sunny's palace?" Glider asked. Krennicx slowly turned to look at Glider in a strong way that gave Jacob the chills.

"Well, goodnight!" Lighter said, jumping up.

"Goodnight!" Glazer said, doing the same thing.

"Goodnight!" Tortoise said, also jumping up.

"What time is it?" Jacob asked.

"I don't care, goodnight," Lighter responded hurriedly. Jacob followed as everyone except for Glider almost ran out the door.

"What was that all about?" Jacob asked as they were getting ready for bed.

"Listen, you're new here," Tortoise said, "so you haven't witnessed the wrath of Krennicx yet."

"He got pretty mad at the Cloud Kingdom," Jacob responded.

"You mean Cloudairia?" Tortoise asked.

Jacob just stared at him.

"Oh that?" Lighter asked. "That was his simple back-off-and-leave-me-alone. You haven't seen him with more dangerous situations. In other words, Glider."

"Glider?" Jacob asked.

"Yeah, let's just say it took years for Glider to figure out how to get to him," Glazer said. "And let's just say he's mastered it now."

"He's still pretty slow to get too mad," Lighter added, "but he can have some bad days though. At least he'll show a warning for you to stop."

"But Glider *NEVER* obeys it!" Glazer said.

"He thinks it's funny," Tortoise added.

"It was a little funny," Jacob said quietly.

No one said anything as they grabbed their own blankets from each chest.

"Which do you prefer, top or bottom?" Tortoise asked.

Jacob opened his mouth to respond but was interrupted by Glider walking into the room.

"So unreasonable," Glider mumbled.

"How'd that go?" Lighter asked.

"Meh, nothing really happened," Glider said, disappointed. "He didn't budge."

"That's a good thing, isn't it?" Lighter asked.

"He might have not this time, but just you wait. After tonight, he'll budge," Glider said sneakily.

"That is so weird," Lighter observed.

"Well, I guess I'll go to bed," Glazer said, yawning.

"Night, Glazer," Lighter said.

"Night," Glider said.

"Aren't you going to come kiss me goodnight?" Glazer asked. Glider's eyes widened and his face turned red from embarrassment.

"Come on Glider, you do it every night," Glazer said.

"Come on Glider, if you do it every night then why don't you?" Lighter asked, not in a teasing way. "There's nothing to be embarrassed about, if I had a sister I'd do it every single night."

"I would say that I do with Aqua every night, but uh...." Tortoise trailed off.

"Aqua?" Jacob asked.

"Yeah, my sister," Tortoise responded.

"Huh," Jacob said curiously.

"You know you don't have to make this weird," Glider said. "Come on, Glazer."

"Yes!" Glazer said, happily following Glider out of the room.

"So what about you, Jacob?" Tortoise asked. "Do you have a sister?"

"Yes," Jacob responded.

"Is she your only sibling?" Tortoise asked.

"No, I have a brother too," Jacob answered. *Wait, is he tricking me?* Jacob thought horridly.

"Cool," Tortoise responded, "so now I'm not the only one with a brother and a sister."

"Are you the middle child?" Jacob asked.

"No, I'm the youngest. My sister is the middle. Are you the middle?" Tortoise asked.

"Yep," Jacob responded.

"Which blanket do you prefer?" Lighter asked.

"Is the temperature here going to be the same as at your house?" Jacob asked.

"Yeah…although it's more like air conditioning here."

"Then whichever is biggest," Jacob said.

"See!" Tortoise said. "It's so cold!"

"If none of you like it," Jacob said, "then why do you do it?"

"To meet certain…..standards," Lighter said.

"Like what?" Jacob asked.

"Like….. well, you see, Glider and Glazer are Ice Dragons," Lighter explained, "so they need to be at a certain temperature or else they'll overheat."

"It's called a compromise," Krennicx said, all of the sudden in the middle of the room.

They all jumped in surprise. "Where did you come from?!" Jacob shrieked, surprised.

"Where do you think?" Krennicx asked.

"How is it a compromise if not even they are happy?" Tortoise asked, continuing the conversation.

"Because everyone's equally *miserable*," Krennicx responded with pure evil in his eyes. "But if you don't like compromises then I guess I can always take away the steam room……"

"No! No, no, no! Compromises are great!" Tortoise said.

"Why do you need a steam room?" Jacob asked.

"Isn't it so weird that everyone here except for Jacob need's some specific care?" Krennicx asked thoughtfully.

"It's so Tortoise's scales don't dry up and cause him to dehydrate," Lighter answered.

"Oh," Jacob said thoughtfully.

"Anyway," Krennicx said, "tomorrow morning we'll get to Sunny's, and if I know her, she'll unfortunately most likely try to have us stay the night."

"Are we?" Lighter asked.

"Not planning on it," Krennicx responded.

"I don't think we've ever been in there during your meeting before," Tortoise said.

"And that will continue because I do NOT want any of you in there," Krennicx responded.

"What? Are you embarrassed by us?" Glider chimed in at the doorway.

"Well, perfect," Krennicx said, "you just so happen to show up at this exact moment."

"I have perfect timing," Glider smirked, "but don't change the subject. Are you?"

"Of course not!" Krennicx said. "I just know exactly what would happen if you guys were in there."

"Which is……?" Glider asked.

"None ya business," Krennicx responded. "Now, if you wake up and I'm not here, don't touch anything except for the pantry and the fridge in the kitchen. Got that, Glider?"

"Ok, I won't touch anything except for food," Glider responded, annoyed.

"And don't pour any of the food on anything either!" Krennicx called, walking away.

"Oh, come on! How did you know I was going to do that?" Glider called angrily.

"Night, Glider!" Krennicx called back.

Glider moaned, "How does he always know what I am going to do?"

"Maybe you're getting a little predictable," Tortoise suggested.

"No, I'm not!" Glider interjected. "Just you wait, I'm get'n him tonight."

"Ok…" Lighter said.

"What's going on between you guys?" Jacob asked.

"I don't want to talk about it," Glider said.

"Ok," Jacob said.

"Welp," Tortoise yawned, "I'm going to go ahead and get in bed. Night guys." Tortoise hopped sleepily onto the bottom bunk on the right side of the room.

"Alright," Lighter said, "I guess we all should."

Lighter climbed onto the top of Tortoise's bunk, leaving Glider and Jacob with one left.

"Top or bottom?" Jacob asked, knowing which one he wanted.

"What do you think?" Glider asked, climbing on the ladder to the top.

"Oh...ok," Jacob said.

"Hey, Jacob, can you turn off the light right there?" Tortoise asked, sleepily pointing to the knob on the wall.

"Ok," Jacob said, turning it.

Hey, this is actually a pretty comfy bed, Jacob thought in relief, putting his blanket on top of him.

"Ah," Glider said, finally laying down above him.

"Oh, Glider! *EW!*" Lighter shrieked when there was a terrible smell in the room.

"That wasn't me!" Glider rejected. "Wait a minute! This is the same stink bomb I put in Krennicx's room!"

"Unpredictable, huh?" Tortoise asked, covering his nose and making his voice sound funny.

"Man, that is like the worst smell ever," Jacob said, covering his noise.

"It should be," Glider said, "I made it."

"Not helping!" Lighter said.

"Whoo, man this is bad," Glider said.

"Ya think?" Jacob responded.

They all moaned and hid under their blankets for the rest of the miserable night.

It might have been because of the terrible smell or the fact that he was flying through space as to why Jacob's dreams were full of poisons, crashes, and death. The smell definitely didn't help with his nightmares. At one point it felt like the stink bomb was the smell of blood. Jacob shot up and banged his head on the top bars. He clutched his head and laid back. "Ow," Jacob said, rubbing his head. He felt his stomach growl in hunger. *Krennicx did say to just go eat.* He slowly and quietly got out of the bed and tip-toed out of the room, trying not to wake anyone up.

"What are you doing up so early?"

"Ah!" Jacob shrieked in surprise.

"Are you always an early waker?" Krennicx asked.

"Do you always sneak up on people?" Jacob asked.

Krennicx only smirked.

"It's a little creepy."

Krennicx smiled, "Why are you up so early?"

"I don't know," Jacob responded. "Sometimes I just wake up from....."

"Dreams?" Krennicx guessed.

"Yeah."

"Dreams are a strange thing," Krennicx said. "Sometimes they are ones that you like and don't want to wake up from. Others are full of ultimate horror, and some..... possibly even your past... the worst of them all."

"Yeah," Jacob said. "Do you understand them?"

"It's not something that you can just study," Krennicx responded. "Best to talk about it another day, but to answer your question: no."

"Ok, where did you say the kitchen was?"

"I'll show you," Krennicx said, leading the way. Jacob followed Krennicx along the hall.

"Is the BeetleWing the only ship there is?" Jacob asked.

"Hmm? No," Krennicx answered. "No, there are actually a lot of ships, but none are as fast as this."

"Really?" Jacob asked. "You sure?"

"Absolutely positive," Krennicx said, patting the wall.

So, a lot of dragons have ships? Jacob thought, horrified. "Did you make it?" Jacob asked.

"In a way," Krennicx responded, "but I didn't design it or put it all together. But I did finish it."

"Cool," Jacob said, thinking of what Krennicx just said. "So, did you make the engine?"

"I guess you can say that" Krennicx responded. *I should tell King Luther that.*

"Did you already eat?" Jacob asked.

"No, but I'm about to."

"I thought you were eating breakfast with someone?"

"Supposed to," Krennicx answered, smiling.

"What is that supposed to mean?"

"It means it's none of your business," Krennicx responded.

"Of course," Jacob accidentally said out loud.

Krennicx smiled, "Here, this is for you." Krennicx handed him a small bag.

"What is it?" Jacob asked. *Wait…where did this come from? He wasn't holding it or anything. How did he just hand it over?*

"Well, I was thinking… now that you are probably being hunted by the Cloud Dragons….. it'd be really easy for them to find you if you were wearing the same clothes so…… I hope you like black, cuz that's the only color I have," Krennicx said, smiling.

"Wait," Jacob said in excitement, "is that what is black?"

"Nope."

"Of course it's not," Jacob said, rolling his eyes. He was never going to play Eye Spy with Krennicx *ever* again.

"But it is yours," Krennicx said.

"Thanks. It doesn't have a tracking device on it, does it?"

"Huh, I never thought about that," Krennicx said thoughtfully.

Is he joking?

"Well, the kitchen is in there," Krennicx said, nodding to the door in front of them, "but I should probably get going."

"Hey, Krennicx," Glider said sneakily behind him.

"Yeesh," Krennicx turned around nervously. "Glider……. What are you doing up?"

"Trying to leave so soon, are we?" Glider questioned.

"Whaaaaaaat?" Krennicx asked nervously. "Why would you think that?"

"Oh, I don't know……. Maybe the fact that you just so happen to ask for the meeting to be early enough for us to still be asleep?" Glider said.

"You better not think you're coming with me," Krennicx said.

"Oh, I don't think," Glider said, "I know."

Krennicx did a small laugh, then quickly sprinted away.

"After him!" Glider shouted.

"But I'm hungry," Jacob said. Glider ignored him and chased after Krennicx. Jacob moaned and sleepily ran after them.

Krennicx ran across the ship and into the pilot area where the way out was.

"Hey Krennicx," Lighter said, standing in front of the door, "going somewhere?"

Glider ran to a stop behind them, "Told ya you're not going anywhere without us."

"No, no, no," Krennicx said miserably. "You can't come!

"Can and am," Glider said. "Isn't that right?"

"Yep," Ben said.

"*Ben!*" Krennicx yelped in betrayal.

"What? I've never been in any of your meetings with her before," Ben said.

"The one time you actually want to be in one of my meetings!" Krennicx said.

"So, Krennicx," Glider said, "why are we going to Sunny's palace?"

CHAPTER 13

SUNNY'S PALACE

Jacob was surprised at how beautiful the kingdom was. Most of it seemed to be a massive beach with huge palm trees everywhere, but there was still plenty of grass and fields. Sunny's palace stood facing the beach. It was big and beautiful with white bricks and pink swirls. Jacob noticed that with all of the kingdom's beauty, it seemed relatively small.

"Is this the whole kingdom?" Jacob asked as they left the BeetleWing.

"Yeah, it's not the biggest anymore," Lighter responded, "but it is the calmest."

"What is this place called again?" Jacob asked.

"It's called many different things," Lighter said, "but it's official name is Sunillia."

"Where are all of the guards?" Jacob asked, noticing that there weren't anyone around.

"Yeah, that's the thing about this kingdom," Lighter said.

"What?"

"You'll see."

Krennicx led the way to the gate of the palace, while Glider kept asking him annoying questions.

"Why are you walking so slowly, Krennicx?" Glider asked. "Why do you walk with your front claws first? Why are you growling? Why are we going this way? Why did you just look behind you? Why are you taking deep breaths Krennicx? Why are we here? Huh? Why, Krennicx? Why? Why?"

"Shut up!" Krennicx snapped.

Glider held in a laugh, but in his eyes, Jacob could tell that he was totally horrified.

"I'm here to see Sunny," Krennicx said—still annoyed from Glider—to a dragon in the gate box.

"Okie dokie, artichokie," a voice from the box said. "You don't have to tell me, the gate is open to anyone."

"Yeah, great," Krennicx said a little sarcastically. "Would you... by any chance take them to one of the guest rooms?" Krennicx asked.

"Everyone is welcome to meet her," the dragon responded. "I think she'd love to see them."

"Really?" Krennicx asked miserably. Glider started to laugh but stopped when Krennicx looked at him.

"Walk in whenever you're ready," the dragon's voice said cheerfully.

"Alright," Krennicx said eagerly, "no matter what happens in there, Don't. Say. A. Word. You got that Glider?"

"Why do you always look at me?"

"Ya got that?" Krennicx asked again.

"Alright, fine," Glider said.

"Good," Krennicx said. "Same goes for all of you."

"Ok," Sky said.

Krennicx took a deep breath, then opened the gate to the palace.

Jacob was surprised to immediately see the Queen in the first room. It was a large room layered with seashells and pink corals. At the end was a giant pile of pillows instead of a throne, where a dragon lay.

"Not. A. Word," Krennicx murmured.

The dragon on the pillows slowly sat up and looked at them. *Now that is Hazel's dream kind of dragon*. The dragon was a sunset yellow with some pink here and there. It had red feathers around its head, feet, and tail. It looked like a piece of a sunset.

Her face brightened tremendously. "Krennicx! I was wondering when you were going to come back," she said brightly.

Krennicx took a deep breath, then bowed deeply, "Bonjour, Your Majesty," he said extremely politely. "How are you this fine morning?"

Everyone's jaw dropped.

Queen Sunny's face brightened, "Queen Icicle told me she was going to send someone, but she didn't say it was going to be you." She stood up and continued to smile.

"I hope I am of no disappointment," Krennicx said calmly.

Everyone turned slowly to each other in pure shock.

"No, I'm rather pleased for it to be you, you are most definitely the most polite," Queen Sunny said.

"Heh," Glider said, disbelievingly.

"Prince Glider and Princess Glazer, what a pleasant surprise," Sunny said, noticing their presence. "We've met before, right?"

"Yes, ma'am…" Glazer said, trying to recover from Krennicx, "we were here last month."

"Hmm, must have slipped my mind," Sunny said thoughtfully. "Now you two, I don't believe I've met," she said, looking at Jacob and Sky.

"As much as I would love to introduce you," Krennicx said, still so polite, "I believe we have some business to attend to this fine morning?"

"Of course!" Queen Sunny said. "The tea table is now set."

"He *does* have an accent," Jacob said quietly. "I knew it."

"Yeah, but it's not that kind," Glider whispered.

"Then what is it?" Jacob asked.

"No idea," Ben whispered, "but from the moment I met him I *knew* he had to have some kind of accent."

"Has he ever told you?" Jacob whispered.

Ben shook his head.

"Tea, Your Highness?" Krennicx asked.

"Of course!" Queen Sunny said. "Surely you and your friends are starving."

You have no idea, Jacob thought. Last time he ate was lunch in the Sky Kingdom.

"I would hate to interrupt your very lovely morning," Krennicx said.

"Oh nonsense," Queen Sunny responded, "you are my guest, and as such you must be fed appropriately."

"Did you know he could talk like that?" Glider asked Ben.

"I've known Krennicx for ten years," Ben said slowly, "he's *never* said 'fine morning'."

"At least we're going to eat because I am starving," Jacob whispered to Lighter.

Lighter nodded.

Krennicx must have known that there was no way out of breakfast, because he kept silent.

"I didn't know there was going to be more of you," Queen Sunny said, "I'm afraid everyone might not get their own chair." She nodded towards a long table in the corner. *Ya think?* Jacob thought, noticing that there were only two chairs.

"Well, then it appears they might need to go to the dining room," Krennicx said.

Sunny opened her mouth to say something but was interrupted by Glider. "We can sit on the floor," Glider suggested, eyeing Krennicx.

"That's an amazing idea!" Queen Sunny said. "In fact, I can lower the table, and we can all sit on the floor!"

"Perfect!" Krennicx said enthusiastically, but in his eyes, he was *miserable*.

"I know, right!" Sunny said, not noticing Krennicx's misery.

Jacob sat with his stomach growling at the table. *Give the food already!* Jacob thought in misery. Sunny sat at the end of the table with Krennicx at the side.

"So Glider," Queen Sunny said politely, "how has the kingdom been?"

Glider wasn't paying any attention, well, at least he wasn't saying anything. *Probably because Krennicx said not to talk,* Jacob realized.

"Ahem," Krennicx said, "Prince Glider, the Queen asked you a question."

"Hmm?" Glider said, giving Krennicx a sneaky look, "I'm sorry Your Majesty, but I was told not to talk."

"Well, whoever told you that is mistaken," the Queen said. "Go ahead, Glider."

"Mistaken, huh?" Glider glared at Krennicx. The smile that was glued to Krennicx's face twitched for a second. "But if you insist, it has been great. In fact, I am preparing for the race. And of course..... as usual....... I'm gonna win."

"Everybody wins, don't they?" Sunny asked.

Glider raised an eyebrow, "Uh.... No."

"Well, that's odd," Sunny said. "Here, everyone wins, and no one is an L word."

"L word?" Glider asked in shock.

The Queen nodded, "We don't dare say that word."

"Ya mean loser?" Glider asked.

Sunny gasped, "My, my, such language!"

Glider's jaw was open with his face blank. "You do realize," Glider said with a sneaky smile, "if everyone wins, then everyone los..."

"This is Jacob and Sky, Your Majesty," Krennicx quickly jumped in before Glider could finish. "If you can, Sky actually has a wound that needs to be tended to."

"Oh," Queen Sunny said, "what kind?"

Krennicx thought for a second. "A very fast moving small thing hit him in the shoulder," he somewhat answered.

"Oh," Sunny responded, "how did that happen?"

"It was an accident, Your Majesty," Sky said calmly. "They didn't mean to hit my shoulder."

"Oh, poor thing, he must feel so guilty!"

"I'm sure he does," Sky said with a nod.

"Well, we shall get right on to that shoulder, right after tea, of course."

"Tea?" Krennicx either asked or commented. Jacob couldn't tell.

"The usual, of course," Queen Sunny said.

"Of course," Krennicx said.

Glider laughed silently as Sunny and Krennicx grabbed a cup.

"What?" Jacob whispered.

"Krennicx all caps *HATES* tea," Glider said, still laughing. "This just keeps getting better and better."

"Cheers to the fact that Queen Icicle always just so happens to send you whenever she needs me for something," Queen Sunny said, holding up the teacup.

"I am the most lucky man in the world," Krennicx said, clinking the teacup against hers. Krennicx took a deep breath and drank the tea down. At that point everyone but Sky was laughing extremely quietly at Krennicx's facial expression. He was obviously disgusted but was hiding it *very* well. Whenever Sunny would look at him he'd smile like nothing happened.

"So, who wants to hear about my beautiful plants?" Queen Sunny asked.

Krennicx burst into their room and ran to the fountain, dunking his head into it.

Glider burst out laughing, "That was hilarious!"

"Ew, ew, ew, *EW,*" Krennicx said, lifting his head out. "That was horrible."

"That was awesome!" Glider corrected, still laughing.

"The tea or my misery?" Krennicx asked, lifting his soaking wet head out of the water.

"Your misery!"

"Oh really, huh?" Krennicx shook his face violently, splashing water onto Glider.

"Ew!" Glider yelped, rubbing his face. "Keep your kitty water to yourself!"

"*Kitty?!*" Krennicx barked. His somewhat normal raspy voice was back.

"When were you going to tell us that you could talk...... er....... Etiquette?" Ben asked.

Krennicx growled, "Just because I haven't been to school in ten years don't mean I don't know a thing!"

"Only ten years?" Glider asked.

"School?" Jacob asked.

"Yes, Jacob," Krennicx said, aggravated, "dragons have school too. And yes, Glider *and* Jacob, I have been to school before."

"But I didn't think you were a dragon," Jacob said.

"I ain't!"

"Then why were you at a dragon school?"

"Well, why are you at a Dragon Queen's palace?"

Jacob paused and kept his mouth shut. "Now," Krennicx said, "I will be going to the bathroom and gargling for around thirty minutes." Krennicx calmly went through a door and shut it.

"I actually thought that tea was delicious," Glazer said quietly.

"I heard that!" the voice of Krennicx called.

"We know!" Glider called back.

"Wow," Jacob said, looking around. "This is a nice place." Even though the color was white and pink, it was nice. The fact that there was a big water fountain in the middle of the room was a little odd. There were a couple of half-circle, red pieces of furniture around the fountain. There were also a lot of wide openings to bedrooms around the room. Jacob counted five. At the end of the room was a big sliding glass door to the outside patio. Flowers twisted along the wooden railings and up the wall.

"Wow," Jacob said, walking onto the patio, looking out towards the massive, beautiful beach and palm trees.

"It's pretty, isn't it?" Lighter asked, walking up next to him.

"Yeah," Jacob responded. "Where are all of the dragons?"

"Probably in the palm trees, asleep," Ben said from inside.

"Hey look, Tortoise, there's your beach you were wanting," Jacob said.

"No!" Tortoise shrieked. "You can't make me!" He dove underneath a sofa and covered his face with his wings.

"Make you?" Jacob asked. "What's wrong with that beach?"

"We don't speak of it," Glider said disgustedly.

"Why? What's wrong with it?"

"Lighter," Ben said, "I'm not sure if he's ready yet."

"Ready for what?" Jacob asked, badly wanting to know.

"For the worst battle you ever heard," Krennicx said behind them.

"Battle for what?" Jacob asked, jumping in surprise a little.

"The only thing every kingdom wants," Krennicx responded. "Power, respect, land. Otherwise known as…. Annorlia…. And everything in it."

Jacob's heart pounded in fear. *Is he referring to my king and kingdom?*

If he is, than he's going to be the first King Luther wants to….. Krennicx's eyes met Jacob's, then chills went through his body and Jacob gulped in fear. *No! My king is different…..right?*

Jacob was silent and didn't say anything.

"Is anyone else still hungry?" Tortoise asked, getting up from the floor and breaking the silence.

"For good food, yes," Krennicx said.

I am still extremely hungry, Jacob thought.

"Yeah, me too," Lighter said.

"I would love to sneak out, get some fried chicken, and never come back," Krennicx said.

"Krenn*icx!*" Lighter said in a funny way.

"Just being honest."

"I can take the BeetleWing and get some," Ben volunteered.

"No!" Everyone except Jacob said at the same time.

"Oh, come on!" Ben said.

"I'll just be right back," Krennicx said. He flared his wings and took off *fast* from the deck.

"He really likes fried chicken," Lighter said.

"Yep," Ben agreed.

"I hope Sky's ok," Glazer said, worried.

"You always worry so much," Ben said.

"What? No I don't."

"Yeah, you kind of do," Ben said. "I'm sure he's going to be fine. The Sun Dragons are like the best doctors in Annorlia."

"Oh."

The Cloud Dragon had already gone to the doctors. They didn't know how long he'd be gone. Jacob wondered about Sky and who he spies for. *The dragons? But that wouldn't make any sense, why would he be at a dragon kingdom? And how would he even be able to spy on the humans? That would be impossible!* Jacob wondered why he never thought of that. *How is he a spy if he isn't in the human kingdom? Well, I guess I'm in the dragon kingdom as a spy, but dragons are much more stupid than humans. Especially considering that they are letting me stay with them.*

"You seem quiet," Lighter observed while Jacob was in deep thought.

"Hm? No, I'm fine," Jacob said.

"You sure?" Lighter asked.

"Yeah," Jacob said. "So what all is there to do here?"

"This isn't exactly what I had in mind," Jacob said in a hammock high in a tree. Other than flying on top of Glider and King Luther's castle, this was the highest he had ever been in his life.

"Welcome to the life of the Sun Dragons," Glider said in a different hammock.

"What does that mean?" Jacob asked.

"Glider……" Lighter warned.

"What? It's true," Glider said. "The Sun Lazies are always sleeping." Lighter kicked Glider's hammock, causing it to tip over. "Oi!" Glider said after he caught himself in the air.

"Glider," Glazer said as if he was in trouble.

"It's true!" Glider defended. "They are ALWAYS sleeping and you know it!"

"Well…. It's just…… that doesn't mean you have to……… well…….what's the word?" Glazer said, thinking.

"Say it out loud?" Tortoise asked, relaxing in a hammock.

"Yeah! Yeah, that's it," Glazer said.

"But we all know it," Glider said, getting back in the hammock.

No one responded.

"What do Sun Dragons do?" Jacob asked.

"Absolutely nothin," Glider said.

"They sleep under the sun," Glazer said, ignoring Glider, "except for sunrise and sunset."

"See? Exactly what I mean," Glider said.

"But," Glazer added, "they actually need to so they can get all of their energy."

"But they don't use it for anything."

"Glider!"

After a long, boring time on the hammocks, Ben suggested to play some weird game called circle-square.

"Circle-square?" Jacob asked. "But that doesn't even make any sense."

"Does football?" Ben asked.

"Uh……. Yeah," Jacob said. "I love football."

"Well, that explains a few things," Ben grumbled.

"What things?" Jacob asked.

Ben didn't say anything.

"I like football," Tortoise said.

"Yep, yep you do," Ben said, glancing away.

"We should probably explain to you how this works first," Lighter said, changing the subject. "Let's see where's a good place…" Lighter looked around, then ran over to a large patch of flat grass right before the start of the beach. "This should be good."

"Ok," Ben said, "this isn't going to be as good as usual because we don't have everything like what we normally do, but this *should* still be fun." Ben pulled out a strange, black, pen-like thing that put out a huge square hologram onto the middle of the small field. Each corner was separated with a line, making a diamond shape inside the square. Inside the diamond shape was a circle. Glider, Lighter, Glazer, Tortoise, and Ben touched the hologram. To Jacob's surprise, somehow the circle in the middle of the hologram turned into a large circular stand. "Alright, here's how it works," Ben said. "A team of four will have one member on each corner. And then a team of two will have one on the circle and one in the diamond. The rules are simple. The first team has to hit the one in the middle with a ball without stepping over their line. If you do, you're out. The one in the middle has to dodge the four balls while the one in the diamond has to protect the middle, catching the balls and throwing it back at the other team. Anyone hit with the ball, except for the one in the diamond, is out. The game is over whenever the one in the circle is hit or all four of the other team is out."

"So…. It's a little bit like dodgeball," Jacob said.

"No, it's nothing like dodgeball," Ben said, seriously.

"Where are the balls?" Jacob asked.

"Hold out your hand," Ben said weirdly.

"Ok….," Jacob said, holding out his hand. Ben attached a strange metal band to Jacob's wrists. "Sooo now what?"

"Tap them against each other."

"Whoa," Jacob said after he did it. The same kind of hologram appeared on Jacob's wrists like a glove, then a small, red, glowing holographic ball appeared in his hand.

"Still think it's like dodge ball?" Ben asked.

"So who's going to play against who?" Glazer asked.

"I don't know, but I do know who ever it is, I'm going to kick their butts," Glider said.

"Really, eh?" Ben said. "Well, in that case, I know exactly who should play who."

"How many times do I have to tell you!?" Glider asked for the thousandth time. *"Dodge* the ball!"

"I'm trying!" Jacob yelped on top of the circle platform. *How is this thing holding me up?*

"Well, try harder," Glider said, very strongly reminding Jacob of Michael.

"I'm not good at this!" Jacob said.

"I've noticed."

"I thought you said whoever it is you'd kick their butts?" Tortoise asked from his corner.

"How can I kick anyone's butt if his butt keeps getting hit with a ball?" Glider asked.

"Well, this butt would happily throw the ball!" Jacob said.

"Nah, your butt's good where it is," Ben said from his corner.

Jacob moaned quietly. *This seems like a pretty fun game,* Jacob thought, *too bad I'm just terrible at it.*

"Alright, you guys ready?" Ben asked.

"Ready to do all the work," Glider murmured.

"Ok," Ben said. "Three, two, one."

"Who's hungry?" Krennicx asked in the diamond next to Glider.

"AAAAAH!" Everyone shrieked at the same time in surprise.

"How do you even do that?!" Ben asked.

"Where did you even come from!?" Glider asked.

"Uh… Annorlia," Krennicx responded in an obvious tone.

"But you weren't right here a second ago!" Glider said.

"Or was I?" Krennicx asked with a grin. "Who's hungry?"

All in all, Jacob had a strange day. After everyone finally stopped asking Krennicx how in the world he sneaks up on everyone, Jacob was finally able to eat…….. fried chicken. Now Jacob laid in a real bed in his own room (that, he was very happy about) in their guest apartment. Jacob stared down at the tracker King Luther had given him. He had no idea how it got there, but Jacob found it in his pocket. Why would Krennicx give it back? He tried not to think about it. *What all should I say? Can this thing even do a long text?* Jacob took a deep breath, then began to type out everything onto the tracker: Dear King Luther, I am very happy to inform you that I am alive and well. Michael and I were separated when we entered the Dragon Forest, or in rather when one of the dragons named Lighter kidnapped me. The day before yesterday we went to the Cloud Kingdom, where I met a dragon spy named Sky and the king tried to kill me. But for some reason this talking panther sacrificed himself and saved my life, showing everyone that he is really the criminal called Severein. There's a lot of things I need to tell you, so be prepared for a very long report.

Then Jacob typed out everything he learned.

Jacob woke up to see bright red eyes right in front of him, "AH!" He shrieked.

"Oh, hey young'n," Krennicx said calmly, as if *sitting* on someone was normal.

"What in the world are you doing?!"

"I didn't think you'd want to miss breakfast," Krennicx said, tilting his head. "Of course, I want to."

"What?" Jacob was starting to feel Krennicx's heavy weight.

"Although, my aunt used to say, 'breakfast fixes your mind for the day,'" Krennicx said thoughtfully.

"You must never eat breakfast," Jacob said.

Krennicx gave him a funny smile, "Welp, come along young'n." Krennicx hopped off Jacob's chest and left the room.

"Ow," Jacob squeaked, quietly laying back.

"And then when I found the poor little thing," Queen Sunny said sniffling, "it was too late." She wiped her teary eyes, "The mosquito was already dead."

"Such a terrible loss," Krennicx said, patting her hand. His eyes were teary and his face looked like he was holding back from sobbing.

"Nice to have someone who understands," Sunny said, starting to cry. "I'll be right back, I think the coffee is ready," Sunny said, running out of the dining room.

Everyone looked at each other, then burst into laughing.

"Oh and Krennicx," Sunny said, poking her head back into the room. Everyone's lips slammed closed. "Do you want the pink cup or the purple cup?"

"Either is quite fine," Krennicx responded as if nothing just happened.

"Ok," Sunny smiled, then left again.

Everyone continued to laugh but a lot quieter.

"Are you *crying*?" Glider asked.

"If laughing was crying," Krennicx said, "then yes."

"Man, do you know how many mosquitos I've killed over the years?" Ben asked.

"Don't tell her that!" Krennicx said.

"What? You've done it too," Ben accused.

"Of course I've done it, who doesn't?"

"Have a good night's sleep, Jacob?" Glazer asked, changing the subject.

"I guess," Jacob responded, thinking back to last night. *I wonder if he got the message?*

"Have you heard anything from Sky yet?" Glazer asked.

"Nah, not yet," Krennicx responded. "My guess is that they're not letting him come down because he needs to rest."

"What exactly happened to him?" Jacob asked.

"Something hit him in the shoulder."

"Seriously?" Jacob asked, annoyed.

"Seriously," Krennicx smirked."Ok, I'm back," Queen Sunny said, walking back into the room holding a tray of coffee.

"Great," Krennicx said, amazingly sounding happy.

"Now the pink and the purple cup were dirty, so I got the bedazzled one instead," Sunny said, handing the cup to him.

"Oh, that's awesome," Krennicx said, everyone but Sunny knew he was being sarcastic. "I just love sparkly cups with… coffee… in it."

"Oh, that just points out how well I know you!" Queen Sunny said. "I knew you'd love it!"

Glider choked on his coffee in laughter.

Girl, you don't know him at all.

"Oh, is that a new portrait?" Krennicx asked. "I don't remember that one being there before."

"Oh, I'm so glad you noticed!" Queen Sunny said happily. "I actually just finished it last night."

Whoa, Jacob thought, looking at the big painted picture on the wall, *how can it only be a whole bunch of splatters…… but yet look so terrible?*

"I mean look at it," Krennicx said, sounding impressed, "it has so many colors."

"It does, doesn't it," Sunny said, admiring her artwork. Jacob started to stare at the picture like everyone else for a few seconds, but something Krennicx did caught his attention. In a swift movement Krennicx dumped the coffee into a potted plant behind him, then reached underneath his chair and pulled out a cup with some different kind of hot liquid in it. He poured what was in the other cup into the now empty one, then winked at Jacob.

"Well, enough about that," Queen Sunny said, turning back around. "Cheers to this wonderful day, and for safe travels."

"Cheers," Krennicx said, clinking their cups. Krennicx smirked a smile as he drank his cup that Jacob knew was not coffee.

CHAPTER 14

RETURN TO THE DRAGON FOREST

"Now make certain she sends you next time," Queen Sunny said as they prepared the BeetleWing.

"I shall do my best," Krennicx said with a bow. "Now, are you sure Sky's not ready to leave yet?"

"Of course!" Queen Sunny responded. "The poor guy's wound nearly hit his spinal cord; he's very fortunate to be alive."

"I'm sure in your hands he'll be just fine," Krennicx said.

"Well, *my* hands would most likely not be the best, but I know that my doctor's hands are."

"Thank you," Krennicx said with *another* bow. "Let me know whenever he's ready."

"I'll try my best," Queen Sunny said, returning the bow. "It just might take a while for the letter to deliver."

"You can send a text," Krennicx pointed out.

"Oh silly willy, you know a single text message is terrible for the environment," Sunny said, as if she knew Krennicx was joking. "Paper is the only thing I trust."

Krennicx's face was frozen, "Of... course."

"Bye, Krennicx," Sunny said as they entered the BeetleWing.

"Bye, Karen," Krennicx said.

"Bye," Sunny said, as the BeetleWing lifted into the sky.

"I thought your name was Sunny?" one of the Sun Dragons next to her asked.

"Oh, he likes to call everyone by their middle name sometimes."

"But I thought….."

Sunny smiled as she watched the BeetleWing fly into space.

"Ah, home sweet home," Lighter said, walking out of the BeetleWing ramp in the Dragon Forest. "The Sun Kingdom is beautiful and all, but there's just something about forests that's so homey."

"What?!" Tortoise asked, walking out. *"Nothing* is more homey than an ocean."

"Both of you are wrong," Glider said. "The *only* places that are homey are places full of ice and snow."

"That's not true at all!" Tortoise yelped.

"You do realize that each one of you are going to like wherever your kind is from?" Krennicx asked.

"So…… what does *your* breed like?" Glider asked. As usual, Krennicx's face was blank and he just kept walking out of the BeetleWing. Everyone looked at Ben, who shrugged. *Does anyone know what he is?* Jacob wondered. They walked for a little while till they reached a small waterfall flowing into a little clearwater pool.

"Yes!" Tortoise said, immediately jumping into it.

"Tortoise, you do realize that's where a lot of dragons get their water, right?" Glider asked.

"Yep," Tortoise said, relaxing.

"Then why are you get'n yo yucky germs in the water I was about to drink?!"

"Glider does have a point on that one," Ben said.

"Thank you!" Glider said.

"Oh, relax," Krennicx said. "Just get it out of the waterfall before it gets to Tortoise." Krennicx tossed something to Jacob that hit him in the face.

"What was that?!" Jacob yelped.

"Oh, I thought you'd catch that," Krennicx said. "It's just a cup."

"Where does all of this stuff come from?" Jacob asked, picking the cup up from the ground. "And what were you drinking at Sunny's palace?"

"Not coffee, that's for sure!"

"Then what was it? Some kind of dragon drink?" Jacob asked.

"No," Krennicx said, "more like some kind of hot chocolate, otherwise known as regular hot chocolate."

"But that's so unhealthy!" Jacob said, curious to see if dragons hate sugar.

"Unhealthy?" Krennicx asked. "Un*healthy*? Dude, I run at *least* twenty miles a day, I don't think a little hot chocolate is gonna kill me."

"You drank her tea, why couldn't you drink her coffee?" Jacob asked.

"There's only one thing that's worse than tea, and that, dearie, is *coffee,*" Krennicx said. "Otherwise known as the worst tasting thing in the *universe.*"

"What?" Tortoise asked. "How could that possibly be the worst thing?"

"I bet there's *something* that you think is worse," Jacob said.

"You see, that's the thing," Krennicx said, *"nothing* is worse. It's by far the worst thing ever."

"I love coffee!" Tortoise said.

"I don't!" Krennicx mimicked.

"I'm sure you'd rather drink coffee instead of *something,*" Jacob said.

"Nope," Krennicx said. "I'd rather drink *anything.* I'd even rather drink the water that Tortoise is swimming in, and that's really saying something!"

"That's disgusting!" Glider yelped, grossed out.

"Not as disgusting as coffee!" Krennicx said. "And who are you to say that hot chocolate is too unhealthy? I saw you eat five rice cakes this morning!"

"I was hungry!" Jacob defended. "And I'm still hungry! And thirsty!"

"Here's your water, Mr. Thirsty," Krennicx said, dumping a cup of water on Jacob's face.

"Ew!"

"And that was Tortoise water."

Jacob groaned while he walked to the edge of the waterfall and filled his cup with its flowing water. Krennicx followed and did the same, "Ah, delicious, fresh, clear, un-Tortoise water," Krennicx said, taking a sip.

"Krennipoo?" a soft voice of a girl asked behind them.

Krennicx choked and nearly lost all the water in his mouth, "Oh *no."*

Tortoise quickly hopped out of the water and shook off.

"How long has it been since I've seen you?" the dragon asked, running up to them. She was completely black with purple eyes, and shape-wise looked somewhat similar to Lighter, except bigger.

"Matilda!" Krennicx said with a scared expression. "Hi….er…….how are you?"

"Extremely happy to see you!" Matilda said. She wrapped her arms and wings around Krennicx in what looked like a dragon hug.

"Let's not do that," Krennicx said, not moving at all and looking extremely uncomfortable. "Please let go. Ok, don't touch me. Seriously, just stop doing this." Krennicx stretched out his wings and gently pushed her away.

"Ok sweetie pie, I guess you're in a no touchy mood today," Matilda said.

"I'm kinda always like that. Especially with you," Krennicx responded, annoyed.

"Oh silly willy," Matilda said, ignoring him. "So what time are you coming to my party?"

"Party?" Krennicx asked. "What party?"

"The party I just told you about," Matilda said. "So you'll be bringing the snacks, mkay?"

"Not 'mkay,'" Krennicx said, "I'm not going to any of your parties."

"Um, sweetie, we talked about this. You are," Matilda corrected, sounding sassy.

"I didn't think Krennicx had a girlfriend," Jacob whispered to Lighter.

"He doesn't," Lighter whispered with a cold expression. "She's always had a massive crush on him and expects him to feel the same about her."

"She's a diamond digger," Glider whispered. *What in Annorlia is a diamond digger?*

"When exactly was this conversation?" Krennicx asked. "Cuz I don't remember that, and trust me…. I remember *everything*……and don't call me sweetie."

"Must have slipped your mind," Matilda said.

"I don't think it was ever *in* my mind," Krennicx said, sounding annoyed, but insanely stern.

"Well, I guess it is now, sweetie."

"Don't call me sweetie," Krennicx said sternly.

"Ok, honey," Matilda said.

"Don't call me honey," Krennicx said, still very stern.

"See you at the party Krennipoo!" Matilda said, lifting into the air.

"And don't you *DARE* call me Krennipoo!" Krennicx called angrily.

"Yeah! Krennipoop would be much better!!!" Glider called out. Everyone cracked up, hoping Krennicx wouldn't notice.

"Really, Glider?" Krennicx asked, sounding miserable.

Everyone was still cracking up, but then Krennicx started to crack up…..so…..then everyone lost it.

To Jacob's relief, another day passed with the dragons, and to Jacob's surprise, the day really didn't feel long…… except for the night, that was feeling very long. Jacob laid on the bare grass underneath a massive tree with so many leaves that it formed walls that went to the ground. Jacob groaned, rolling back and forth. *Why did they have to decide to sleep under a tree? There's so many big bumpy roots! And why are Tortoise's and Ben's snores so LOUD?!*

"Pssst."

Jacob looked up to see Krennicx dangling from his tail on one of the massive branches. "What?" Jacob asked.

"Come with me and I'll tell you everything you want to know," Krennicx said, then he disappeared into the branches. *Everything? Jacob thought. Anything I ask? Surely he's joking, but I guess it's worth the risk. I guess there really isn't a risk.* Jacob stood up and walked to the trunk of the tree. Looking up, it looked a lot bigger than Jacob thought. He gripped onto the hard bark and pulled himself up in between the split in the tree. Jacob prepared himself and jumped for the nearest branch and tried to grab onto it……well…..tried. Jacob immediately lost his grip and fell. In a swift movement, a sharp furry talon caught his hand and flung him up into the tree onto a branch. Jacob breathed hard as he held on for dear life.

"You have climbed a tree before, right?" Krennicx asked, already dangling above Jacob.

"Nothing like this!" Jacob said. *I guess the risk is falling. That's not bad at all!* Jacob thought sarcastically.

"Sure you can handle this?" Krennicx asked like he was talking to a little kid. *I can pretty much only see his eyes, but how do I just KNOW he's doing that little smirky smile he's annoyingly really good at?* Jacob ignored him and started to climb again. Again, Krennicx disappeared into the leaves. *He sure is a lot like a panther.* Jacob stopped high in the tree and looked up, "How much further?" Jacob stood up and looked around.

"Krennicx?" Jacob's foot slipped and he fell backwards. Krennicx instantly grabbed his hand and pulled him up next to him.

"Little word of advice," Krennicx said. "Don't stand while you are climbing in a tree, especially when you're a rookie."

"I'll try to remember that," Jacob said. Krennicx grabbed Jacob's hand again and jumped higher into the tree, dragging Jacob behind him, then pulled him next to him again. "Ok, you've got to quit doing that."

"If that's what you want." Krennicx disappeared again. *Wait, now where am I supposed to go?* Jacob looked around and noticed a wall of moss. *Does that go somewhere?* Jacob pushed the moss aside and climbed through.

"Whoa." The moon and stars shone brightly as Jacob stepped onto a strange deck high in the tree. The deck had moss and leaves layered on top, and it had no railings.

"Of all the beautiful places in Annorlia," Krennicx said, sitting at the very edge of the deck, "this might be my favorite."

"Did you make this?" Jacob asked, walking over to Krennicx.

"No…. I guess," Krennicx responded. "Well, I did, but not alone. My dad and I made it together. This was the only place I could come to that was even close to the village, but we could only come at night."

"Why?" Jacob asked. Krennicx looked at him in a way that said he didn't want to talk about it. "Oh, come on," Jacob said. "You said that you'd answer any question."

"Yes, but are you sure you want to waste it on my childhood?" Krennicx asked cleverly.

Whoa, nice move. He hated that Krennicx was right, but it was true. *Why would I want to waste it on Krennicx's past?*

"Ok," Jacob tried to remember everything he wanted to say. "How exactly did the war start?"

"Nice question," Krennicx said. "But in order to answer that, you'd have to know about the Diammonites."

"Ok," Jacob said, "then what are the Diammonites?"

"Aliens, but no one knows what they look like," Krennicx responded. "You see, they *look* kind of like dragons with armor on, but they're not from Annorlia."

"Where are they from?"

"A planet far away, but no one really knows where. One day they just attacked and killed every single Diamond Dragon."

"What are Diamond Dragons?"

"Ok, I'm just going to have to stop for a second," Krennicx said. "Before the Diammonites came, the Represenetor had three military forces."

"Represenetor?"

"Ok, High King."

"High King*?!*"

"Oh my *goodness!*" Krennicx said. "Look, Annorlia has three levels of authority; the Represenetor, the representatives, and kings and queens. There's one representative for every kingdom."

"What do they do?"

"I'm get'n there," Krennicx said. "The representative watches over the kings and queens, and the kings and queens watch over their subjects. Basically, whenever the representative feels that the king is making the wrong choice, he goes to the Represenetor."

"What does the Represenetor do?"

"Quit interrupting. If the Represenetor feels that it is needed, he will send in one of the three military forces: the Diamond Dragons, the Formwings, or the Golden Dragons. So, see it like this: the representative is there to make sure that the king won't make everyone do whatever he wants and enslave everyone."

"I guess that makes sense," Jacob said thoughtfully. "But then what does that make the Represenetor?"

"The Represenetor is over pretty much everything," Krennicx said. "The representatives and kings and queens answer to him. So, basically he's like the High King over *all* of Annorlia. Although, there are things that he couldn't do. Usually, everyone would meet up once a year to discuss everything."

"But then doesn't that mean the Represenetor can do whatever he wants with the military?"

"I have to say it is a very confusing and somewhat stupid setup," Krennicx responded. "But it worked for a long time.......until the Diammonites."

"What did they do?" Jacob asked.

"Nobody really knows exactly what happened," Krennicx said, "but we know they immediately killed the Diamond and the Golden Dragons, and stole their lands. Right after that, a few of the kings allied themselves with them, sparing their kingdoms. With their help, they murdered every representative they could find. It took them years for them to find the Formwings, but when they did.... no one was spared."

"What happened to the Represenetor?"

"No one heard from him for months," Krennicx responded, "but just as Annorlia was about to fall forever, a prophesied Fighter appeared, and Annorlia has been hanging on by a thread ever since."

"Is that the Fighter of Peace?" Jacob asked. "But I thought there were more than one."

"It didn't take long for the rest of them to be found," Krennicx said, smiling. "But even then, they're still having a pretty hard time."

"So, is the Represenetor dead?" Jacob asked.

"No one really knows," Krennicx answered. "But some think that the Represenetor *is* the Fighter, that's why some call him the Lightning Prince."

"So, the humans aren't the only ones at war?"

"All of Annorlia is at war with each other, whether they're humans or not," Krennicx said. "Anything else you want to know?"

"Hmm," Jacob said thinking, "I feel like I had so many questions to ask, but now I can't think of anything."

"Well, then I guess we're…"

"Wait," Jacob said, "what was Sky spying for?"

"Sky? Well, he…..er," Krennicx said, hesitating.

"Anything I want to know," Jacob reminded.

Krennicx sighed, "He kind of works for the Fighters of Peace. He's *highly* trained."

"Oh," Jacob said, "I guess that makes sense. So, why did *you* and Ben have to pick him up?"

"Because they told us to."

"What?! You *know* the Fighters of Peace?"

"Who doesn't?"

"So that's why they saved you!" Jacob realized out loud. "It wasn't because you were innocent!"

"Ouch."

"It was because you were doing what they said to do," Jacob continued, *"and* the reason they used you is because you're a criminal so no one would think anything about the Fighters of Peace! And if you *were* killed, they really wouldn't lose anything!"

"Huh," Krennicx said with his face blank, "way to go to make me feel unimportant."

Jacob laughed, "That makes sense, because I was wondering why it was you who came to pick him up. I guess at first you didn't want to go, so you just sent Ben, who failed, miserably."

"Are you a detective or something?" Krennicx asked, looking like he got caught. Jacob tried to copy Krennicx's smirky smile, but figured he failed miserably when Krennicx started laughing.

"How do you do that?" Jacob asked.

"Do what?"

"That smile you do all the time."

Krennicx gave him the smile, "Everyone always said that I was the master at facial expressions."

"Yes, but how do you *do* it?"

"I don't know," Krennicx said, shrugging. He stared at the stars. "First time in space, huh?"

"*Last* time in space," Jacob corrected.

Krennicx laughed, "That bad, eh? But you didn't even get to go to a planet."

"And throw up? No, thank you," Jacob responded

"Which one would you ever want to go to?" Krennicx asked.

"I don't know much about space stuff."

"Does school teach *anything*?" Krennicx asked.

"Yeah, misery," Jacob answered.

"Oh so true," Krennicx said, shaking his head. "You'll have to come to this one planet I found, it smells a lot there."

"What's it called?"

"Uranus."

"What?!" Jacob burst out laughing, "You're joking!"

"No."

"So there's *actually* a planet call Uranus?!"

"Yeah," Krennicx said, calmly smiling, "it's the most smelly one there is."

"No, Michael, I don't want to get up," Jacob sleep-talked, hugging his pillow. "I want to sleep on this soft pillow forever."

"AHHH!" Krennicx shrieked.

Jacob's eyes opened and he realized he was hugging Krennicx. "AHH!" Jacob screamed. Krennicx accidentally rolled over the edge of the deck, trying to get away.

"WHAT IN THE WORLD!" Krennicx yelled, hovering next to the deck. "Don't *DO* that! That's dis*GUSting*!"

"I didn't *mean* to!" Jacob said, standing up to Krennicx's eye level. "It is just as gross to me as it is for you!"

"Well, it's gross and you should *never* do that again."

"Trust me, I won't," Jacob responded, trying to rub his clothes clean.

They both moaned disgustedly.

"Oh that was the most disgusting thing *ever,*" Krennicx said, hours later as everyone walked along the trail.

"Will you *ever* get over it?" Jacob asked.

"It was *gross*."

"Hate to say it, but I'm with Krennicx on this one, that's gross." Glider winced, "That literally hurt to say."

"Not as much as it hurt to be hugged," Krennicx said, smiling.

"I don't see how this is a big deal," Glazer said.

"Of course you don't," Ben said, "you're a girl."

"And how does that have anything to do with this?" Glazer asked.

"Well, I mean come on! You hug Glider all the time," Ben pointed out.

"Yeah, because he's my brother," Glazer responded.

"And Glider just loves to be hugged," Ben said, patting Gilder's back.

"You touch me again and I'll punch you in the face," Glider threatened.

"Don't worry Ben," Krennicx said, "Glider's punch isn't that hard. It won't hurt."

"Oh, I'm not worried," Ben said calmly.

Glider growled, "Why does everything always come back to me?"

"Because you're you," Ben responded.

"What's *that* supposed to mean?"

Nobody responded as they just kept walking. Jacob was still unsure about everything Krennicx had told him last night. *It just doesn't make sense! Was he accusing that my king is a murderer? Was anything he said true? If so, then what does that make my king?*

"Oh, I love this spot!" Glider said as they walked off their trail to the left.

"Krennicx!" Ben said, realizing where they were. "Why?"

"Just because you can't fly doesn't mean nobody else can," Krennicx said.

"But Krennicx," Tortoise started.

"Just because you're afraid of heights doesn't mean that everyone else is," Krennicx said.

"What is it?" Jacob asked.

"The drop off," Lighter responded. They came out of the trees into a small patch of grass; the grass and the land dropped into a massive cliff.

"How high is this?" Jacob asked looking down the cliff, then took a few steps back when he felt queasy.

Glider shrugged, "I don't know, but I usually practice for my races in it."

"You mean you *jump* off?" Jacob asked.

"I am a dragon," Glider reminded.

"Ben, I forgot something in the BeetleWing, can you go get it?" Krennicx asked.

"You? Forgot something?" Ben said, surprised in a teasing way.

"Please."

"Fine." Ben turned around and walked back the way they came.

"Thank you!" Krennicx called.

"When's dinner?" Jacob asked.

"Oh yeah, that's what I forgot," Krennicx responded calmly.

"What!?" Everyone yelled miserably at the same time.

"How in the world can you forget that!" Glider asked unhappily. *Oh great, another day of starvation*, Jacob thought. *Although….. King Luther might have gotten my text……. So I might be going home as a hero today.* An odd stab of guilt hit Jacob. *Although, is it the right thing?* Jacob thought of everything Krennicx had said about the kings. *Is my king like that?* Jacob pushed the thought away. *No! My king is NOT like those stupid pathetic dragon kings! Why should we care about what's going on between the dragons and some sort of alien thing? Plus, we haven't done anything! But they've been burning down buildings for years! It's about time they pay!*

"Made up your mind?" the voice asked as the buzzing turned on.

"As a matter of fact, I have," Jacob thought in return. *"King Luther sent me as a spy to befriend and then betray the dragons, and I'm not going to disobey him."*

"But what about everything they told you about the war?"

"I'm sure that was either lies or not our problem, but I'm a human, not a dragon."

"So?"

"So I have to do what is best for my people, so why should I care about the dragons even if what they said is true? My brother was right, every dragon deserves to die."

"Are you sure?"

"Positive," Jacob thought, ignoring the small twinge of…no, he couldn't feel guilty.

"Then you have caused your wish to come true," the voice said. **"Enjoy."**

"Tortoise!" Glazer shrieked in horror. Tortoise fell to the ground, unconscious with a small strange arrow on the side of his neck. When Glazer knelt beside him, she too was struck by an arrow and fell unconscious. Glider growled in fury and tried to run to her, but Lighter quickly grabbed onto him and pulled him back.

"Glider, wait," Lighter said.

"Well, well, well," a very familiar voice said, "I knew you couldn't hide from me forever." With a crossbow in hand, King Luther walked out of the bushes and into the light.

"How *DARE* you do that to my sister!" Glider said angrily, nearly flinging Lighter off.

"Glider, stop," Lighter said firmly.

"Ah Jacob, my dear boy," King Luther said noticing Jacob. He walked over in front of them. "I was so happy to see your text, and that you are alive. We just had to come as soon as we could."

"What text?" Glider asked, looking furious.

"You see, my good boy Jacob here is such a loyal boy," Luther said. "He does everything he's told."

"Oh, you little backstabbing human!" Glider furiously broke away from Lighter and went for Jacob.

"Stop it," Krennicx said, quickly getting in between Glider and Jacob. "It's going to be ok," Krennicx said quietly.

"How?" Glider asked. Krennicx whispered something into Gliders ear. Glider took a deep breath, then nodded.

"Now there's the worthy opponent I've been looking for," King Luther said. "What to do, huh Severein? You escaped the Cloudairian King, but that doesn't mean you can escape me."

"What makes you think you're any different?" Krennicx Severein asked.

"Because I am prepared." Hundreds of soldiers in armor revealed themselves behind King Luther, with swords and bows in hand.

"What makes you think I can survive a Lyvith but not your soldiers?" Krennicx asked.

"You had help, and as far as I can tell," King Luther said, "no one is coming to help you, making this the end of this little war stage with the Peace Forest."

"If I know my village," Lighter said, "they won't surrender to you."

"So tell me, Jacob," King Luther said, walking over to him, "didn't you tell me the precise location of the dragon village and it's weaknesses?"

"You wouldn't," Lighter said, realizing what he was saying.

"Oh, but I would," King Luther said daringly. "Unless a certain hybrid surrenders." He turned to Krennicx.

"You know I will never surrender to you," Krennicx said calmly and sternly.

"Not to me," King Luther said. "But what about him?" King Luther, the king of the humans, kicked Jacob hard in the gut. Jacob fell back in shock and pain. As swift as a soldier, King Luther pushed Jacob over the side of the deep, dark cliff.

"No!" Lighter shrieked.

Glider ran for the edge, but Luther shot him with a sleep arrow before he could dive after Jacob. Then he put a blaster against Lighter's throat. "Which one Severein?" King Luther asked. "You know you can come back and save your *only* family, but the kid will be gone forever."

Krennicx looked concerned at Lighter. "You know what you have to do," Lighter said.

"Tic tock, tic tock, every second is a risk of his life," Luther reminded. Krennicx shook his face angrily at King Luther, then dove after the kid who betrayed him.

CHAPTER 15

THE ANSWER

Krennicx dropped Jacob onto the ground then angrily landed in front of him, not facing him. Jacob breathed hard in fear as he clutched the ground. The smell of smoke gagged him. "What just happened?" Jacob asked himself.

"What just happened? *What* just happened? I'll *tell* you what just happened," Krennicx said angrily. "You just gave Luther the one thing I worked for years to keep away from him."

"And what could that be? Defeat?"

"No, the only one I have that's even close to an actual son."

"And what is that supposed to mean?"

"Has it ever occurred to you why Lighter is a kid, but lives alone? Or why he *never* talks about family?" Krennicx asked. "It's because he doesn't have any! And do you want to know why?"

Jacob shook his head, "No, we'd never do anything like that. We would never leave a kid to die."

"And yet the king just tried to kill you," Krennicx said. "Luther betrayed Lighter's parents and killed them. After that, he was nearly smashed, that's why his wing is broken."

"And how did you not see this coming?" Jacob asked, standing up. "You had the tracker I used to tell him. You gave it back to me! How in the world did you not expect this? At the arena, you *said* I was sent here by King Luther."

"You see, you see that's the thing," Krennicx said. "I knew you were going to do this. I *knew* that you were going to allow Luther to take them, but, but I guess I figured you'd immediately regret it. I don't know, I guess I just thought you'd change after all of this, especially having a friend like Lighter."

"Krennicx, I..." Jacob started.

"Don't, just don't," Krennicx interrupted. "I've had enough of this. You can go home now. But what I do want to ask you this, what do you think the humans would gain with all dragons dead?"

"What are you going to do?" Jacob asked, not bearing to answer the question Hazel had always asked.

"Well, thanks to you, I have a massive forest fire to put out. Goodbye, Jacob Bennett." Krennicx spread his wings and took off into the sky and out of sight.

It was dark as Jacob tried to find his way home through the Dragon Forest. *What just happened?* Jacob thought, bewildered. *Why did my king try to kill me? What did I ever do to him? Could Krennicx actually be right? But why? Why would he do this?* Jacob looked back. *Should I go back? I don't think Krennicx put out the fire yet. I still smell smoke. Should I help him?* Jacob jumped when he heard a twig snap. "Krennicx? Is that you?" Jacob asked. There were growls as a dragon stepped out of a bush. "Oh, hello," Jacob said, stepping back in fear as the dragon got closer. "Can you talk?" The dragon continued to growl and walk closer. "Wait a minute," Jacob said, recognizing its dark blue scales. "You're that dragon I let out in the Cloud Kingdom, aren't you?" It stood up onto its back legs and acted like it was going to breathe fire. Just when Jacob thought it was the end, the dragon sat on the ground and stuck its tongue out and panted like a dog.

"What?" Jacob asked in shock. The dragon jumped onto Jacob and started to lick all over him like a happy, loving dog. Jacob realized its growls weren't growls at all, but purrs.

"Ok, ok, I think that's good," Jacob said, covering his face from the dragon's slobbering licks. It jumped off him and stood in front of him, still panting with his tongue out. "So, you don't want to eat me?" It tilted his head and looked at him curiously. "*Errr!* What am I supposed to do?" Jacob asked sitting on a log. "Is it possible that everyone *is* wrong about dragons?" The dragon sat down in front of him, staring into his eyes as it rested its snout on Jacob's legs. Jacob rubbed its head with his mind made up. "I have to make this right," he said, standing up. "Can you do me a favor and let me ride your back?" The dragon stood up and crouched in front of him. Jacob climbed on to his back and leaned forward. His hands grabbed onto two strange spikes on the back of its neck, pointing outward like a handle. A vision of a person dressed in black riding on the back of a dragon flashed in Jacob's head. *I wonder why he has this.* It was like the dragon used to have normal long spikes, but they got bent somehow. He held on tight and pulled up, trying to angle the dragon to the sky. The dragon's wings spread wide and they launched into the sky, causing Jacob to almost scream.

As the fire spread, Krennicx worked hard to protect as many things as he could from the devouring flames.

"Krennicx!" Jacob yelled as they flew above the fire.

"You shouldn't be here!" Krennicx called as he caught a branch before it could fall on a retreating fox.

"I tried to leave, but I couldn't stop thinking about everything you said!" Jacob said. "You were right, not all dragons are bad!"

"I can see that," Krennicx said, flying in front of him.

"I'm sorry! I never should have gotten myself into something I didn't fully understand!" Jacob confessed. "And I didn't know about Lighter's parents, I'm so sorry. I knew they were gone but I didn't know it was Luther who killed them. I guess all this time I thought this war was the dragons' fault, but I guess it was the human's."

"It has never been the human's fault," Krennicx said, his accent was bleeding through. "The truth has been hidden from them for years."

"Then I guess it's time for us to put an end to Luther's lies," Jacob said.

Krennicx smiled, "I guess it is."

"We can't save the dragons if there isn't a dragon home."

"I have an idea about that," Krennicx said. "Go to the village and ask them to gather as much Zillow plants they can find."

"Wait a minute," Jacob said, "what happened to the whole dragons hate humans?"

"I think they'll like you more than me," Krennicx said.

"Yeah, I guess that's true," Jacob said.

"Plus, dragons don't dislike humans. A lot of people actually live here."

"What?!" Jacob yelped.

"Do you think you can find your way to the village?" Krennicx asked, cutting him off.

"Probably not," Jacob answered.

"I wasn't talking to you," Krennicx said. The dragon did a small roar that Krennicx seemed to understand. "Good luck," Krennicx said. The dragon closed its wings, then flew fast through the fiery forest with Jacob absolutely terrified. They came up to the village that seemed to be unharmed.

"Excuse me!" Jacob called. "We need to find as much Zillow plants as possible!"

"Why in Annorlia do you need Zillow plants?" one of the dragons asked. All of the dragons were shiny black, similar to Lighter.

"It will help with the fire!" Jacob answered.

"Help?!" a different dragon asked. "Child, don't you know that the Zillow is highly flammable?!"

"All I know is that someone told me to get it," Jacob responded.

"Who?" the first dragon asked.

"Er...," Jacob hesitated on which name he should say, *Krennicx having two names is confusing.* "Krennicx?" Jacob responded hesitantly.

The dragon thought for a second, then nodded, "Come with me." He spread his wings and took off with Jacob following. "Can I trust you to not show any of this to anyone?" the dragon asked as they flew. Jacob thought for a second, then nodded. Jacob was terrified as they flew fast through the dark forest where fire somehow hadn't reached yet. For some reason they dove down towards something he couldn't see; it felt like they were in a tunnel. There was the sound of a waterfall as the tunnel came out to a huge cavern with a gigantic waterfall. *How in Annorlia are there so many tunnels here?!*

"Hope you don't mind getting wet!" the dragon called out, heading towards the waterfall. Jacob ducked as they flew into the hard beating water. They came out into a massive cave lit with torches.

"How many does Krennicx need?" the dragon asked, landing on the ground with water dripping off his scales.

"He said as much as we can get," Jacob responded, flicking his wet hair out of his eyes.

"Well, hope this is enough," the dragon said, unlocking a chest right at the edge of the cave where it was wet.

"Why does that chest have holes?" Jacob asked.

"If the Zillow isn't moist, there's a very high chance it will explode," the dragon answered, pulling a big sack out of the chest.

"Oh, then why in Annorlia does Krennicx want it?"

"Not sure, but I've learned to listen to him…… most of the time." He murmured the last part with a slight eye roll.

"Well, let's hope we don't blow up."

The fire raged as Jacob, the dragon he was on, and the other dragon looked for Krennicx.

"Scott!" Krennicx called flying over to them. "You brought them, right?"

"I brought them," the dragon who's name apparently was Scott said. "Not sure how it's supposed to help you, but I brought them."

"Good," Krennicx said. "Now I need you to go around and sprinkle the powder around the entire fire."

"What?" Scott shrieked. *"Are you crazy?!"*

"Yes."

"If that fire touches that powder it will blow up, causing an even larger flame!" Scott said.

"Yes, but if that new fire is *already* under control...." Krennicx trailed off.

"Are you seriously trying to fight fire with fire?" Jacob asked.

"Who said anything about fight?" Krennicx asked. "If you can *contain* it, it won't spread, then all you have to do is wait for it to burn out."

"Yes, but how in the world can you contain something like that?!" Scott asked.

"Listen, you're a doctor, right?" Krennicx asked.

"A medical doctor, but yes," Scott answered.

"Then you know that the Zillow fire does not like the trickery vine."

"That's... not at *all* what it's called but, yes," Scott said. "But how would that.....oh..."

"You can't fight fire with fire, but you can contain it with fire, because..... fire hates other fire," Krennicx said.

"You'd have to cover the entire thing with the vine."

"Already have," Krennicx said, smirking his smile.

"Krennicx!" Scott said in excitement. "You are a genius! Wait, how did you get that many vines and cover it so fast?"

Krennicx smiled, "Alright doc, I need you to start spreading the powder while I show Jacob how to do something."

"Ok," Scott said, flying towards the fire's edge.

"Alright, Jacob," Krennicx said, flying closer. "This is called the fruit of the Zillow," Krennicx said, showing him a small, strange, purple onion shaped fruit-like thing with orange dots. "Now when he finishes with the powder, all you have to do is carefully slice it completely in half down the side, then slide them against each other like what you do with rocks, alright?"

"Ok," Jacob said uneasily.

"Now, just try not to blow up, alright?"

"Wait, what!" Jacob yelped in alarm.

"I think it's all ready," Scott said, flying back over to them.

"You know what, I think I'll just do it," Krennicx said. "Just be ready to fly fast." Krennicx disappeared into the edge of the fire that had already gotten further back. He landed in front of the vine he had already put down. He dug his claws into the middle of the squishy Zillow fruit and ripped it open. "Please don't blow anyone up," Krennicx whispered. He slammed the two pieces together, then slid them against each other violently. Sparks exploded onto the ground as the Zillow also caught on fire. Krennicx quickly dropped the Zillow fruit and launched into the sky, flying fast. A massive and tall wall of fire exploded around the forest fire like a ring. Jacob and Scott quickly bolted out of the fire's way and over to Krennicx.

"Genius, genius, GENIUS!" Scott said, flying over to him.

"Now all we have to do is wait for the rain to take care of it, if it does rain," Krennicx said as they landed on the ground away from the fire. "I think it is supposed to rain."

Jacob carefully got off the dragon, shaking. "Still not the biggest fan of flying."

"Oh yeah, I don't think I fully introduced myself," Scott said, turning to Jacob.

"I don't think I did either," Jacob said.

Scott reached his talon out in a shake position, "Barton," Scott said. "Scott Barton."

"Uh…. Bennett," Jacob said awkwardly, "Jacob Bennett." He awkwardly shook his talon.

"Nice to meet you, Mr. Bennett," Scott Barton said. "You look very familiar, like you've been to my office before."

"Pretty sure I haven't," Jacob said. "Like one hundred percent sure."

"It's just, you really remind me of someone….recently too," Scott said thoughtfully. "Who was it…."

"Well, thanks again Barton," Krennicx said, saving Jacob. "Probably couldn't have done it without you."

"Anytime," Scott said. "Don't forget about everyone's appointment this time."

"I don't forget," Krennicx said with a grin, "I just get busy."

"Uh huh, sure," Scott said. "Better get going."

"Wait, what kind of dragon are you?" Jacob asked.

"Nyychthemeron."

"What?" Jacob asked, confused.

"It means night," Krennicx said.

"Good evening," Scott said, spreading his wings and flying away.

"Evening?" Jacob asked.

Krennicx shrugged, "Well, I guess I better get home."

"Where am I going?" Jacob asked.

"Home," Krennicx responded, walking away.

"Krennicx I…" Jacob started.

"Yes?" Krennicx asked, stopping.

"I, I can't go back," Jacob said. "I want to help you save them. I want to come with you."

"You realize," Krennicx said, "if you help me, your life will never be the same."

Jacob thought for a second, "I know."

Krennicx smiled, "Well, you better mount your friend."

"Oh, this was just a favor," Jacob said. "He's probably going to go now."

"Sure about that?" Krennicx asked. Jacob looked at the dragon curiously as it sat, staring at him.

"What? Do you want to stay for now?" Jacob asked the dragon. The dragon crouched for him to get on its back.

"I think he likes you," Krennicx observed.

"I guess it's a he," Jacob said, getting on the dragon's back.

"Uh… yeah," Krennicx said. Krennicx and the dragon spread their wings and took off into the dark smoky sky.

Jacob sat on the couch drinking ice water in Lighter's cave as the dragon laid by the fireplace. He stared blankly at the fire. *I don't really like fire anymore.*

"Dude, get off that couch," Krennicx said, noticing him.

"What?"

"Off!"

"Why?" Jacob asked, standing up.

"You *stink*," Krennicx said, disgustedly. "When in the world was the last time you've taken a shower?"

"Shower!" Jacob asked in surprise. "But I didn't think you *had* showers."

"Why would we *not* have showers?" Krennicx asked. "Dragons are gross, but not *that* gross."

"So this *entire* time, I could have taken a shower?"

"Yep," Krennicx responded calmly.

"Why didn't you tell me?"

"Why didn't you ask?"

Grrr," Jacob said. "Too bad I don't have my clothes."

"Oh, yeah, I found something in the BeetleWing," Krennicx said, grabbing a bag from the couch. "And I don't think it was an accident." He smirked his smile.

"I don't like long sleeves," Jacob confessed.

"Well, those clothes stink," Krennicx said, slapping the bag into Jacob's face. It was the bag Krennicx had tried to give him from the BeetleWing. "There's soap in there you can use."

"Conditioner?" Jacob asked.

"What do you think?" Krennicx asked.

"That..... dragons use conditioner even though they don't have hair?" Jacob said in a hopeful way. Krennicx rolled his eyes, "Or," Jacob said, "maybe a certain thing with fur would have some?"

Jacob dramatically walked out of the steaming hot bathroom, "Oh, that felt so good, just *so* good!"

"Dude, did you just use up *all* the hot water?" Krennicx asked.

"Wait, what?" Jacob asked with his happy moment ruined.

"Dude, I can't do the dishes with no water!"

"Oops."

"I mean, come on, man," Krennicx said. "Hasn't your mom ever told you not to use up all the hot water?"

"Yeah but...." Jacob started.

"Especially as a guest! Why would you use all of the host's hot water?!"

"I'm sorry!" Jacob apologized in panic. "I didn't mean to! I was just trying to relax having the first shower I've had in a few days!"

Krennicx laughed, "I'm just mess'n with ya, I never run out of hot water. Never. Long sleeves and pant-skirt looks good on ya." He calmly walked away to the kitchen.

"Skirt?" Jacob asked looking down. "It's not a skirt." The clothes Krennicx had given him was completely black with long sleeves. The sleeves were too long so Jacob had to ruffle them in a way that he kind of liked. The pants were almost the same way except it had a cool, long black cloth wrapped along his waist that came before his knees.

"Sorry dude, but that's a skirt," Krennicx said.

"Not a skirt," Jacob said. "I do like that if for some reason my pants fall down it'll cover my butt."

"You're weird," Krennicx said with a laugh.

"You're not?" Jacob asked.

"I'm not wearing a skirt."

"It's not a skirt," Jacob said, laughing.

"Sure."

Of all of Jacob's nightmares, this was the worst. Jacob rolled in his sleeping mat as every single dream he ever had turned into one. Jacob ran through a hallway, running away from a pure white dragon. Then he found himself running through a forest and into Luther's castle. He ran into the Throne Room where it was too late; King Luther had already killed Michael. Fire burned the scene, revealing the same pure white dragon standing in the middle of a huge city. Death followed the dragon everywhere it went. The dragon's voice was terrifying and unforgettable when it spoke. Then Jacob was in a middle of a war, where the pure white dragon killed Hazel. Again, the scene changed as the dragon shouted, "Watch your world burn!" Jacob watched his house explode, knowing his parents were still inside. Fire burned the scene and Jacob found himself sword fighting King Luther. Fire burned as the top of the castle crumbled, and Jacob fell into darkness.

"No!" Jacob shot up in his sleeping mat. *It can't be real! I can't let them die!* He thought about Michael, how he was just laying there in front of King Luther. *Has that already happened! No! It can't! I have to stop him! Or is it even real? And what was that white dragon?! It wasn't Sky, its wings were different. He killed Mom, Dad, and Hazel! I can't let them die! Please,* Jacob thought, trying to reach the voice, *I need your help. Can we please meet now? I need you to explain to me what is going on.*

"So you have finally come to your senses?" the voice asked as the buzz cut on.

Jacob had never been so happy to hear the voice. *Did I just start a conversation?*

"No, I had already been listening to your thoughts."

"What do I do?" Jacob asked out loud. He tried to not think about the fact that whoever the voice was, it was literally *reading* his mind.

"You know." The buzz became stronger ahead of him. Jacob got up and went where the buzz was strongest. His dragon friend woke up and looked at him curiously. The buzz became stronger as it led him against the stone fireplace.

"Why would it lead me here?" Jacob asked himself. He remembered something that Lighter did in the first cave they were in. Jacob put his ear against the stone wall and tapped it three times. Nothing happened.

Jacob thought back to what the pattern was that Lighter did. *I think it was faster.* He made a fist with his fingers and knocked it fast three times. There was a rumble as the stone and the fireplace split apart, revealing a hallway. The dragon jumped up and walked to him, peering into the hallway. The buzz became stronger and Jacob went in with the dragon following. The buzz led him through the hallway past a lot of doors and rooms, until it stopped when he passed a door on the left. "I guess I'm supposed to be in here?" Jacob asked the dragon. The dragon made a sound that just felt like it meant 'I don't know.' The buzz cut back on as Jacob opened the door that went towards stairs going down. The dragon crouched for Jacob to climb on, then they flew down the stairs and landed on the ground. Huge lights cut on one at a time on the ceiling. "Well, this isn't creepy," Jacob said, looking around. It was a huge room with a tall ceiling, aisles and aisles of huge shelves went around the entire room. The shelves were layered with strange metal-looking parts. "Hello, is anyone here?" Jacob asked, walking along an aisle. There was the sound of something gliding above him.

"I have been waiting to meet you like this," the sound of the voice said.

"Do you hear that too?" Jacob asked the dragon. The dragon did a small nod. *So this isn't in my head.*

"No, it is not," the voice said.

"So you really *can* hear thoughts," Jacob said out loud.

"Yes, and I believe you have a gift as well. Though I don't think it's mind-reading," the voice responded.

"What do you mean?"

"Do you think it's a coincidence that *you* ran into me instead of your brother? Do you think it's a coincidence that *you* hear me and no one else?"

"What is that supposed to mean?" Jacob asked, confused.

"You have a gift," the voice said, **"and I will teach you how to use it."**

"But who are you?" Jacob asked in fear. Smoke and lighting whirled on one of the shelves above him as the same Fighter of Peace from the arena appeared. Krennicx had called him the Lightning Prince.

"Want to guess?" the Fighter of Peace in the shape of a dragon of pure lightning asked, walking along the massive shelf. It wasn't at all see-through, but it was still pure lightning.

"I need a clue first," Jacob said walking along with him.

"Continue."

"Do I know you?" Jacob asked.

"We've met, but you do not know me completely."

Jacob thought for a second, "I think I know who you are."

"Do you now?"

"There's been six dragons I ran into in the forest," Jacob said. "Three of them tried to kill me, so that rules them out. The other three were Lighter, Glider, and Scott Barton. Scott is just, well….. not exactly the type. But, there's one that chose me instead of my brother, and I felt your presence when we met, and at the Cloud Kingdom…. He disappeared before you arrived. And I never saw Luther take him. I know who you are," Jacob smiled, "you are Lighter."

290

The Fighter of Peace chuckled, **"So close, yet** so far." His voice changed, and Jacob immediately knew precisely who it was. "Hello, kiddy."

CHAPTER 16

THE INSANE TRAINER

"But that's impossible!" Jacob yelped as black smoke circled around the Fighter of Peace, showing the one that matched its *real* voice.

"Is it though?" Krennicx asked, flying onto the floor in front of him.

"But, but, but you were there!" Jacob stammered. "You were right next to me in the arena!"

Krennicx smiled. "I understand," he said. "Most Annorlians don't know that I can, well..." Lightning flickered around Krennicx and the same dragon-shape of pure lightning appeared behind him, flickering as pure lightning. It flew into the air, circling around them, then it disappeared.

Jacob was bewildered. "Then why didn't you fight back against King Saul? He was terrified of the Fighters of Peace, but he wasn't scared of you that much."

"I wanted to know how bad the Cloud Kingdom was," Krennicx said. "And there were innocent dragons *and* people in the dungeons that needed to be rescued."

"But the only ones you rescued were me, Sky, and..... well, you," Jacob said, thinking back to the arena when the Fighter of Peace leader rescued them from the Lyvith. *Whoa, I guess Krennicx really can beat that thing*, he realized, thinking back to when the lightning bolt beat the beast.

"Was it though?" Krennicx asked thoughtfully. "Not how I remember it."

"Well, it's how *I* remember it," Jacob said.

"Well, I guess not everyone's memory is perfect," Krennicx said with a smirk.

"But still! Even with all of that, why did you need any of us? And why didn't you tell me? How does not telling me help you in any way?"

"Oh……. I don't know…. 'Hey King Luther,'" Krennicx said, pretending he was typing on a phone, "'I am very happy to say I am alive and unharmed, although I haven't eaten much. I am also very happy to say that I found out the Fighters of Peace are real! And man have they told me everything! I found out that Severein, your 'nemesis' is also this insane talking panther I met in the forest, *and* he's the *leader* of the Fighters of Peace! He's the Lightning Prince!' I'm not sure if I'm the smartest, but at least I know I'm smarter then *that*….. I hope."

"But you trust me now?" Jacob asked, surprised.

"Not entirely," Krennicx responded. "But we'll see how you do in tomorrow's training. If you're gonna help me save our friends, you need some work."

"Training?" Jacob asked.

"Better get some more sleep, dearie," Krennicx said, "you got a long day tomorrow." There was a flicker of lightning and Krennicx disappeared.

"What. Just. Happened?" Jacob asked in amazement.

"Day one, wake up sleepy head!"

"Ah!" Jacob shot up in his mat, alarmed.

"I told you we are starting training so that's what we're gonna do," Krennicx said.

"But the sun isn't even out yet!" Jacob said, pointing to the window.

"Well, I did say you're going to have a long day, didn't I?" Krennicx asked, smirking.

Jacob gulped.

"Run! Run! Run! RUN FASTER!" Krennicx called from in front of him.

"I can't run any faster!" Jacob called back.

Krennicx stopped, "I thought you love running?"

"I do, BUT I'VE NEVER RAN UP A MOUNTAIN BEFORE!" Jacob said, glancing down where they already ran. "When you said that you run at least twenty miles a day, I honestly didn't believe you."

"Believe me now?" Krennicx asked, smirking a smile.

"I can't do twenty *miles,* especially up a *mountain!"*

"Hm," Krennicx said, then started to run again.

"Uhhhh," Jacob moaned. He forced himself to start running again. "My shoes aren't even good for this!"

Jacob fell on to the floor on his back, breathing hard. "I never want to run again."

"Oh, quit your whining," Krennicx said, calmly hopping over him. He wasn't even breathing hard.

"Do you *really* do that every *day?*"

"If I'm not busy, but I usually don't on Saturday and Sunday," Krennicx responded.

Jacob groaned. He tried his best to walk to the table to sit. "Ah!" he shrieked in surprise. He fell to the ground face first. "What was that?" Jacob asked, trying to stand back up. There was a loud squeal as something else scrambled up. "What is *that?!*"

"Oh, hi Pix," Krennicx greeted, as if a pig in the house was *normal.*

"Why do you have a pig in the house?" Jacob asked as 'Pix' ran in circles around his feet. The pig had a long snout and a lean body. It was white with a black straight tail, black hooves, and black ears. Its height was a few inches below Jacob's knee.

"It's not just a *pig,*" Krennicx said, reaching down and rubbing Pix's chin. "It's a *mini* pig."

"I thought those things were a myth!" Jacob said, staring at the small, adorable pig. It had to be around the size of a small or medium-sized dog.

"Well, you also thought the Fighters of Peace were a myth," Krennicx reminded. He patted Pix's head, then whispered something in its ear. Immediately, the pig ran to the fireplace, tapped it three times with its hoof, then ran through the secret hallway.

"How in Annorlia…" Jacob started.

"Welp, you ready for breakfast?" Krennicx asked before Jacob could finish.

Jacob's legs felt like jelly as he tried to walk to the couch to rest. The dragon walked along with him, making sure he wouldn't fall. As Jacob dramatically fell onto the couch and moaned, the dragon jumped up and sat with him. "He is insane," Jacob said. "Can you help me?"

The stone fire place opened and Krennicx walked out, then it closed behind him, "All right young'n, time to continue your training."

"What?!" Jacob shrieked in alarm. "But I was about to get in the shower!"

"Oh, I wouldn't do that if I were you," Krennicx advised. "You'd just get sweaty all over again."

"But this isn't even healthy! My body is supposed to rest!"

"We have to find out how much you can handle."

"Found it!"

"And then…" Krennicx said, smirking his smile, "we have to make you able to handle *more*."

"I've got a bad feeling about this," Jacob said nervously.

"Heard that before," Krennicx said with a smirk. "How 'bout we take it easy for today."

"What's your version of easy?" Jacob asked warily.

Krennicx smirked, causing Jacob to gulp. *That's not a good sign.* Krennicx walked over to the stone fireplace with the secret passageway. "Why do you have to tap it three times to get it to open?" Jacob asked.

Krennicx raised an eyebrow, then with a flicker of lighting, he *touched* the fireplace. The fireplace rumbled and instead of moving apart, it rose into the ceiling, revealing an elevator.

"How many secret passageways do you have?" Jacob asked.

Krennicx smiled, "After you," he said, nodding to the elevator door.

"Dragons have *elevators?*" Jacob asked, walking in.

"It used to not be here," Krennicx said walking in and pushing a button on the wall, "but I put it in after we had a……er….. incident with Ben," Krennicx smirked. "But I had to prank him in some way." The elevator shot up, feeling almost as fast as the BeetleWing.

"AH!" Jacob shrieked, immediately falling over. It suddenly stopped, causing Jacob to feel even more sick. The door slowly opened in what felt like more than a minute.

"Man did he get a kick out of it," Krennicx added when the door finally finished opening. Jacob moaned, laying on the floor. "Well, come along young'n, we don't have all day," Krennicx said, jumping over him and out into the pitch-black darkness. Jacob dizzily stood up and walked after him, feeling like he was going to fall over.

"Are you *trying* to make me throw up?" Jacob asked. "First it was the BeetleWing and now this?"

"Technically, I succeeded with the BeetleWing," Krennicx said with a small laugh. "That was awesome."

"Especially the fact that I hadn't eaten *anything* that day so it refused to come out," Jacob said, annoyed.

"Well, at least you did drink some water so that was something that could come out," Krennicx said, smiling.

"Please don't mention it," Jacob said miserably.

"Good times….. good times. THINK FAST." Krennicx threw something that hit Jacob in the face.

"Hey!" Jacob yelped in surprise. "What was that for?"

"Just what I thought, we need to work on your reflexes," Krennicx snapped his claws and lightning flickered, somehow causing the beginning part of the room to light up. "Now, one of the most important things you need to fight is reflexes. You need that so you can use your sword at the right moment."

"Sword?" Jacob asked.

"Well, for right now we'll use a stick." Krennicx walked to the wall on the left side of the room. "Pick which one." He waved to a couple of bamboo sticks against the wall.

"How is a stick going to help me?" Jacob asked, picking up a long bamboo stick.

"Ready?"

"For what?"

Krennicx smirked a smile, "Anything." A massive glass wall closed in between Krennicx and Jacob, leaving Jacob in the other side of the room. Jacob immediately turned around to the dark side of the room. Bright lights flashed down on the room, revealing a massive obstacle course.

"This training course will help your reflexes, fighting skills, and good decisions," Krennicx said. "Things you really need to work on."

"Wait, fighting?" Jacob asked, alarmed. "Why do I need to know that?!"

"You can't beat King Luther without knowing how to *fight,* can you?" Krennicx responded calmly.

Jacob stared at him in shock, then took a deep breath and faced the obstacle course. Before Jacob even started, a fast, small ball hit him in the face. He fell from the shock and hit his face on the wall. Jacob moaned on the floor clutching his face. "Looks like we got some work to do," Krennicx said.

"Day two! Now, I know yesterday didn't go very well," Krennicx said the next day. "But if we're going to save everyone, we really need to get better, well, you really need to get better."

"I'm sore," Jacob said.

"Too bad."

"I can't do it!" Jacob hollered in pain.

"It's not if you can, it's if you will! Now push!" Krennicx commanded, flying above him. Jacob moaned as he continued to lift himself up and down on the tree branch. "Ninety-seven, ninety-eight, ninety-nine, done!" Krennicx said. Jacob dropped to the floor and laid there in pain.

"First my legs, now my arms! What else are you going to do?" Jacob asked, breathing hard.

Krennicx smirked a smile.

"AHHH!" Jacob shrieked, trying to run away.

"You're supposed to fight the dummy! Not run away from it!" Krennicx called out.

"Well, if the *dummy* would stop chasing me, I would stop running!" Jacob called. The dummy rolled on fast wheels and it had a set of four sticks spinning on the top and bottom of it. It also had two boxing gloves trying to punch him in the middle. The dummy stopped and stood still. "Seriously?"

"Well, go on," Krennicx said in a baby voice. "Use your little stick and fight him."

"Ok," Jacob said, nervously walking up to it. "This thing's not going to start spinning its sticks around again, right?"

"All you have to do is hit it," Krennicx instructed.

"Ok," Jacob said, raising his stick to hit it. But before he could, a boxing glove stretched out from the dummy and punched Jacob in the stomach. Jacob clutched his stomach, out of breath; then the spinning sticks on top of it hit him in the head, then the bottom sticks hit his legs, causing him to fall.

Krennicx cracked up, shaking his head.

"Day three!" Krennicx announced. "We need to find something you're good at."

"Well, I *was* somewhat good at running," Jacob said. "But thanks to you I never want to run again."

Krennicx smirked a smile that made Jacob scared.

"AHH!" Jacob screamed in terror as he ran for his life from a bear.

"Keep it up," Krennicx said, calmly sitting down, looking at his claws. "It's interesting how much faster you can run when your life is being threatened."

"HEEELP!"

"You seem to be doing fine so far," Krennicx said calmly.

"You're insane!" Jacob tripped over a tree root and rolled onto the floor. The bear went to pounce but somehow Jacob found himself sitting on a soft velvet couch in a nice house.

"Not exactly ready for running faster yet," Krennicx said, sitting on a couch in front of him reading a book. "We'll try something else."

Jacob bewilderedly looked around the room, breathing hard. The room looked like a library with its walls completely covered with shelves of books. At the end of the room was a nice stone fireplace where Jacob sat on the couch. In front of him was a large coffee table with another couch behind it, facing him. The room was dark except for the fireplace and a couple of candle lamps. *That's smart having fire lamps in a library,* Jacob thought sarcastically. Jacob looked at Krennicx, confused, "What just happened?"

"What do you mean?" Krennicx asked, looking up. He sat on the couch across the table.

"You tell me," Jacob said.

"Tell you whaaat?"

"I, I just appeared here," Jacob said, confused.

"And?" Krennicx asked as if it was completely normal. "Hm, I think I know what to do next." Faster than an eye could blink, Jacob found himself standing in the room with all of the training tools. Jacob shook his head, confused. "Now," Krennicx continued, standing next to him, "another thing we need to look at are your kicks."

"My *kicks?*" Jacob asked.

"They are more important than you realize," Krennicx gravely said. "Now, show me your best kick."

"Er, *show* you?" Jacob asked awkwardly.

"Yes," Krennicx responded. "Now, go on."

"Now?"

"Now."

"Uh…" Jacob said, trying to angle his foot. "How do I do this?"

"Just act like you're kicking down a door," Krennicx instructed.

"Ok," Jacob said. "Uh…" He awkwardly tried to kick thin air.

"Wow," Krennicx said. "That was terrible."

"I'm trying, ok!" Jacob said. "This is weird!"

"What's weird?" Krennicx asked, tilting his head curiously. "All you have to do is raise one of your legs and *kick.*"

"It feels weird!" Jacob said, putting his foot back down. "I mean, like what *kind* of kick? And why does this have to be right now? And this feels awkward!"

"What? Would you like to do a butt kick? Because that is what's happening to you right now!"

"I am not getting my butt kicked!" Jacob defended. "You're getting *your* butt kicked!"

"Not by you, that's for sure!"

"Well, how about I kick your head!"

"Yes, *please!*"

Jacob tried to kick Krennicx's head but failed miserably and ended up falling. "Wow," Krennicx said. "That was pathetic."

"You try it!" Jacob said, standing back up.

"With pleasure." Krennicx expertly jumped up and kicked Jacob against the stomach, sending him across the whole room. He landed with a loud and painful thud. How in Annorlia can a four- legged animal kick so *hard?!*

Jacob moaned, trying to get up, "I didn't mean literally!"

Krennicx chuckled, "Not to bring you down or anything, but you really need to know how to kick."

"Sounds like I really need to know everything," Jacob said, standing up.

"You do."

"Sometimes you're going to be on a rescue mission," Krennicx said, "and unfortunately, they might be very annoying, especially when you need them to escape."

Sirens went off and everything was glowing red while Jacob was going through a whole bunch of wires in the wall to unlock the door.

"If you're trying to unlock the *door* you're not doing a very good job," Krennicx said, acting like someone Jacob just rescued. He was standing behind him being very annoying.

"Can you please tell me which wire I need to cut?" Jacob asked frustratingly, for he had been trying to cut the wires for a few minutes already. Time was running out.

"*Not* that one, that's for sure," Krennicx said. He was *very* good at acting annoying.

"Is it this one?" Jacob asked, showing another one.

"If it was *that one,* I would have *said* so."

"How 'bout this one?"

"No."

"This?"

"No."

Jacob moved his hand back and forth but would immediately be yelled at.

"No. No. No. No. No. The one I'm pointing at," Krennicx said, then rolled his eyes. "No. No. No. No."

"You're pointing at all of them!" Jacob yelped in aggravation.

"No, I'm pointing at the one you need to cut."

"Is it *this* one?"

"No. Is *that* the one I'm pointing at? News flash, it's not!"

"Can't you just touch it?!" Jacob asked, about to lose it.

"No!"

"Why not?!"

"I don't want to get my claws dirty."

"Are. You. *Serious?!"*

"Ok, I can do this one now," Jacob said, starting to run through the obstacle course. Balls flew violently at him as he ran. He dodged a few until one of them got him in the face, causing him to fall over.

"Fail," Krennicx said.

"I can't do it!" Jacob said, laying down on the running trail.

"Fail," Krennicx said.

"Whoa, whoa, whoa!" Jacob yelped, toppling over after trying to do a big kick.

"*Soo* fail."

"Naaah," Jacob confidently chased the dummy, trying to hit it with his stick…. "AHHHHH!" Jacob ran the other way as the dummy chased him.

"Fail."

"Fail."

"Fail."

"Fail."

"Fail."

"Fail!"

"And fail!"

"*KRENNICX!!!*" Jacob yelled as loud as he could. "THIS IS INSANE EVEN FOR YOU!"

Jacob's hand nearly slipped as he dangled on the side of the cliff, holding on for his '*darling* dear' life.

"Sometimes your best weight is yourself," Krennicx said calmly. "Especially when dumbbells are extremely expensive these days."

"GET ME OUT!" Jacob yelled.

"Oh, calm down," Krennicx said, flicking his hand like it wasn't a big deal. "You really have nothing to lose."

"EXCEPT MY LIFE!"

"No, because if you *do* fall, I'll catch you. Isn't that right?" Krennicx asked Jacob's dragon sitting next to him. The dragon grunted. "What do you mean I wouldn't be able to catch him?" Krennicx asked. "Oh, so it's going to have to be *you* to catch him?"

The dragon nodded.

"But out of the few days he's known me I've already caught him twice. Plus, at the rate he's at, I bet ya he'll have to catch someone *by* hanging over a cliff," Krennicx said with a calm laugh.

"WHAT IS IT WITH ME AND CLIFFS?!" Jacob shouted, trying not to look down.

"You see that's exactly why we're doing this," Krennicx responded calmly. "You've already been pushed *three times*, so you need to know how to catch yourself and pull yourself up. You have to train yourself because you'll never know if an enemy is going to push you over the side of a cliff."

"WELL THIS TIME THE ENEMY WAS *YOU!*"

Krennicx smirked a smile as he calmly scooted a little closer to the cliff. He was about five feet away. "You know the sooner you pull yourself up, the sooner you can go back to all the other wonderful training courses."

"Fine," Jacob said, trying to pull himself up. He tried to put his foot onto a rock and pull himself up on a tree root sticking out. To his horror, the root began to wobble, "Uh, Krennicx." The root snapped and Jacob fell, screaming in horror.

Krennicx continued to sit, calmly looking at his claws. He glanced next to him, then jumped up, "I thought you said you were getting him?"

The dragon jumped up and said the same thing to Krennicx in dragon tongue. Krennicx's eyes widened.

It turned out that Lighter's place was a lot bigger than what he thought it was. What Jacob thought was the living room where he had been sleeping was actually just a decoy, and the real living room was up the secret elevator on the top floor…. or, well at least Jacob *figured* it was the top floor. The real living room was *way* nicer. The living room itself had one long couch, a smaller couch, and a recliner in front of a huge TV. The side of the wall where the village was, was extremely dark, tinted, thick glass. Jacob guessed it was the kind you can look out of, but not into. The other side had the same glass but with a large door that had white glass framing it. The door went to a huge balcony that overlooked the large pool. Jacob had no idea how he didn't see it when he swam in that pool. At the end of the living room was a good sized dining room, kitchen, and a huge walk-in pantry. It was a *ridiculously* nice place. Jacob moaned, tiredly laying down on the long couch, "I hope you're not going to ask for a survey on how good you are at training."

Krennicx sat on the other side of the couch, strumming a ukulele on his lap. "If I let everyone else train the way they wanted to, there'd be a lot of dead people."

"That didn't sound creepy at all," Jacob said sarcastically. "And you know that's not how to play the ukulele, right?"

"And how do *you* know how to play the ukulele?" Krennicx asked, continuing to strum it with it on his lap. He wasn't even doing any actual chords.

"I play the guitar," Jacob responded.

"Well, that ain't no ukulele now is it?"

"I don't think I have to know how to play it to know that's *not* the way you play it," Jacob pointed out.

The elevator door at the beginning of the room slooowly opened. "Man, you've got to fix that," Ben said, walking out and throwing a bag on the floor. "Sup, butt."

"Turd 'n toot," Krennicx welcomed.

"Hey would ya look at that, the kid's still alive," Ben noticed, shocked. "That's surprising."

"Barely," Jacob snorted.

"We had a few disagreements," Krennicx said calmly.

"He pushed me over the side of a cliff!" Jacob accused, standing up and pointing to Krennicx.

"Seriously?" Ben asked in excitement.

"Seriously!"

"Did you really?" Ben asked.

"I can neither confirm nor deny," Krennicx responded, *still* strumming.

"Awesome," Ben said.

"No! Not awesome!" Jacob yelped. "Have you gone through his trainings before? They're terrible!"

"I've gone through a few teachings," Ben responded.

"And how was it?" Jacob asked.

"I don't want to talk about it."

Krennicx chuckled as he continued to annoyingly strum the ukulele strings.

"Well, did he throw you into a bear's den?!"

"Not exactly."

"Ben's training was hilarious!" Krennicx said, bursting out laughing.

"Hey we agreed not to talk about that," Ben said.

"Yeah I know, I know, it's just when you were screaming it was just so…." Krennicx said laughing.

"Wait, what did you do?" Jacob asked, interested.

"You see, what happened was…." Krennicx started.

"Kren*nicx*!" Ben yelped in alarm.

"I'm just kidding," Krennicx said. "You know I'm not going to actually tell anyone right?"

"Uhh… Oh yeah, who's that?" Ben asked, pointing at the dragon… and changing the subject.

"Oh, yeah this… huh, I guess he doesn't have a name yet," Krennicx said.

"He doesn't have a name already?" Jacob asked.

"I mean he *does* but it's in dragon tongue so it doesn't mean anything in our language," Krennicx responded. "And I really don't think you can even say it right."

"True," Jacob agreed, "but isn't he going to just fly away?"

"If he wanted to leave," Krennicx said, "he would have already. You might want to name him before you're falling from the sky and all you can yell is 'help me dragon friend that's following me around everywhere!' And by the time he hears what you're saying you'd already be dead… Just give him a name."

"Fine," Jacob said, getting onto the floor in front of the dragon. "Spike? Nah, err… how 'bout Blue? Nah, don't like that one either…"

"Seriously Krennicx," Ben said. "Glider and Glazer aren't here, so why do you have to make it so cold in here still?"

"Burn? No… Kyle? Nah," Jacob continued.

"You know I never would have let it be cold in here if I didn't like it," Krennicx said. "You know I like the cold don't you?"

"Yeah, but it's the beginning of summer!" Ben said. "You don't have to make it as cold as winter!"

"Winter!" Jacob jumped up. "Do you like that?"

The dragon jumped up and stuck his tongue out in a happy way.

Krennicx smirked a smile, "Well, at least someone likes the winter."

"It's not that I don't like the winter," Ben said, "it's just I also like the summer too."

"Well, if you want summer just walk outside," Krennicx said, "I'm sure you'll love it when it gets to ninety degrees tomorrow!"

"How hot does it get here?" Jacob asked, rubbing Winter's snout.

"It can get pretty hot," Krennicx answered. "Although, normally the temperatures stay around seventy."

"That's not bad!"

"Tomorrow is supposed to be pretty rough," Ben said. "It's supposed to be hot and humid."

"But I thought you like it?" Krennicx asked, smirking a smile.

"I didn't say that!"

Krennicx laughed, "Did you bring the pizza?"

"Yep."

"Good," Krennicx said, "I think me, Jacob, and Winter can agree that we're hungry."

CHAPTER 17

THE RETURN

Jacob yawned as he calmly sat up from the long couch in the real living room. "That was actually a pretty good night's sleep….. and the sun is actually out… oh no! The sun is actually out!" Jacob jumped up and ran to the clock on the oven. "Twelve o'clock! Oh *no!*" Jacob ran to the elevator and went down to the decoy living room and ran out the back door. "Krennicx, I am so sorry!" Jacob said, finding him sitting by the pool. "I don't know what happened! I guess that couch was just so soft, I kept sleeping!"

"Don't be sorry," Krennicx said. "You can't be tired for what we're going to do today."

"What are we doing today?" Jacob asked, surprised.

"Everyone learns things differently," Krennicx said, starting to walk along the pool. "I try to make sure everyone knows how to fight regularly before this, but we're kind of on a time limit."

"Learns what?"

Krennicx smiled, "After the Diammonites invaded, the only hope for Annorlia was this small prophecy that no one even believed existed. They said that it came from Diamond—the leader of the Diamond Dragons."

"What was it?" Jacob asked.

"It wasn't like those rhyming prophecies you know of, it was more of a vision." The water whirled around in a small circle. "Diamond never really explained it, the only thing he had shown was the symbol." The water stopped moving, and a shape of a triangle that was missing the tip of the three ends appeared. At the opening of each corner, a line floated where the tip of the triangle should have been.

"What does it mean?"

"All he had said was that each part was a powerful fighter, equipped with powers that can save Annorlia," Krennicx responded. "Five of the six are already pretty well-trained."

"What about the sixth?" Jacob asked.

"He's been found. I wouldn't call him pretty well-trained, but I'm working on it."

"Why are you looking at me like that?" Jacob asked warily.

Krennicx smirked a smile.

"Wait, wait a minute," Jacob said, realizing what he was saying. "You think *I'm* the last Fighter of Peace?"

"I don't think," Krennicx said, "I know."

"No," Jacob said disbelievingly. "No, no, no. I am, I am not a Fighter of Peace."

"Why would you think that?" Krennicx asked, tilting his head curiously.

Jacob laughed, "I don't have powers! I'm not a super hero! I can't even kick with somebody watching me!"

"So we need to work on your awkwardness, so what?"

"So that's why you've been training me?" Jacob realized. "You think I can become a Fighter?"

"You just now realized that?" Krennicx asked. "I figured you'd know that already."

"Another reason!" Jacob pointed out. "As you can see, I'm not the smartest."

"Who said you have to be extremely smart?" Krennicx asked. "And who said you aren't smart?"

"Look, I am not who you're looking for," Jacob insisted. "I'm a human. I don't have any powers."

"Oh really?" Krennicx asked. "Says the one who has visions about things before they even happen."

"Visions?" Jacob asked. "They're not visions! They're just bad dreams! They're not real!"

"Just because they haven't happened yet doesn't mean they won't," Krennicx said. "But that's why you have them, to warn you so you can stop it."

"No, no, no!" Jacob yelped in panic. "They're not real!"

"But do you really want to take that chance?" Krennicx asked. "I know you've seen everyone you care about die. There might not be a way to stop it, but don't you at least want to try?"

"But that can't happen! The dreams can't be true!"

"Oh but they are," Krennicx said. "And they're starting now."

At that exact moment, a few miles away, the DragonStaff was found. There was a bright flash as all of Jacob's dreams came to him while he was still awake. Fire raged across Annorlia as buildings crumbled. Dragons and humans fought with swords against other dragons and humans. A dragon in pure white emerged out of the fire, with a white flaming sword in hand. It destroyed anything in its path, including

Jacob's own sister. "No!" Jacob shrieked. The visions moved on through every single terrible dream Jacob had, from the two dragons fighting to the Fighter getting onto the dragon. All the way to Jacob running into the Throne Room where King Luther had just killed his brother. "No!" Jacob fell to the ground and covered his eyes with his hands. The ground rumbled and rocks fell as the visions went away. Jacob looked up to see rocks floating in the air, then they fell to the ground in front of him. Jacob sat on his knees, looking at his hands, "Why? Why does this have to happen?" he whispered.

"I don't know," Krennicx said, "but it hasn't yet, so maybe it won't… we don't know yet. The only thing you can do is your best and what is supposed to happen will happen."

"But why me?"

"I've asked that question about myself many times," Krennicx said, sitting next to him. "I still don't know, trust me. It's highly possible that I will never know. But it doesn't change the fact that for some reason, I was born with these powers. It's up to us to decide what we're going to do with them."

"What do I do?" Jacob asked.

"It's your choice," Krennicx responded. "I'm going to go to Luther's palace to rescue them tonight. You can either come with me or go back home. It's all up to you."

"I need a second." Jacob got up and ran into the woods.

"I understand," Krennicx said.

Jacob continued to run for what felt like a few miles. He barely even knew what direction he was going. Finally, he stopped and sat on a tree stump. "How is this possible?" Jacob asked himself. *These dreams can't be real! They just can't! What should I do? Should I go home or go with Krennicx? Which one would cause Michael to die?* Jacob leaned his head into his hands. *Maybe I should stick with Krennicx. If I can learn how to use these so-called-powers, maybe I can stop all these nightmares from happening.* Jacob looked at his hands, "What kind of powers could they be?" Jacob had just made his decision of what to do when a twig snapped. Jacob jumped up to see what it was when, to Jacob's huge surprise, Michael ran out. "Michael?!"

"Jacob?!" Michael asked, surprised. "Is that you?!"

"Michael!" Jacob nearly cried, happily giving his brother a hug.

"You're alive!" Michael said happily. "Mr. Samual look it's my brother!"

Jacob hadn't even noticed the soldiers that were behind his brother. *Oh no.*

"I thought you said he was taken by the enemy?" a different soldier asked. Jacob guessed he was the commander.

"He was!" Michael said, still very happy. "How in the world did you escape?!"

"Yeah, I'd like to know that myself," the commander said uneasily.

"They didn't hurt you any, did they?" Michael asked. "Man, I can't wait to find that dragon and kill it!"

"What do you mean?" Jacob asked, trying not to sound concerned.

"Jacob," Michael said, "we found the DragonStaff!"

"You did?!" Jacob asked in alarm.

"We did!" Michael said excitedly. "We're taking it back to King Luther now, and then after that, we can come back and kill every single dragon alive!"

"No!" Jacob shrieked in panic.

"No?" Michael asked, confused.

"Michael, you have to listen to me," Jacob said. "The dragons aren't what we thought they are!"

"I know!" Michael said. "They're worse!"

"No!" Jacob said. "They're not evil at all! Some of them are, but not all of them!"

"Are you joking? Because this isn't funny."

"I'm not joking," Jacob insisted. "They're actually nice! A little weird, but nice!"

"What are you talking about?!" Michael asked. "They kidnapped you!"

"Lighter didn't mean to scare us!" Jacob defended. "He was trying to help me!"

"Lighter?" the commander asked. "I heard word that Lighter had already been captured."

"So that means we can kill it when we get back!" Michael said happily.

"What? No!" Jacob yelped in panic. "Don't kill Lighter!"

"Why not?" Michael asked. "He kidnapped you! Did they brainwash you or something?"

"I'm not brainwashed!"

"Then why are you acting like this?" Michael asked.

"Because they're my friends!"

"*Friends*?" Michael asked. "Dragons can't be your *friends*."

"But they are!" Jacob insisted. "Especially Lighter! I think he just might be my best friend!"

"The one that kidnapped you?" Michael asked.

"He didn't make me do anything I didn't want to do!" Jacob tried to defend. "He let me leave anytime I wanted to!"

"Maybe we should take him to King Luther, he could be dangerous," the commander said.

"Michael, please, you have to believe me," Jacob said. "You can't use the DragonStaff! You can't kill all of them, it's not right!"

"Jacob would never say anything like that," Michael said, taking a few steps back. "You've always helped me with this."

"Michael, please, I can explain everything," Jacob said, walking towards him. "You have to believe me."

"I wouldn't get too close," the commander warned, "it might be contagious."

Michael looked hesitant and heartbroken. "I'm sorry," Michael said, "but they've done something to you."

"Trust me, they didn't," Jacob said. *Except for push me over some cliffs, but you really don't need to know that.*

"I'm sorry kid," the commander said, "but we're doing this for your own good."

"Wait, just let me explain," Jacob said, but it was too late. There was a prickly sensation as the commander blasted a stun gun, causing Jacob to fall unconscious.

Jacob moaned, "What happened?" he asked, rubbing his head.

"I honestly don't know why everyone has such a hard time with Severein," a familiar voice said. "As long as you know what he loves, you can get him pretty easily."

Jacob shot up off the floor and faced King Luther, who had been staring at him. "Why does everyone want him?" Jacob asked, terrified.

"Severein and I have some unfinished business to attend to," King Luther said.

"You want to kill him," Jacob said.

"No, as a matter of fact I don't mean to kill him," Luther said.

"Then why do you need the DragonStaff?" Jacob asked, surprised at himself for talking to the king like that.

"The DragonStaff is merely to protect my kingdom," Luther said.

"*Merely?*" Jacob asked. "But that's not the whole reason."

"I always forget that kids don't know what all the words mean," King Luther said. "Merely *is* the whole reason."

"Then what is the whole reason?"

"Merely."

"What does merely *mean?*"

"The whole reason."

"Then what *is* the whole reason?" Jacob asked.

"Merely!" Luther said, aggravated.

"But what does merely mean?" Jacob asked, confused.

"Oh my goodness, this is why I don't like kids," King Luther said. "Merely means the whole reason! Which means the whole reason of finding the DragonStaff is to protect my kingdom!"

"Ohh....," Jacob realized. "Why didn't you just say so?" *Wow! So this is why Krennicx loves testing everyone! It's actually kind of fun to act like you know nothing and see how easily it is to drive someone crazy! I need to do this more often!*

King Luther took a deep breath, "So I've heard you care about Lighter? I guess he is a weak spot for two now."

"What do you mean?" Jacob asked.

"Listen kid," King Luther said. "Don't ruin your life forever; if you leave now, you can return home and forget all of this ever happened."

"What about Lighter and the rest of them?"

"Are you seriously going to let *them* ruin you and your family?"

"Wait, my family?" Jacob asked, terrified. "They don't have anything to do with this."

"They won't if you leave now and never even mention dragons or Severein again," King Luther threatened. "So, are you going to pick the side of your family you've known and loved all your life? Or a few dragons you met in the woods a few *days* ago?"

"What are you going to do to them?" Jacob asked, feeling like crying.

"That is none of your concern," Luther said. "Now unless you want me to kill you *and* your family, I suggest you leave."

Jacob stared at the floor as he left the palace and ran along the trail that led to his favorite bench in the park. He sat down and dug his face into his hands. He wanted to cry, but he knew that someone would ask why he was so upset. He knew he wouldn't be able to help pouring out everything he was going through. With a bark, Spot ran out of a bush and jumped onto the bench next to him. "Hey, Spot," Jacob greeted, petting his favorite dog. "I don't feel like running right now." Spot tilted his head as if he was asking why. "I'm just not up for it." He patted his head. "Why can't any of my best friends be human?"

Spot barked.

"Oh, how could I have been so stupid! I should have just stayed with Krennicx," Jacob sighed. "I am such an *idiot*."

"You got that right."

"*AHHHH!*" Jacob screamed, jumping off the bench. He stared at the dog in horror, "You can *talk?!*"

"Yeah, sometimes I just want to say, 'shut up' and then just puke," Spot said with a *very* familiar voice. "Have I ever mentioned how much I *hate* dogs?"

"*Krennicx!*" Jacob shrieked in pure horror.

"Heyo kiddo," Krennicx as Spot said.

"You have *got* to be *kidding* me?!"

Spot laughed, "I told ya I knew everything about ya!"

Jacob gulped, "I've told you a lot."

"Yes, yes you have," Spot said, looking miserable, "and I seriously felt like puking."

"Well, being a dog, you'd have to eat it," Jacob said.

"Yeah, that's what kept me from doing it."

"So *all* of this time it's been you!?" Jacob asked.

"Sadly," Krennicx answered with a dog sigh.

Jacob groaned, "So all this time my best friend has been a dragon?"

"No," Krennicx said, *still* able to smirk a smile, "it's been me."

"Now *I* feel like puking," Jacob said.

Krennicx laughed, "Well, being a human you'd have to *clean* it up! Something you *hate* doing!"

"What are you even doing here?" Jacob asked. "And why in Annorlia did you have to be my 'best friend' dog!"

"Well, if you liked cats I wouldn't have to be a dog!"

"I never said I don't like cats," Jacob said, "I just like dogs better."

"Well, I guess it's a good thing we all have our own opinion," Krennicx said, "cuz I hate dogs, love cats, and love mini pigs."

"*What?*" Jacob asked in confusion.

"Anyway, I'm here to help you," Krennicx said with a dog grin.

"Well, I can't help you," Jacob said. "King Luther threatened that he'll kill my family if I help you. I can't let my vision come true."

Krennicx sighed, "Doing the right thing is a very hard thing to do. Trust me, I know."

"But how is putting my family in danger the right thing?"

"They're already in danger," Krennicx responded. "Everyone is, but it's up to you if you're going to protect them or not. You and your family aren't the only ones threatened by King Luther, there's thousands across your kingdom. None of them will fight, so it's all up to you."

"But why me?"

"I don't know why you were chosen, it's up to you to figure it out," Krennicx responded. "I need your help, but I'm not going to make you do anything you don't want to do. It's all up to you."

Jacob took a deep breath, "What do you want me to do?"

CHAPTER 18

SPOT

Jacob and Krennicx—in the form of a dog, formally known as Spot—ran along the sidewalk towards the city. "Don't you think they would notice us running?" Jacob asked the Krennicx-Spot-dog.

"That's kind of the whole point," Spot said. "We run all of the time, almost every single day. There's nothing un-normal about it."

"I guess that's true," Jacob responded. "So what am I supposed to call you?"

"What do you mean?"

"Do I call you Krennicx or Spot?"

"Well, you know no one would think anything about you first calling your dog Spot and then a few days later calling him by the name of a weirdo panther," Krennicx said sarcastically.

"Yeah, I guess I'll just call you Spot," Jacob said.

"Yeah… that'd be a good idea."

Jacob moaned, "I still can't believe all this time my dog has been you! This means I've known you like, forever!" Jacob still felt like puking. "I've told you absolutely everything that's been going on in my life. *Everything!* Even my love life!"

"Hehehe! That you have!" Krennicx's voice was still accented and scratchy even when he was a dog.

The more he thought about it, the more he felt sick…and *embarrassed.* He told that 'dog' more about his feelings than he told his parents! Forcing himself to change the subject, Jacob stopped. "What are we even supposed to do here?"

"There's a few people I want to talk to, a few questions that I want answered, a few places I want to go to, and above all, there are some things I *have* to do," Krennicx responded. "But we can kill some time and act normal, you know we do have a whole day…buddy."

Jacob sighed. Oh, how many times he had called Spot buddy! He smiled, "You know there is a vet in the city, I doubt you've had your rabies shot and flea preventative."

"Haha, very funny," Krennicx said. "And for the record, fleas are too afraid of me to *ever* bite or even get on me."

"What would you do? Turn into one and smirk them to death?" Jacob asked mockingly.

"Actually, it's very easy to hit them with a bolt of lightning," Krennicx said.

"Seriously?"

"Seriously."

They both laughed. "Well," Jacob said, laughing, "at least you don't have to speak their language and just *tell* them to not touch you!" Spot's face was blank. "Right?" Jacob asked. Spot started to walk again with his face blank. "Krennicx?" Jacob asked again, walking after him. "Krennicx? Spot! Spot? Krennicx?! *SPOT?!*"

They walked along the busy city sidewalks as cars drove fast along the four-lane road. Jacob always liked the city and hated it at the same time. He didn't mind the hustle and bustle much, but he didn't like that he was constantly bumping into someone. "Sorry!" Jacob said for what felt like the twentieth time.

"Are you sure you can handle this?" Krennicx's voice buzzed in his head.

"What's that supposed to mean?" Jacob thought in return.

"I know first missions are hard, but it must be even harder to know your family is on the line."

"Yeah, it is kind of hard, I don't want to be the reason they die. I don't want that to happen!"

"I know what you mean."

"Really?" Jacob asked, shocked. *"How do you know?"*

"You're not the only one like this my friend; every mission puts all of our families at risk."

"Then is it even worth it?"

"Every single one of us thought that at first," the voice of Krennicx said with a sigh, **"until the first time we saw what the Diammonites have done and are doing right now."**

Jacob sighed, *"It's that bad, huh?"*

"Unfortunately."

Jacob thought for a second, *"Why can't I start a conversation with anyone? I've been trying to talk to Hazel to see if she's ok."*

Krennicx chuckled, **"First off, it takes a little bit for you to learn how to start a conversation. Second, it's even *harder* to start one with someone that isn't a Fighter of Peace."**

"So, I'm just going to assume that Glider, Lighter, Glazer, and Tortoise are the rest of the Fighters of Peace?"

"Yes, yes they are, and you can only imagine what their powers are."

"Pretty obvious."

"Yep."

Their conversation was interrupted when Jacob tripped over someone's foot.

"Watch where you're going!" the man barked.

"Sorry," Jacob said, getting off the floor. He looked for Spot, but the crowd was so thick he couldn't see him. *Krennicx?* Jacob tried to think, but the buzz was off, and he didn't know how to start a conversation yet. "Spot?" Jacob called. He tried to copy Krennicx's smirk as he yelled. "Come here, boy! Spot!" Jacob called again, starting to get worried, "Spot!" He was nowhere to be seen. *Did he keep walking when I fell?* Jacob thought. *But wouldn't he notice I wasn't there?* Jacob began to panic. *What if I can't find him? What if Luther decides to come after me and everyone else? I can't protect us!* "Spot!" Jacob yelled loudly. "Where are you?"

Krennicx sat patiently waiting for Jacob to come back from wherever he was. *Why is it that I always have to wait on a human to come back?* Krennicx thought, rolling his eyes. He smiled when he noticed a small child stare at him. *I guess it is a little un-normal to see a dog rolling its eyes.*

The kid's eyes widened when he smirked his signature smile that everyone was amazed with. The kid's jaw dropped, staring in pure shock. Noticing her son had stopped, the child's mother quickly grabbed onto his hand, scowled at Krennicx, and continued to walk along with the kid. *I guess I'm not the only one that's not the biggest fan of dogs,* Krennicx thought. *Oh good grief, what is taking that kiddy so long?* Krennicx didn't look behind him, but he knew what was there. Krennicx whirled around and, using his dog mouth that he *hated,* he caught the stick of the dog catcher's net in midair.

Jacob stopped when he heard a commotion behind him. He turned around to see a crowd of people watching something with great interest. Jacob immediately ran towards the crowd and made his way through it. *Oh, you've got to be kidding me!*

"Come on man, you're stronger than that!" a rude person yelled in the crowd.

"I'm trying!" the struggling dog catcher said.

Spot, the dog who was actually Krennicx, stood with a long stick that was attached to the net in his mouth. Spot stood firm as the dogcatcher pulled with all his strength. The crowd laughed and made fun of the dogcatcher, but Jacob knew Krennicx, and he knew he was full of surprises. The dogcatcher relaxed, then pulled with all his strength. But Krennicx, who had to be the smartest dog ever, let go at that precise moment. The dogcatcher fell backwards with a thud. The crowd exploded with laughter and mockery at the poor dogcatcher. This had to have been the most embarrassing moment in the poor fella's life! Spot noticed Jacob and ran to him.

"So much for keeping a low profile!" Jacob scowled.

"Surely he saw that coming," Krennicx murmured.

"We should probably get going."

"Yep."

They ran along the sidewalk while the dogcatcher scrambled to his feet and chased after him.

"Let me guess," Jacob said as they ran, "you know this dogcatcher, don't you?"

"I usually don't go into the city, so no, but I do know your country dogcatcher," Krennicx said with a smirk.

"So you're the dog Davis is always talking about?"

"I am his worst nightmare."

Jacob laughed. He glanced behind him. "I don't see him anywhere," Jacob said.

"That's what he wants you to think," Krennicx said in Jacob's head. He was right. The dogcatcher jumped in front of them and tried to throw a net on Spot. But Krennicx was ready. Spot jumped into the air and kicked the dogcatcher in the face. The dogcatcher fell back in surprise. He scrambled to his feet and stared at him in shock. Spot smiled and ran in between his legs.

"Get back here!" the dogcatcher yelled, still not noticing Jacob. Jacob was about to tell him that he was his dog, but Krennicx stopped him. **"That wouldn't be a good idea,"** Krennicx said in his head. **"He** would have to report it to his boss. King Luther would hear about me being with you and he'd know it is me."

"Ok," Jacob responded, *"then what do I do?"*

"I think this man's biggest fear is heights, so meet me at the nearest apartment building. Second floor."

"Apartment building!" Jacob thought in panic. *"You know I'm not the biggest fan of heights either!"*

"I know," Krennicx responded, **"even though you literally *have* a pet dragon."**

"It's not official yet," Jacob thought, smiling.

"Sure," Krennicx said disbelievingly. **"Now act like you're just going for a run and go to the top floor of the closest apartment building. Go up through the front. I'll go up through the back. You know, where the emergency exit is."**

"Glad it's not me," Jacob responded. He ran fast and Spot slowed down, causing a distance between them. The first tall apartment building he saw was next to him on the left. He turned and went to the other side of the building where the regular stairs were and began to run up them.

Krennicx ran much slower than he liked, but he knew that he couldn't outrun the poor, exhausted dogcatcher if he wanted the plan to work. He did not want to put Jacob's family in danger. Krennicx continued to slow down until the dogcatcher was a few feet behind him.

He sped up a little to be safe from the net. Krennicx closed his eyes to think of what the man's name was. Ned. *Well, that matches him pretty well.* Again, Ned tried to catch him with his net. Krennicx quickly dodged it. He saw the apartment building he wanted and, speeding up, he ran to the foot of it. He tested the rickety escape stairs on the side of the building and began to run up it the best he could. Ned paused and looked up, gulping. He took a deep breath and began to slowly climb up. *Sorry dearie,* Krennicx thought, *but I'm not exactly in the mood of being caught.* Krennicx ran up the steps as Ned tried to run too. But he was way too out of breath. Ned tripped and almost fell off the building. Krennicx stopped and looked back when he made it to the second floor, concerned, but not too much.

Jacob ran up the stairs as fast as he could without falling. He made it up just in time to see Krennicx, as the dog, Spot, pull the leaver to the small stairs. The stairs began to fold and the dogcatcher quickly ran back down to the ground with a yelp. Spot smiled.

Jacob shook his head, "You're lucky he didn't fall."

"*He's* lucky he didn't fall," Krennicx said. Jacob rolled his eyes. *Oh no!* "Hey," Krennicx said smirking, "isn't this Jasmine's apartment?"

"Oh, shut up," Jacob said, remembering everything he had told Krennicx over the many years. It made him feel sick. Krennicx's ears perked up and his eyes widened. Jacob heard it too. Footsteps. Panic rose inside of him; he stared at Krennicx to see what to do. Krennicx glanced at the stairs and Jacob shook his head. Jacob pointed towards the way he came and began to walk that way. Krennicx rolled his eyes and started to reluctantly follow. The door slammed open on Krennicx's face and knocked him over the side of the balcony. Jacob gasped in panic.

"Jacob?" a familiar voice asked.

Jacob paused and slowly turned around, "Jasmine! Hi, nice…..er….nice to see you!"

She's even prettier than a Sun Dragon. Jasmine had dark skin and beautiful long black hair. She wore a bright, light blue gown with white patterns on the bottom. "Nice….to see you too?" Jasmine said slowly. "What are you doing here?"

"I was……. uh," he glanced over to see with relief Krennicx hanging on to the side of the balcony.

"Uh…… What?" Jasmine asked. "If you were coming here to see me for some reason, then why didn't you come to the front door? Are you trying to break into my house?"

"No! No, of course not!" Jacob yelped, watching Krennicx. "I was……. looking for my dog."

"You have a dog?" Jasmine asked in disbelief.

"Yes," Jacob answered. "He got scared and ran off and I thought I saw him come up here."

"Ok……," Jasmine said, "do you need any help?"

"I should be fine," Jacob responded.

Krennicx began to slip but caught himself. "Hurry up!" he said quietly. "These dog paws are terrible!"

Jacob shook his head.

"Are you ok?" Jasmine asked. "You're acting really weird."

"I'm fine," Jacob responded, trying hard not to lie. "I just hope my dog is ok."

"He is *not* ok!" Krennicx said so quietly, and *so* raspy. "Want to know why? Cuz he's a dog! Their paws are terrible! Now hurry up!"

"As long as he has a collar and doesn't get hit by a car, he should be fine," Jasmine responded, "but if he doesn't have a collar then he's most likely dead."

"Dead?" Jacob asked in alarm. "They wouldn't kill him, would they?"

"Well, not right away," Jasmine said, "but they would in a few days if no one claims him."

"Well, then, I guess I better go make sure he's not at the pound," Jacob said, stepping back.

"Ok," Jasmine said, not caring in the least bit.

"Bye," Jacob said awkwardly.

"Bye."

Jacob tried to calmly walk away, but he knew he was walking weird. *Why do I have to be so awkward?!* Jacob walked loudly down the stairs, then he paused and listened. After a few seconds he heard the door shut. He sprinted up the stairs and back to the balcony.

"Took you long enough, lover boy!" Krennicx said angrily.

"Oh shut it." Jacob smirked as he grabbed onto Krennicx's dog paws and pulled him up. "You're welcome."

"Did you hear me say thank you?" Krennicx asked.

"Come on," Jacob said, leading the way back the way he came.

"You really weren't lying when you said you don't know how to talk to her."

Jacob took a deep breath. "You know," he said, "I think I know how to fix the dogcatcher problem."

Krennicx moaned, "Let's get this over with."

"Hi, I was wanting to register my dog," Jacob said to the vet associate at the desk. "What all do I need to do?"

"Has he had his rabies shot?" the lady asked.

"No ma'am."

"Well, he's going to need his rabies shot, microchip, and flea medication," the lady said. "What breed is he?"

"A mutt," Jacob responded, looking down at Krennicx, "an *ugly* mutt."

Spot growled.

"Is he fixed?"

Spot chocked and coughed. "Errr," Jacob said, staring at the dog. *Awkward!* Jacob cleared his throat. "I….don't know," he finally said when she gave him a weird look.

"Alright….. I'd advise to schedule an appointment to do it if he isn't, but it's not as important as the rabies shot."

Jacob took a breath with relief, "Ok."

"I think the doctor should already be ready so if you can just sign here." The lady gave him paperwork and a pen.

"Is there any way I can just get an ID tag and reschedule an appointment?"

"I'm afraid if he doesn't get his rabies shot, he would have to go to the pound," the associate responded.

Krennicx nodded.

"Ok," Jacob said, taking the paperwork, "I guess you can go ahead and do it."

"Well, just go ahead and fill that out while the doctor sees him."

"Thank you," Jacob said, sitting down on the waiting bench while they led Spot away.

Krennicx sat on a raised bed, waiting for the veterinarian. He flinched at the thought of a 'veterinarian' *I. Hate. Being. A. Dog. Haha! At least Jacob got uncomfortable. If this dude tries to 'check' me, I WILL bite his face…. off!!*

As if he was summoned by the thought, the doctor walked into the room. He had short, golden blond hair and wore a long white doctor's coat. "Alright Mr. Spot," he said putting on rubber gloves, "I'm just going to give you a little shot that will protect you." *Heard that before,* Krennicx thought. The veterinarian picked up a shot with white liquid in it. "This is how it's going to work: I'll do the shot first, then the microchip, ok?"

"Ok *doctor,*" Krennicx said, smirking at his shocked face, *"this* is how it's going to work."

"Here you go," Jacob said, handing the associate the paperwork, "and I'm going to get this collar and leash."

She gave the bright pink leash and the brown leather collar a funny look, "Ok," she said, scanning it.

Jacob smirked.

"Here you go," the doctor said walking out. Spot walked next to him. The doctor looked terrified, "He's all good. Take care." He turned around and speed-walked away. Jacob stared at him warily as he walked away. He looked at Spot. He was smirking his smile. *Oh boy.*

"Well, I guess you guys are good to go," the associate said.

"Ok, thank you," Jacob said. Smiling, he bent down and attached the collar around Spot's neck. Krennicx's eyes widened when he attached the hot pink leash to the collar. Jacob tried hard not to laugh as they left. When they walked past the property, Jacob burst out laughing.

"That was just too good!" Jacob said laughing.

"No one hears of this," Krennicx said, walking along. It was so satisfying to walk him on a leash. "Man, I wish Glider was here to see this! Krennicx Severein, in the palm of my hand…on a leash!"

"Seriously?"

"Did you actually get a rabies shot, flea medicine, and a microchip?" Jacob asked, starting to laugh even more.

Krennicx smirked his smile, "Poor doctor."

Jacob wasn't sure if he really wanted to know what happened, "So," Jacob said smiling, "how do you like your leash?"

"How do *you* like *your* leash?"

"What do you mean?" Jacob asked. He heard laughter behind him. *Oh no!* he thought, realizing in horror who it was.

"Well, well, if it isn't little Jackie."

Jacob took a deep breath and turned around to face the group of teenagers. "Brian, Gary, and the gang," Jacob greeted, "nice to see you."

Brian and Gary had to be the most popular kids in school. Brian had curly, blond hair and Gary had brown, curly hair. Brian had to be the most muscular kid in school, and Gary, well… he was probably the biggest in school, but it wasn't exactly muscles. They were definitely opposites in size. But they both did have brown eyes. Not only were they brothers, but they were BEST friends. The two of them were bad enough, but when they were surrounded by their army of ten cool kids, things got rough.

"Terrible to see you," Brian said.

"Nice hot pink, loser," Gary said.

"Wait, what?" Jacob asked realizing the leash. "It's not like that!" Jacob could feel Krennicx's laughter.

"Check it out!" Brian said to their army. "This kid likes hot pink!"

Brian, Gary, and their gang all laughed. "What kind of dog *is* that?" Gary asked. "It's ugly."

"He's not ugly!" Jacob defended.

Brian raised his eyebrow at him, "You like him?"

Jacob gulped, "Yes." He could feel Krennicx snicker.

"Hm," Brian said. He pushed Jacob away and the gang immediately pinned him against a tree.

"Don't hurt him!" Jacob shrieked.

"Now why would I hurt it?" Brian asked.

"I wasn't talking to you," Jacob responded.

Brian laughed, "I doubt it would have to come to that." He unhooked the pink leash and tossed it to the entourage. "Be free, ugly dog!" Spot raised his eyebrows, sat down and stared at Brian. "Shoo!" Brian said, trying to scare him away. "What is wrong with this dog?"

"What is wrong with *you?*" Jacob was glad Brian and Gary couldn't hear Krennicx like he could.

"Well," Gary said with a small laugh, "if you can't break it, then they will." He pointed to a group of large Rottweilers. *Oh no!* Jacob thought in terror. He wanted to run but they pinned him to the tree. He knew these dogs. They were mean. They were huge. They were weapons. And they were heading right for Krennicx.

CHAPTER 20

DAY WASTED

Of all of the dogs Krennicx didn't like, Rottweilers were the worst. He sat straight and acted calm, even as eleven monstrous dogs ran towards him barking loudly. But Krennicx didn't even flinch. They stopped in front of him and growled angrily. Krennicx stared at the two in the front, their name tags dangling from their collars. Bolt and Flash. Krennicx waited for them to make the first move.

"Hello, wimp," Bolt said hoarsely.

"Bonjour imbecile," Krennicx greeted calmly.

They barked a laugh (literally barked) "It seems this one doesn't know how to talk to us!" Flash said, laughing.

"That must be why he isn't terrified!" Bolt said. "He doesn't understand us!"

"He'll understand this!" said Flash. He let out a massive bark right in Krennicx's face.

"I can assure you," Krennicx said, calmly swiping the spit off of his miserable dog face, "I understand every word. It is you, my friend, that does not understand me."

They stared at him in shock, unable to say anything. *Probably because they're not used to anyone fighting back. Especially the fact that I am not afraid. That must be very shocking.* Recovering, they barked, "You dare mock us!" Bolt said angrily. "You're not even a purebred!"

"You have no right!" Flash joined in. "You're merely a mutt!"

"Well," Krennicx said, keeping his calm, "if I am a mutt, then I guess that makes you a butt, does it not?"

That did it. They barked angrily and circled around him in a frenzy, growling. Krennicx could hear the laughs of Brian, Gary, and the gang. He could feel the fear in dear Jacob. Krennicx smiled. He had made a promise. He *will* protect this kid with his life, even if it's from a gang of idiotic teenagers and their stupid pets.

"Ready to die?" Flash asked.

"I'm always ready."

"Wait," one of them said, stopping the circle.

"What?!" Bolt barked.

"Aren't we supposed to do the sniff?" the dog asked. "You know, the code?"

Bolt sighed, "We have to obey the code." There was an impatient groan among the pack.

"The *code?*" Krennicx asked. *Stupid dogs have a code? Of course!*

"Have you been sniffed yet?" Flash asked, ignoring his question. *You've got to be kidding me,* Krennicx thought, realizing what they were talking about.

"What," Krennicx said, "you want to sniff my butt?"

"It is tradition," Bolt said with a grave nod.

"Yeah, I think I'd rather be eaten," Krennicx said.

They growled, "You *will* be sniffed!" They stepped forward, expecting to get what they wanted.

Krennicx chuckled. He stood up on his four paws and allowed his voice to sound humorous, "You want to sniff my butt, eh? Well, then."

Krennicx burst into a creepy laugh that seemed to make them scared, "You sniff my butt, you sniff my fart! Now sniff it baby!" He jumped onto the nearest dog's face, sending it back in a howl. He jumped off and over the entire pack, landing behind them. There was a gasp from the gang that held Jacob against a tree. Krennicx smiled and turned around to face the dogs. They spun around in pure shock and fear. Krennicx began to chuckle again. "How did that sniff feel?" Krennicx asked. "Do you want more sniffs? Or do you want a bite?"

They growled furiously, "You *will* die!" They ran towards him in a stampede. Krennicx smiled. He knew what these dogs were expecting, so he did the opposite. Bolt himself came first, expecting to bite his prey. But Krennicx was no prey. He was predator. Krennicx fell to his back on the ground just as Bolt reached him. Krennicx pushed hard against Bolt's stomach before Bolt had time to realize Krennicx was underneath him. Bolt yelped in pain and flew through the air, landing on the ground with a whimper. The stampede stopped in surprise. Krennicx chuckled and climbed up the tree, above where they held Jacob. They let go and staggered back in surprise. Krennicx stood on a long thick branch and continued his strange and creepy chuckle. "Apologies dearie," Krennicx said, only allowing the dogs and Jacob to understand him, "but it appears this is the only thing you can eat." He jumped off the tree and landed gracefully in front of Jacob, "Eat my dust ya idiots!" Jacob and Krennicx took off running alongside each other. Krennicx could hear Gary yelling at the dogs to chase after them, but they were too afraid. Krennicx smiled, *I promise you dear one, I will protect you.*

"That was amazing!" Jacob said as they ran along the sidewalk. "No one has ever stood up to them like that! How did you *do* that? No one has ever been able to beat those dogs!"

"I believe you have forgotten who your partner is," Krennicx said jokingly. Jacob laughed. "So, did you learn anything?" Krennicx asked.

"Yeah," Jacob said. "Why in the world does Glider keep trying to prank you?"

"That is a good question."

"I am *never* going to try to do that again," Jacob said, laughing.

"Good boy," Krennicx responded as if he was talking to a dog.

Jacob laughed again. What was this? Even though his family's lives were in danger, Jacob had never felt so safe in his life. Sure, Krennicx was insanely weird and a little……well, a lot crazy, but somehow he felt so…*fatherly*. Jacob didn't know why, but somehow it felt like Krennicx really would die for him. Jacob smiled, "So what next?"

"Waste our time," Krennicx responded. "After we eat lunch, of course."

"Good," Jacob said, "I'm starving."

Eating was really weird for Jacob, due to the fact that a *dog* ate off a plate right next to him. And of course they ate at a fried chicken restaurant! After they ate, they did what Krennicx had said they'd do, they wasted the day. As they sat on the side of the road and stared off into the distance, no one said anything. "So....," Jacob said, trying to break the silence. "Why are we doing this?"

"Doing what?" Krennicx asked.

"Sitting on the side of the road looking homeless," Jacob answered flatly.

"You tell me."

"What do you mean?"

"Well," Krennicx said, "you're the one that said you were tired of walking."

"What!" Jacob yelped standing up. "You're telling me that we've been sitting here doing nothing, for nothing?!"

"Yes."

Jacob groaned, "Why?"

"I told you we have to waste the day," Krennicx responded.

"But why?"

"Oh quit whining."

"I'm not whining!" Jacob defended.

"Sure."

"Hey...."

Krennicx chuckled, "So what do you want to do, Mr. Whiny?"

Jacob smiled.

"Seriously? A baseball game?" Krennicx asked as they sat on the highest bleacher.

"The school baseball game," Jacob corrected, as the crowd of mostly parents cheered for their kids.

"That's even worse," Krennicx said. "I thought it was the beginning of summer."

"It is," Jacob said, "so, it kicks off with baseball."

"Hmm," Krennicx said.

"YES!" Jacob screamed standing up. "GO JASMINE! WAHOO!" Krennicx raised an eyebrow at him. "What?" Jacob asked innocently.

"What did I tell you about young crushes?" Krennicx asked.

"To run to them?" Jacob asked, sitting back down.

"To run *away* from them."

"So you had a bad experience, so what?"

"Boy," Krennicx said, "I know nearly every. Single. Thing. That happens in Annorlia. Trust me, the percentage is around ninety-nine.... point nine.."

Jacob rolled his eyes, "It's not like I'm actually going to try to *date* yet. Besides, what's so bad about cheering for her? She just gave her team a point?"

"Wait a minute," Krennicx said, shooting up. "Team?"

"Yeah," Jacob said, confused. "Baseball is two teams." Krennicx's eyes widened. "What?" Jacob asked.

"Do I know more about your family than you?" Krennicx asked, panicked. *Oh no!* Jacob realized, *Hazel.* Bat in hand, Jacob's sister Hazel walked to home base, determination on her face.

"How could I have forgotten?" Jacob asked in panic. "How could I forget that my own sister is on this team?"

"I was wondering the same thing."

"You're not helping."

"We need to go," Krennicx said.

"Hold on."

"Seriously?!"

"Let me watch her first," Jacob said. Krennicx sighed. Jacob smiled and watched his sister. With the bases loaded, the pitcher took a deep breath and basically danced till he threw the ball towards Hazel. Hazel swung the bat and sent the ball flying, "Yes!" Jacob cheered. The ball was gone! Hazel ran. A grand slam home run.

"I'm guessing that was good?"

"That was amazing!" Jacob said with pride for his sister. The crowd cheered loudly and congratulated everyone. Everyone but Hazel. Jacob frowned and glanced at Krennicx. He was frowning too. Jacob sighed, "So that's why she never wanted us to come to her games." They stared at his sister. She sat alone and looked at no one. *How dare they!* Jacob thought angrily, *SHE is the reason they got those home runs. SHE is the best player EVER! Why didn't she ever tell me about this?*

"How long has this game been going?" Krennicx asked.

"I don't know," Jacob said, still staring at his lonely sister. "It was already going on when we got here."

"Then isn't it about time for...." Krennicx was cut off by a loud buzzard.

"Seventh inning stretch!" Jacob said, panicked.

"Oh no!" Krennicx said in Jacob's head. Jacob saw it. Hazel was coming their way.

"What do I do?" Jacob asked in alarm. Hazel wasn't looking up, but if she did…..she would totally see him. Instead of responding, Krennicx jumped onto Jacob, causing him to fall off the bleacher. Jacob didn't even have time to scream, for he had already landed painfully on the ground with Krennicx on top of him. Jacob winced, "Ow."

"Come on," Krennicx whispered. He jumped off and ran. Jacob stood up painfully and ran after him. *He's a lot heavier than I thought,* Jacob thought, clutching his stomach. Jacob followed Krennicx as they ran underneath the rows of bleachers. "Ow," Jacob yelped as he bumped his head. "Where are you even trying to go?" Krennicx stopped and signaled to be quiet. "What?" Jacob asked. Krennicx glanced next to them where Hazel was walking by.

"Where are you even going?" Jacob mouthed.

"We're leaving, aren't we?"

"Yeah, but what direction are you going?"

"Out," Krennicx responded. **"Just follow me."** Jacob still didn't understand why he couldn't start a conversation like Krennicx did, but he obeyed and followed. They climbed out of the back of the bleachers and darted for the fence. Jacob knew that he had to be fast. He did *not* want Hazel to see him. He did *not* want to explain everything to her yet. But he knew he'd eventually have to explain everything. Krennicx quickly jumped completely over the fence without even touching it. Jacob remembered what Krennicx had taught him and tried to climb and then jump. He tripped at the top of the fence and fell over the side of it, landing on his stomach.

"Ow," Jacob winced. He looked up to see Krennicx's blue dog eyes.

"Quite the fall there, dearie," Krennicx said with a dog smirk.

"Oh stop it."

Krennicx chuckled, "Not safe yet young'n. Come on." He ran along the sidewalk of the road. Jacob moaned and scrambled to his feet and ran after him.

"I feel kind of bad," Jacob said, walking along the sidewalk with Krennicx. "Hazel needed me, but I wasn't there."

"Well, you were there, you just didn't do anything."

"Oi!" Jacob barked. "You made me run! You said she couldn't see me!"

"I don't recall saying that," Krennicx said with a smile, "you just assumed that."

"Seriously?! You mean I could've talked to her!"

"Well, it would have ruined absolutely everything. She would tell your mom, your brother would find out, and then he'd tell King Luther. Luther would send his soldiers out, they'd kill you and then your family... So, yeah, I guess you could've talked to her."

Jacob sighed, "How could I not tell she didn't have any friends? She *never* has anyone over to see her, and she never talks about anyone. All she really talks about is drawing and..."

"Dragons?"

"Oh, how could I not realize this! It's not that she *only* wants a dragon it's……she wants a friend. And she's always said that when you earn a dragon's loyalty…"

"They'll never leave you," Krennicx finished for him.

"I have not been the best big brother, have I?" Jacob asked. "What am I supposed to do?"

"I'm sorry, young'n," Krennicx responded, frowning, "but I don't have a sister to be with, so I don't know what it's like. I'm not the right one to ask."

"I'm sorry," Jacob said. "Do you have a brother?"

"No," Krennicx said, not looking up. Jacob frowned. Krennicx never really said anything about his own family. Jacob figured something bad had to have happened.

"So," Jacob said, trying hard not to ask family questions, "was this day well wasted?"

Krennicx chuckled, "I don't know, that game was a lot."

"So now what are we going to do?"

"The night is coming," Krennicx responded. "Now we save our friends."

"And Glider?"

"And Glider," Krennicx sadly agreed.

CHAPTER 21

THE RESCUE

"I still don't see how this is going to work," Jacob said. Kings Park was lit by many beautiful lights. "Explain to me how two teenagers are going to break into the king's castle?"

"Trust me," Krennicx said in his head. **"Now, are you in position?"**

"You can say that," Jacob responded, "though, I have no idea how I got up here." Jacob sat high in a tree out of sight from the guards. He looked down, then regretted it.

"Yeah, starts with k and ends with x," Krennicx responded.

"Krennicx?"

"You don't know how to spell my name, do you?"

"Nope."

"Now, when you see the signal, I want you to get in through the main entrance."

"The main entrance, are you insane!" Jacob yelped a little too loudly.

"Yes."

"They're going to kill me!"

"Oh ye of little faith, relax," Krennicx responded. **"Your best weapon right now is trusting me."**

"May I remind you that's also my *only* weapon?" Jacob asked, panicked.

"Then I guess you better use it wisely."

"Haha very funny…where are you anyway?"

"The king's personal power tower."

"What?" Jacob yelped. "How did you even get in there?"

"Like you said," Krennicx responded, **"I'm insane."**

"I'm guessing I don't really want to know."

"Do you?"

"Nah, I'm good."

"Ready?" Krennicx asked. All the lights shut off and it became pitch dark.

"No countdown?" Jacob asked. There was an uproar as all soldiers realized there was no power in the entire castle. Jacob obeyed what Krennicx had instructed and waited in the tree. He could hear the commands of captains telling everyone what they needed to do. Groups of soldiers ran in all directions to figure out what happened. Jacob waited till the last group ran by underneath him. He took a deep breath and jumped from the tree. He landed crouched with his right hand on the ground and his left leg in a split position, "Wow." Jacob said quietly, impressed with himself. He got up and ran towards the entrance of the castle, the moon lighting his path. He hid behind a tree and looked at what he was up against. There had to be around ten soldiers or more guarding the gate. He had no idea how he was going to get through, but then he heard it. A roar. A dragon roar. The soldiers looked terrified as they stared into the sky with their spears at ready. Jacob knew this was his chance. He had to take it. He ran for the gate as fast as he could. He knew they would still see him, so he was going to own it. "HELP!" Jacob yelled, getting their attention. "I'm being chased by a dragon!" He continued to run for the gate without slowing down. They looked at him scared and confused. They were about to stop him but were interrupted by another roar. This one right behind Jacob. A black dragon with blue spikes and red eyes flew over Jacob and hit all of the soldiers with its tail in one swift movement. The guards went flying a couple feet, allowing Jacob to go through the gate. The dragon flew ahead of him and busted the large door of the castle down into shards of metal and wood. "Wow," Jacob said, running inside of the castle.

"What?" the dragon asked, turning into his regular form.

"It's just….that door was made to stand against many dragons," Jacob said, staring at the broken door. "They said no dragon should have the strength to break it."

"Well, remember young'n, I am no dragon," Krennicx said. He looked at his wings with a smile.

"Where are all the guards?" Jacob asked warily. He looked uneasily around the large entrance room.

"They're probably all huddled with Luther where Lighter and everyone else is." Krennicx chuckled, "They knew we were coming, but I guess they might have figured we'd come through a window or something."

"So this is a trap?" Jacob asked.

"Of course," Krennicx answered. "I always knew it'd be a trap."

"I didn't."

"Well, you do now dearie," Krennicx said. "The question is, do you want to turn back or keep going?"

Jacob took a deep breath, "We came here to save our friends, and that's exactly what we're going to do. It's my fault they're here, so it's my responsibility to get them back. Even if it is a trap."

Krennicx smiled, "It's funny how quickly someone can change within a few days."

"It all depends on how quickly you learn the truth. Now let's save our friends."

"Lead the way," Krennicx said with a bow.

"Where are we going?"

"Where your lovely journey began."

Jacob smiled and ran into the first tunnel on the right. The Throne Room. Jacob was relieved that Krennicx was his normal form again. It was strange and somewhat uncomfortable to talk to his 'best friend Spot' who was actually Krennicx. It felt like Deja vu as Jacob ran along the twisting hallway towards the Throne Room. It was hard to believe that only a few days ago he and his brother Michael had come to beg the king to let them find the DragonStaff so they can kill the dragons. Now here he was, *helping* Luther's enemy *rescue* a group of dragons! Jacob didn't know why he turned his allegiance so quickly, but for some reason it just felt like it was the right thing to do. Jacob stopped as they came into the first room that went into the Throne Room. He took a deep breath, nodded to Krennicx, and burst the door open. They barged into the Throne Room, expecting a lot of guards. No one was there. He looked around the Throne Room, expecting someone to jump out and kill him. But it was empty.

"What kind of trap is this?" Jacob asked.

"I guess he was expecting us to go to the dungeon or something," Krennicx responded, smirking his hilarious smile. "I guess we really have surprised him."

"I guess so."

Krennicx frowned and walked to the right side of the room, where the statue of himself was. He looked upset. "Why is it that so many suffer just because you made a mistake?" Krennicx asked with a sigh.

"Is that real?" Jacob asked.

Krennicx sighed, "Nothing in this castle is fake, my friend."

"Did you know him?" Jacob asked. "Was he one of your kind?"

"No," Krennicx responded. "He isn't my kind. But I did know him. I know all panthers from the forest. Honestly, I kind of know everyone."

"You do?" Jacob asked.

"Well, I haven't *met* everyone, but I know everyone."

"How?"

"Let's not talk about that right now," Krennicx said. "I think I know where he wants us to go."

"Where?" Jacob asked, rolling with the conversation change.

Krennicx smirked a smile, "Funny, it's pretty much where I began."

"I can't believe we're doing this!" Jacob said, following Krennicx as they ran up a winding staircase.

"It's the only way."

"How?" Jacob asked. "How can it be the only way?"

"You'll understand soon," Krennicx responded. "Just trust me."

"Ok," Jacob said with a sigh, "I trust you."

"Good boy," Krennicx said. The stairs ended into a large, half-circular, open room with three large doors.

"What is this place?" Jacob asked.

Krennicx smirked, "An arena."

"Sooo, how did you 'begin' in an arena?"

"Oh hush!"

King Luther sat on the first row of his arena, tapping his finger on the armrest while hundreds of soldiers around him surveyed the area. Luther knew Severein was strong, but even he had weaknesses. He wondered about his plan. He expected sacrifices, but he wasn't exactly expecting all the power in his castle to be one. At least he still had power for prison cells and stuff like that, but all lights and outlets were gone. He knew it had to be part of Severein's plan, but there were still no reports on any break-ins. The last time he tried to get Severein he had underestimated him, causing many complications. This time would be different. He learned his lesson last time. Now he knew more about him. He had studied him for years. He knew his darkest secrets. He knew the one thing that could beat him. The one thing that can silence Severin forever. He had done this once, he can do it again. The last time he had tried to do this…it was a disaster. He had no idea just how much the small creature was capable of. The microphone from the glass box that overlooked the arena rang, and there was a familiar chuckle that surprised everyone. Luther jumped to his feet and the guards did the same. "Miss me?" the voice of Severein asked from the microphone. Soldiers immediately ran up the steps to the glass box. King Luther took a few steps ahead and looked around. It was still dark, but the farthest large light in the arena cut on. And then, one by one, every single light cut on, lighting up the entire arena. King Luther knew that the power couldn't be fixed that fast.

"Hello darling."

Luther and the soldiers jumped in surprise and fear. He whirled around. On the very chair he was just sitting on, sat Krennicx Severein.

Jacob couldn't help but smile at the terrified response of King Luther when he saw Krennicx sitting where he himself just was. He guessed Krennicx's plan was working, for all of the soldiers who were in the arena were now with King Luther. Jacob crept along the wall of the arena. Krennicx had said that even though the lights would be on, as long as he stayed close to the wall, he should be unseen. He reached the end of the arena and, like Saul's, there were a few dragon cells.

"Jacob?" a familiar voice asked.

"Lighter!" Jacob said, putting his hands on the bars. Lighter stared at him with a worried expression. Even though Jacob met him a few days ago, he was still really happy to see him.

358

"What's going on?" Lighter asked. "I heard Krennicx."

"We're getting you out of here," Jacob responded. He tried to break the lock that kept the cell closed. "Well, that's definitely not working."

"No, Jacob you can't."

"I'm trying, ok," Jacob said. "It would be nice if you could give me ideas on how to break this."

"No, that's not what I'm talking about," Lighter said. "I mean it's a trap. You shouldn't have come."

"Krennicx told me to trust him," Jacob responded. "He seems really sure that his plan will work."

"I know it'll work," Lighter said. "That's exactly what I'm worried about."

"You know Krennicx's plan?"

Lighter nodded, "He didn't tell me everything, but he said what he wants to do."

"Can he talk in anyone's head?"

"Yes, but I think only we can respond. I think."

"Oh," Jacob said, still feeling weird about the word 'we.'

"So what is his plan?"

"If you knew, you probably wouldn't want to do it," Lighter responded.

"That doesn't make me worried," Jacob said, still trying to break the door open.

"Don't worry," Lighter said, "it's all going to somewhat make since after it's done."

"Somewhat?"

"Trust him."

"So I've heard you've made quite the appearance in Cloudairia," King Luther said, recovering himself. "The only reason I didn't come is because I knew that the foolish king would fail."

"That he will," Krennicx said, staring into Luther's eyes.

Luther laughed, taking his eyes away. "You are still so erratic, aren't you."

"Why is it that kings use fancy words?" Krennicx asked.

"Said 'dear darling.'"

Krennicx smirked his smile, "I'm guessing you got the letter."

"I did," King Luther said with a nod, "and the answer is 'never.' So go tell your little friend that I will never step down. I will always put my people first."

"You are still so un-erratic, aren't you?" Krennicx mimicked.

"Mock me all you want," King Luther said, "but I will always protect my people."

"Then why threaten a kid and his family?" Krennicx asked, changing his voice to serious. He stared into Luther's eyes. "Why harm so many innocent people and dragons who have done nothing to you? The more you harm those who are good, the more your land will become miserable. I can assure you, all people are not idiots, though most are. They will figure out what's going on. They will know it isn't what they asked for. The kingdom will fall, and who do you think it will all point to?"

"Your presence always brings out the worst in everyone," King Luther said, losing his regalness.

"I don't know how, but I bring out the truth in everyone," Krennicx said, still staring into Luther's eyes. "The truth that is hidden behind your shield of lies. Stop the treaty. Stop lying. Then maybe he'll let you keep your precious crown. But this is your last warning."

"And this," Luther said smiling, forcing his eyes away as he failed miserably at not looking afraid, "is your last night of life." Arrows whizzed from the ceiling towards Krennicx. Krennicx swiftly jumped from the chair and landed gracefully behind Luther, unharmed. The soldiers immediately tried to slice him with swords, but Krennicx was far too quick for them. He never hit back, he only dodged and jumped over them.

"Dear *darling*," Krennicx chuckled, "this is unavoidable."

"*This* is unavoidable." Luther reached out his hand, and with a flicker of light, something appeared in it. It was a long, wooden, dark grey staff. A black stone dragon rested on the top with its bottom claws holding onto the wood and its tail curled around it. Its eyes were emerald stones. Its wings were folded back, and in its top claws it held a glowing orb that swirled white and dark purple. There was no doubt. It was the DragonStaff.

"King Luther, stop!" Jacob jumped out of his hiding spot from beneath some chairs. "It's not right! The dragons are innocent!"

Luther frowned, "Jacob, my dear boy. I thought you would heal once you came home. I thought the spell they cast would wear off. But it appears you have given me no choice. Kill him."

"No," Krennicx said, jumping in between the soldiers and Jacob.

"Stay away from him!" Lighter jumped into the scene between the soldiers and Luther, growling at the soldiers. The soldiers didn't know whether to attack Krennicx to get to Jacob or attack Lighter to get to King Luther.

"This is just too good," King Luther said with a laugh. "Such a beautiful family reunion."

"King Luther, you've given us no choice," Lighter said with authority in his voice. "Surrender the throne or we will take it by force."

"Force it is," Luther said. There was an icy roar as the gate to the arena sprang open. A chill spread as icy mist sprang into the arena.

"Get down!" Lighter barked. Jacob obeyed as icy mist that looked somewhat like white fire flew above him, clashing onto the chairs. It froze them into pure ice. The dragon stepped out of the mist, revealing who it was. Jacob could see the pain in Lighter's expression. It was Glazer. Jacob realized that all the soldiers were making their way into the rows of chairs, out of the arena floor. King Luther went with them. Roaring, Glazer flew into the air towards them, preparing to let out more ice.

"Glazer would never betray us," Lighter said painfully.

"Of course she wouldn't," Krennicx agreed. They quickly jumped out of the way from another ball of ice.

"It's the Staff, isn't it?" Jacob asked.

"Most likely," Lighter responded. Glazer shot onto Lighter, sending him onto the ground. Lighter shrieked and kicked her off, "I don't want to hurt you!" he called. Glazer only roared and breathed out more ice. They got out of the way, but this time the ice began to spread as it hit the ground. They ran until it stopped spreading. "You guys should go," Lighter said, stopping. "I can hold her back."

"It's not like we'd be able to make it out," Jacob said, glancing at the soldiers. He was mad to see that most of them were actually enjoying the chase.

"I can take her," Krennicx said.

"I know you can," Lighter responded with a worried expression. "I don't want you to hurt her." As if King Luther knew what they were thinking about, another gate opened.

"Now him I can hurt," Krennicx smirked. Glider bolted into the arena and immediately went straight for Krennicx. The second Glider reached him, Krennicx bolted into the air, causing Glider to skid across the arena sand. Glider roared and took off after Krennicx. Glazer returned and blasted a massive amount of ice fire. There were flickers of lighting as Lighter took a deep breath and breathed out fire mixed with lightning. There was an explosion as they crashed together, a ring of lighting caused the ice to shatter in midair. Glazer fell to the ground in surprise. Lighter immediately ran to her to make sure she was ok, looking worried. Jacob was amazed, he had never seen a dragon breath fire, especially with lighting in it. Jacob looked around for Krennicx, then nearly laughed when he saw him staring at one of the cells that now held Glider in it.

"Is she ok?" Jacob asked as Lighter walked back to him.

"Yeah, she's fine," Lighter said. They moaned when there was another roar and Tortoise ran into the arena.

"Will this ever end?" Jacob asked.

Lighter shrugged, "He's the last one of us." Lighter paused and didn't move.

"Are you ok?" Jacob asked, stepping back. Lighter began to growl and stepped closer in a pounce position. "Lighter?" Jacob asked, panicked. "Come on Lighter, fight it." He continued to walk backwards. Lightning flickered around Lighter's mouth as he took a deep breath. Jacob dove out of the way as a ball of lighting and fire shot from Lighter's mouth, piercing a massive hole in the wall. Lighter roared and charged after him, with Tortoise coming up behind. Jacob got up and ran for his life through the hole Lighter had made. He didn't know where he was running, and he didn't even think he would be able to get away from the soldiers. All he knew was that there was a dragon, his friend, that was trying to kill him. He ran and jumped on top of the chairs that faced the arena. He didn't dare look behind him, he knew Lighter was right there. Jacob jumped onto the stairs and ran. He ran out of the door to the arena and for some reason turned left and ran up a spiraling staircase. The stairs ended into a balcony in the dark open sky. Jacob was terrified to look behind him, but when he did, nothing was there. Jacob sighed in relief. *What happened?* Jacob thought. *Did the guards not see me? What happened to Krennicx? Where did Lighter go?* Jacob didn't know what to do. If he went back down there, Lighter might be waiting to kill him. If he stayed on the balcony, the soldiers and Lighter might kill him. He moaned and leaned against the railings, staring at the park below. Past the park, with its leaves rustling in the wind, was the Dragon Forest. He didn't know why, but he longed to be in the beautiful woods. He breathed hard, the adrenaline pumping so hard it hurt. He was too distracted. He didn't know there was a watch tower above him. He didn't hear the arrow draw and fire. He didn't see it flying towards his neck. He didn't have to. Krennicx flew faster than any arrow. Jacob shrieked in surprise when such a strong force hit him and tipped him over the side of the balcony. Jacob nearly screamed in fear as he knew with no doubt Krennicx was gripping onto his shoulder and falling. Krennicx flared his wings open, but something felt wrong. Krennicx nearly fell from the sky as he glided towards the forest. Krennicx's grip was loosening, and he seemed to be having a hard time staying in the sky. The moonlight reflected on a lake just past the edge of the forest. Krennicx's grip loosened, and he was losing altitude fast. The second Jacob saw the lake below, Krennicx let go.

CHAPTER 22

HOME

Jacob gasped for breath as he pulled himself onto the shore of the lake. He was tired and soaked from head to toe. His eyes were blurry from the unexpected water. When he regained his vision, he expected to see Krennicx, but he wasn't there. "Krennicx?" Jacob asked. *Why did he drop me in a LAKE?! Why was he in such a hurry?* Jacob was beginning to panic. *What happened?* He wanted to call out to Krennicx but was afraid someone else would hear him. His body was sore from the fall, but he still got up and looked for his friend. He remembered that Krennicx was acting like he was about to fall. *So if he fell he would have fallen…..* he pointed his finger in the sky where Jacob fell and angled it in the direction Krennicx was heading, *there.* The top of a tree was broken and the one behind that one was snapped completely in half. Jacob ran in that direction, hoping his friend was ok. "No," Jacob breathed. He ran over and got on his knees in front of where Krennicx lay limply on the ground. His eyes were closed, but he couldn't tell if he was alive or not. He hoped he was, but that really did look like a nasty fall. "Krennicx!" Jacob shrieked in panic. Krennicx moaned and rolled over. Jacob was relieved. "You're alive. What happened?" Jacob asked, worried. Krennicx rolled onto his feet and tried to stand up, but he fell right back down. Then Jacob realized what was wrong. "Krennicx," he said in alarm. An arrow had gone deep into his back. Krennicx looked at him and forced out a smile. Jacob realized what had happened at the balcony. "Why?" he asked. "You got in front of me?"

Krennicx looked tired, "You would have died."

"But now *you'll* die." He had only known Krennicx for just a few days, but now, he realized that he didn't want to lose him. He tried his best to fight back tears as he stared at his insane trainer. Krennicx closed his eyes, "The juice of the Zillow plant is powerful enough to kill a human."

"But is strong enough to put a dragon to sleep for a few hours," Jacob finished, remembering what he had been told.

"I'm no dragon, dearie," Krennicx said with a tired smile.

"Sure, but I'm no doctor, and even I can tell that arrow should kill you," Jacob said, worried.

Krennicx smirked, "Look who cares."

Jacob smiled wearily, "We need to get you somewhere safe."

"Nowhere is."

Jacob sighed, "You might not be a dragon, but you should still rest, and maybe I know somewhere you can."

Krennicx smiled wearily, "To your house it is."

Jacob smiled, "You really need to stop reading my mind."

"Hm."

Jacob rolled his eyes, "Let me go scout the area to make sure no one is following us. Wait here and rest." Jacob ran back to the lake and looked around. Seeing nothing, he turned to walk back, but then he heard a twig snap. Jacob jumped and looked around, his heart pounding.

"Jacob!" Michael ran out of the tree line across from the lake.

"Michael?" Jacob asked, relieved.

"What are you doing out here?" Michael asked. "Come on, let's go home."

Jacob paused, remembering what had happened the last time he saw his brother, "Hold on, I need to go get something." Before Michael could say anything, Jacob ran back to Krennicx.

"What are you doing?!" Jacob nearly screamed. Krennicx yanked the arrow from his back and winced. Jacob felt like throwing up even though it was too dark to see any blood.

Krennicx took a deep breath in pain, "Ow."

"Why did you do that!?" Jacob almost shouted. "You're going to bleed to death!"

"Just trust me," Krennicx said, grinning in pain. Krennicx's ear perked up.

"I know," Jacob said. "It's Michael. He wants me to come home with him."

"Well, you are……with me."

"He's not going to approve of that."

"He doesn't have to," Krennicx said with a smirk.

Jacob rolled his eyes.

"What's going on?!" Michael asked, standing in front of them. His eyes widened when he saw Krennicx. "Get away from him!"

"Michael, this isn't what it looks like," Jacob said, standing between Michael and Krennicx. "He's not going to hurt me or you."

"*He* is a dragon!" Michael said. "And dragons hurt everyone!"

"No, they don't!" Jacob defended.

"Come on, Jacob," Michael said, annoyed and afraid. "They literately kidnaped you!"

"They gave me the choice to leave whenever I wanted to, and King Luther told me to go with them and spy on them," Jacob said. "When I tried to run, I was attacked by wolves, but then *he* saved my life."

"No, they've tricked you," Michael said, taking a step closer to them. "You've been brainwashed, but maybe when you come home, you'll realize that."

"I am coming home," Jacob said, standing his ground, "but Krennicx is coming with me."

"Krennicx?" Michael asked. "You *named* it? Never mind. Don't worry." Jacob noticed Michael was reaching for something strapped to his waist. "I'm sure everything is going to be ok." There was a blaster shot, and Michael fell to the ground.

"Michael!" Jacob shrieked. He ran over and got on the floor next to him. "What did you *do?!*"

"Relax," Krennicx said calmly, "it was just a stun." He held out his blaster that he had used in the Cloud Kingdom. Jacob sighed with relief as he felt Michael's heartbeat in his chest, then he saw what Michael was holding. It was a dagger. Krennicx had saved his life....again. Jacob's eyes welled up with tears, *he was going to kill me*. Krennicx stood up to walk, but nearly fell. He sprang his wings open for balance, then winced from the movement. He folded them back and made his way to Jacob, sitting next to him. "There was a rumor," he said, "that if one who was brainwashed were stabbed by a specific dagger on any part of their body, they would be set free from their captors."

"You think King Luther told him that and gave him this?" Jacob asked, holding the dagger.

"I know he did," Krennicx said, taking the dagger. "I know something poisonous when I see it."

"So no matter where he stabbed me," Jacob said, staring at his older brother, "it would have killed me?"

"And he would have had to live with that terrible regret for the rest of his life," Krennicx added with a nod.

Jacob sighed, "King Luther really does want to kill me, doesn't he?"

"Yes," Krennicx responded with a sigh.

Jacob took a deep breath, "Then we have to stop him. First you need to rest and somehow we have to get you *and* Michel home."

"Yeah, I guess I didn't really think about having to carry him."

"I'm guessing you won't be able to turn into a dragon and fly us both there?" Jacob asked. Krennicx smirked a tired smile. "I'll take that as a no."

"Well, you ready to learn how to carry someone to safety?" Krennicx asked with a grin.

Jacob moaned.

"Ow!" Krennicx barked.

"I am so sorry!" Jacob yelped, trying to get Michael's head off of Krennicx's arrow wound. They walked down the road where Jacob's house was. It had been a miserable thirty to forty minutes of walking from the edge of the forest. Jacob held onto Michael's legs as his head and back was on Krennicx's back. Jacob knew Krennicx wasn't a dragon, but he could tell that the Zillow arrow was still affecting him. Jacob tried as hard as he could to hold most of Michael's weight, but he just did not have the strength to hold him. Jacob felt terrible putting so much of Michael's weight on Krennicx's hurt back; he could tell he was already having a hard time keeping his own balance. He looked like he was about to tip over and fall asleep. Jacob couldn't help but smile at the thought of how *weird* the scene looked. "There it is!" Jacob announced with relief when he saw his house. He had never been so happy to see that dirty, white, two-story home. They walked into the yard and sat down. "How are we supposed to get in?" Jacob asked, staring at his bedroom window.

"I'll take care of it." With a wince, Krennicx spread his wings and clumsily launched with one flap to the window. He held onto the shudders and somehow got the window open and jumped in.

Don't I keep my window locked? A few minutes later, Krennicx ran out of the front door. "Come on," Krennicx said, "if we hurry, we can make it."

"Make what?" Jacob asked.

"They're in the playroom," Krennicx responded. "If we hurry, we can make it to your room unseen."

"That's a risk," Jacob said.

"You think it wasn't a risk when we broke into Luther's palace?"

"Good point."

They grabbed Michael again and went as fast as they could into the house. They came into the kitchen where they could hear the TV playing in the playroom. Jacob longed to go in there and hug his mom and Hazel, but he had to do this. His heart nearly stopped when the floor squeaked. They paused and looked around, then took a deep breath and went for the stairs. They crept along until finally they made it into his bedroom. Jacob slowly closed the door behind them and flipped the light on. He took a deep breath. They had made it. Jacob was home. Krennicx laid Michael somewhat gently on the floor.

"Careful," Jacob said.

"If you wanted to be careful you would have kept the light off," Krennicx said. Jacob rolled his eyes. Krennicx still looked extremely tired, especially since he almost fell.

"You can rest on the bed," Jacob offered.

"You sure?" Krennicx asked, looking relieved.

"Unless you'd rather sleep on the cold floor."

Krennicx seemed too tired to do his smirky smile. He hopped onto Jacob's bed and laid on his stomach. "Where are you going?" he asked, noticing Jacob gathering his clothes and going to the door.

"I've been holding it in for toooo long," Jacob responded. "And I guess I'll go ahead and shower.... if you'll be ok."

Krennicx rolled his eyes. Then rested his head on his talons like a cat. He was out. He even slept like a panther. Jacob smiled and left the room.

Krennicx was tired. Really tired. And on top of the tiredness, his back burned a *lot*. He didn't lie when he said it was poisoned with the juice of the Zillow, but it wasn't the juice. It was the heart. Deadly to *all.* The heart of the Zillow can kill anything. Well, almost anything. He had originally thought that it was the juice of the Zillow, but even though it wasn't, he didn't regret doing what he did. The heart was very, very strong. It was almost strong enough to do to him what the juice does to normal dragons. Almost. He had dozed off when Jacob left the room, an uneasy sleep. If it was just the Zillow juice, it really wouldn't have affected him at all. Not only was the arrow filled with the heart of the Zillow, it was filled with a *ton* of it. Though tired, the second there was a sound on the floor, Krennicx forced himself to be awake. He really wanted to sleep, but as long as someone else that he didn't trust was in the room, he wouldn't let himself. Plus, he didn't want to miss talking to Michael when he woke up. He laid on his side and stared at Michael as he regained consciousness.

"Hello, darling," Krennicx greeted with a toothy grin.

"*Ah!*" Michael shrieked. He jumped up, then fell right back down again. Krennicx smirked his smile. Michael was terrified. "You can *talk?!*" He made his way off the floor and stared at him in fear. "What did you do to me?!"

"I shot you," Krennicx responded flatly and honestly.

"You *what?!*"

"Careful young'n," Krennicx advised, "Jacob would prefer to explain everything to you and your parents himself."

"You monstrous dragon!" Michael said, scared but trying to be brave. "I don't know *what* you've done to my brother, but it *has* to stop. I know him, and he would *never* betray me!"

"You're right," Krennicx agreed, "he would never betray you. But tell me dearie, will you betray him?"

"What kind of question is that?!" Michael asked angrily.

"Michael," Krennicx said. Michael's face froze in terror at the sound of his own name. "I know you think I'm going to hurt you, but I promise you I won't. Jacob isn't betraying you, he's trying to help you. There are things you don't understand, but I can explain everything to you. Trust me."

"I will *never* trust a dragon."

"Well, I think there's something you need to know about me," Krennicx said, grinning his smirky smile. His smile grew at the sight of Michael's shocked face. "I am no dragon."

Jacob silently crept along the hallway from the bathroom back to his room. He had a nice shower, and it was weird being in his own clothes again. The weirdest part was that he actually *missed* the other clothes that Krennicx had given him. He was definitely going to have to wash them. Jacob walked into his room during a scene he was not expecting. "What are you *doing?*" Jacob asked. Michael had a dagger in his hand as Krennicx held it in the air while pinning him against the bed. He seemed to be enjoying Michael's horror.

"Jacob, run!" Michael said. "I'll hold it back. Now run!"

Krennicx seemed to be on the verge of laughing.

"Let him go," Jacob said. Krennicx released Michael and smiled. Michael immediately tried to stab Krennicx, but he was expecting that. Krennicx grabbed the dagger out of his hand and kicked him in the stomach. Michael fell back in surprise.

"It has a weapon now!" Michael announced in panic. "If we work together, we can take it!"

Krennicx looked amused.

"Doubt it," Jacob said calmly, "but we don't have to. Michael, he's my friend."

"Not this again!"

"He is!" Jacob said, aggravated. "Trust me."

"It's hard to trust someone who's brainwashed!"

Krennicx finally let out his laugh, "Brainwashed? That's what ya think? I'd say that's the funniest thing I've been accused of, but it isn't. Ha, one time someone claimed that I *stole* their brain. That was hilarious, but still not the funniest thing I've been accused of."

"You're not helping," Jacob said.

Krennicx shrugged, "I'm not good at first impressions."

"I've noticed."

Michael jumped at Krennicx for the dagger, but Krennicx was ready for him. Krennicx caught his hand and tossed it right back at him, causing Michael to hit himself in the face. Michael tried to come back, but Krennicx kicked him again. "Let him go!" Michael yelled angrily.

"Michael, stop," Jacob said, concerned that Krennicx might hurt him. "Even if I am brainwashed, this isn't the way."

Michael ignored him and tried for Krennicx again. Jacob didn't want him to hurt Krennicx, especially on his arrow wound. Jacob tackled his brother before he had a chance to go for his friend. Michael was bigger than Jacob, but even though he only had a few days of training, Jacob was already getting stronger. He gripped onto Michael's wrists and held him back. Michael was difficult to hold as he tried to get out of his grip. Jacob was about to lose his temper, but that was when the bedroom door unexpectedly opened.

"*What* is going on in here?" Hazel stood in the doorway looking at the unexpected scene of her two brothers fighting for real. Michael stopped struggling and Jacob let go.

"Hazel!" Jacob said, happily running over and hugging his sister. Michael eventually did too.

"You're alive!" She said happily with tears in her eyes. She hugged them both at the same time, until her eyes widened, "Oh. My. *GOODNESS!*" She ran in front of the bed where Krennicx sat, "A d-dragon!" She stared disbelievingly at Krennicx as he looked calmly at her. Jacob had never seen her look so happy. "It's a *DRAGON!*"

Jacob smiled, "I met him in the forest." He took a deep breath, "He's my friend."

"YOU MET A DRAGON?!" Hazel was beaming. "Oh my goodness! I. HAVE. SO. MANY. QUESTIONS!"

"Wow," Krennicx said, eyes wide. "You remind me a lot of Glazer."

Hazel was about to blow up, "YOU CAN TALK?! Oh my GOODNESS! I HAVE SO MANY QUESTIONS!"

"Well, I guess it's time for your dreams to come true, dearie." Krennicx lifted his hand/talon for a handshake, "Name's Krennicx."

Hazel grabbed his talon and shook it violently, "My name is Hazel," she said, continuing to shake it. "I am so happy to meet you. I don't know if Jacob told you, but I have always wanted to meet a dragon. Sure, you don't look like how I expected, but I don't care. I have *so many* questions. Oh my goodness! I have finally met a dragon!" *She IS a lot like Glazer,* Jacob realized.

"Hazel, I think that's enough shaking," Jacob said.

"Sorry!" Hazel apologized, letting go. "I'm just so happy to meet you! A dragon!"

"It's fine," Krennicx said with a kind smile. "But the first thing you should know about me is that I am no dragon. Well, at least not full-blooded."

"Oh," Hazel said. "That's ok. You're still from the Dragon Forest, right?"

Krennicx smiled and tilted his head in a nod.

"Wait," Jacob said. "Did you say, 'not *full*-blooded'? Does that mean you have some dragon in you?"

"I'll explain later," Krennicx said.

"This is still so cool!" Hazel said. "You just have no idea how long I've waited to meet a dragon…. or something that HAS some dragon blood….or even just something that knows *anything* about them."

"I know everything about them," Michael said.

"Have you *met* any?" Hazel asked.

"Yeah, Michael," Jacob joined in, *"have* you ever met one?"

Michael glared at Krennicx uneasily.

"Well, ask away dearling," Krennicx said. "I am someone who knows just about everything of dragons."

"Perfect," Hazel said happily.

Michael sat on the window bed looking uncomfortable. Jacob frowned and sat next to him. "You know," Jacob whispered, "if you can't do this for me, then do it for Hazel. She has always wanted to talk to something like a dragon. I'm not going to make you believe me, but Michael please. At least give us tonight. Please?"

Michael sighed.

"Maybe," Jacob continued, "you could get some information through Hazel's questions?" That seemed to have done it, for now at least. Michael leaned back and didn't meet Jacob's eyes. He sighed. *Now I think I know how it feels to be Hazel.*

"What am I doing?" Hazel realized, "I need to get paper! I *have* to draw you! I'll be right back." She sprinted out of the bedroom.

"I don't know if I've ever met someone who likes me this much," Krennicx said with a proud smile.

"I can see that," Michael murmured. Jacob agreed. Hazel ran back in holding a stack of paper and drawing pens.

"Ok," Hazel said, sitting next to Krennicx on the bed. Krennicx eyed her uncomfortably. She immediately went to work drawing. "First question," she said. "Why are your eyes red and scary?"

"Why is your hair long and brown? Krennicx asked.

"Ok, moving on," Hazel said. "If you're not a dragon, then what are you?"

"Krennicx."

"Ok…… moving on," Hazel said with a funny expression. "How many kinds of dragons are there?"

"Depends," Krennicx responded, "there's some that technically aren't counted as dragons."

"Like what?"

"Can we save that one for later?" Krennicx asked.

"Ok…" Hazel answered, confused.

"We don't really have enough time for that one, it's very long," Krennicx added.

"Alright," Hazel said, "I have a weird question."

"What?" Krennicx asked, concerned.

"Do dragons lay eggs?"

Krennicx gave her a funny look, "Actually, they don't. They give birth."

"*Really?!*" Hazel asked, surprised. "Man, I really thought they laid eggs. Since they have scales….wait, *do* they have scales?"

"Yes," Krennicx answered, "but some also have feathers."

"Are there any…..er……*pink* dragons?"

Krennicx smiled, "Jacob, would you like to answer this question?"

Hazel slowly turned to Jacob, eyes wide, "You've *seen* a pink dragon?"

"Maybe….." Jacob said, smiling.

Hazel looked like she was going to explode……again. "I want to see one."

Jacob frowned. *It should have been her to see all the dragons. She was the one who believed in them. Why was it me?* Hazel continued to ask question after question until Jacob finally interrupted, "Krennicx should probably rest," Jacob said, noticing that he was looking *very* tired.

"Why?" Michael asked. "Isn't this what Hazel's always been waiting for?"

Jacob glared at him. Hazel looked a little upset, but Jacob couldn't tell if it was at Michael or Jacob. "Michael, you don't understand," Jacob said.

"Oh I understand plenty," Michael said, standing up. "You're just trying to make excuses so that this *Krennicx* can't accidentally say something important!"

"That's not what I'm doing!" Jacob defended, extremely aggravated. "You didn't let me say *why* he needs rest!"

"So he can make his grip on you *stronger?*" Michael asked.

"He doesn't have a grip on me!"

"I know you!" Michael said. "You would never do this!"

"Well,I am," Jacob said, "and you want to know why? Because I chose to."

"Please stop fighting," Hazel said with a frown. "This should be bringing us together, not breaking us apart. Besides, Dad wouldn't want to see you are fighting on the third day he's here."

"Wait," Jacob realized, "Dad's *here?*"

"Yes," Hazel answered. "He's been worried about you. He can't wait to see you."

"Why didn't you tell me that right when I got here?" Jacob asked.

"I guess I kind of got carried away," Hazel said, glancing where Krennicx had been. *Had* been, "Where did he go?" Hazel asked. Krennicx was gone.

"What have you *done*?" Michael asked, terrified. "He's going to Dad!"

CHAPTER 23

THE ANNORLIAN WAR

Jacob, Michael, and Hazel frantically ran down the stairs in search of Krennicx.

"What have you done!" Michael repeated.

"Nothing," Jacob responded. He didn't know why Krennicx disappeared, but surely he wasn't going to do anything. Jacob trusted Krennicx, but if he was hurting his dad…. They turned left from the stairs and ran through the kitchen till they made it to the guest bedroom. Krennicx sat on the side of the bed next to a tall, tan man with short black hair. Jacob's dad. Michael nearly shrieked at the sight. Krennicx and Jacob's dad were *hugging!*

"What is going on?!" Michael demanded. Jacob's dad pulled away and smiled at his kids. Jacob could feel his eyes tearing. He hadn't seen his father in months.

"Jacob, Michael," Dad said, eyes tearing and opening his arms, "you're ok!" Jacob ran into his arms and hugged him. Michael hesitated, then gave up and hugged him too.

"*What* is going on?" Michael asked, pulling away. "What did you do to him?!" Michael asked, turning to Krennicx.

"Nothing," Krennicx responded.

"You've brainwashed him too, haven't you?!" Michael asked, about to lash out.

"Brainwashed?" Dad asked, wiping his teary eyes. "That's what you think?"

"It's what I know!" Michael said. "Jacob was *never* for the dragons! And now all of a sudden he's brought one to our house? He's brainwashed! And you've been injured by a dragon for weeks! Why in Annorlia would you be *hugging* one?"

Dad sighed and looked to Krennicx, who nodded. "There's something I need to tell you," Dad said.

"I found some bandages and some pain killer for your wound," their mom said, walking into the room. She paused and saw Jacob and Michael, then began to cry. "You're ok! He didn't kill you!" She threw her arms around them and hugged. Jacob never knew she had such a tight grip.

"He hasn't killed me yet," Michael said, eyeing Krennicx.

"He didn't hurt you, did he?" Mom asked, pulling away and checking for injuries.

"Not yet," Michael responded, "but I think he's brainwashed Jacob and Dad."

Mom gave him a weird look, "He hasn't even been here. I don't see how that would be possible."

"What do you mean?" Michael asked. "He's sitting right there!"

"Krennicx?" Mom asked glancing at him. "Oh, I almost forgot! I need to bandage you."

"It's fine," Krennicx insisted as she unwrapped a bandage. "Trust me, it doesn't really need anything."

"Kind of like last time?" Mom asked. "If I hadn't bandaged you up you would have died."

"This time is different," Krennicx said with a smirk.

"Because you're grown?" Mom asked, placing her hands on her hips. "Last time you were a baby."

Jacob chuckled.

"Don't laugh too hard, young'n," Krennicx warned, smirking a smile. "Don't forget she gave birth to you. And you were naked."

Jacob laughed. Mom went to Krennicx's back and frowned, "I'm sorry," she said, "I forgot about that. Is there anything else you might need?"

"Do you have anything that could make me stay awake?" Krennicx asked.

"I have coffee and tea, how's that?" Mom asked.

Krennicx and Jacob exchanged looks, trying not to laugh. "No, thank you," Krennicx responded, "I'm fine."

"You sure?" Jacob asked. "Cuz we both know you just adore tea and *love* coffee."

Krennicx rolled his eyes.

"Is *anyone* going to tell me what is going on?" Michael asked.

"There's something we should have told you a long time ago," Dad said with a sigh.

"What is it?" Hazel asked. Dad nodded to Krennicx, who pulled out a small silver ball. Krennicx tossed it onto the ground, falling to the ground, it opened in half. A large blue hologram of a planet rose above it: Annorlia.

"What's so secretive about Annorlia?" Michael asked.

"Show him," Dad said to Krennicx. Krennicx nodded and hopped off the bed with a wince.

"Annorlia isn't what you think it is," Krennicx said, "it's far more." The map of the planet zoomed out to reveal hundreds of planets around it. "Annorlia is the capital of the Annorlian System, which is pretty weird if you ask me. The Annorlian System and the capital are ruled by the Represenetor, and the kings basically take care of each of their kingdoms. Each king has a representative that looks after the king and pretty much keeps the king in line. Whenever the king does something that the representative doesn't like, he would report it to the Represenetor. Then the representative, the king, and the Represenetor would discuss the matter. And if anything happened in Annorlia or the other planets, the Represenetor would take care of it and well, *represent* Annorlia's government."

"And *how* would he 'take care of it?'" Michael asked.

"If needed, he would use his military," Krennicx responded.

Jacob remembered when Krennicx was talking about all of this, "Wasn't it the Diamond Dragons, Gold Dragons, and the Formwings?" Jacob asked.

"Yes, dear student," Krennicx responded with a smile. "But each of the kings had an army of his own, too."

"I still don't see how this is a huge deal," Michael said, trying to sound uninterested.

"Don't worry kidden, I'm get'n there," Krennicx said calmly. "Annorlia had peace for many years with each other and to the aliens of the galaxy, until…. the unexpected happened."

"What was that?" Hazel asked, interested.

"The Diammonites." Krennicx swiped his hand and blackness covered the map, consuming most of the planets and half of Annorlia itself. "No one knew they existed; they came out of nowhere. They literally blew up the land that the Diamonds lived in, hence the name Diammon*ite*. After they killed all of the Diamond Dragons, they did the same to the Golden Dragons. And then finally……to the Formwings." Krennicx sighed, then continued, "Everyone thought they killed the Represenetor, but no one knew because no one knew who he was. Many rulers signed a treaty with the Diammonite ruler, Omega. But the rest of the kings worked together and brought their own army to the beach of the Sun Dragons, otherwise known as the Sunilians. That was their last stand. *None* of them made it out alive. The Diammonites won. It was over."

"That's why Tortoise was terrified of that beach," Jacob realized out loud. "That was where it was, wasn't it?"

"Yes," Krennicx responded.

"Is that the end?" Hazel asked, "I've never seen an alien walking around before. Do they really rule?"

"Not quite yet," Krennicx said with determination. "For months everyone thought that the Represenetor was dead, until his new military came."

"Who are they?" Hazel asked.

Krennicx grinned, "Why, the Fighters of Peace, of course."

"Fighters of Peace!" Hazel yelped. "I thought that was a myth!"

"They are a prophesy," Krennicx said. "I can assure you, they are real. They are the tiniest hair that is keeping Annorlia from falling completely. They work for the hidden Represenetor, who I can also assure to you *is* alive."

"Have you met him?" Hazel asked.

"That answer is classified."

"I'll take that as a yes," Hazel said with a grin.

"So how would any of this have anything to do with us?" Michael asked.

"Because your king was the first to sign the treaty and kill his representative," Krennicx answered. "Your war isn't against the dragons. It's against Annorlia. And you, my dear friend, are on the side of the Diammonites."

"Are you *blaming* my king?!" Michael asked angrily. "How could we even *believe* any of this? Why would we trust you?!"

"Because I was there," Krennicx responded. "You wanted to know what I am, this is it. My mother was a dragon and my father was a Formwing. I was there when Omega found the Formwings. I am the only one with the blood of the Represenetor's old military."

"This is *not* happening," Michael whispered. He was red hot with anger and Jacob didn't dare talk to him. After Krennicx told him the truth about everything, their dad told them the truth about himself. He wasn't working for King Luther, instead, he was his prisoner. He was never hurt by dragons from the Dragon Forest; instead, it was King Luther who used dragons that worked for him to do it. Everything they had wasn't their own, it was a disguise. Not even their last name was real! They didn't own anything. They were prisoners. Nothing was real. Apparently, Krennicx had been wanting to rescue them for years, but their dad had said no. It had been just a few weeks ago when their dad finally somehow sent a message to Krennicx, begging him to help his kids. Krennicx was immediately on it. The box of Dad's stuff wasn't Dad's at all, but Krennicx's. Somehow, he got the box to their mom. Somehow, he knew that Michael and Jacob couldn't help but look inside it. Somehow, he knew that they would give the bad map to King Luther, then find the real map afterwards. Somehow, he knew that they wouldn't give the real map to King Luther. Somehow, he knew that Luther would send them into the forest. Somehow, he knew that Michael would be found by a group of soldiers. He knew that he would have to get Jacob alone in order to convince him the truth. He knew Jacob would betray them to King Luther, but he also trusted that he would realize the wrong he did and allow Krennicx to train him. It was all the master plan to get to them and save them from the hands of King Luther. Jacob knew Krennicx was smart, but this? This was insane. The dragon war was fake, but Krennicx *used* it for his advantage. Surely there were other ways, but this way seemed to be working so far, for now, here they were. Together.

"We're sorry," Dad apologized. "We wanted to tell you, but if we did, they would kill you. I know this is different, especially since this is against everything you've been taught in school, but please believe us."

"Even if any of this is true, how could we believe you if you've lied to us!" Michael got up and stormed out of the room. Dad began to get up to run after him.

"You should give him a minute," Krennicx interrupted. "This is new to him, he needs to think."

"But shouldn't I comfort him?" Dad asked.

"I won't stop you from anything you think you should do," Krennicx responded. "If you think you should go talk to him, then go ahead. I just learned from experience that sometimes they need space, but sometimes they don't. It's up to you to decide which one he needs."

"Which do you think?" Dad asked.

"I already told you," Krennicx answered. "But he is not my son. He is yours."

Dad sighed, "I don't know. I haven't been with him as much as I should have."

"It's not your fault," Hazel said with tears in her eyes. "You were forced to stay away."

"Let's just hope Michael believes that," Dad said, getting up and walking after his son.

"We really are sorry," Mom said, about to cry. "We *never* wanted to do this."

"I believe you," Hazel said. "It's kind of hard to go against a king, even when what he's doing is wrong."

Jacob took a deep breath, "I believe you too. And I'm sorry for not believing you, Hazel. You were right the whole time."

Hazel smiled, "That felt good."

Jacob laughed, "So…. Our last name is really *Specter*?"

"Yes," Mom answered. "We were constantly disguising it, but Specter is the real one."

"Why were you constantly changing it?" Hazel asked.

"I… think it's best if you don't know," Mom said.

"Ok," Hazel said.

"So how did y'all meet?" Jacob asked.

Krennicx and Mom exchanged a funny look. "I doubt I'm allowed to tell that story," Mom said with a smile.

Krennicx smirked, "You got that right."

Jacob rolled his eyes, "So, the great non-dragon-Krennicx is a Formwing/*dragon* hybrid? I guess Formwings look like panthers?"

"Nope," Krennicx responded.

"Then what do they look like?" Hazel asked.

"They look like they are classified," Krennicx responded with a smirky grin.

"Is anything not classified with you?" Hazel asked.

"Not much."

"How many secrets do you have?" Hazel asked.

"That my dear, is a secret," Krennicx responded, continuing his smile.

"Of course it is," Hazel said, rolling her eyes.

"Krennicx is a pile of dirty secrets," Jacob said.

"Yep," Krennicx agreed.

"How are you injured?" Hazel asked. "Or is that a secret too?"

Jacob stared at the floor, somewhat embarrassed.

"Um…" Krennicx said, glancing at Jacob, unsure if he should answer.

"He saved my life," Jacob answered for him. "It was a poisonous arrow, one that would have killed me. But Krennicx jumped in front of it."

Hazel stared at Krennicx in awe. "You saved my brother's life? After everything humans have done to you? Thank you so much! But why did you do it though?"

"Like I said," Krennicx responded, "this isn't a human vs. dragon war, it's an Annorlians vs. Diammonites war."

"But, if that arrow was poisonous," Hazel said, now concerned, "won't you die?"

Krennicx half smiled, "The poison has enough power to kill a human, but to me, it….. doesn't really affect me *too* much. The most it'll do is make me very tired and…. well, it's not that big of a deal."

"But still, if that went into your back, how are you not dead?" Hazel asked.

"I guess there's more I have to do in this world," Krennicx responded, "and protecting you is one of them."

Jacob still didn't understand why Krennicx always seemed to be hiding something, especially about his past. He already said something about his family, but was that really all that could be said? And he seemed to be hiding something about the poisoned arrow, but what? Jacob's thought was interrupted when his dad walked into the room, head down.

"How did it go?" Mom asked.

"You were right," Dad said with a sigh to Krennicx, "I should have let him be."

Jacob yawned and opened his eyes to see green dragon eyes, "Ah!" he shrieked in surprise. *"Winter?"* Winter stuck his tongue out, looking happy. "Hey, buddy!" Jacob said, rubbing his dragon's head. "What are you doing here? Did you find me?" Winter panted and licked him. "Hazel is going to freak," Jacob said excitedly. "Come on, buddy." He jumped off the bed and ran downstairs with Winter right behind him. Hazel sat on her usual chair at the breakfast table, with Krennicx sitting across from her. Hazel was intensely studying the blue hologram that was glowing from the silver ball in the middle of the table. Krennicx seemed to be showing her all the different kinds of dragons. Michael was sitting in the corner next to Hazel, eyeing Krennicx warily.

"Morn'n," Krennicx greeted, noticing them walk in.

"Morning," Jacob responded.

"I wasn't talking to you," Krennicx said.

"Then who were you talking to?" Jacob asked.

"My friend."

"And who is that?" Jacob asked.

"Winter," Krennicx responded.

"Who's Winter?" Hazel asked, looking up. Her eyes widened when she saw Jacob's dragon, "I-I-Is that an *actual* dragon?!" she asked, standing up.

"Full-blooded," Krennicx responded with grin.

"Whoa," Hazel said, standing in front of Winter. "Can he talk?"

"No," Krennicx answered, "he's one of the speechless ones we were talking about, a Dragonese. They aren't exactly the same as other kinds of dragons."

"Can I touch him?" Hazel asked.

"If he lets you, and if Jacob says you can," Krennicx responded.

Hazel gave Jacob a surprised look, "Is, is he your pet?"

"Er…" Jacob said as Winter was nudging and rubbing him while purring.

"I'll take that as a yes," Hazel said. She reached her hand out, "Hey, Winter." Michael stared intensely at Winter as if he was debating on attacking it. *Don't do anything stupid,* Jacob thought, eyeing him. Winter warily sniffed Hazel's hand like a cat, then put his forehead against it and purred. Michael stared at it in shock.

"They can't talk, but they are really good at smelling," Krennicx said. "They can even tell if you are trustworthy or not. The only ones they'll ever fully trust are their owners, but unless you make an idiotic move, they will be nice to you." Krennicx seemed to have glared at Michael when he said 'an idiotic move', for Michael tried not to look at them.

"How did you meet?" Hazel asked, running her hand along Winter's scales.

"In the Cloud Kingdom," Jacob answered. "He was one of the prisoners there. I was still a spy when I did it, but for some reason I still let him out of his cage. The next time I saw him was after King Luther took everyone. I ran into him in the forest while I was heading back home, feeling terrible. That was when I made up my mind to go back and help Krennicx put out the fire. Winter brought me there, and he stayed with me ever since. How did he find me here though? And how did he even get in?"

"He came tapping on your window last night," Krennicx responded. "I let him in."

"Did you ride him?" Hazel asked, studying his majestic wings.

"Yeah," Jacob answered with a smile. "It was terrifying, but amazing."

"Can I fly with him?" Hazel asked.

"I don't think you'd want to do that," Krennicx said, "Jacob and Winter don't even really know how to fly together yet. You'd probably want to wait. For your own safety."

"Ok," Hazel said.

"What is there we have to learn?" Jacob asked.

"Well, for one thing you have to trust each other," Krennicx said. "And you also need to know how to….oh I don't know……get *on* him."

"I know how to get on him," Jacob said. "See?" He grabbed onto one of Winter's spikes on his back and pulled himself up. He nearly fell over the other side as he tried to position himself.

"Well, that was sad," Krennicx said, "and very slow. Don't forget, most of the time when you're going to mount him, you'll probably be running for your life."

"Good to know," Jacob said sarcastically, jumping off.

"What will he be running away from?" Hazel asked.

"Probably dragons," Michael murmured with a snort.

"Are you ready to tell them?" Krennicx asked in Jacob's head.

"*Not really*," Jacob responded. *"I haven't even eaten breakfast yet. Plus, that would be a bit much for Michael to take in so close to each other."*

"Ok, but the longer you keep it secret, the more difficult it will be."

"You never know what you could be running for," Jacob said out loud. "The king does want to kill us, after all."

"True," Hazel agreed.

"Which is why today is a training day," Krennicx said.

"No!" Jacob yelped. "Not again! I need a rest."

"You just had one," Krennicx said with a smirk.

"I need at least a *day* of rest," Jacob corrected.

"You had yesterday."

"No, I didn't! That was *not* rest."

"We didn't do too much yesterday," Krennicx responded, almost sarcastically.

"Except for walking around the entire city!" Jacob corrected. "Not to mention the failed attempt of breaking Lighter and the others out!"

"Ok, first off, that was not a fail."

"Well, what about you?" Jacob asked, desperately trying to escape training. "You were literally shot with an arrow last night! Don't *you* need rest?"

"I am fine." Krennicx grinned, "Besides, I'm not the one training. You are."

"But...we don't want to leave the house unguarded!"

"I never said that we were going to go anywhere. We're staying here."

"Oh," Jacob said with relief.

"What kind of training?" Hazel asked.

Krennicx smirked his sneaky smile, "The kind that ol' Jacob hates."

CHAPTER 24

THE UNBELIEVER

"Ah!" Jacob shrieked. "Would you stop that?!"

"Man, am I enjoying this," Hazel said, shaking her head. Hazel grabbed another baseball and threw it hard at her brother. Jacob tried to clasp his hands around it but missed, causing it to canon on his stomach.

"Ow!" Jacob shrieked. "Isn't there something that isn't as painful!"

"Nope," Krennicx said, amused. Winter sat behind the hybrid on the steps and did a roar that sounded like laughing.

"Really! You too?" Jacob asked, annoyed. A ball whacked him in the head after a failed attempt to catch it.

"You're trying too hard," Krennicx coached. "Just relax and let your instincts take over."

Jacob closed his eyes and took a deep breath, *"AH!"* He shrieked, falling to the ground after a ball hit him right where it hurts.

"Ooo, sorry about that one," Hazel said.

"Or you could also make yourself get new instincts," Krennicx observed.

Jacob clutched his face and tried hard not to throw up, "Ow."

"Let's take a break from that," Krennicx said.

"Yeah, I agree," Hazel said.

"But I was kind of enjoying it," Michael complained, walking out of the house door.

"Look who decided to show up," Hazel said.

"Might as well spy," Michael said with a shrug, sitting on the step as far away from Krennicx as possible.

"Rather bold," Krennicx observed, "I'll give ya that."

Michael glared at him and Winter uneasily, "You'd be surprised what you would do to save your family's lives."

"Agreed," Krennicx said, glaring back. *Michael doesn't know how much Krennicx cares about Lighter*, Jacob realized. *I think he would do anything to save him.*

"Er…," Hazel said, trying to break the awkward tension between the two of them. "Is there anything else we could do?"

"Actually," Krennicx said, glaring at Michael, "there is." Krennicx opened his claws, where two bamboo sticks immediately appeared.

"Whoa," Hazel said in amazement.

Krennicx smirked his sneaky smile, "Sword fight."

"Oh *no,*" Jacob said, standing back up.

"How did you do that?" Michael asked, eyeing the two long bamboo sticks in Krennicx's hand.

Ignoring his question, Krennicx tossed one of the sticks to Jacob and said, "Sometimes whenever me and Glider get into an….er… argument, we fight it out….. literally."

"So that's why he's terrified of you," Jacob said thoughtfully. "But why *does* he argue with you? You're annoyingly always right."

"That is something I've always wondered."

"But I'm not in an argument with you," Jacob said. "Why do we have to fight?"

"We won't," Krennicx responded sneakily, "you and Michael will." Krennicx handed the other stick to Michael, who took it out of fear.

"What?" Michael angrily asked, standing up. "You want me to fight my own brother? No! You're just trying to rip us apart! Is that your evil tactic?"

"It's a tactic, but I wouldn't call it evil," Krennicx said with a shrug.

"Ok," Michael said seriously. "I'll fight, but I want to fight *you.*"

Krennicx's facial expression changed to the slick, clever, and cunning face Jacob had met in the woods. "You want to make a deal, don't you?" he asked smoothly.

"So, you're familiar with deals?" Michael asked. "Yes, I do."

"And what is this...deal, you want?" Krennicx asked, keeping his creepy voice. Jacob rolled his eyes. He was starting to figure out why Krennicx made things so creepy. He wants to see their reactions. He wants to know everyone by seeing how they react in *very* uncomfortable situations. That or he just loved torturing people. Either way, he was *ridiculously* good at it.

"If I win, you tell me everything I want to know *and* you'll release my family from your curse," Michael said. *Oh boy,* Jacob thought. He knew what Michael thought he wanted, for he had done something similar with Krennicx. He thought about warning Michael, but figured he needs to learn this on his own.

"And...if I win?" Krennicx asked.

"Er…," Michael said thinking. *Don't do anything stupid! Well, I guess you already are. Just don't do something you'll regret!* "What is it that you want?" Michael asked.

"Before anything is done, I want you to know what you're getting yourself into, young'n," Krennicx said. "Are you sure you want to do this?"

"Positive," Michael answered. "Now what do you want?"

Krennicx sighed, "There is nothing you can give me but your help," Krennicx said. "All I ask is that you do not harm your own family, so don't tell anything about them or me to King Luther. And don't be mad at Jacob for his decision that he has made or will make."

"That's it?" Michael asked, shocked.

"I have done deals many times, dearie," Krennicx said. "I know what I am doing."

"Ok," Michael said with a shrug.

"Michael," Jacob said, "are you *sure* you want to do this?"

"Yes," Michael responded confidently. "Don't worry, I *will* set you free." Michael turned to Krennicx, "Deal."

"Very well," Krennicx said. "It might be best if the three of you went inside. This might get dirty."

Michael gulped. Hazel looked worried as she, Winter, and Jacob went inside. *Dirty?* Jacob thought, alarmed. Jacob wanted to stop it. He didn't want any of them to get hurt. Even if he could convince Michael to back down (even though he probably already wanted to) he wasn't sure if Krennicx would be happy about a deal being broken. Even if it was for show, he still didn't want to mess up the hybrid's plans, for this was probably a part of his plan somehow. He was afraid for Michael, but he was also a little afraid for Krennicx too. He was injured after all. Winter followed them inside as they glanced one more time at Michael and closed the door.

"Dirty?!" Hazel yelped in worry. "Is he going to *hurt* him?"

"I don't know!" Jacob said, also worried. Krennicx had never exactly *hurt* Jacob in his training, although…..he wasn't exactly very *gentle* either. He never really hit back much, but when he did……yeesh.

"Oh, why does he think we're brainwashed!" Hazel asked, sitting down at the breakfast table. "And why does he think acting like a dimwit and fighting Krennicx will set us free!"

Jacob shrugged, "I mostly trust Krennicx. I *know* he won't kill him, well….er…..*shouldn't*."

"Seriously!"

"Sorry," Jacob yelped. He paced back and forth. *Please, Krennicx. I trust you. Please don't hurt my brother! Don't get dirty!*

Michael tried to stay calm as Jacob and Hazel, followed by that stupid dragon, walked inside. What was he doing?! Fighting a dragon thingie? No way! But yet here he was, alone with something that most likely wants to kill him. And possibly will. He gulped in fear. The thought of running entered his mind, but he pushed it away. *I can't let this psycho take my brother away from me. Not now, not ever!*

"Whenever you're ready, dearie," so-called-Krennicx said.

Michael clenched his jaw, *"Never* call me dearie!" He jumped for the hybrid with his bamboo stick stretched out. He slammed the stick hard on his opponent's face, well, so he thought. Krennicx held Michael's stick with a firm grip.

"You truly are Jacob's brother," Krennicx calmly observed. Krennicx released the stick and allowed Michael to back away. Michael's hatred for the hybrid grew significantly. *I HAVE to kill this thing. For King Luther. For my friends. For my family.* Michael clinched his jaw, *For Annorlia.* Krennicx tilted his head and his face expression was something Michael had never seen before. It was grinning, cunning, sneaky, and charming all rolled up into one smirky smile. Michael felt chills running up his skin. "What are you looking at?" Michael asked, pointing his stick uneasily at the creepy hybrid. "Can you read my mind?" Michael asked, alarmed.

"Unfortunately," Krennicx said, almost teasingly.

"Do you *want* me to hate you?" Michael asked, ready to fight.

"You already do," Krennicx said, sounding annoyingly wise. "No point in trying to change your mind."

"You got that right!" Michael lunged for Krennicx to hit his back with his stick. Krennicx caught the stick with ease, and, to Michael's surprised, pushed it *towards* Michael, nailing him in the gut. Michael yelped and jumped back, clutching his stomach.

"Dearie, dearie, dearie," Krennicx said smoothly. "Is that really the way you want to fight?"

"You said it would get dirty," Michael said, "now FIGHT ME!" Michael attacked Krennicx full force. Michael wanted Krennicx to fight, but what the hybrid did was unexpected. A smooth black stick appeared in Krennicx's claws. Krennicx slammed Michael's attacking stick with such force that it flung out of Michael's hand. Krennicx jumped and twirled in the air, banging Michael in the face. It hurt, but Michael didn't realize that Krennicx was still being extremely gentle, for the hit wouldn't even bruise.

"Ow!" Michael shrieked falling to the floor. Krennicx pointed his stick to Michael's neck in a sword stance.

"You are not very well with a sword," Krennicx observed.

"You are?"

Krennicx tilted his head again, "I've had practice, but I wouldn't call myself great."

"Oh, stop it!" Michael demanded. "Drop the humble act!"

Krennicx raised an eyebrow, "What?"

"We all know you're just faking it!" Michael said. "You're just trying to earn our trust with all your smooth-talking words!"

Krennicx studied Michael as if he was reading a book. "Is that why you don't like me?"

Michael paused. What was the reason why he didn't like him? Was it because of his odd accent? Or his smooth but hoarse words? No! It was because he was a dragon thing. He cast a spell on his brother and is tricking everyone. Michael didn't like Krennicx's character at all, but more importantly, he HATED what Krennicx was. A dragon. Krennicx seemed to notice what Michael decided, for he frowned. *I will kill this thing.* Michael grabbed the stick and jumped up, trying to slam Krennicx in the face. Krennicx caught the stick and held it in the air. "Oh darling," Krennicx said holding Michael's stick firmly, "will you ever learn?" Krennicx kicked Michael in the stomach and snapped his stick in half. Michael fell to the ground again and clutched his stomach in pain.

"'Dirty' can mean many different things, dearie. It doesn't have to be physical. I believe this fight is over," Krennicx said, walking towards the door.

"No!" Michael shrieked. "Please! Set them free! Please!"

Krennicx frowned sympathetically, "Our deal is done."

"How about a different one!" Michael asked, panicked. "Take me! Do whatever you want to me! Just set them free from your curse!"

Krennicx sighed, "What Jacob has chosen is nothing you nor I can control. He has made up his mind all by himself. I have not done anything to him."

"Please!" Michael begged, feeling like he would sob. "I *know* you've done something! Undo it!"

"Goodbye, Michael," Krennicx said, trying to walk away.

"Take me instead!" Michael nearly screamed and ran in front of Krennicx. "Let him go! Please! I'll do whatever you want! Just let him go!"

"There is nothing you can do that can change this," Krennicx said. "Now please, do not ruin your relationship with your family. What you and Jacob have is something you do not want to lose."

"You're a *monster!*"

Krennicx sighed, "I know."

Michael stormed inside, slammed the door behind him, and ran.

"How did it-" Hazel started. Michael was already running upstairs and slammed the door of his room. Hazel gave Jacob a worried look. Jacob returned the look. The same door Michael came in from opened and Krennicx calmly walked inside.

"What happened?!" Hazel asked worriedly.

"What did you do?" Jacob asked. Krennicx didn't look at him.

"Nothing," Krennicx responded.

"Did you hurt him?" Hazel asked.

Krennicx didn't respond.

"*Did* you hurt my brother?" Hazel asked.

"No, well, not exactly.. physically," Krennicx responded.

Jacob sighed, "I should talk to him, shouldn't I?"

"Yep," Krennicx responded. Jacob took a deep breath and headed upstairs to Michael's room. Jacob gulped and opened the door without knocking. Michael sat on the side of the bed with his elbows on his legs and his hands covering his face. Was he *crying?*

"I'm sorry," Michael said, muffled by tears, "I failed. I couldn't get it to set you free."

"Oh Michael," Jacob said, sitting next to his brother, "it's going to be ok."

"No, it isn't!" Michael said, waving Jacob's arm that was going to hug him away. "Everyone is brainwashed! Nothing is going to be ok!"

"Is there any way I can prove to you that I am *not* brainwashed?" Jacob asked, trying hard not to sound annoyed.

"Unless you killed that thing downstairs, no," Michael responded.

Jacob sighed, "What if I prove that something Krennicx said is true?"

"Like what?" Michael asked, looking at him.

Jacob sighed, "Like the Fighters of Peace?"

There was silence until Michael shrugged and whispered, "I don't know."

"Please, just promise me you won't freakout?"

Michael looked worried. "Unless your head pops off, ok."

Jacob ignored the head thing and lifted his hand and closed his eyes. Michael shrieked. Jacob opened his eyes to see it was working.

"*What* is happening?!" Michael asked, panicked. Everything on his dresser and floor were floating in midair. Jacob smiled, pleased. He lowered his hand and everything fell back in place."*What* was that?!" Michael, asked terrified.

"Michael, *I* have Fighters of Peace powers," Jacob said. "That is why Lighter took me instead of you. They knew. They were protecting me from King Luther."

"By *kidnapping* you?!" Michael asked. "Either they've cursed you more than I thought, or they were keeping you from us so you don't hurt their chances at winning the war! Plus, the Fighters of Peace *can't* even be real."

"There is no human-dragon war!" Jacob nearly yelled. "It's fake! It's a cover up so that King Luther can use all emergency powers to make us do *anything!* And the Fighters of Peace are real! I've been with them for a week! Did you even pay *attention* to *everything* we said last night?"

Michael seemed aggravated, "Of course I paid attention! If I was cursed, it would be *very* convincing!"

"Ugh!! Would you *stop* with the curse?! I don't even know if Krennicx *can* curse anyone!" Jacob said, losing it. "All I've seen him do is shoot lightning, shape shift, and disappear!"

Michael looked at Jacob with interest, "Shape shift?"

"He *is* a Formwing, well, half Formwing," Jacob responded. "It's kind of what they do."

"Ok....," Michael said in deep thought. "What did I get you for your birthday last year?"

"You have got to be *kidding me!!!* I am not Krennicx!!!!"

"Well, then, what *did* I give you for your birthday?" Michael asked again.

Jacob took a deep breath, "I'm sorry. I shouldn't have yelled. I'm just really aggravated that you don't believe me. That you think I'm lying. And it was socks."

"What kind of socks?"

"Hearts and smiley faces. The day I wore them to school is the day Spot decided that he wanted to steal my shoes off my feet while we were on the way there. I had to walk in those socks the whole day without shoes. I was the laughing stock," Jacob responded. *Wait a minute......... KRENNICX!!!!!!!!!!!*

Michael sighed, "Sorry. It just *really* seems like you're cursed. When we left, you wanted to kill *every* dragon. And now that you're back, you don't. Now you want to fight against the *humans,* your own kind!" Michael grinned, "And that day was awesome."

Jacob sighed, "I know it seems odd," he said, "but please believe me. I *did* betray them to King Luther."

Michael's eyes widened in excitement, "Really?"

"Don't get excited," Jacob advised, "I had made a mistake. He came and took Lighter, Glider, Glazer, and Tortoise."

"Am I supposed to know who those are?"

Jacob ignored him and continued, "But when he took them, he....," Jacob trailed off and took a deep breath, "he pushed me over the side of a cliff. Then he caught the forest on fire."

Michael stared at Jacob in shock. "What happened?" Michael asked.

"Krennicx saved me," Jacob answered. "Even though I handed over his friends, including Lighter, he went after me. He could have saved the others, but instead he saved *my* life. I owe him for that."

Michael looked like he didn't know what to believe, he just stared at the floor. "Surely it was a misunderstanding. King Luther wouldn't push you."

Jacob thought back to when King Luther kicked him so hard he fell, then how he pushed him over the cliff. Jacob shook his head, "He did, trust me. Krennicx caught me just in time. If he was a second later...."

Michael sighed, "I still don't believe you."

Jacob felt his eyes wanting to tear, but he held them back, "It took saving my life several times for them to convince me," Jacob said. "I just hope it won't be too late for you." Jacob got off the bed and left Michael to his thoughts. *Krennicx the Spot dog, is there any embarrassing part of my life that you DIDN'T cause?!*

Jacob had thought the dinner with Ben and Krennicx was awkward, but this.....sheesh, this was the next level. Dad, Mom, Hazel, Michael, Jacob, and Krennicx sat at the dinner table eating lunch. Krennicx sat at

Jacob's right, and Mom sat at Jacob's left. Dad sat at the end of the table, next to Mom. Hazel sat right across from Jacob, and somehow, Michael sat at Hazel's left, right *smack* in front of Krennicx. There was silence. Pure, awkward silence. Jacob sat next to Krennicx as they silently ate. Nothing was heard except for the crunching of food. Jacob glanced at Krennicx, who seemed to be trying so hard not to burst out laughing. Jacob felt the same. Jacob stared at his nachos, trying hard not to look at Krennicx. He knew if he did, they would *not* be able to keep themselves from laughing. Jacob felt the smile sneaking on his face as he almost let out a laugh. He was getting sweaty from holding it in. He wanted to glance at Krennicx, but was it worth the risk? He couldn't help it. Slowly he looked at Krennicx. At the same time, Krennicx was slowly starting to look at Jacob. Their eyes met, and they lost it. Krennicx was laughing, but not like Jacob. Jacob was all out. All but Michael joined them in their laugh. They recovered themselves and the silence fell. *Again.*

"So…..," Dad said trying to break the silence. "How is…. Glider?"

"Annoying as always," Krennicx responded.

"Uh-huh," Jacob agreed.

Dad cleared his throat, obviously trying to think of something else to say.

"How are you feeling?" Krennicx asked.

"Good," Dad responded. Jacob glanced at Michael and nearly laughed in surprise. He was giving Krennicx the biggest death stare Jacob had ever seen in his life. Krennicx smiled kindly at him as if he was amused. Michael's face turned red and he stared at his food. *There is DEFINITELY some tension going on.* Krennicx tapped his claws on the table, thinking.

"So…what's the battle plan?" Hazel eagerly blurted out.

"Battle plan?" Mom asked.

"Well, somehow we have to break out these other dragons y'all are talking about. So how?" Hazel asked. To this, Michael seemed interested. He looked up to see what Krennicx's response would be. Krennicx glared at him and Michael looked down again.

"Krennicx and I will handle it," Jacob said, *not* wanting them to be anywhere near the palace.

"But I want to help," Hazel said eagerly. Jacob looked worriedly at Krennicx for help. Krennicx shrugged.

"How about you try to stay out of it for now," Krennicx advised, glancing at Jacob with a frown. "I don't think Jacob wants you to get hurt."

Hazel sighed, "Ok."

There was silence again, until Dad broke it, "I really am glad you're here. It's been so long and so hard. Now that you're here, it already feels much better."

Krennicx smiled, "It's my pleasure."

Dad smiled.

"This is nuts," Michael murmured quietly. Dad frowned.

"Couldn't agree more. Especially with Jacob here," Krennicx said playfully. He was very good at lightening up moods when he wanted. "He's one of the biggest nuts in the world."

"Oi!" Jacob yelped playfully. "You're a pine nut without a spine!"

"That makes zero sense whatsoever, lover nutty boy," Krennicx said, looking at him.

"I'm a Hazelnut!" Hazel announced. Everyone laughed. Michael looked embarrassed. The joke wasn't funny in the least bit, but the awkwardness….it made *anything* funny.

"Cheer up, son," Dad finally said, "you used to always want to meet a dragon-like-thing."

"I wanted it to meet my sword," Michael murmured.

Krennicx's eyes widened and he smiled.

"Michael," Mom scowled.

"It's fine," Krennicx assured, "I'm used to threats. Some I enjoy."

Michael raised an eyebrow at him in surprise. *Michael is trying so hard to scare him*, Jacob thought in amusement, *he just can't*. Krennicx continued to tap his claws on the table. He had been doing it for a while.

"Would you stop that!" Michael exploded.

Krennicx smirked. He didn't stop though. Jacob felt a nudge on his lap. "What are you doing?" Jacob asked Winter as the dragon rested its snout on his lap. "Are you begging like a dog?"

"Should be," Krennicx observed, "I haven't seen you feed him a single time."

"What do I feed him?" Jacob asked.

"Not this again."

"What? I seriously don't know what in Annorlia to feed him."

"What are you eating?" Krennicx asked.

"Nachos."

"Then feed him that!"

"What?" Jacob yelped, "I am *not* giving him my nachos! That can't be healthy!"

"I'm eating nachos," Krennicx pointed out.

"My point exactly."

"Oi," Krennicx said with a laugh. "Didn't we already go over this? He likes fish."

"Mom, do we have fish?" Jacob asked, turning to her.

"Tuna fish," she answered, "but probably not enough to fill him up." She paused, then added, "Are you sure you'll be able to care for him?"

"Of course I can!" Jacob immediately said, not wanting to give Winter up. "Let me go see if we have anything good for now. But don't worry, I'll buy some real dragon food later." Jacob got out of his chair and looked in the kitchen for some food. *There's some leftover chili? Nah, that would probably give him gas. Uncooked steak? Good grief, no! That stuff is expensive! Leftover pizza?* Jacob thought back to when he ate pizza with Krennicx and Ben. Krennicx had given Winter some and he seemed fine. *Pizza it is.* He grabbed some pieces out of the pizza box, he didn't even bother warming it up. "Here you go, Winter," Jacob said going back to his chair. "I think you liked pizza —HEY!" Krennicx had the most mischievous smile as Winter gulped down the last bit of Jacob's nachos, "Kren*nicx!"*

"I didn't do it," Krennicx said innocently.

"But you let Winter do it!"

Krennicx shrugged, "Finder's keepers, loser's weepers."

Winter hopped off Jacob's chair, jumping up and grabbing the pieces of pizza out of Jacob's hands. He gulped it down in a heartbeat. Jacob shook his head at him. Everyone but Michael laughed. Winter yawned and walked to a corner and laid down. Jacob rolled his eyes.

The next day, Jacob and Spot crept along the sidewalk of Jacob's neighborhood. "I don't see any soldiers," Jacob observed. It was still *very* uncomfortable to talk to his old pal Spot knowing that he's actually Krennicx. But the fact that Jacob had him on a leash was pretty satisfying.

"They are hiding," Krennicx responded. "He probably has his best soldiers on the job."

"If that's true," Jacob said, "then don't you think you should be protecting the house? You are the reason why they haven't attacked. The second they see you away....."

"I know," Krennicx said, "I was just wanting to check. Plus it puts him on edge."

"You *want* him on edge?" Jacob asked, surprised.

"Of course," Krennicx responded, "it's way more satisfying."

Jacob rolled his eyes. *Only Krennicx would want a king tracking his every move.* "So how are things looking with Michael?" Jacob asked.

"He's a little more buttheaded than you, but I think I can break 'em."

Jacob snorted, "You better. His dream has always been to kill every dragon in the world."

"Well, I guess after he's done here he'd have to buy a ship to get to the rest of the planets," Krennicx said sarcastically. Jacob laughed.

They came to the end of the neighborhood and stopped. "So, what would happen to the humans?" Jacob asked. "You know, without King Luther?"

"You'd be free," Krennicx responded. "The wall will be broken."

"What wall?"

"Have you ever noticed that no one moves away?" Krennicx asked. "Have you ever noticed that for a city where a king lives, where *supposedly* all people live, this town is a little small? And you know how large Annorlia really is. How is there only one small town with supposedly *all* of the people's population?"

Jacob had never really thought of that before, but now that he did, it was true. No one *ever* left the town, except whenever King Luther sent soldiers to the forest, but other than that.... "Are you saying that everyone here is a prisoner?"

"Not all of them, but most of them," Krennicx answered. "The only ones that aren't are the ones that chose to work for King Luther."

"So where is the wall?" Jacob asked. "It sure does seem like I would notice it."

"It's because it's invisible," Krennicx responded. They turned around and began to walk home, "But past it is the biggest city in all of Annorlia. Humans and dragons live there. Have you ever noticed that whenever the kids reach sixteen, they disappear? It's because they get sent across the border, where they will be unable to fight Luther."

Jacob had actually noticed that, but he never really thought about it too much. "Why would they do that?" Jacob asked. "Then they would discover the truth."

"Because as long as the people grow, so does their strength. Strength is a threat. So they end it."

Jacob sighed, "But…. kids?"

Krennicx frowned and nodded, "That's why that brother of yours is in the wrong grade."

"Because he's sixteen," Jacob realized. "You said our dad begged you to help us, is that why? Is King Luther trying to take him away?"

Krennicx didn't look at him, "Yes."

Jacob took a deep breath, "Thank you."

"For what?"

"For helping us. And also for not taking anything from Michael. When he stupidly challenged you, you knew you would win, but even though you did, you didn't ask for anything in return. Thank you."

Krennicx smiled, "My pleasure. You have no idea what your father did for me. Seriously, there is *nothing* I can do to match what he's done."

"What did he do?" Jacob asked curiously.

"That's a long story for a different time, for now we need to focus on helping you," Krennicx responded.

Jacob nodded, then asked, "Can you really turn into anything?"

Krennicx paused, then worriedly nodded, "I think so. Why?"

Jacob smiled sneakily, "I think I know how to help prove to Michael that you're on our side."

"Is this payback or something?" Krennicx asked. Krennicx was *not* happy about what Jacob wanted to do, but at least he was willing to do it. They slipped into Jacob's yard and looked for Michael. "See him anywhere?" Jacob asked.

"Unfortunately."

"Where?" Jacob asked. Krennicx sighed and nodded to a tree. Michael sat on a long tree branch where he and Jacob used to sit. Jacob frowned. Michael looked so...*sad*. Jacob looked at Krennicx hopefully. "Fine," Krennicx said. Faster than a blink of an eye, Krennicx turned into a massive Philippine eagle and flew to the branch where Michael was.

Michael's eyes widened at the sight of his favorite animal. He gaped at the large bird that sat next to him. He looked like he was about explode with excitement, then he frowned, "You're not real, are you?" Michael asked.

Krennicx—the eagle—shook his head. "Jacob thought that you might listen to me if I didn't look like your enemy," Krennicx said, "so he wanted me to talk as your favorite animal."

Michael looked mad, but he still couldn't keep himself from staring in awe at the beautiful bird, even if it was someone he hated. "Well, it's not working," he finally said.

"I figured it wouldn't," Krennicx responded. "Aaanyway, what ya do'n up here?"

"Thinking," Michael answered quietly.

"That's a surprise, I didn't know you had the ability to do that."

Jacob slammed his hand on his face and shook his head, *Why? Why is he so terrible at this?!*

Michael stared at Krennicx in shock, "Are you *mocking* me?"

Krennicx shrugged with his feathered wings. "What? Do you want me to be a mocking bird? If you want me to, I could burn you to the crisp. Although, I really don't have to, you always do it to yourself."

He's hopeless!

"Are you *trying* to make me hate you?" Michael asked, annoyed.

"If you already hate me, there's no use for me to change myself." Krennicx switched from the eagle to his weird but ridiculously cool-looking self, then continued, "I've learned that it's hard to change someone's mind, so why do I have to change myself so you can change your mind? You can't like me if you don't *know* me for who I am." Michael stared at Krennicx, shocked. It was still hard for Jacob to figure Krennicx out. At one moment, he's a sneaky, crazy, cunning, insane… *thing*. Then the next moment, he talks so smooth and is so….*wise*. "Hate me if you like," Krennicx added. "Just, don't hate your family." Krennicx turned back into the eagle and glided off the tree branch, leaving Michael alone. Krennicx flew onto Jacob's shoulder, then whispered, "Happy?"

"Er," was all Jacob could say. He wouldn't exactly call that a win, but at least Michael *looked* like he was debating on what Krennicx had said. "I think we should leave Michael alone for a while."

"Agreed," Krennicx said, ruffling his feathers.

"Can you turn into a pink dragon for Hazel?" Jacob asked turning to walk inside.

"I could, but I won't."

Jacob laughed and walked inside.

CHAPTER 25

ATTEMPT 2

"Are you sure about this?" Mom asked, giving Jacob *another* hug.

"It's the right thing to do," Jacob said. He had told everyone about the fact that he's a Fighter of Peace in training. Apparently, Mom and Dad already knew, so it was really just telling Hazel. Sure, Hazel acted excited for Jacob, but he could tell she was worried sick. Krennicx had warned him to go ahead and say goodbye. Krennicx said he was planning to immediately get to the palace right after this mission, which was a weird one. Krennicx said he wanted to visit the wall guardian and warn him of what's coming. Apparently the 'wall guardian' surveyed around the wall and reported whenever something seemed off. Jacob wasn't sure *what* was coming, but by the sound of it, something big.

"Remember," Dad said, "if someone is acting like they're going to hurt you, don't hesitate to punch them in the face."

Jacob stared in shock at his father. He never knew he was a fighting person. To be honest, he never really knew much of anything about him. *After all of this is over, I really want to spend time with him… If I survive this.* Jacob nodded.

"Don't you need a weapon?" Hazel asked, wiping the tears from her eyes. "It's kind of hard to fight without a bat or something.

"When he's ready," Krennicx said, "his weapon will come to him." Jacob remembered Krennicx telling him that. He had said every Fighter of Peace can harness a blade that can cut through *anything*. Although, they had to have something strong to use as a handle.

"Ok," Hazel said, confused.

To Jacob's surprise, Michael came over and gave him an awkward hug. "Don't let it hurt you," Michael whispered in his ear.

"I won't," Jacob whispered back. Michael pulled away and frowned.

"Ready, dearie?" Krennicx asked. Jacob nodded and tried hard to keep himself from crying.

"Ready," Jacob responded.

"Now remember, as long as you stay in this house, the border will protect you. Do not leave," Krennicx warned, "because if you do, he will kill you."

Dad took a deep breath and nodded, "Thank you."

"Don't thank me yet, all I've done is cage you in a house." Krennicx glared at Michael, "Do. Not. Leave."

Michael looked mad. *Please, Michael, please obey him.*

"Bye, love you," Jacob said to his family. He mounted onto Winter's back and nodded to Krennicx. Krennicx nodded back. The front door of the house opened by itself, allowing them to walk out into the sunshine. Jacob glanced one more time at his family before the door shut. He sighed.

"You sure you're ready?" Krennicx asked.

Jacob nodded, "I am."

"Alrighty then." Krennicx spread his wings and bolted into the sky. Jacob took a deep breath, then tugged on the strange spikes on Winter's shoulder that he held onto. Immediately, Winter shot into the sky after Krennicx. "Ready for it?" Krennicx called.

"As ready as I'll ever be," Jacob called back. There was a strange tickling feeling as Krennicx turned them invisible and they flew unseen through the sky.

Jacob shifted uncomfortably on the wooden chair he sat on. He glared at Krennicx-disguised-Spot laying on a large cushioned leather chair. Why, *oh why, does the wall guardian have to be old Marty?!* It's not that Jacob didn't *like* the old man, in fact he had spent a lot of time with him. That was just it though, a *lot* of time. Really, you did *not* visit the old man unless your schedule was completely free. In this situation, it was not. It felt like Jacob and Krennicx had been sitting there for *hours*. And it was *hot*. He tried to swipe his sweaty forehead without the man noticing. Not only did his cabin not have air-conditioning, but it also had a campfire going right smack in the middle of a *wooden* house. Who in Annorlia *does* that?! Especially during the *summer?* On top of all of that, the house *stunk*. The walls of the small lodge were *layered* with dead stuffed animals. Jacob knew the man was a *huge fan of hunting,* but this was ridiculous! Jacob noticed Krennicx staring uncomfortably at a stuffed cheetah staring *directly* at him. Was that a gulp?

"Yer doggie seems to take an interest at d-dat 'there cheetah," old Marty said across the hot fire. He seemed to be *at least* five hundred and forty years old with a smushed green hat on top of his balding head. He sharpened a knife as he talked. He was making Jacob nervous as he stared at them without looking at the knife, "Wonder what he'd do if he saw my future prize."

"Future prize?" Jacob asked with a gulp.

"In dees walls hold many things," old Marty said studying the creepy walls, "except one, a black panther." Krennicx's dog eyes widened and he gulped loudly. Old Marty's eyes looked at him curiously. "That there really is a pretty thing, interested in sell'n?"

"No," Jacob immediately said.

"When it dies, let me know."

Jacob had never seen Krennicx look so terrified.

He isn't scared of kings, but yet he's terrified of an old man? Of course, Jacob couldn't judge, for he himself was horrified. *How are we supposed to warn this guy if he wants to kill us?* Jacob was so lost in thought he nearly jumped when the buzz came on.

"He's about to go hunting," Krennicx said in his head. **"Tell him to be careful. And when danger comes, seek cover behind a wall. He'll know what you mean."**

"Ok," Jacob responded.

"Well, I best get hunt'n," old Marty said, standing up. "Deer an't goin to kill 'em'selves."

"Be careful," Jacob quickly said, "when danger comes, seek cover behind a wall."

Old Marty looked at him curiously, "Ok....," he said awkwardly. *Does he not know what I'm talking about?* "You too..... I guess." He awkwardly left the cabin through the back door.

"Well, that went well," Jacob said, sarcastically standing up and stretching. "Did he not know what I meant?"

"Who knows," Krennicx said with a shrug.

"So…..now what?"

"I want to leave this creepy place," Krennicx responded. He hopped off the chair and also stretched.

"You looked so terrified," Jacob said with a laugh.

"It's not a comfortable feeling to be targeted for the next stuffed toy," Krennicx responded. "Let alone the fact that I can *talk* to any kind of animal in this room," he added with a shiver.

"Yeah, it's pretty creepy," Jacob agreed heading for the door. Though the outside was also hot from summer, it still felt so good and relieving. Jacob moaned, "How long were we *in there*?"

"An eternity," Krennicx responded. "We only have an hour till sundown."

"*Seriously!*" Jacob yelped. "We left home right after lunch! We were in there for *hours!*"

"That's a surprise?"

"No, I thought it'd be longer."

Krennicx laughed, "Call your dragon."

"Winter!" Jacob called. Immediately, Winter jumped from a tree and licked him, "Not now bud, I'm really hot." Winter looked at him curiously. Jacob rolled his eyes.

"You ready?" Krennicx asked, turning back into his normal Dragon/ Formwing shape.

"Yeah," Jacob answered. "Although, I do want to know the plan this time."

"No, you don't."

"Yes, I do," Jacob insisted. "Last time went terrible! It'd be a lot better if I knew what I'm *supposed* to do."

Krennicx gave him an unsure look, "You sure?"

"Yes," Jacob responded, "I want to know the plan."

"Oh how I wish I didn't know the plan!" Jacob moaned as he ran. He knew Krennicx was crazy, but this was outrageous! *Not to mention obvious! Everyone calls Krennicx clever at planning, but this sure was expected. Is that why he's good? Sometimes he does the unexpected and sometimes he does something so expected to where you don't even expect it?* Jacob did know one thing, he did *not* want to do it this way. He sighed and shook his head. *Here we go again.* He took a deep breath, then yelled as he ran up the road to the castle, "A dragon's coming! Help me! It's chasing me!"

"Not this again!" a guard grumbled. Jacob smiled as he continued to run. He came into view of the same gate that he ran to last time. "It's coming!" Jacob called again.

"Not falling for it," another guard said. They jumped in Jacob's way and grabbed his wrists and cuffed them.

"He's coming!" Jacob warned, trying to act insane. "He's coming for you! You're all going to be fired! Literally!" They rolled their eyes as they led Jacob inside. Jacob tried hard not to smirk at the broken door that the construction workers were trying to fix. *Dragon proof ain't Krennicx proof!* Jacob didn't dare fight back, but he wasn't making things easy for them either. He hummed and rocked his body back and forth like a little kid. The two soldiers that led him eyed each other curiously. Jacob smirked. *So this is what it feels like to act like Krennicx. It feels very childish. Makes sense I guess.* They walked for a few minutes through the winding hallways and stairs. They seemed to be going lower. Jacob tried hard not to gulp too loudly. They came out into a massive prison. The many hallways were lined with too many cells to even count. They were *all* filled with dragons. Dragon roars echoed everywhere. It smelled like smoke. *These dragons must have tried to save us from Luther,* Jacob thought with a stab of guilt. *How has King Luther kept his lies believable for so long?* It felt like forever as they walked past all of the rows of cells. Finally they made it to the end and turned into the last row against the wall. This row was different. It also *felt* different. It was cold. All of the cells were empty, except for the one in the middle, where Jacob seemed to be going. Jacob also realized that the soldiers seemed to be afraid of this prisoner. *I have a bad feeling about this.* Jacob felt like he heard a gulp as one of the soldiers unlocked the door with shaking hands.

"Good luck," the soldier said, opening the barred door and pushing Jacob in. They immediately stepped back as far as they could go.

Jacob stayed at the edge of the door inside the cell and looked around. It was cold. Jacob could see his own breath as he studied the cell. Icicles were growing everywhere and the floor was almost completely frozen. There was a growl that sounded like ice scraping against each other. Jacob gulped, "Hello?" he asked into the darkness.

Something moved. Everything got colder as the growl began to get louder. The light gleamed off frosted silver eyes with a hint of blue. It had shimmering silver scales that looked like ice. *Glazer.* "Hey, Glazer," Jacob said in a puppy voice. "Remember me?" Glazer only continued to growl and come closer. Ice followed her every step. Jacob gulped and stepped back as much as he could. "Come on, Glazer," Jacob tried. "It's me, Jacob, remember?" Glazer lunged. Jacob shrieked and ran to the other side of the cell. "Glazer, stop! It's the Staff! You have to fight it! Snap out of it!" Glazer roared and lunged again. Jacob had nowhere to go. He was cornered. "Glazer, please!" Glazer took a deep breath and the sound of ice scrapping roared. Misty ice fired from her mouth like fire at Jacob, and there was nowhere to run.

The soldiers sighed at the ice block that had frozen the kid. "Well, I guess that's the end of that." They left out of sight and went back to their positions.

Glazer continued to growl, then curled on the floor and smiled. "You can come out now," she said brightly. Breathing hard in cold and fear, Jacob stepped around the wall of ice in the corner. Somehow Glazer had created a wall of ice around him, to where it *looked* like she froze him, or in other words, killed him. Jacob's body shook violently from the freezing ice that was so *close* to freezing him. "Are you alright?" Glazer asked, concerned.

Jacob shivered, "You're....f-f-free?" Jacob asked with his teeth chattering.

Glazer frowned, "I'm sorry I scared you, it just had to look real." She tilted her head towards where the guards were. But they were gone.

Jacob nodded, "I-I-I understand."

"I didn't hurt you, did I?" Glazer asked, studying him closely. Jacob could feel the ice forming on his clothes. She frowned.

"I'm f-fine," Jacob responded, trying *hard* to not clatter his teeth. He was freezing *cold*. Glazer didn't look convinced. Jacob felt the need to say something else, "How are you?"

"Tired," Glazer responded honestly. "You have no idea how hard it is to *not* freeze these walls and shatter them into pieces."

Jacob looked at her, shocked. He realized there was something about her tail that was odd. He remembered noticing that it kind of glowed before, but this time it was glowing a *lot*. He didn't want to sound rude, but he was curious. "Is your tail glowing?"

Glazer sighed, "Yes."

Jacob wanted to know more, but he felt like it was a tough subject. "Did you know I was coming?" he asked instead."

Glazer nodded, "I wasn't sure if you'd come to me, but Krennicx warned all of us to be prepared."

Jacob nodded, "He didn't tell me that part, but I guess it is smart to guess that King Luther would use one of my friends to kill me." Glazer's face seemed to brighten at the mention of 'friend.' Jacob smiled, then added, "Now that he thinks I'm dead, things will be a lot easier." Jacob paused, then asked, "You *did* freeze the cameras, right?"

"Of course," Glazer said. "They kind of already were." She nodded at the frozen wall.

Jacob smiled, "Do you think you can get me out of here?"

She gave him a smile, then glanced at the large glowing snowflake on her tail and tapped it against the barred door. Immediately, the entire thing froze and shattered into shards of ice.

"Good luck."

Jacob nodded, trying hard not to marvel at the work of her odd tail. "I'm guessing you can do that for all of the prisoners here?"

"Of course," Glazer said with a nod, but Jacob could see concern in her face.

"We'll be fine," Jacob comforted.

"I know," Glazer said with a smile, "this isn't my first time breaking out of a prison. And I highly doubt it will be the last."

"Well… good luck anyway," Jacob said, shocked.

"Thank you. You got this."

I hope I do. Jacob nodded and left the way he came.

Michael moaned frustratingly. *What am I supposed to do? I can't leave Jacob with that, that, thing! It will kill him!* Michael wanted to leave. To get to Jacob before he's gone forever. But what about the so called 'border' that is supposed to 'protect' them? *It's a cage! Meant to keep me from saving Jacob!* Michael did *not* want to sit on his bed and wait for Jacob to come back after killing the king! *That's it! Krennicx is using Jacob to kill King Luther! Then the dragons would win the war without having to do the work themselves! That way they wouldn't look like they did it. It would look like it was Jacob who did it. Then everyone would be so distracted by Jacob that they won't even realize 'Krennicx' stole the throne!* Michael was angry. He did *not* want Jacob to have to go through this. He did not want King Luther to die. He did *not* want the dragons to win. *I have to stop this! Protected border or not, I will save my country! Even if it means killing that stupid Krennicx Severein!* He smiled, *But I don't see that as a negative.*

"Michael you idiotic *dummy!*" a hoarse, raspy voice that Michael hated yelled. Michael grinned in hatred as he turned to face the angry speaker.

"Ahha! I knew you were acting with that smooth-talking voice!" Michael shouted.

Krennicx growled, "You mock my voice?!"

Michael smiled, "I mock your fake attitude. *And* your voice!"

Krennicx chuckled creepily, "You think I wanted to act towards you differently? I didn't. I only did it because your brother asked me to." Krennicx sat on the sidewalk and smirked in a scary way. "Want to see how I act on my own?" His voice was smooth and icy, even more than before. His smile felt terrifying. Michael tried not to gulp.

"H-how?" Michael asked, failing at not sounding scared.

Krennicx's face was scary as his smile grew larger. Krennicx stared at Michael as if he was about to kill him. Michael felt like running away but thought better of it. *I'm about to die,* he thought in horror. Something snapped in Krennicx's facial expression and he burst into laughter. *That was unexpected.*

Krennicx laughed as he tried to talk, "You should see the look on your face! It's priceless! You're so *terrified!*" Krennicx's voice changed. It wasn't as icy and hoarse but dazzled with laughter and his strange accent. Michael stared at the hybrid in shock. "Oh *dearie!*" Krennicx continued, still brightened with laughter, "you have no idea how many times I've done this! I've seen it all!"

"What do you mean?" Michael asked, dazed.

"You think that I'm not acting usual so you try to make me stop! When really I *am* acting normal, want to know why? I have no normal!"

That's it! This thing's insane! "No *normal?*" Michael asked, confused. *"Everyone* has a normal."

Krennicx smirked and chuckled, "Oh darling dearie, you don't understand. You don't know how many things I've gone through in my life. You don't know anything about me! How would *you* know what's normal for me?"

Michael stared at him in confusion. *What in the world is going on?* "Er…," Michael said not knowing what to say. "Um…"

"Exactly."

Michael switched from confusion to frustration, "I do know one think that must be normal with you!"

"And what is that?"

"You brainwash children!"

"You're still on that?" Krennicx asked calmly.

"You're not denying it!" Michael observed.

Krennicx rolled his eyes, "What would be the point? You won't believe me no matter what." He stood and smirked, "I can't bring you back to your house because you'll just leave again, but I don't want you near the palace either," he sighed. "Unfortunately, your safest bet is with me. Aren't you so happy?" Krennicx smirked his smile at Michael's annoyed face.

"Where is my brother?" Michael demanded.

"As long as he is doing what I told him to, he's fine," Krennicx responded. "He should be leaving the dungeons by now."

"Dungeons!?"

"What? Want me to explain to you what a dungeon is?" Krennicx asked annoyingly. Michael clenched his jaw and tried not to moan. *I hope this wasn't a mistake.*

"Oh darling dearie, it was one of the worst mistakes of your life."

Michael stared at him in horror.

How many turns did I take before? Jacob stopped running in the winding halls and scratched his head. He had been running for a few minutes from the dungeons, but he couldn't remember exactly which way he had come. *Was it right? Or was it left?* He tried hard to remember. *Krennicx just might kill me for being so terrible at directions!* Jacob took a deep breath. *Maybe my 'powers' could tell me where to go?* Jacob rolled his eyes. He knew he had *some* sort of power, but he still didn't know what it was, let alone how to use it! He had already learned a lot from Krennicx, but he knew nothing about his powers. *Worth a shot, I guess.* Jacob took a deep breath and closed his eyes. He tried to feel for that tug that Krennicx had said would come whenever he needed it, but he also said sometimes you have to look for it. Nothing. Jacob moaned and opened his eyes. "I'm lost," he said out loud. Then something inside him snapped and he could feel it. *Movement.* He couldn't see them, but he could *feel* soldiers marching throughout the castle. Jacob took a deep breath. This was it. His powers. The quiet buzzing hum filled his mind. Similar to the buzz whenever Krennicx talked to him in his head. Except, this one felt very….soothing. *Ok, I have to find the entry hall. I should be able to make it around from there.* He focused on the strange feeling of things moving. He felt many different people marching along hallways. Soldiers, probably. Then he felt something coming from outside into the castle walls. It felt not too far away. The entry hall! Smiling, he opened his eyes and ran in that direction, trying not to let go of that feeling. The tunnels began to rise into floor level. After a few moments he came into the entry hall. A tug on his strange powers warned him that someone was there. Jacob stopped and hid behind a pillar. He took a deep breath.

It feels like there's only one. I can take him, right? What am I thinking? No! They're all armed soldiers! I can't take any of them! *But how am I supposed to get through? I can't let him see me and alert the others.* Jacob checked again to make sure it was just one. He felt the person coming and wandering in his direction. It felt like he was just behind the pillar. *Ok, I can do this. I have to do this!* He took a silent deep breath. *Here we go.* Relying completely on his feelings, he jumped from the pillar and gave his first punch in the face. To finish it, he kicked the intruder in the gut, sending him to the ground. "Dah!" Jacob shrieked, "Michael?!" His brother moaned on the floor. "What are you *doing* here?" Jacob asked bending over and giving him a hand. "You're supposed to stay at the house!"

"That's what I said."

"Dah!" Jacob shrieked again. *"Krennicx!?"*

"What?" Krennicx asked.

"How are you here?"

"What do you mean?"

"It's just….I didn't feel you," Jacob responded awkwardly, "I only felt one person."

Krennicx's face brightened, "You used your powers!"

"I guess so," Jacob said, looking at his hands, "but how did I not feel you?"

"That's a question for another time," Krennicx responded.

"Alright," Jacob said, "but the question for right now is *WHY DID YOU BRING MICHAEL?!*"

"I didn't *bring* him," Krennicx defended, "he brought himself."

"*What?!*" Jacob turned to Michael. "Why did you do that? You were supposed to stay at the house! It was protected!"

"I wasn't just gonna leave you with this…*thing,*" Michael said, recovering himself. He rubbed his face with a wince.

"*Ughhh,*" Jacob moaned.

"Besides," Michael continued, "it's not like I'm in danger of anything. It's you who's in danger."

"Krennicx, can we talk?" Jacob asked.

"Isn't that kind of what we're doing?" Krennicx asked.

"I *mean* without him," Jacob said, nodding towards Michael.

Krennicx shrugged, "I guess."

"Excuse me," Jacob said to Michael, "Please allow us to discuss the consequences of your stu*pidity.*" Satisfied, he turned and walked away.

Behind a different pillar, he checked to make sure they were not within hearing range but could still see Michael. He nodded.

"Not happy, eh?" Krennicx asked.

"Of *course* I'm not happy!" Jacob barked. "This is exactly what I didn't want, remember?"

Krennicx frowned, "Yes, I know."

Jacob sighed, "What are we supposed to do? If they really *are* visions, then that would mean...." Jacob trailed off, unable to say the words.

"I know," Krennicx said with a sigh, "which is why.....I don't think it would be a good idea to put him back in the house."

"Why?!" Jacob asked, alarmed.

"He's made it perfectly clear that he won't stay," Krennicx explained. "He would come right back and we wouldn't be there to protect him."

Realizing what he said was true, Jacob groaned, "Why does he have to be so difficult!"

"I can definitely see the family resemblance."

"Oi!"

Krennicx smiled, then frowned, "Remember, visions don't *always* come true. Sometimes they are warnings to be prepared for it, so you can stop it."

Jacob sighed. "I know, I just, I just don't want to risk it," Jacob said, looking at his brother. "I don't want him to die."

"Death is kind of unavoidable."

"What?" Jacob asked, turning his attention back to Krennicx. "Why would you *say* that?!"

"I'm just saying it will eventually happen," Krennicx said with an innocent shrug. "I'll die, you'll die, he'll die. Although, him probably before me."

"Kren*nicx!*"

Krennicx chuckled. Jacob shook his head, *only Krennicx…* "Look," Krennicx said soothingly, "just because you saw it, it doesn't mean you can't stop it. I believe in you."

Jacob took a deep breath, "Ok," he said. "I'd rather not bring him to the Throne Room though, just in case."

Krennicx frowned, "Whatever we do, it will happen."

"Well, that's reassuring," Jacob said sarcastically.

Krennicx smirked, "It's one of my specialties."

"Ha!" Jacob laughed. *I can do this. For Michael. I have to do this.*

CHAPTER 26

KING LUTHER

"If you don't want him to talk to you then *don't* look him in the eye!" Jacob instructed.

"But they're scary!" Michael complained.

Jacob moaned. They walked as slowly as they could, taking long hallways to somewhere Jacob did not know. "Then *why* are you looking at them?!"

Michael shrugged, "Because they're *creepy*."

"Hmph," Krennicx said. "Want to see something creepy? Go look in the mirror."

"Why you little!"

"Ok," Jacob cut him off. *He's acting like a child.*

Krennicx chuckled, "Listen to your brother, dearling."

"*Dearling?*" Michael asked, horrified.

Krennicx smirked his smile.

"What is it with you and 'd'?" Jacob asked.

Krennicx shrugged, "I can make a lot of people aggravated."

Michael groaned. Krennicx looked amused. Jacob rolled his eyes. *When is he going to realize that Krennicx enjoys this?* Jacob wondered. "Where are we even going?" Jacob asked. "And how have we not come across any guards?"

Krennicx glared at Michael, **"I'm not exactly sure your dimwitted brother should know our plan,"** Krennicx said in Jacob's head, causing the buzz to turn on.

"You think he'll betray us?" Jacob asked.

"Of course he will. It's for the best he doesn't know exactly what we're doing."

Jacob thought for a second, then nodded, *"I guess you're right."*

"As always."

Jacob rolled his eyes.

"Er....what is going on?" Michael asked, confused. He looked from Jacob to Krennicx, then back again. *This probably looks weird.* Krennicx smirked but didn't respond. Michael looked annoyed as they continued to walk without answering his question. Jacob held in a chuckle, *Michael hates Krennicx.* For a few minutes they walked in silence. Jacob had an uneasy feeling that this was just too easy. They were literally walking around the *king's* castle and haven't run into any guards. He remembered last time was kind of like this and shivered. *I hate Krennicx's plan.*

"What's the goal here?" Michael finally abruptly asked.

"You seriously haven't figured it out?" Krennicx asked.

Michael gritted his teeth, "It's kind of hard to when no one's telling me anything!"

"I guess that's what happens when you're not invited," Krennicx responded. Michael growled. Jacob rolled his eyes, *Krennicx isn't helping his cause.*

"Ready?"

"Oh boy."

As Krennicx walked, he flat out disappeared. Either he was invisible, or he was gone. Michael jumped in surprise, "What happened?"

"You sound concerned," Jacob said teasingly.

Michael groaned. There was a familiar shriek up ahead, and following was a *very* familiar laugh. Smiling, Jacob ran towards the commotion. Sure enough, Glider stood scowling at a laughing Krennicx, "Pay back baby!" Krennicx said, pleased.

Glider moaned, "I'm still not sorry."

"That's a *very* dangerous thing to say," Krennicx warned.

Glider groaned. "Sup Jacob," he said, noticing him.

"Nice to see you too, Glider," Jacob said with a nod.

"Who dis?" Glider asked, nodding towards Michael.

"Oh, this is my brother, Michael," Jacob said. "Michael this is Glider. Oh, and this is also Glazer and Tortoise," Jacob added when he noticed them behind Glider. "Where's Lighter?"

Glazer frowned, "He wasn't in the dungeons."

"He's probably stuck with Luther," Krennicx said with a scowl. "We'll get him."

"What are we supposed to do?" Tortoise asked.

Krennicx tapped the floor thoughtfully. "There's a few options, I'll leave it up to you," Krennicx said turning to Jacob.

"What are the options?" Jacob asked.

"Well, for one, Michael here can go with 'em," Krennicx responded.

"What?" Michael asked, alarmed.

"What? I thought you wanted to get away from me?" Krennicx teased.

"I do!" Michael said. "It's Jacob I don't want to get away from!"

Krennicx rolled his eyes, "How adorable. Most brothers aren't exactly touchy with each other, but you want to be as close as possible!"

"Ugh!" Michael groaned. "Not that kind of close! Seriously! Do you have any idea what it's like having a brother?"

"No," Krennicx responded. For a split second, Jacob could see *pain* in Krennicx's eyes. *I really don't know anything about him and his family, do I? I guess I should have asked about it on that night.*

Jacob sighed, "Would y'all mind taking care of him?" he asked, turning to Glider, Glazer and Tortoise.

"Another human to babysit?" Glider asked with a groan.

Glazer gave him a kind smile, "Of course not." She glanced to her brother and added, "Although, it seems the two might be a bad influence to each other." She nodded towards Michael.

"I agree," Krennicx said, smirking his insane smile. "Glider's already unbearable, but with Micky's help… sheesh, the planet just might crumble from annoyance."

Glider pursed his lips in irritation.

Krennicx grinned mischievously.

Michael clenched his jaw, *"Micky?* Do *not* call me that! And do *not* compare me with a dragon!"

Krennicx smirked sneakily. *Oh boy. Michael, what have you done to yourself? He's going to call you Micky forever now!*

"What's wrong with dragons?" Glider asked.

"What isn't wrong with them?" Michael asked, staring at him. Nothing!" Glider growled, "Ha! Look who's talking! A boy that betrayed his own brother!"

Ouch.

"Betrayed?" Michael was offended now. "How *dare* you! I am trying to save my brother from the likes of *you!* You probably don't even know what it's like to have a family! You probably leave them like birds or fight them to the death!"

Now Glider was mad. "How *dare* you talk about my family!" Glider defended. He angled himself between Glazer and Michael in a defensive position. "I'll have you know, you are *talking* about one of the best families in Annorlia!"

"Hah! Is that so, *Glider?"*

"Prince Glider to you," Glider snarled. Michael's eyes widened in shock. Glider smiled in satisfaction. *Wow,* Jacob thought, *I kind of thought they would get along. Wait, Glider's a PRINCE?!*

"Anyway…Micky," Krennicx said, awkwardly eyeing the two of them, "is that what you want?"

Jacob thought for a second, "What do you think?"

"Whatever you think," Krennicx said. "This is, after all, your mission."

Jacob frowned, "What do you mean?"

"Well, *technically* I'm not exactly supposed to be the one doing this."

"What?!"

"But we do need to get going," Krennicx immediately changed the subject.

Jacob wondered if he should change it back, but Krennicx seemed to be right. They needed to get going. *Fine, you win.* Jacob nodded, "Alright, Michael, please go with them," Jacob pleaded. "Please, if you want to keep me safe, then do exactly what they say. Understand?" Michael grumbled something Jacob couldn't hear. "Understand?" Jacob repeated.

"I guess," Michael finally said.

"Be ready to suit up," Krennicx said to his team. Jacob could see the slight confusion on Michael's face. *Right, he doesn't know that they are the Fighters of Peace.* Glider, Glazer, and Tortoise nodded. Krennicx turned to Glider, "Do *not* punch him."

"No promises," Glider smirked.

Krennicx rolled his eyes and turned to Michael, "Good luck, butty."

Michael groaned, "I'm not your buddy."

Krennicx smirked his signature smile. It took a second for Jacob to realize that 'buddy' wasn't the word the hybrid said. Glider was snickering.

"Jacob…" Michael started.

"Sorry," Jacob cut off, "but this seems to be the best option. I'm sorry."

"You know, if you wanted Michael to like you, you could act more…..well…"

"Likable?" Krennicx finished for him.

"Precisely," Jacob said with a grin.

Krennicx rolled his eyes, "Makes sense."

Jacob let out a small laugh. They continued to walk, even though everything seemed very familiar. "Are we walking in circles?" Jacob finally asked. "And why have we not run into any soldiers?"

Krennicx smirked.

"What did you do?" Jacob asked suspiciously.

"Don't worry," Krennicx said, "this is our last round. We'll get there soon."

Jacob sighed, "What was it you said back there? Something about this is my mission?"

"It is."

"How? I thought it was both of ours?" Jacob asked, confused. Krennicx didn't respond and kept walking. Jacob groaned, "Why don't you answer when you don't want to talk?"

Krennicx stopped and raised an eyebrow at him, "Really?"

"I didn't mean to sound…."

"Exactly what you meant?"

Jacob grinned, "In my defense, you do it a lot."

Krennicx smirked. "Here we are," he said, stopping at a door.

"Wait a minute," Jacob said. "We've walked by this door so many times! Why have we been walking in circles?"

Krennicx chuckled crazily, "Have to keep things interesting."

Jacob rolled his eyes. *Of course.* "Sure….."

Krennicx smirked, "Are you gonna open the door or what?"

"Why didn't you just ask?" Jacob asked, twisting the door handle.

"Just did."

Jacob rolled his eyes and opened the door. His eyes widened in shock. It was a large, red and gold hallway with soldiers running everywhere. In the middle of the hallway was a huge muscular man holding something down in a headlock. It was Lighter. Lighter smiled in a way that somewhat resembled Krennicx. Soldiers with chains surrounded him, trying to muzzle him. Lighter stopped struggling with the muscular one and eyed the others. When they went to throw the chains, Lighter backflipped, slipping straight out of the soldier's grip. There was a yelp as the chains meant for Lighter banged into the muscular soldier's chest. Lighter smiled threateningly. The soldiers recovered their chains and threw them at Lighter again. This time, Lighter caught one in mid-air and yanked it out of their grip, sending one of the soldiers head-over-heals. Not like he wasn't before, but now that Lighter had a weapon, he was unstoppable. Using the chain, he dodged swords and whipped the attackers in their faces. Soon, all the attacking soldiers were on the ground, unconscious. Jacob stared, shocked at his dragon friend. He had no idea he could fight, let alone have the *guts* to fight. Krennicx clapped. Lighter noticed them and smiled kindly. He dropped the chain and ran to them, "You're ok!" he said happily.

"Yeah," Jacob said, bewilderedly eyeing the fallen soldiers.

Lighter frowned. "They aren't dead….right?" he asked Krennicx.

"Nah," Krennicx said, swatting his hand as if it was nothing. Krennicx smiled, "You did good."

Lighter's smile was more weary than happy. "You are ok, right?" Lighter asked, turning to Jacob with concern in his eyes. "That was quite a fall."

It took a second to realize what Lighter was talking about. "Oh, when I fell over the side of the tower? Yeah, I'm alright." Jacob was still somewhat embarrassed about when he had stood at the side of the tower, not knowing there was a poisonous arrow aimed for his heart. Jacob tilted his head to Krennicx. Lighter's eyes widened. He turned to Krennicx. "Are *you* ok?" Lighter asked worriedly.

Krennicx smiled, "I'm fine."

Lighter turned back to Jacob, "What happened?"

Jacob caught Krennicx's eye roll. "Krennicx jumped in front of a poison arrow," Jacob answered. He couldn't help but smile when Krennicx slammed his talon into his face. "He saved my life."

"Poisonous arrow!" Lighter turned abruptly back to Krennicx, who smiled innocently. "You *jumped* in front of a *poisonous* arrow?! It could have killed you!" Lighter studied Krennicx with a worried expression. "Is there anything else I need to know?"

"No," Krennicx responded flatly.

Enjoying this, Jacob responded for him, "He also crashed.....into a tree."

"Why you little snitch," Krennicx said with a laugh. "I love it. Although, you aren't very accurate. It was several trees."

"Kren*nicx!*" Lighter said, as if he was Krennicx's mother.

"While this is so much fun," Krennicx said, "I believe we are running short on time, correct?"

Lighter took a deep breath, "I hate that you are so good at changing subjects."

"Me too," Jacob said.

"Me not!" Krennicx said, happily skipping along the hallway, effortlessly jumping over the fallen (but not dead according to Krennicx) soldiers.

"It really is nice to see you," Jacob told Lighter.

"Nice to see you too," Lighter responded with a warm smile. "Has he broken you yet?"

"Ha! He broke me the second it started!"

442

Krennicx was whistling loudly as he was *still* skipping along in front of them. "Er, Krennicx?" Jacob asked. "Aren't we supposed to be more…..stealthy?"

"Oh dear Jackie, have you lost your fun?" Krennicx asked in his odd and insane voice.

"Ugh," Jacob moaned quietly. "Has he always been like that?"

"Like what?" Lighter asked next to him.

"One second he acts calm and talks politely…the type of politeness that doesn't even exist," Jacob responded, "but then he acts like a madman! And *then* like he's some cunning and slick genius."

Lighter chuckled, "Oh, that. Yeah he's always been like that. Which part of him do you like?"

"What?" Jacob asked, confused.

"Well, some of the crazy part was the panther you met in the woods," Lighter explained. "And the politeness act was obviously with Queen Sunny. And then the other part was….er…. how do I describe it? Let's go for *'sweetniblets Glider!'*" Lighter tapped his lip thoughtfully, "Yeah, that sounds about right."

Jacob chuckled, "You even did his raspiness and accent right….almost."

Lighter grinned, "What kind of accent *does* he have?"

"No idea."

They laughed. It felt nice. Jacob never had a good friend before. Sure, Lighter was a dragon, but Jacob had never laughed this much around any human friend. It was odd though, he only knew him for a few days, and here they were! On their way to face *King Luther*? To Jacob it felt like it took a while for him to turn, but when he thought about it, it really only took him a few days!

"Why is it that I feel like the two of them are talking about me?" Krennicx asked thoughtfully. "Oh yeah, I guess it's because they're talking extremely *loud.*" He looked behind him and scowled at them, *while* somehow also smirking. *HOW does he DO THAT?!* Krennicx didn't have two mouths, of course, but somehow he made many facial expressions at once. Jacob glanced up at Lighter to ask how. Before he even started to speak, Lighter shrugged. Jacob rolled his eyes and shook his head. *How? Just how?* Jacob was so distracted from looking around the hall that he almost tripped over Krennicx's tail. "Sorry!" Jacob yelped. Krennicx ignored him and looked around, twitching his ears.

"Krennicx……," Lighter asked worriedly, "what is it?"

Krennicx smiled a mischievous smirk, "Exactly what we want." With an excited expression on his face, he speed-walked along the hallway with Lighter and Jacob struggling to stay behind.

"Should I be worried?" Jacob asked.

"Depends," Lighter responded. "In other words……yeah, probably."

Jacob gulped. Lighter smiled. The hallway finally stopped at a red and gold double door. Krennicx glanced at them with pure mischief in his eyes. *Oh boy.* Without any warning, Krennicx launched for the doors and yanked both sides open at once, even though they would be able to fit thru just one of them. Krennicx just *loved* to make an entrance. The doors slammed into each side of the wall with a loud clang.

"What happened to stealth?" Jacob asked, wincing at the noise.

"They were going to find out anyway. Now hush, you're ruining my thunder," Krennicx said with a smirk. He flicked his wings towards the outside of the hallway's opened doors. Jacob couldn't even gulp due to the lump in his throat. Soldiers. Everywhere. It was a large, shiny room *filled* with soldiers looking their way. *Krennicx, what have you done?*

Krennicx let out a chuckle that brought chill bumps to Jacob's skin. "You dearies really don't disappoint!" He smirked at the soldiers' surprised expressions. They slowly walked towards them with spears and swords stretched out. Krennicx paid no attention to them and calmly walked towards them. *What are you DOING?! Why am I surprised?* Jacob thought shaking his head. He glanced at Lighter, who rolled his eyes. The soldiers looked like they had no idea what to do as Krennicx walked with no intention of stopping. Somehow, Krennicx made it to the other side of the room. "Dearie, dearie, dearie." Krennicx calmly walked up the two-step stage. It took a second for Jacob to realize that they were standing in the Throne Room. *How did we end up here? It sure didn't feel like we were heading in this direction, unless that was a back door we came in.*

"How you doin?" Krennicx asked.

Krennicx stood calmly in front of the throne of King Luther.

King Luther raised an eyebrow at the hybrid in front of him. "I have to say," King Luther said, "I'm impressed. I knew you'd get here, but the fact that no one seems to have seen you is….remarkable."

Krennicx smiled threateningly, "Wish I could say the same for your guards, or rather, their leader."

There was a streak of fear that ran down Luther's face, it immediately disappeared, "I'll think about hiring a different commander."

Krennicx tilted his head, "You really are clueless, aren't you?"

King Luther bit his lower lip to cover his anger. "If only you knew the amount of strength it takes to not kill you where you stand," Luther snarled.

"Temper, temper," Krennicx sneered. "I adore your hatred. It's amusing." Krennicx didn't pay any attention to the shuffle of soldiers pointing their crossbows at him, he kept his eyes staring directly at the king. *I feel like I'm supposed to be doing something while they're distracted.* Jacob looked around the room trying to remember the plan. *I remember I hated it…..so….what was it?* He thought for a second, then remembered, *oh…..NOW I remember.* It took everything in Jacob's strength to not moan. *I do NOT want to do this.* Jacob took a deep breath, then shouted, "Smell my stanky pits, you idiot!" He immediately ran to the other set of doors on the other side of the room.

Judging by the sound, a few soldiers were chasing him. *I hate Krennicx's plan!* He ran down the hallway until one of the soldiers tackled him to the ground. "Smell my pits has been bothering me!" Jacob said like a madman. He rolled onto his back and looked at the soldier, "Mr. Samual?"

"Jacob?" Samual said, helping him up. "What are you doing with Severein?"

"It's a long story," Jacob said, brushing his clothes off. He counted five soldiers that had followed him, all of them looking ready for a command.

"What's your command?" Samual asked.

"Command?" Jacob asked, shocked.

"You said the code, so, what does the Represenetor need?"

Jacob stared at the soldier in shock. *Krennicx didn't tell me that was a code.* He thought of what Krennicx had told him to say, then taking a deep breath, finally answered, "It's time."

The soldiers nodded in agreement. "Of course," Samual said. "We will take up our stations and report to the others."

"Others?" Jacob asked, shocked.

Samual nodded, "I don't know what is you are doing with the Represenetor's code, but good luck. And don't worry, when all of this is over, we won't tell anyone you were a part of it."

Still shocked, Jacob forced himself to say something. "Thank you?"

"Don't mention it," Samual said, not noticing it was a question. "Now, do you need anything?"

A memory of something Krennicx had said came in his mind, he pushed it back and thought about the question Samual just asked. "I could use…. A sword, maybe?"

Again, Jacob ran along a *long* hall trying to find his way, but this time he had a scabbard thumping his side. While he appreciated the soldier's kindness, he found the weapon very annoying. Krennicx had said once that a sword would probably be his main weapon, so of course, Jacob believed him. He just wasn't expecting it to be so stinking annoying! Jacob sighed as he slowed to a jog. *So far, it seems Krennicx's plan is working. Although, I'm not exactly sure how his side is going. Or Michael's! I hope he's not being TOO hard on the others,* Jacob grimaced, *although, I wouldn't mind too much if he gave Glider a hard time.*

Michael moaned in aggravation, *Next time I see that brother of mine I'm going to throttle him!*

"Stop stepping on my tail!" the annoying one Jacob said was Glider barked.

"Well, if you didn't walk so *close* and so *slow,* I wouldn't have to!" Michael said, purposefully stomping his foot on the dragon's stupid tail.

Glider whipped around and snapped his jaw at him threateningly. Michael forced himself to not look afraid. He found all three of these dragons annoying, but he was still afraid of them.

"Are you alright?" a too-sweet-to-be-true voice asked. Michael looked up to see the dragon Jacob had called Glazer walking next to him. Her frosty eyes sparkled, staring directly into his.

"I'm fine," Michael said with too much flatness. He bit his lower lip when he realized that did *not* sound convincing. It wasn't.

"I see….," Glazer said with a frown. Clearly, she did not believe him. "I know it's probably weird talking to us and all. I understand, trust me."

Michael looked up at the girl dragon in shock. What was she talking about? Was she around humans often? Why? *Probably attacking them!* Something still didn't feel right though. Then he realized what he was feeling was….cold. Cold was radiating from the dragon's scales. He was getting chill bumps. "Ok," Michael finally said when he realized Glazer was waiting for some sort of answer.

"You're a lot like him, you know," Glazer said, studying him.

"Who?"

"Jacob."

"Really?" Michael asked.

"Well, yeah. Both of you are willing to do anything to save each other, even if it means getting out of your comfort zone. You're always thinking about him, hoping he's ok. And Jacob sacrificed himself for you, even though he didn't have to. Even when you wake him up extremely early to do dragon research, Jacob is willing to do it because it makes you happy. And you are also willing to go for a run with him sometimes. And *both* of you are willing to play baseball with your sister."

For a second Michael smiled, and then he realized exactly what she just said. "Wait, how did you know all of that? You just met me."

Glazer's face went from sincere to panic. "Whoopsies, blew that one didn't I?"

Michael stared at Glazer in horror, "You can read my *mind?*"

Glazer opened her mouth to say something but was interrupted by Tortoise, "They're coming."

Glazer frowned, "How many?"

"Pretty good bit," Tortoise responded.

Glider rolled his wings. "Let 'em come," he said daringly. "I want to kick some human butt."

"Glider!" Glazer scorned.

"What? I do!" Glider responded innocently.

Glazer rolled her eyes. "We have specific orders," she said, shifting her weight to the side in a way that reminded Michael way too much of Hazel. Michael frowned at the similarities. *I hate that she would LOVE this dragon.*

"So?" Glider asked.

"*So* you have to obey them!" Glazer responded. *Yes, she would want to be best friends.*

"Hmph," Glider paused and smirked, "I guess it's too late, sis." Thumps of soldiers' footsteps filled the hallway. Tortoise was right, there was a lot. Michael's mind whirled with his options. *I don't want the soldiers to die, but I really do need to escape. And it's not like I would be able to help them in any way.* His mind was made. When the battle started and the dragons were distracted, Michael ran.

The sun was beginning to set as Jacob and a squad of Smell-My-Pit-turned-soldiers marched along the trail in the thick trees. Apparently, the wall was behind King Luther's castle, so in order to get there, they had to go through some of the Dragon Forest. Jacob's feet hurt from so much walking and running. "So, how long has this wall been here?" Jacob asked, afraid of the answer.

A soldier sighed, "Longer than you've been alive."

"Do you remember when it wasn't here?" Jacob asked.

"Yes," a different soldier said, "but that's about all we should say. You never know what's hiding around the corner."

Jacob nodded, "I understand." *I hope Michael and Krennicx are ok!* Sure, Krennicx had told him *most* of the plan, but he still didn't know all of it. He mainly only heard a little bit, but to be fair, Jacob *did* tell Krennicx to stop explaining it. He was afraid that if he heard any more than what he already heard, he would refuse to do it. But come on! Screaming out 'smell my pits!' is *not* something you'd want to do. Especially in front of soldiers *and* the king! But reluctantly, he did it. And it *worked*. Now he had a few squads of soldiers on his side and helping. With the amount they had, they just *might* be able to accomplish their goal. Whatever the 'goal' was. Jacob figured it was to release everyone from this wall that he had never heard too much about, but something told him that wasn't all.

"Report," one of the soldier leaders said as a scout came back.

"It seems safe. Nothing has breached it from any sides. And the guardian is still in place."

"Good," the leader said. He nodded towards Jacob and added, "We seem to be all set."

"Thank you," Jacob said with a smile.

The soldier nodded once like a small bow, "Let's move out!"

Jacob went to follow them when a vision struck with so much strength it sent him to his knees. He had already seen this vision before, but it felt *stronger*. As if it was happening now. Michael was running along hallways that led to the Throne Room, where King Luther waited. The vision hazed, then went to the worst part: where King Luther stabs a sword through Michael's heart. "NO!" Jacob cried. It was happening. Michael was running to his death. He didn't know how, but he could just *feel* that Michael was doing it. The vision fogged and faded away.

"Are you alright?" the soldier asked.

Jacob hardly even noticed. *NO! He can't die! He can't! I can't let it happen. But it IS happening! And I'm so far away! I would NEVER make it in time. But I have to try! I have to save him!* Jacob looked up to see all of the soldiers staring at him curiously. Jacob wiped his teary eyes. "I have to go," Jacob said, forcing himself to stand up. "I have to go back to the castle."

The soldier shook his head, "It's too dangerous. Soldiers will be everywhere and nightfall is upon us."

"I am going," Jacob said, staring up into the soldiers eyes. "I *have* to."

The soldier nodded, "Ok, but don't think we didn't warn you."

Jacob nodded, "Thank you."

The soldiers nodded in return. Then Jacob sprinted. His legs screamed in tiredness. They wanted to rest. But Jacob pushed on and ran faster. His vision began to blur from his hot tears. His mind was filled with all the precious moments he had with his brother. All the times that Michael had embarrassed him at school, yelling at him through the window about how they would kill the dragons together. Michael was wrong about the dragons, he was wrong to try to kill Krennicx and stab

Jacob, but Jacob didn't care. He loved Michael. He couldn't let him go. Jacob used all his strength to keep running, even when he tripped on a tree root. He fought hard to not break down and sob. He could hardly see. He thought of what Krennicx had said about visions, trying to have hope that it wouldn't happen. He had said that they were warnings, and that they would happen unless he figured out a way to stop it. He had said that sometimes they *will* happen, but sometimes they won't. There's just not much you *can* do about it, just the right thing. *I have to stop this! That's the only right thing to do!* He forced himself to run faster, even when his tired legs tried to drop. He was too focused on his brother. Too terrified that he would die. He barely noticed when everything became a blur and he rammed into a wall. Jacob moaned on the floor and looked around, "What in Annorlia?" He looked around, then his jaw dropped. He was at the castle! *How did I?...* He shook his head, pushed his question aside and stood up. *It doesn't matter. I'm here. I'm coming Michael!*

"King Luther!" Michael called to the king that sat on his throne.

King Luther smiled, "Michael, what brings you here?" He stood up and walked towards him.

"It's the dragons!" Michael said, panicking. "They're here! I think they want to kill you!"

King Luther tapped his lip thoughtfully, "Sounds about right. They already came, Jacob with them. Three got away. But the most important one is contained."

"Severein?" Michael asked.

"Yes," King Luther said with a dark smile.

"Where did my brother go?" Michael asked.

"I'm not sure, but we are searching," King Luther responded.

"Thank you," Michael said with a sigh of relief. King Luther was still coming closer, which was odd. He put his left hand on Michael's shoulder.

"Don't worry. We will find your brother and save him from their grasps. No matter the cost," King Luther smiled warmly. "And the ones responsible will die. You have done well."

"It was my honor, my King," Michael said, going for a bow, but King Luther held onto his shoulder too tightly.

"Those responsible will die, no matter the cost."

"Of course," Michael said awkwardly. "Although Jacob can be saved, right?"

"He will no longer be used against us," King Luther assured.

"And you won't let the dragons kill him?" Michael asked.

"Of course not! I'll kill him myself," King Luther responded happily.

"Wait, what?"

King Luther's sword was unsheathed, and it went to stab him in the heart. But a blur came in between them, blocking the strike with a sword. *Stay away from my brother!* Jacob snarled.

454

Jacob was furious as he held the sword against King Luther's. He had never been more mad in his life. He had respected the king, loved him, really. But here he was, trying to kill his own brother! Jacob gritted his teeth in pure fury.

"Well, well, well, Jacob," Luther sneered. "I see you're figuring out your powers. That speed was pretty impressive."

"Shut it, Luther!" Jacob said angrily.

"That's *King Luther* to you," King Luther said angrily.

"You are *not* my king!" Jacob snarled. "Now stay away from my brother!"

"I'll stay away from him when he's a dead carcass!" King Luther sneered. Jacob jumped and spun, sending a devastating kick in King Luther's face. King Luther fell back and clutched his face in pain. He cackled a laugh as he recovered himself. "Well, done, dear boy! Very impressive! I can definitely tell who your teacher is!"

Jacob had no idea where that came from, but honestly, it felt *good*. He clenched his fists angrily at the terrible king. "Where. Is. Severein?" Jacob asked as stern as he could.

Luther laughed, "Afraid to face me alone, are you? You *should* be. No one can help you. Not even Severein."

"I wouldn't be too sure of that."

King Luther's face turned to absolute terror as he turned to face the most terrifying thing in the world. "B-but y-you were…" Luther stumbled.

"'Contained'? Seriously, the King of Cloudairia couldn't 'contain' me, do you really think *you* can? Now, unless you want to be panther meat, I'd expect you to *back off."*

Showing absolutely *no* bravery, Luther, the king of the humans, ran in horror into the back left door. Jacob knew where the stairs went.

"Well, that went well," Krennicx smirked hilariously.

Michael fell to the ground and breathed hard, "H-he just tried to…"

"I know, and I'm glad you're ok," Jacob said hugging his brother. "I'm sorry, but I have to go. I have to stop him." Without another word, Jacob ran after the king. *He's safe*, Jacob thought as he ran up the spiral staircase. *Now, I just have to keep it that way. King Luther, I'm coming for you.* Again, everything blurred and Jacob found himself already standing in the room where he and Michael first talked to the king. He saw Luther's back as the king ran for the window.

"Leaving so soon?" Krennicx asked, standing in front of the window. King Luther shrieked in surprise and fear. He turned around to go the other way, but Jacob stood there. Luther's eyes searched the room in fear, then he rolled his eyes and laughed. "How could I forget? You can't hurt me." He reached out his hand, and the DragonStaff appeared. He laughed when Krennicx eyed it.

Jacob unsheathed his sword, "It's over King Luther. Your reign of lies has come to an end."

"Lies?" King Luther asked. "My dear boy, all I have done is for the good of my people."

"Creating a wall to entrap all who are threats and making their kids go to a school where they are taught about a war that doesn't exist? Sounds *perfect* for your people," Krennicx said sarcastically.

"Shut it," Luther said, thumping the floor with the DragonStaff. Immediately, Krennicx's mouth slapped closed and he rolled his eyes, his facial expression annoyed. *I might be in trouble,* Jacob realized in horror. Luther laughed.

Jacob took a deep breath, *I have to do this. Even if he turns Krennicx against me. I can't let King Luther hurt anyone anymore. This has to end. But how?* Jacob tried not to think about it. "Why are you doing this?" Jacob finally asked. "Why? Why do you have to rule the people this way? Why are you lying? Why are you *making* people lie to everyone? What will you gain?"

"Foolish child! Are you seriously asking this? Isn't it obvious? People don't know how to follow correctly. They don't know how to do exactly what I want. They need fear to obey. That's why the war exists," Luther sneered. "As long as they're terrified of what the idiotic dragons do to them, they will hand *everything* over to me. They won't even *question* what I do. That my dear, is how you rule."

"But what if you gave them a reason to obey? If you treated them with the truth and made the right decisions, they would *choose* to obey," Jacob said. "Why would they obey someone who lies?"

"Am I seriously being taught how to rule by a kid? Really Jacob, what has made you so sappy?" King Luther asked.

Jacob clenched his teeth, "I don't care. This has to stop. *Now.*"

"For you, I'm afraid that's not possible. As long as I have this staff, you'll be too busy trying to save your own life. But with who you'll be up against, that would be impossible." King Luther smiled, "Now, with this Staff, your very own *teacher* will have no choice but to kill you." Luther glanced at Krennicx and sneered, "Because now, thanks to you and your pathetic brother…..*I* can control the second most powerful…"

A highly accented voice burst out in pure laughter. Krennicx wiped his eyes, "I'm sorry, I'm *so* sorry! You see, I practice my acting for when it's actually needed, but this? I just....I can't," Krennicx laughed again. "But, oh dear *darling*, is that really what you think?"

King Luther whipped around and gaped at the 'talking' and *laughing* Krennicx, "Y-you are s-supposed to be..."

"Silent?" Krennicx's chuckle brought goosebumps to both Jacob and Luther. "I suppose my mouth is very hard to shut. Don't you agree?"

"B-but the Staff is supposed to c-control," King Luther stammered like a terrified child.

Krennicx let out a laugh that was absolutely horrifying, "You really did fall for that, didn't you? The great King Luther, fell for a cute little bedtime story."

"But it is real!" King Luther stepped back. "It worked on all the dragons I tried it on! But, maybe because...." He trailed off in horror when he realized what it meant.

"I am no dragon," Krennicx smirked. "And may I ask, which dragons did you try it on? The one's who already work for you? Your prisoners? Or...could it be......Glider, Lighter, Glazer, and Tortoise?"

"B-but it worked on them!" King Luther stammered. "You're just trying to scare me! It isn't fake! It's real! It has power..."

"It *does* have power in it, but not the kind you'd expect," Krennicx cut him off. He looked at the orb on top of the Staff as it swirled purple. "Yes, it *does* tell dragons *what* to do, but it doesn't have the power to make them do it."

"Where's the power from?" King Luther asked, but he seemed to know the answer.

"There is power in the Staff, *my* power," Krennicx responded, his eyes looking so satisfied. "I knew you figured out who I was those several years ago, so I decided to make a diversion. I made the DragonStaff because I needed to keep you distracted from me and the Fighter of Peace in your kingdom. So I decided to distract you from me by, well, me. I knew that if I could make you think that if you found this *legendary* relic that could control dragons, you'd go after it so much that you would forsake one of the biggest secrets of Annorlia. You decided to not blow my secret of being the Lightning Prince because you wanted to use the Staff to take me yourself. You hoped that you could control me and kill Omega, making you the ultimate ruler of Annorlia. But if I wasn't powerful enough to kill Omega, the King of Shadows, you'd simply gift me to him in return of the position of second in command," Krennicx grinned. "You fell for the creation and scheme of an eight year old. Oh darling dear! You know what that technically makes me? *I* am the DragonStaff. And I believe it's time to take it back." Krennicx raised his talon. Lightning flashed as the small stone dragon holding the orb spread its wings and flew to its creator, placing the orb in his talon. Krennicx smiled as the little stone dragon crawled onto his back and rested there.

Luther's eyes widened in terror while taking several steps back. "Y-you can't kill me! It's illegal!"

Krennicx let out another terrifying chuckle, "I'm not much of a killing type."

"Illegal?" Jacob couldn't help but ask, even though his mind whirled with questions about Krennicx being *THE* DragonStaff?! *He made it when he was eight?!* "What's that supposed to mean?"

"You might have been sent by the Represenetor," King Luther was starting to sound like a child, "but that doesn't mean you have the authority to take the thro—"

"We have every authority we need," Krennicx grimaced.

"That's impossible," King Luther snorted. "For one thing, the Represenetor never accepted the vote. So, only a representative can dethrone the king, but even then, he doesn't have the power to do anything once the king doesn't have the throne. Only the prince can. And we all know that won't be happening." Luther swiped his hand like he was pushing the matter away. "Besides, our representative is dead, and it's a *very* long process to even try to elect a new one. *Especially* with the Represenetor never showing his face to do anything, for he is the only one that can elect a new one."

Krennicx laughed, "Oh *dearie!* Whatever will we do? If only the Represenetor chose and elected a new representative!" He smiled threateningly at the king. The way the hybrid stood without an ounce of fear…something seemed weird in a way he had never seen before.

"That would be impossible," King Luther said in panic. "The so-called 'High King' hasn't gotten himself into politics in years. He's too distracted with the war."

Krennicx sighed, "The war is draining, but I think he can manage, well I *hope* so."

He sure does seem to know a lot, unless….. Jacob nearly gasped. Could it be?

King Luther wasn't done uselessly talking, "*Only* the representative, with permission, can dethrone a king. You might be the leader of his 'new military,' but that doesn't give you authority over me. Only the dead representative has that type of authority."

Krennicx smirked, "You think I don't know that? With permission, the representative *will* dethrone you." Krennicx glanced at Jacob and smiled. King Luther whipped around and stared blankly at him. *It's me,* Jacob realized, *I'm the representative. That would also mean that I was chosen. That I've MET the Represenetor, but who?* Jacob looked up and realized what was always so weird about Krennicx's stance. He looked *regal.* Far more regal than any other king, including King Luther. He wasn't prideful looking, but yet when he needed to be, he was fearless and authoritative. He was like that in Cloudairia too, but Jacob hadn't put his finger on it until now. Jacob took a deep breath. *It's him. Krennicx is the High King of ALL Annorlia. The Represenetor.*

CHAPTER 27

THE TRUTH

How is this possible? Krennicx? ME? A representative? KRENNICX? THE REPRESENETOR AND THE DragonStaff?! Well, he's not exactly a staff….but still! THE REPRESENETOR!? He looked at King Luther to see if he figured it out. He immediately looked away when he met Luther's gaze. *Why? Why me? Why was I chosen?*

"You don't have to do this if you don't want to," Krennicx said in his head, turning the buzz on.

"Did, did I just….."

"No, I just so happened to be looking into that cute little head of yours."

Jacob rolled his eyes, *"How? How am I supposed to 'dethrone' a king?"*

"Since he killed the last representative, drastic measures can be taken. Emergency power is given to the next representative."

"You mean…. Permission to…kill him?"

There was a pause, until Krennicx finally responded, **"Yes."**

Jacob sighed, *"How am I supposed to beat him?"*

"You don't have to do it alone, I can help you."

Jacob hesitated. *Can he? He's the Represenetor! Is it legal?* "But….you're the Represenetor! Are you allowed to?"

Krennicx sighed, **"I can help, and I wouldn't hesitate to, even if it is somewhat illegal,"**

Jacob took a deep breath. He just confirmed it. He was right. Krennicx truly was the Represenetor. All those times Jacob made fun of him and tried to kill him, he was *really* doing it to *the* High King of Annorlia! **"The *only* problem is...."**

"What?"

"The only ones that know is you, Lighter, Glider, Glazer, Tortoise, Ben, and Queen Icicle, and a small amount of others that would kill you if you found out their names. If Luther found out... his mouth is very..."

"Big?"

"Yes."

"I understand." Truthfully, he did. It would be a disaster if everyone knew all of Krennicx's secrets. And out of four kingdoms he's been to (Jacob assumed the Dragon Forest was a kingdom) *two* of them had a wall, entrapping their citizens. *Plus,* he didn't even know of any others. All of them hated Krennicx, or some part of him. Obviously, Annorlia was crumbling, and Krennicx seemed to be the only one keeping it together. What a burden! But if everyone knew exactly who he is, and where he lives, Annorlia wouldn't stand a chance. Jacob could *feel* that this was the right thing to do, but it was still terrifying. Jacob caught Krennicx's unsure gaze. Jacob nodded.

"I'm guessing the two of you have a way of communicating," King Luther said, looking at them curiously. "You are just staring at each other."

Krennicx ignored him, **"Are you *sure?*"**

"Yes," Jacob responded, he was *actually* starting to believe he could do it. *"I'm also sure your help will be needed breaking down the wall. I doubt they can do it without you."*

Krennicx still looked unsure as he stared at him worriedly. "Go!" Jacob said out loud.

Krennicx sighed, then gave King Luther a dark glare, "Hurt him in *any* way…"

Luther gave him a smug look, "Run along, little prince. I have a few things I want to say to, well, my representative,"

Krennicx cast one more worried look, then there was a flicker of lighting, and he was gone. "I thought he'd never leave," King Luther smiled. "Now, where were we?"

Jacob tried to calm his fast beating heart, *Probably should have asked him how in the world I'm supposed to do this! HOW am I supposed to dethrone a king?!* Jacob took a deep breath. No matter what, he couldn't show he was afraid. He looked up at King Luther, who was studying him *intensely. Why does this feel so AWKWARD?* He was starting to open his mouth to say something when King Luther sighed. Jacob gulped, "What?"

"It's just sad," King Luther said. He walked to the large window wall and stared at the darkness of night.

Jacob hesitated, "What is?"

"When a kid is killed."

Jacob shrieked in alarm when a dagger came flying for his face. Somehow, he managed to miss it when he jumped to the ground. He got on his knees and looked up just in time to see Luther's boot slam him in the face. He fell to his back and clutched his face in pain. He was *not* going to cry. The slight sound of a sword unsheathed warned him of the present. He rolled over as the sword stabbed the ground with a loud clang. He crouched on the floor with his left leg spread out next to him and his right hand on the floor. It felt odd but….*right*. Refusing to let himself be distracted, he jumped from his position and just barely dodged another attack. His hands were sweating so much he forgot he was holding a sword. He felt like slapping himself in the face when he realized he still had it. At least he remembered in time. There was a loud clang as Jacob blocked Luther's sword with his own. His hands vibrated from the force, but he kept it in place, at least until King Luther kicked him in the gut. Jacob shrieked and fell to the ground, clutching his airless stomach. It would have been the perfect time for King Luther to go for the kill, but a roar greeted his ears like beautiful music. He looked up to see dark, midnight-blue scales. Jacob felt like kissing his pet dragon! Winter roared angrily at the king and clamped his teeth onto the king's sword, flinging it across the whole room. Now, with Winter's help, maybe Jacob could win. Winter was about to pounce Luther when the king blew on a whistle that was strapped around his neck. Another roar echoed. The glass wall shattered as a crimson red dragon rammed into Winter and sent him flying into a wall. This one was far bigger than Jacob's beloved pet. "Watch out!" Jacob shrieked. But it was too late. The red dragon pounced onto Winter and bit him. Winter roared and clawed at the attacker. Jacob was too distracted to remember his own fight. *Bang!* The lights began to dim as his head felt like it was spinning. He fell to the ground in pain. He could hardly remember where he was. His head hurt too much to remember anything. Darkness clouded his vision like claws. He was hardly even aware of the sword being taken out of his sweaty hand. Had he really been holding onto it that long? His eyesight was too clouded to see the sword that was about to slice his neck, but that was when something inside him clicked. His hand shot up, making the sword stop in mid-swing. Jacob took a deep breath as his vision began to clear, allowing him to see the shocked expression on Luther's face. Jacob couldn't help but smile, "What was it you wanted to talk about?" Jacob swiped his hands like he was moving something aside. King Luther went *flying*. There was a loud and painful thud as Luther slammed into the wall and fell to the floor. Was he unconscious? Jacob stared at his hands and gulped in fear. *Did I just do that?* He stared at his hands disbelievingly. *Krennicx said I had powers.... And I remember lifting those rocks....but THIS?* He just *threw* the king of the humans against a wall and knocked him unconscious! Jacob took several deep breaths, then he walked to the king. He glared at the DragonStaff that no longer held the stone dragon or the orb. It had gone flying with King Luther. *Why couldn't Krennicx have taken all of it?* Jacob wondered, rubbing his head. He cleared his throat, "King Luther, by order of the Represenetor and representative, I erm, *arrest* you." Jacob honestly didn't know if Krennicx was arresting the king, but he figured he was. Jacob gulped. King Luther wasn't responding. *Did I kill him?!* Jacob thought in horror. *Maybe I should call Krennicx.* The only problem about calling would be because he *couldn't* call. *Well, that's aggravating.* Another deep breath, *I can do this.* He reached out his hand and thought about what he wanted and where it was. Immediately, Jacob's sword flew to him. He had to ignore the fact that he was actually able to do it. *Just to be safe*, Jacob thought, positioning his sword against the king. "King Luther?" Jacob asked, studying the unconscious king. Somehow, the king was still holding the fake DragonStaff. *Did he glue it to his hand?* he wondered. Jacob paused in horror when he realized something. It was quiet. Too quiet. A loud roar echoed off the walls as the crimson dragon pounced at Jacob. Jacob shrieked and tried to get out of the way.

"Oh, dear Jacob, did you really think it'd be that easy?" Jacob whipped around in horror. King Luther stood with a smirk on his face. Next to him, on both sides, stood black dragons. *Night Dragons*, Jacob realized. They looked a lot like Lighter, except Lighter had the blue on the tip of his scales. Their body shape was a *little* different, but not much.

"The DragonStaff doesn't work!" Jacob mostly reminded himself. "You can't control them!"

"I don't have to," King Luther sneered, "they *work* for me. You see Jacob, not *all* dragons are bad. But some are far more superior. Kill him." In unison, both Night Dragons opened their mouth, and, for the first time Jacob had ever seen, they *breathed* fire. Red, scorching hot flames flew towards him. It should have hit him immediately, but it didn't. Jacob looked up to see dark, midnight blue scales circling around him. When the fire stopped, Winter roared in fury. Smoke stung his lungs as fire erupted out of Winter's mouth at King Luther. Smoke flared from Winter's nostrils as he growled angrily when his fire was blocked. Jacob gagged as smoke burned his lungs. It took him a second to realize that the room was catching on fire. He looked around in fear. Panels on the wall caught fire and was quickly spreading. Jacob coughed. "We should probably leave," Jacob said, turning to Winter. Winter nodded and began to lead him to the large shattered windows. Something struck Jacob's head hard....again. Jacob again fell to the ground in pain.

"Leaving so soon?" King Luther asked, emerging from the fire. Winter went to pounce him but was pounced by one of the Night Dragons. "Honestly, I thought you'd be smarter than that." King Luther unsheathed his sword. It took all of Jacob's strength to rise from the floor and hold his own sword in a defensive position. He shook his head dizzily, trying to stop everything from spinning. Luther laughed, "Just like your father."

"Don't talk about my dad!" Jacob defended.

"What? The person who *lied* to you?" King Luther asked.

"He didn't lie! And even if he did, it was because of you!" Jacob snarled.

"Oh, please! He did it to himself when he disobeyed. He might not have lied, but he wasn't honest with you about his past."

"I don't care," Jacob snapped.

"Really? Want to know the reason why Krennicx owes him?"

Jacob took a deep breath, "No." He launched an attack on the king.

"Feisty," Luther sneered, blocking his swing. Luther kicked him and expertly fought back. Jacob was *not* an expert, but somehow he was doing fine at blocking. He was vaguely aware of Winter's fight with the Night Dragons as Jacob fought for his life. Somehow, he sent an impressive kick in Luther's face. Luther fell back and rubbed his face, "Severein is training you well!"

"I guess he is," Jacob said with a smile. He was about to end the fight with another kick, but the ground rumbled and sent him off balance. "What is that?!" Jacob shrieked. The floor was cracking and the castle was groaning. He tripped as everything began to lean forward. The fire had spread almost everywhere now, but surely it wouldn't cause this, would it? Luther looked just as terrified as Jacob was. "What did you do?!" Jacob asked in terror.

"This isn't me!" Luther promised in horror.

"Who is it?!"

Luther's eyes widened. "Traitor," he mouthed.

"What?"

"That traitor!" King Luther shouted angrily. He struggled to his feet and whistled for one of the dragons. None of them came. King Luther looked furious. All of the dragons were gone.

"Winter!" Jacob called. Nothing. Jacob went into a coughing fit as the fire raged toward them and the castle began to crumble. Jacob and Luther shrieked as the castle leaned completely to the side as it crumbled. They fell to the floor and slid to the shattered windows. Jacob grabbed onto a loose window panel with his right hand and caught Luther's hand with his free one just in time. The tower was completely leaning as Jacob and King Luther dangled out of it. Jacob's muscles screamed in pain as he held onto both of their weight. "You've got to be kidding me!" Jacob said when he remembered Krennicx telling him to practice dangling over the side of a cliff in case he ever needed to save someone. Except this time, he wasn't on Krennicx's training wheels. "Hold on!" Jacob called to the heavy king.

"Why are you saving me?" King Luther asked. "If you let go you will finish your mission and possibly save yourself!"

For a split second he was tempted. *NO*. "I'm not going to let you die! You can't have your throne anymore! But this is *not* the way. You might be worthy of death, but it's wrong! I'm not going to let go!"

Luther gaped at Jacob as if he was staring at pure gold. Jacob took a deep breath, ignored his tired muscles, and pulled the king to the edge next to him. Luther grabbed the edge and started to pull himself up, with Jacob's help. Jacob wasn't aware of the sword that had fallen into Luther's reach. "You're a good kid, ya know that?" King Luther asked.

Jacob smiled. Then an indescribable and horrible pain erupted in his left shoulder. Jacob was in too much pain to even scream. King Luther kicked him in the face. Jacob lost his grip and fell.

Jacob was hardly aware of anything as he fell through the dark sky. Just pain. And near darkness. He hardly noticed the small flash of light below him. He fell into the arms of something furry and gentle, inspecting him with worried eyes. He recognized the fur. "Don't worry," a familiar voice said. Then something cold pricked him. *Clever,* Jacob thought as he fell into a deep dark sleep.

CHAPTER 28

THE THRONE SLAYER

With a moan, Jacob slowly opened his eyes to see pure red. "Morn'n sleepy beauty," Krennicx said with a bright smile. "Will there ever be a time when you *don't* fall off a cliff?"

Jacob smiled wearily, "This time it wasn't a cliff."

Krennicx snorted, "Yeah, like a tumbling castle is any better."

Jacob smiled, "Wait, where are we?" he asked, looking around the long room with many other beds like the one he was laying in. It seemed like a hospital room.

Krennicx opened his mouth to respond but was interrupted.

"*YOU!*" a familiar voice shouted. "I thought I banned you?"

Krennicx smirked, "A band? Great! I'll go get my ukulele!"

"NO!" Jacob and Scott Barton yelled in unison.

"Tough crowd," Krennicx snorted.

Barton rolled his eyes and turned to Jacob with a warm smile, "How are you feeling?"

"I'm not sure," Jacob responded. He went to scratch his face with his left hand but froze.

Krennicx heaved a large sigh. **"Deep. Breath,"** Krennicx transmitted.

Jacob obeyed, then slowly reached for his left arm. Nothing was there. His stomach churned. He closed his eyes and forced several deep breaths. His memory raced back to the pain he felt when he saved Luther's life. It took a second to feel the similar pain, but it was distant. Barton must have used some *strong* numbing medicine. Jacob's heart was racing. He kept his eyes closed as the queasiness was becoming unbearable.

"Here, let me just grab this and I'll give you two some privacy. Call me if you need me," Scott Barton said, grabbing something underneath Jacob's bed. Just when Barton was standing back up, Jacob lost all control. He threw up all over the poor doctor.

"Ummmmm. I think we need something," Krennicx said, breaking the frozen silence.

Krennicx had been laughing the entire time Dr. Scott Barton was cleaning himself. Jacob held it back for a while, at least until he finally gave in and laughed too. It wasn't until Barton came back with a bucket when Jacob realized that his body wasn't prepared to laugh so hard yet. His stomach churned when Scott placed the bucket at the side of his bed. To be honest, he was *aiming* for Krennicx. Poor Barton. After that, Krennicx *could not stop laughing*. He laughed so hard he Couldn't. Even. *Talk*.

"It's not funny!" Jacob said, as a laugh escaped his mouth. He was tired of Krennicx's non-stop laughter.

"You're right, IT'S HILARIOUS!" Krennicx burst into another laughing fit. Jacob rolled his eyes, trying *hard* not to laugh. His stomach *obviously* did *not* agree with laughter. But when he wasn't laughing, reality would hit. Jacob looked at where his arm was supposed to be. The queasiness churned in his stomach and he yanked his eyes away. Krennicx sighed, "I'm sorry I wasn't there to stop it."

Jacob looked at Krennicx, shocked. Krennicx stared at him, *zero* laughter in his eyes. *He's trying to distract himself*, Jacob realized. *Does he think it's his fault?* Yes, if Krennicx was there, it *would not have* happened. But not only would it have been illegal, all of Annorlia would know his secret. Jacob just *knew* that if Annorlia knew, everything would crumble. "Krennicx, this is *not* your fault," Jacob said, staring into Krennicx's scary eyes. *"Trust me,"* Jacob transmitted, then his eyes widened. *"Did I just?..."*

"Congratulations," Krennicx said with a warm smile. "You've accepted who you are. A Fighter."

"Really?" Jacob asked, shocked. "That's how you learn? Why didn't you tell me? I would have accepted sooner."

Krennicx chuckled, "It doesn't work like that, dearie," his faced turned serene. "I really am sorry about what happened."

Jacob took a deep breath, "Thank you." He hesitated, "So, what exactly happened?"

Krennicx hesitated, "Well…. I didn't stay, but when the wall was broken, it got *pretty* chaotic. When I checked on it yesterday, it all still seemed pretty crazy, but I think it's coming along just fine."

Yesterday, Jacob realized, "How long have I been out?"

Krennicx smiled, "Three days."

"Three *days*?" Jacob asked, alarmed.

Krennicx laughed, "Better than Barton's estimate. He said it'd be around a week."

Now that he thought about it, he figured it *was* pretty impressive that it was only three days. With the fact that Jacob wasn't in *too* much pain, it was truly amazing. "Barton must be a good doctor," Jacob murmured.

Krennicx smiled sneakily, he opened his mouth to say something but was cut off…again.

"Why are you still here?!" Scott barked. "How many times am I supposed to ban you?"

Krennicx snorted, "Do you *really* think you can get me out?"

"Why can't he be here?" Jacob asked. He was surprised to realize he *wanted* Krennicx's company.

"He *LOCKED* me out of the emergency room!" Barton hollered.

"He *what?*" Jacob yelped in surprise. But when he thought about it, it really wasn't surprising at all.

Krennicx smirked, "You weren't doing it right."

"'Doing it right'?! *I* am the one who has a doctorate! *You* wanted to work for *me!* REMEMBER? *How* was I not *doing* it right?!" Dr. Scott Barton yelled. He frowned, "What did you do anyway?"

Krennicx smirked maliciously, "I did it right."

Jacob was shocked to see how red a Night Dragon's face could get. Barton clinched his jaw, gave Jacob some sort of medicine, and stomped out of the room. "Temper, temper," Krennicx said as Barton left. Jacob was pretty positive Barton heard him, but he was probably supposed to.

Jacob shook his head.

Krennicx gave him an innocent smile.

"Why didn't you want him working on me?" Jacob asked, somewhat afraid to know.

"It's not that he's a bad doctor or anything. He's amazing. I'm not a doctor, but I have some experience. It's just…." Krennicx hesitated, "there's special elixirs I've made over the years that help, *tremendously.*"

"Is that why I'm not in too much pain? And why recovery is so much faster?"

"Yes," Krennicx responded with a smile. It looked like he had more to say but was debating on it.

"What is it?" Jacob asked.

"Well…. it sounds weird, and pretty awkward."

"What?" Jacob asked, getting nervous.

"And I knew I had to put a few things inside so I can make a replacement arm. I had to do it before he fixed it up," Krennicx responded hurriedly.

Jacob felt like throwing up again, "You *put* stuff *in* me?" Jacob asked disbelievingly.

Krennicx stared at the floor as he nodded.

"*While* I was bleeding?" Jacob asked.

Krennicx continued to nod.

"*And* you didn't let the doctor do anything till you were done?"

Krennicx kept nodding.

"You realize I was bleeding to death, right?"

Still nodding.

"Are you *insane*?" Jacob asked.

Krennicx kept his head down and looked at him with his eyes and smiled toothily.

Jacob shook his head disbelievingly. *Gross*

"You seem disgusted."

"Of *course* I'm disgusted!"

Krennicx smirked, "Would you rather me *not* make you a new arm?"

Jacob glared at him. Talking about a 'new arm' was still grossing him out. Jacob sighed. This was the question he wanted to know, but he was afraid to ask. "So," Jacob hesitated, "what happened with King Luther?"

Krennicx smiled, "He got away."

"He *what?!*" Jacob yelped. "How could you say that so calmly! You mean to tell me all of that was for nothing!"

"Hold your horses kiddy!" Krennicx barked. "That was *not* 'nothing'! Your job was not to kill him! It was to *dethrone* him. Thanks to you, there isn't even a throne to sit on! It's been blown to smithereens!" Krennicx smiled sneakily. "I better watch out, you might become a better Throne Slayer than me."

"Now *that* makes me feel better!" Jacob said sarcastically.

"You're welcome."

Jacob groaned, "What if he comes back and takes the throne again?"

"Dude, did you not hear me?" Krennicx asked. "There is no throne. It's gone! The castle along with it! I'm not sure what you did, but you did it great!"

Jacob paused, "I, I didn't do that."

Krennicx's face turned serious, "I'll check into it." In his eyes, Jacob could see that Krennicx already knew. Jacob thought about asking but decided not to. *Krennicx clearly knows what he's doing. If he thinks I shouldn't know, then I shouldn't.* There was a familiar roar and stomps.

"Winter!" Jacob called happily. Winter ran through the row of beds and rested his snout on Jacob's lap, panting happily. "Hey buddy! Where did you go?" Jacob asked as he rubbed the dragon's snout.

"Found 'em in the crumbled ruins," Krennicx said rolling his eyes, "along with three dragon bodies. That dragon of yours has some strength."

Jacob smiled, "Thanks, bud," he whispered in Winter's ear. "Ew!" Jacob yelped when Winter licked his face. Winter pouted and rested his snout where Jacob's arm was supposed to be.

Krennicx frowned, "I'll get working right on that."

"Wait a minute! What happened to Michael!" Jacob realized in horror. "He was still in there!"

"It's alright," Krennicx promised, "he's fine. Glider, Lighter, Glazer, and Tortoise got him out. He is just fine."

Jacob sighed with relief, "Thanks."

"For what?"

"Saving my life….again."

Krennicx smirked, "Don't worry. The amount will build and build to where there's really no point in 'thank you's.' You'll lose count soon enough."

Jacob snorted, "Kinda already have."

Krennicx smiled, "Get some rest. At this rate, I'm sure you'll be good to go home in a day or two….maybe three. But the real question would be ol' Barton. We might have to sneak ya out."

Jacob smiled, "Are you leaving?"

Krennicx smirked, "Sad to see me go, are you? Don't worry your cute little face. I'll just go tell your family you're awake. They're worried about you. Especially your annoying brother."

Jacob smiled, "I'm guessing him and Glider in the same room is rough, isn't it?"

"Actually, it's pretty relaxing. Both of them end up fighting each other. They're so distracted by each other, they forget about me." Krennicx frowned, "Glazer and Hazel on the other hand, *yeesh*. They're inseparable. You can only imagine how annoying they can be. After Hazel asked Every. Single. Question. Possible, she finally left me alone."

Jacob smiled; he was hoping Hazel and Glazer would become friends. He hated seeing his sister alone at the baseball game. No more. Things were about to change. But change didn't sound bad at all.

As Krennicx predicted, Jacob felt up to going home two days later. But Dr. Barton *insisted* staying a few more days. Once that time was over, Jacob had a happy reunion with his family.

"Jacob," Dad said with a smile after an hour of their reunion, "I'd like for you to meet Bailey." He motioned towards the Night Dragon that had just walked up.

"Hello," Bailey said with an elegant bow. He was a lot larger than Lighter, and somehow he looked ancient.

"Hi," Jacob greeted. He debated whether or not to bow in return.

"It's a pleasure to meet you," Bailey continued. "Your family has said many good things about you. Is there any way I can show my appreciation?"

"For what?" Jacob asked, surprised.

"I was trapped underground in the castle, trying to find my way through the maze. You may not realize it, but you ran by me." Bailey gave him a friendly smile, "You led me out."

Jacob was about to ask more questions, but then he realized something about the dragon's eyes. They were a faint, light green. They were empty. *He's blind*, Jacob realized. Jacob smiled, "It is my pleasure. There is nothing to repay me for. Really, there's no need." Jacob added the last part when Bailey opened his mouth to argue.

Bailey smiled and turned to Jacob's parents, "You've done well in raising your children. I'm proud of you."

Jacob was shocked to see his dad do an elegant bow, "Thank you. For everything."

Bailey smiled and turned to Jacob, "It was my pleasure." He paused, then added, "Good luck with your 'rascals.'" Bailey spread his wings and took off into the sky.

"What did he mean by 'rascal-*AH!*" Jacob shrieked and jumped back, everyone else did the same.

"I like Bailey, don't you?" Krennicx asked, completely unbothered by the terrified faces.

"You have *got* to quit doing that," Jacob said, still trying to get his heart to calm down.

Dad shook his head, "I think that's impossible for him."

Krennicx smirked, "If it brings terror to you, then of course it's impossible."

Jacob rolled his eyes, then he remembered something. "I need to go talk to Michael." Without another word, he ran inside and made his way up the stairs to Michael's room. Michael hadn't come outside when Jacob came home. He hoped he wasn't still mad. He nearly tripped when he twisted the door handle. He hadn't exactly figured out his new balance yet, due to his arm being, well, gone. Jacob took a deep breath as he entered his brother's room. As Jacob figured, Michael sat on his bed staring at his hands. Jacob sat down next to him. No one said anything. Jacob didn't even know what to say. All Michael's life he wanted to kill dragons, but now.....now he probably didn't know what to do. Jacob took a deep breath and opened his mouth to say something but was interrupted. "I'm sorry," Michael whispered.

"It wasn't your-" Jacob started.

"But it was!" Michael insisted. "If I had listened to you...." He trailed off when he finally looked at Jacob, staring at where his arm used to be.

Jacob shifted uncomfortably. "Krennicx said he's making a replacement."

"I don't doubt that," Michael said, staring at his hands again. "But it won't be the same." Michael sighed, then continued, "I was a jerk. I didn't listen to you. I didn't even listen to Dad! I only listened to that liar. I didn't realize my mistake until he...." Michael trailed off

"I'm glad you're ok."

"I just wish you were," Michael murmured.

"Look at me," Jacob said. He didn't continue until Michael finally obeyed. "I am fine. You're fine. Everyone is fine. There's no use living in the past. You'll never know when there isn't going to be a future. Let's forget our fights and live in the present. It doesn't last forever."

Michael stared at him in shock, "Where in the world did you get *that!* I've never heard you sound so cheesy!"

Jacob laughed, "I've spent a *lot* of time with Krennicx."

Michael snorted, "I've spent more time than I'd like. I'm *very* grateful he saved you, but I *still* don't like him."

"He kind of grows on you," Jacob said with a smile. When he first met the hybrid, he hated him. He drove him crazy. He really couldn't think of the moment when he decided that Krennicx was his friend, for he really did grow on him.

Michael sighed, "He hasn't, and I kind of hope he won't, but I still owe him an apology, don't I?"

"Yes," Jacob said, nodding over and over.

Michael groaned, *"Fine."* There was a scream that made them both jump up. "That sounded like Hazel!"

They ran downstairs and back outside. Jacob gasped.

"SHE'S BEAUTIFUL! THANK YOU SO MUCH!"

"Don't touch me," Krennicx shrieked when Hazel trapped him in a hug. Jacob smiled. In front of Hazel was a beautiful rose colored dragonese type of dragon with a pink tint. She was around the same height as Winter with small pink spikes running down her back. She didn't have the strange spikes at her shoulder like Winter did, so she would probably need a saddle. "Thank you, thank you, THANK YOU!" Hazel said, squeezing Krennicx harder. Jacob smiled warmly. Hazel's dream came true. She *finally* had her dragon. Michael seemed to be thinking the same thing, for he smiled and shook his head.

"What is the world coming to?" Michael asked as Winter and Hazel's new pet began to sniff each other.

Jacob smiled but was interrupted before he could answer. "Jacob? Can I have a word?" Krennicx asked.

"Sure."

"Your Majesty," Jacob said, bowing before they sat on the roof.

"Oh, please," Krennicx said flicking his hand. "Just because I'm the Represenetor, you don't have to bow. Besides, how many times have we made fun of each other?"

Jacob figured that, but it was still odd to know that *Krennicx* was the High King of all Annorlia. Krennicx and Jacob sat on the top of Jacob's roof. He hoped what Krennicx wanted to talk about wasn't something bad. "I have something for you," Krennicx finally said, handing Jacob a shoebox. It was wrapped in black paper.

"What is it?" Jacob asked.

"You have to open it."

Jacob felt ridiculous, but when he opened it, he shook his head. They were the black leather boots from Cloudairia—the Cloud Kingdom. "Am I ever not going to be tested?"

Krennicx smirked, "Of course not."

Jacob perked up, "Wait a minute! Is *this* what's black?"

"No."

"Oh, come on! Seriously, you *have* to tell me what it is!"

Krennicx smirked, "You really want to know?"

"Yes! I can almost promise you, I *never* want to play that game with you *again,*" Jacob said rolling his eyes.

Krennicx grinned, "You *sure* you can't figure it out?"

"Positive," Jacob assured. He had named *everything* he could possibly think of. *"Please*. What. Is. Black?"

Krennicx's signature smirk had to be the biggest ever, "Your pupils."

"WHAT?!"

Krennicx laughed outright. "You should see the look of your face right now! Especially your pupils! It's priceless!"

Jacob shook his head disbelievingly. *Only* Krennicx would choose something like *pupils.*

Jacob rolled his eyes, "Thanks… I guess."

Krennicx smiled, "That's not everything you got."

"Really?" Jacob asked lifting up the boots. His eyes widened. He took a deep breath as he grabbed the black sword-like handle on the bottom of the box. It was a little bigger than a sword handle, but it was a perfect size. It was smooth and black, with dragon scales etched on every part of it. From underneath each scale glowed dark purple and whirled white. The white was constantly moving around inside the purple. "Is this?…"

"A piece of the DragonStaff? Yes," Krennicx said with a smug smile.

"I thought it was destroyed from the castle blowing up," Jacob breathed.

"*I* was not destroyed," Krennicx responded. Of *course;* Krennicx created the DragonStaff.

"Thanks, DragonStaff."

Krennicx laughed, "I'll admit, I went a little dramatic with saying that one. But it was totally worth it to see the look on that king's face. It was priceless!"

Jacob smiled nervously, then glanced away, "So, you really think my powers are…. movement? It still doesn't make too much sense to me."

Krennicx nodded, "We've already been over this, Kiddy. Movement is the easiest way I can describe it. You can manipulate any object with your mind. You can make it *move*. It will probably be easier for you if you channeled it into your hands…er…hand."

"But I still don't exactly see how I was running super fast," Jacob said, trying hard to not feel sick about the 'hand.'

"Because you channeled your movement powers into yourself! So at the moment, you can go super fast, see all the movement around you, make things float, *and* see visions of the future. Not to mention that everyone also has an increased amount of strength as well," Krennicx grinned. "You should also discover more abilities later on, too."

"Whoa," Jacob couldn't help but say, impressed with himself. "What all can you do?"

"How about you try to figure out all of your own powers before trying to figure out mine."

Jacob took a deep breath, staring at the sword-like-handle in his hand. It felt so cool. "So, does this mean…" Jacob hesitated.

"Yes," Krennicx answered without needing to hear the question. "With this handle, you can harness your blade. This is made out of the same orb from the Staff. It's strong enough to hold a little bit of your power for your blade. You decide how sharp you want it to be by the amount of power you put into it."

"Do you think I'm ready to…"

"Be a Fighter of Peace? Yes, I do," Krennicx responded. "But it's up to you. You don't have to do this if you don't want to. It's your decision."

Jacob hesitated. He *knew* what he wanted, but he needed to know… "What about my family?" he asked, staring at Hazel and Michael playing with Winter and Hazel's new dragon. "Will I ever see them?"

"Of course," Krennicx answered gently. "The only reason Glider, Glazer, and Tortoise don't stay with their parents all the time is because Glider and Glazer's mother is always having to lead armies against the Diammonites. Tortoise's parents think that he has a full-time scholarship. It's terrible, but Tortoise doesn't go home much because his parents are on Omega's side. I would like to do more training with you while it's summer, but you can be home whenever you want. Sometimes—if your parents are alright with it— you might do night duty. Other than *that,* I will not keep you away. You have Winter now, you can go almost anywhere. So, kid, ready to save the world?"

Jacob looked at him and grinned. *He has always been involved with my life, hasn't he?* Jacob took a deep breath. This would forever change his life, but something told him his life had already changed. He stared at the handle in his hands. *Movement, huh? I can control anything and everything that is still and moving? I can make myself move super fast?! Super speed?! AND super strength?! Fighter of Peace…huh.* He had always imagined himself as becoming a hero from stopping the 'dragon war,' but that war was a lie. It's actually way bigger than he could have ever thought it was. It was a war between Annorlians and Diammonites. A few days ago, he didn't even know aliens existed! Now he was about to fight them to keep them from wiping out all existence?! He didn't even know that the Dragon Forest—that was actually called Peace Forest—wasn't the only place outside of his city! *I need to learn how to use these powers, so that I can do good with them. We have to stop the Diammonites.* One last deep breath. "I'll do it."

EPILOGUE

The tunnels were dark as the hooded human made his way with a Diammonite escort. He thought he would do it. He thought he would earn his respect. He was wrong.

"Lord Klaus," former King Luther said, lowering his hood, "I need to speak with him."

Lord Klaus was probably the second biggest Diammonite. He was the second in command, after all. Most of his armor was black like the rest of the Diammonites, but he had a white slash mark on his face and white talons. He also had porcupine-like white spikes along his back that grew larger as they wrapped around his tail. "You already are," Klaus said, turning to a glowing black screen on the wall. "Your Majesty, I present to you, *former* King Luther."

Luther cringed at the word 'former' but when the most terrifying figure of all time appeared on the screen, all words left him.

"What seems to be the problem?" the figure asked. His voice was smooth, like the smooth stone wall. There was even a hint of kindness. But all it brought was cold fear.

Luther stared at the floor until he remembered his words. "You betrayed me. We had a deal."

"And what deal was that?" the figure asked.

Luther gritted his teeth, "You know what I'm talking about! I would have had the kid, but *you* betrayed me!"

"Everything happened the way it was supposed to," the figure responded.

"But I *did* as you asked! Now do what you promised," Luther demanded.

"And what is that?" the figure asked.

Luther glared at Lord Klaus, then back to the figure. "You *promised* that if I did what you said, I will be your number two," he said, doing his best to keep his fear out of his voice. Suddenly, Luther was very aware of Klaus next to him, for Luther would be taking Klaus's spot.

"No promises will be broken."

Luther heaved a relieved sigh, "So I'll still be your number two?"

"Of course," the figure said. He turned to Klaus. "If you will, he wants to be in two."

"Of course, my Lord," Klaus said bowing. "It will be done."

"I hope you enjoy being in two."

"Wait," Luther, said realizing what they were saying. But it was too late.

"Annorlians," Klaus murmured as he cleaned his large, shining black stoned sword. "There's one more you need to see." There was a struggle as two Diammonites entered the cave, dragging a struggling Annorlian. "I present to you, the personal spy of Krennicx Cooper, the Represenetor. Sky, of Cloudairia."

The Diammonites slammed Sky onto the floor in front of them with a painful thud. Sky moaned as his shoulder wound throbbed. He glared at one of the Diammonites that threw him. He couldn't help but notice the smallest limp in the soldier's back leg, "Hello there," Sky said with a smirk. Sky imagined the Diammonite would flinch or something. But he didn't. He was as still as a statue. Sky stared threateningly at the figure in front of him. Hatred swelled inside of him, "I will *never* give you what you want."

The figure smiled, "I like this one. He has fire. Bring him here. I'd like to speak with him myself."

"Of course, my Lord," Klaus bowed. There was a tug on Sky's neck as the Diammonites pulled him backwards, causing Sky to gag. *I'm sorry Krennicx. You'll have to find someone else. I wish I had the chance to tell you, but I can't let them know what I know. Trust me, I will NEVER tell them. No threat will break me, I promise. If we're lucky, they'll kill me before they get the truth. If they don't, I'LL do it myself.* Sky glared at the Diammonites as the figure disappeared. *I TRULY hope ALL of your 'kids' are ready. Because I have a feeling things are about to go crazy, and you need all the help you can get. Goodbye, Krennicx Severein Cooper, my High King. And good luck, you'll need it.*

Emily Woods lives in the North Georgia Mountains with her awesome family, loving cat, and chickens that think they're pet dogs. She dreams of being a stay-at-home mom on a farm, with an indoor Mini pig. She is the youngest of five children, a teenager, homeschooled, and plays keyboard for her church. Her goal in writing is to provide family-friendly books for all ages, ones without foul language and inappropriate content, but full of laugh-out-loud humor and thrilling action.

www.ingramcontent.com/pod-product-compliance
Lightning Source LLC
Chambersburg PA
CBHW061854310726
48972CB00004B/1018